Praise for *The 7th Victim*

"I've always been a fan of Alan Jacobson's thrillers, but his latest novel, *The 7th Victim*, is a quantum leap in terror and suspense. Tautly written and brilliantly executed, here is a masterpiece of horror and murder. Read it with the doors locked and the lights blazing."

—James Rollins, *New York Times*
bestselling author of *The Judas Strain*

"In the fictional world of criminal profilers, Karen Vail is a knockout, tough and brilliant. In *The 7th Victim* she truly meets her match, and the twists and turns will astonish you."

—Tess Gerritsen, *New York Times*
bestselling author of *The Bone Garden*

"Alan Jacobson pulls off a winning combination in *The 7th Victim* — a strong, credible, likable heroine; high-velocity narrative drive; a non-stop, twisting, believable plot; and a satisfying surprise of an ending. Thrillers don't get much more thrilling than this one."

—John Lescroart, *New York Times*
bestselling author of *Betrayal*

"Another Jacobson twister. The ending will shock you."

—Stephen J. Cannell, *New York Times*
bestselling author of *At First Sight*

"Jacobson's third novel has all the ingredients for a best-selling psychological thriller: strong female lead, multifaceted serial killer, compelling plot, and just enough secrets and surprises to keep the adrenaline racing."

—*Library Journal*

"...action...plot twists...the ending is a shocker. For fans of Patricia Cornwell, Nelson DeMille, and James Patterson."

—*Booklist*

THE 7TH VICTIM

ALAN JACOBSON

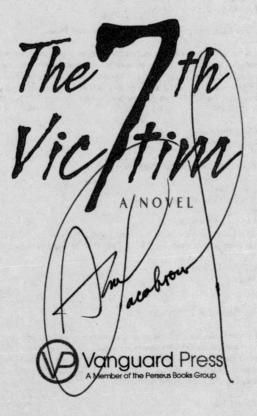

The 7th Victim

A NOVEL

Ⓥ Ⓟ Vanguard Press
A Member of the Perseus Books Group

Hardcover edition first published in 2008 by Vanguard Press, a member of the Perseus Books Group

Mass market edition first published in 2009 by Vanguard Press

Designed by Jeff Williams
Set in 11-point Galliard

Library of Congress Cataloging-in-Publication Data

Jacobson, Alan, 1961-
   The 7th victim : a novel / Alan Jacobson.
      p. cm.
   ISBN 978-1-59315-494-3
   1. Serial murderers—Fiction. 2. Criminal profilers—Fiction. 3. United States. Federal Bureau of Investigation—Fiction. I. Title. II. Title: Seventh victim.

PS3560.A2585A615 2008
813'.54—dc22

2008019462

Mass market ISBN: 978-1-59315-546-9

10 9 8 7 6 5 4 3 2 1

For my grandmother, Lily Silverman, ninety-seven at this writing and still climbing the five flights of stairs to her apartment . . . still refusing to take the elevator. Lily is an inspiration to everyone who's ever met her, a woman who at ninety stood in front of a New York City bus and refused to move until the driver opened the door to let her in. Spunk. Wisdom. And a heart of platinum (apparently, literally). For now, we continue to celebrate your life. But when your time passes, you'll be immortalized by those who knew you and were touched by your soul.

I love you the whole universe.

———

"He who fights with monsters might take care lest he thereby become a monster. And if you gaze for long into an abyss, the abyss gazes also into you."

—Friedrich Nietzsche, *Beyond Good and Evil*

"A profiler puts himself into the mind of the killer to see things as the killer saw them, to understand why he immersed his entire emotional and physical being into the fetid stench of human depravity. When a profiler explores the minutia of pain and death, he's wading knee deep in the blood and guts, and there's only so much he can take before it begins to affect him."

—Mark Safarik, *FBI profiler and Supervisory Special Agent (Ret.)*

"To know the artist, study his art."

—John Douglas, *The Anatomy of Motive*

prologue

SIX YEARS AGO

QUEENS, NEW YORK

"Dispatch, this is Agent Vail. I'm in position, thirty feet from the bank's entrance. I've got a visual on three well-armed men dressed in black clothing, wearing masks. ETA on backup? I'm solo here. Over."

"Copy. Stand by."

Stand by. Easy for you to say. My ass is flapping in the breeze outside a bank with a group of heavily armed mercenaries inside, and you tell me to stand by. Sure, I'll just sit here and wait.

FBI Special Agent Karen Vail was crouched behind her open car door, her Glock-23 forty-caliber sidearm steadied against the window frame. No match for what looked like MAC-10s the bank robbers were toting, but what can you do? *Sometimes you're just fucked.*

Radio crackle. "Agent Vail, are you there? Over."

No, I left on vacation. Leave a message. "Still here. No movement inside, far as I can tell. View's partially blocked by a large window sign. Bank's offering free checking, by the way."

Vail hadn't been involved in an armed response since leaving the NYPD five years ago. Back then she welcomed the calls, the adrenaline rush as she raced through the streets of Manhattan to track down the scumbags who were doing their best to add some spice to an otherwise bland shift. But after the birth of her son Jonathan, Vail decided the life of a cop carried too much risk. She eventually made it to the Bureau—a career advancement that had the primary benefit of keeping her keester out of the line of fire.

Until today.

"Local SWAT is en route," the voice droned over the two-way. "ETA six minutes."

"A lot of shit can happen in six minutes." *Did I say that out loud?*

"Repeat, Agent Vail?"

"I said, 'A lot of sittin' for the next six minutes.'" The last thing she needed was to have her radio transmission played back in front of everyone; she'd be ridiculed for weeks.

"Unit Five approaching, Queens Boulevard and Forty-eighth." Mike Hartman's voice sounded unusually confident over the radio. Vail was surprised Mike and his new partner were responding to this call. She'd worked with Mike for six months and found him decent enough, but a marginal agent in terms of execution. At the moment, she'd take marginal execution . . . the more firepower the good guys had, the more likely the gunmen inside the bank would be intimidated, and the greater the odds of resolving this in the Bureau's favor. Translation: she'd come out of this in one piece and the slimeballs would be wearing silver bracelets . . . tightened that one extra notch—just enough to make them wince when she ratcheted them down around their wrist bones, for all the trouble they caused her.

Dispatch replied: "Roger, Unit Five."

Mike's unit was a block away and would be here in seconds.

With her eyes focused on the bank's windows, she heard Mike Hartman's Bureau car screech to a stop to her left, about thirty feet from the front door. But as her head swung toward the BuCar to make eye contact with Mike, she heard the clank of metal on metal and she pivoted back toward the bank—

—where she saw the three armed men in black sweats blowing through the front door, large submachine guns tucked beneath their arms, and damned if she didn't think she'd called it right, they were carrying MAC10s. But in the next split second, as she ducked down and as glass shattered and rained all over her back, she saw, out of the corner of her eye, Mike Hartman lying on the ground, face up, his right arm tracing the pavement as if searching for something. A glimpse of his face showed raw pain and she knew instantly that he'd not lost anything but rather *gained* something—a few rounds of lead in his body. Still, Mike fared better than his partner, whose head hung limp, slumped back over the seat.

The bank robbers, machine guns and all, were arrayed in a triangle but not going anywhere, strategically positioned behind a mailbox and a row of metal newspaper dispensers, a pretty damn good bit of cover and a huge stroke of luck for them. But they'd just killed a cop—why weren't they getting the hell out of Dodge?

Lying on the ground, with a bird's-eye view of the pavement and Mike's writhing body, Vail spied the cockeyed tires and sky blue rims of another vehicle, to the left of Mike's BuCar. A local NYPD cruiser responding to the call. *And where the hell was SWAT? Oh, yeah, six lonnnng minutes away. What did that make it, another four before they showed up? I told them a lot of shit can happen in six minutes.*

Rounds continued popping all around her. Vail tried to stand—probably not the smartest thing to do while projectiles were zipping through the air at 950 feet per second, but she needed to do something.

As she rose, a couple of thumps struck her in the left thigh. The deep burn of a gunshot wound was instantly upon her, and a wide bloody circle spread through the nylon fibers of the stretch fabric of her tan pants. She didn't have time for pain, not now. She grabbed the back of her leg and felt two tears in the fabric, indicating the rounds had gone right through. Assuming they didn't hit a major artery, she'd be okay for a bit. But shit, right time or not, it sure hurt like hell.

She slithered to her left to gain a better view of what was happening in front of the bank—just as two of the slimebags dropped to the pavement . . . hit by the cops' fire, no doubt. But the remaining asshole kept blowing rounds from his submachine gun, holding it like fucking Rambo, shooting from his waist and leaning back, hot brass jackets leaping from the weapon like they were angry at being expelled for something as mundane as murder.

The final cop went down—she could see him fall from her

ground-level vantage point—and the perp stopped firing. The silence was numbing in its suddenness.

Vail watched as the man bent over and lifted the large canvas bag from his dead comrade's hand and turned to hightail it down the street.

Well, this wasn't good. Mike and his partner down, a couple cops dead, and the shithead was about to make it away with the cash. *Not on my watch.*

Vail rolled left, got prone against the ground and brought her Glock to the front of her body. This would be an insane shot—below the cars and above the curb—but what did she have to lose? With all the shooting, there were no innocents around. She squeezed off several rounds, the weapon bucking violently in her weak grip. And gosh darn it, if the fucker didn't stumble, then limp—he was hit. Vail grabbed the edge of Mike's car door and pulled herself up as best she could, her thigh burning like a red-hot poker, her muscles quivering as she groaned and pushed with her right leg to get herself upright.

Hanging onto the sideview mirror with her left hand, she took aim at the limping gunman and screamed, "Federal Agent. Freeze!"

Did that ever work? Nah. Usually not. But this guy wasn't too smart, because he turned toward her, his submachine gun still in his grasp, and that was all she needed.

Vail fired again and took him out cold, flattened him against the pavement. And then let go of her hold on the mirror and joined him in a heap on the asphalt as she heard the uneven scream of sirens approaching.

She craned her neck back a smidgen and caught Mike Hartman's pale gaze. He managed a slight smile before his eyes wavered closed.

The next morning, after her release from the hospital, she put in for a transfer.

one

PRESENT DAY

FAIRFAX COUNTY, VIRGINIA

Wisps of vapor hung in the frigid night air like frightened ghosts. He shooed away the apparitions, then checked his watch as he huffed down the dark residential street. He'd chosen this house, this victim, for a reason.

Within a few hours, pale-faced neighbors would be staring into news cameras, microphones shoved in their faces for commentary and insight. *Tell us about her. Stir our emotions, make us cry. Make our hearts bleed. Make our hearts bleed just like the victim bled.*

His right hand was toasty warm, curled around the leather FBI credentials case inside his coat pocket. But his suit pants were too thin to fight off the biting cold that nipped at his legs. He shivered and quickened his pace. In a moment, he'd be indoors, comfortably at home with his work.

At home with his victim. Flowing brunet hair and clear skin. Long legs and a turned up cute-as-a-button nose. But buried beneath the allure, the evil was there—he'd seen it in her eyes. The eyes were always the key.

Strong fingers palpated his fake moustache to ensure it was properly placed. He repositioned the small pipe holstered to the inside of his coat, then placed the loose-leaf binder beneath his left arm before stepping up to the front door. He'd been here a number of times over the past few days, inspecting the area. Watching the comings and goings of the neighbors. Measuring the arcs thrown by the streetlights. Gauging the visibility of the front door to passersby. Now it was a matter of flawless execution. *Execution!* Indeed.

He pressed the doorbell and brightened his face for the peephole. Rule number one: look pleasant and nonthreatening. Just a friendly FBI agent out to ask a few questions to keep the neighborhood safe.

An eye swallowed the small lens. "Who is it?"

Sweet voice. *How deceiving these women-slut-whores can be.*

"FBI, ma'am. Agent Cox." He had to keep himself from smiling at the irony of the name he'd chosen. Like everything he did, there was a reason. Everything for a reason and a reason for everything.

He unfurled the credentials case the way agents are taught to do, then leaned back a bit, helping her take in the whole package. A clean-cut FBI agent in a wool overcoat and suit. How easy could it be?

A second's hesitation, then the door opened. The woman wore an oversize sweatshirt and a pair of threadbare jeans. She held a spatula in her right hand, a dishrag in the left. Cooking a late dinner. *Her last supper,* he cackled silently.

"Ms. Hoffman, we've had some reports of a rapist in your area. His attacks are escalating. We were wondering if you could help us."

"A rapist?" pretty little Melanie Hoffman asked. "I haven't heard anything about it."

"We haven't released it to the press, ma'am. We work differently than the police. We believe it's best to keep it quiet, so we don't tip him off that we're on to him." He shifted his feet and blew on his right hand as he hugged the binder close to his chest with his left. It's cold, he was telling her. *Invite me inside.*

"How can I help?"

"I have a book of mug shots here. All I need you to do is look over the photos and let me know if you've seen any of these people in the neighborhood the past two months. Shouldn't take more than a few minutes."

Her eyes bounced from the binder to his face, on which she seemed to linger for just a bit longer than he would have liked. He decided to press ahead. He had a knack for creating a window of opportunity, and the window was now open. He had to move, and move fast.

"Ma'am, I don't mean to be impolite, but I've still got a number of other houses to visit tonight, and it's getting kind of late." He shrugged a shoulder. "And the longer it takes to find this guy, the more women he's going to attack."

Melanie Hoffman lowered her spatula and stepped aside. "Of course. I'm sorry. Please, come in."

HE SNAPPED HIS SHEARS CLOSED and lopped off a lock of brunet hair. He leaned back, admired his work, then grabbed Melanie Hoffman's limp head by her remaining hair and clipped off another handful. Then another. And another.

Snip. Snip. Snip.

The sweet scent of blood was everywhere. He sucked it in and shivered. It was an intense feeling, a sudden euphoric rush.

When he finished with her hair, he moved on to her fingernails. Down to the quick, and beyond. Blood oozed a bit, and he licked it, like a lover slowly lapping off the chocolate from his companion's fingers. He repositioned Melanie's hand, got it just the way he wanted it, then brought the shears up again.

Clip. Clip. Clip.

Blood oozed again, and he drank some more.

An hour must've passed, the need to make things right driving him to perfection. He'd always been like that, for as long as he could remember. Besides, he was in no rush to go back out to the cold. He snatched a sesame seed bun from Melanie Hoffman's kitchen counter and slapped on some cream cheese, peanut butter, and ketchup from her fridge. He squirted on a generous helping—the symbolic affection for the red stuff wasn't lost on him—and he took a large bite, careful not to leave any crumbs, saliva, or other identifiable markings behind.

A soft, tan leather couch that still smelled new sat in the living room. He sunk down into it and flipped on the television, surfed the channels for a bit and found wrestling. *Such senseless violence. How could they allow this junk on TV?*

He left the tube on and sauntered through the rest of the house, munching on the sandwich and admiring the pictures hanging on the wall. He liked Melanie's taste in artwork. It had a looseness to it, abstract yet somehow structured. Organized, but with a randomness inherent in creative expression. He stood in front of one of the paintings and noticed her signature in the corner. She had created these herself. He clucked his tongue against his palate. Tsk, tsk, tsk. Too bad. He wondered what other works of beauty she might have created had she not been so damned evil.

He stood in the bedroom doorway admiring his work. He finished off the sandwich, then crossed his arms and tilted his head from side to side, finding the right perspective, sizing up the room. Taking in the whole view. Yes, it was a masterpiece. As good as anything Melanie had painted. The most complex work he'd ever created.

He moved to Melanie's side and looked down at her eyes, frozen open, staring at the ceiling. No, at him. They were looking at him.

The evil had to be purged. Had to be. Had to.

He lifted the serrated knife and felt its weight—its power—in his hand. Melanie Hoffman had paid dearly, for sure. Just payback for an unjust crime.

It was, it was, it was.

Like a master painter inscribing his name at the bottom of a canvas, he brought back the knife and drove it through Melanie Hoffman's left eye socket.

She must not see.

She must not.

She must.

two

What is it with me and banks?

Supervisory Special Agent Karen Vail's weapon was aimed at the loser, who just stood there, his .38 Special pointing right at her. Sweat pimpled his greasy forehead, matting dirty black hair to his skin. His hands were shaking, his eyes were bugged out like golf balls, and his breathing was rapid.

"Don't move or I'll blow your goddamn head off!" Vail yelled it a bit louder than she'd intended, but the adrenaline was pumping. She wanted the message to get through the perp's thick skull that she meant business. The frightened patrons of Virginia Commonwealth Savings Bank got the message. Those who were still standing hit the ground with a thud.

"Drop the fucking gun," the man screamed back. "Drop it now!"

Vail smirked. *That's exactly what I was going to say to him.* As he shuffled his feet and held the hostage in the crook of his left arm, Vail flashed on Alvin, a skel she'd busted sixteen years ago while a member of the NYPD. It wasn't Alvin—he was doing time at Riker's Island—but, nonetheless, she thought he could be the guy's twin.

"I'm not putting my gun down till you put yours down, pal," Vail said to the perp. "That's the way it's going to work."

"I call the fucking shots here, bitch. Not you!"

Great, she thought, *I got one who wants to fight.* It'd been six years since she'd been a field agent, eleven years since she'd camped behind a detective shield. Though she still trusted her instincts, her skill-set was in the crapper. It wasn't like putting on pantyhose every morning. Dealing with hostage situations took practice to know you'd do the right thing under pressure, without thinking. As Vail had often been kidded by the others in her squad, the "without thinking" part came naturally to her.

"Since you won't tell me your name, I'm going to call you Alvin," she said. "Is that okay, Alvin?"

"I don't care what the fuck you call me, just drop the fucking gun!" He shuffled his feet some more, his eyes darting from the left side of the room to the right, and back. As if he were watching a table tennis match.

Alvin's hostage, a thirty-something stringy blond with a sizable rock on her ring finger, began whimpering. Her eyes were bugged out, too, but it wasn't from drugs. It was raw fear, the sudden realization that, FBI or not, Vail might not get her out of this alive.

And Vail had to admit that so far it was not going well. She'd already blown protocol about as well as any rookie could her first day on the job. She should've yelled "Freeze, scumbag, FBI!" and he would have then just pissed his pants and dropped the gun, surrendering to law enforcement and ending the nightmare before it started. At least, that's the way it always happened in the old TV shows she watched as a kid.

But this was reality, or at least it was for Vail. For the Alvin lookalike standing in front of her, it was some speed-induced frenzy, a dream where he could do anything he wanted, and not get hurt.

That was the part that bothered her.

She kept her Glock locked tightly in her hands, lining up Alvin's nose in her sight. He was only about twenty feet away, but the woman he was holding, or rather choking with his left arm, was too close for Vail to risk a shot.

The other part of protocol she'd screwed up was that she should've been talking calmly to Alvin, so as not to incite him. But that was according to the *Manual of Investigative and Operational Guidelines*—known throughout the Bureau as MIOG, or "my-og." In Vail's mind, it should've been called MIOP, short for *myopic*. Narrow-minded. And if there was one thing Vail was sure of at the moment, it was that the guy who wrote MIOG didn't have a crazed junkie pointing a snub-nosed .38 at him.

So they stood there, Alvin twitching and shuffling, doing what looked like a peculiar slow dance with his hostage, and the level headed Karen Vail, practicing what was sometimes called a Mexican standoff. Was that a politically correct term? She didn't know, nor did she care. There was no backup outside, no tactical sniper focusing his Redfield variable scope on Alvin's forehead, awaiting the green light to fire. She'd just walked into the bank to make a deposit, and now this.

She let her eyes swing to Alvin's left, to a spot just over his shoulder. She quickly looked back to him . . . making it seem as if she'd seen someone behind him, about to sneak up and knock him over the head. She saw his eyes narrow, as if he'd noticed her momentary glance. But he didn't take the bait, and for whatever reason kept his ping-pong gaze bouncing to either side of Vail. She realized she needed to be more direct.

She turned her head and looked to his left again and, reaching into her distant past as a one-time drama major, shouted *(deeply, from the abdomen)*, "No, don't shoot!"

Well, this got Alvin's attention, and as he swiveled to look over his left shoulder, he yanked the hostage down and away, and Vail drilled the perp good. Right in the temple. As he was falling to the ground in slow mo, she was asking herself, "Was this a justified shooting?"

Actually, she was telling herself to get the hell over there and kick away his weapon. She couldn't care less if it was a justified shooting. The FBI's OPR unit—Office of Professional Responsibility, or Office of Paper-pushing Robots—would make the final call on that. The hostage, though frazzled and rough around the edges, was alive. That was all that mattered at the moment.

Once Vail knocked aside Alvin's weapon, she took a moment to get a closer look at his face. At this angle he didn't look so much like Alvin. Could've been because he had the blank deer-in-headlights death mask on, or because of the oozing bullet hole on the side of his head. Hard to say.

Vail suddenly became aware of the commotion amongst the tellers and security guards, who had emerged from their hiding places. The hostage was now shrieking and blabbering something unintelligible. A man in a gray suit was by her side, attempting to console her.

"Don't just stand there," Vail yelled to the closest guard. "Call 911 and tell them an officer needs assistance."

It wasn't entirely true, but it wasn't exactly a lie, either. Still, she thought the cops would come faster if they thought it was one of their own who needed help instead of an FBI agent. Sometimes they don't like fibbies much, the locals. But with banks, the police had to share jurisdiction with the Bureau, so she didn't anticipate much of a tiff over it.

As she stepped away from Alvin's body, her BlackBerry's vibrating jolt made her jump. She yanked it from her belt and glanced at the display. Her intestines tightened. Her heart, still racing from adrenaline, precipitously slowed. The brief text message sucked the air from her breath.

She had hoped she'd never see another day like this. She had hoped it was over.

But the Dead Eyes killer had claimed another victim.

In six years as an FBI profiler, Karen Vail had not experienced anything quite like this. She had seen photos of decomposed corpses, eviscerated bodies, bodies without heads or limbs. Seven years as a cop and homicide detective in New York City had shown her the savages of gang killings and drive-by shootings, children left parentless, and a system that often seemed more interested in politics than in the welfare of its people.

But the brutal details of this crime scene were telling. A thirty-year-old woman lost her life in this bedroom, a woman who seemed to be on the verge of a promising career as an accountant. A box of new business cards from the firm of McGinty & Pollock was sitting on her kitchen counter, the toxic odor of printing press ink burning Vail's nose.

She curled a wisp of red hair behind her right ear and knelt down to examine a bloody smear outside the bedroom doorway.

"Whoever did this is one sick fuck." Vail said it under her breath, but Fairfax County homicide detective Paul Bledsoe, who had suddenly materialized at her side, grunted. The baritone of his voice nearly startled her. *Nearly* startled her, because there weren't many things that did surprise her these days.

"Aren't they all," Bledsoe said. He was a stocky man, only about five-eight, but plenty wide in the shoulders to make anyone think twice about screwing with him. Deep-set dark eyes and short, side-parted black hair over an olive complexion gave him the look of Italian stock. But he was a mutt, some Greek and some Spanish, a distant Irish relative thrown in for good luck.

His trained eyes took in the large amount of blood that had been sprayed and smeared, just about painted all over the walls of Melanie

Hoffman's bedroom. Melanie Hoffman, former newcomer, now dearly departed, recently of the firm McGinty & Pollock.

All Vail could do was nod. Then, as she crouched down to get a different perspective on the scene, she realized that Bledsoe was only partially correct. "Some are more fucked up than others," she said. "It's just a matter of degree."

The photographer's flash flickered off the mirrors in the adjacent bathroom and drew Vail's attention. Without walking through the crime scene, she glanced up and saw that blood had also been smeared on the bathroom walls, at least the parts of them she could see.

Profilers didn't usually get to visit fresh crime scenes. They did most of their work secluded in a small office, poring over police reports, photos, written or transcribed suspect interviews, victim histories culled from relatives, friends, acquaintances. VICAP forms—short for Violent Criminal Apprehension Program—that were completed by the investigating homicide detectives provided background and perspective. Having as much information as possible was crucial before beginning their work . . . before beginning their journey into the depths of a sick mind.

"So you got my text." Bledsoe was looking at her, expecting a response.

"When I saw the code for Dead Eyes, my heart just about stopped."

Another flash from the camera grabbed Vail's attention. They had both been standing near the doorway, seemingly in no hurry to step into the chamber of death.

"Well, shall we?" she asked. He didn't reply, and she figured he was mesmerized, if not overwhelmed, by the brutality that lay before them. She sometimes had a hard time reading Bledsoe and, over the years, had concluded that he preferred it that way . . . erecting a wall between his inner thoughts and someone who made her living analyzing human behavior.

As Vail tiptoed around eviscerated body parts strewn across the floor, the criminalist poked his head out of the shower. "There's

more in here, Detective," he said to Bledsoe, who had moved beside
Vail.

"Peachy," Vail said. As Bledsoe headed into Melanie Hoffman's
bathroom, she took a deep breath and cleared her mind, descending
into the funk she needed to get into to begin her analysis.

Profilers didn't try to identify *who* committed the murder, as the
police did; they tried to ascertain the *type of person* most likely to have
perpetrated the act. What their motivations were; why now, why
here, why this victim. Each one a crucial question, an important
piece to the puzzle.

There were cops who thought profiling was bullshit, psychobabble crap that wasn't worth the paper their reports were written on,
and certainly not worth the salary the Bureau paid, plus benees, car,
and clothing allowance. That talk never bothered Vail, because she
knew they were wrong. She knew that, for some cops, it was a simple
inferiority complex, while for others it was merely ignorance about
what profilers did.

Vail continued to study Melanie Hoffman's bedroom. Several
things bothered her about this murder. She turned to Bledsoe, who
was busy puking into a barf bag he carried in his pocket. She'd seen
him do this before, the last time at a particularly bloody crime scene.
It was a strange thing to happen to a homicide detective, but when
Vail asked him about it, he shook it off the way he brushed aside an
opinion he didn't like: with the shrug of a large shoulder. Bledsoe
had said it wasn't anything he controlled, it just kind of happened.
He thought it had something to do with an "autonomic response"
related to the smell of blood. Vail thought it was baloney, but what
did she know? Maybe it was true, or maybe it was just male ego trying to cover up an embarrassing weakness. At the time, he seemed to
want Vail to ignore it, so she did.

Vail poked her head in the bathroom and forged ahead. Bledsoe
straightened up, borrowed a plastic bag from the criminalist, and
sealed off his sour stomach contents. He wiped his lips with a folded
paper towel he pilfered from the technician's utility case, then

popped a Certs in his mouth. He maneuvered the breath mint toward his cheek, then nodded at the wall above the mirror. "What do you make of that?"

Scrawled in large red strokes were the words, "It's in the."

"Could mean a lot of things."

"Such as?"

Vail shrugged. "I'll need to think on it. I'm not sure we know enough yet to even formulate an opinion."

"You said it could mean a lot of things. You've gotta have some idea about it."

"First off, it's not necessarily what he wrote as much as why he felt the need to write it."

Bledsoe chewed on that a moment, then shook his head. "You guys are gonna have a field day with that one."

"No doubt." Vail stepped out of the bathroom. "Okay, what've we got?"

"No signs of forced entry," Bledsoe said. "Vic could've known her attacker."

Vail looked away, her gaze coming to rest on Melanie's blood-soaked bed. "Could've met the guy yesterday evening and brought him home. Or, he could've used a ruse to lower her defenses. Enough to get her to open the door for him. Either way, your assumption that she knew him wouldn't do us much good."

Bledsoe grunted, then stepped out of the bathroom.

Profilers often found it difficult to have a relationship with someone, let alone have a family. They constantly thought about crime scene photos, wondering what they'd missed—or even what they had seen and misinterpreted. Or what they expected to see but didn't. It was a perpetual state of unease, like when you keep thinking you've forgotten something but can't figure out what it is.

But, it was Vail's job and she did it the best she could. At present she hoped she did it well enough to help catch Dead Eyes. After three murders spread out over five months, the killer had gone silent. For several months, there was nothing. When such a pattern developed, the police figured—or rather, hoped—the offender had either died, or was sitting in a maximum security jail cell, arrested on some unrelated charge.

When doubt intensified that the third victim was the work of Dead Eyes, it left the offender with only two murders to his credit. He suddenly didn't appear to be as prolific, and thus the threat he posed was not as potent. With escalating police department budgets always a concern, the task force was mothballed.

For Vail, it was good timing: nine months of working in close proximity with Bledsoe was enough. Vail liked him, but anytime you were around someone so much, you tended to make that person's problems your own. And with a failed marriage—and serial killers bouncing around inside her head—she had enough stress without Bledsoe's issues invading her thoughts as well.

Vail knelt beside Melanie Hoffman's bloody, mutilated corpse and sighed. "Why did this happen to you?"

Vail stood at the foot of Melanie Hoffman's bed. After the criminalist briefed her on his findings, Vail asked Bledsoe to leave her for a few moments so she could be alone with her thoughts. *Alone with the corpse.* Some would think this was a morbid request, but for a profiler it was a priceless advantage.

As a new agent going through training, Vail had read all the papers written by the original FBI profilers, Hazelwood, Ressler, Douglas, and Underwood. For a profiler, getting inside the offender's head was exciting, almost sexy. The way they figured things out, the way they could put their finger on the offender's personality traits was uncanny. What a rush it must be, she had thought, to write up a summary of an UNSUB, or unknown subject as the Bureau's procedural manual calls them, and discover later that not only did your assessment help nail the killer, but that it was spot on.

As was usually the case, in practice things were a lot different than it seemed they would be. The romantic notions of catching a serial killer were long gone. Vail spent her time in the trenches where psychotic criminals roamed, peering into minds of men who deserved to be gassed. Better yet, to be sliced and diced and tortured like they often did to their victims.

Vail settled into a chair in the corner of Melanie Hoffman's room and took in the scene, looking at its entirety. The blood all over the walls, the grotesque mutilation of the victim. She slipped a hand into her pocket and removed a container of Mentholatum and rubbed the gel across her top lip, masking the metallic blood odor and reek of expressed bodily fluids.

As she sat there, she tried to get into the mind-set of the killer. Though there were a couple dozen FBI profilers who traveled the world educating law enforcement personnel on what profiling could and could not do, word of mouth was slow. And defunct TV shows, where the FBI agent could "see through the killer's eyes" only made their job of education more difficult, their credibility more suspect.

Two years ago, a cop asked Vail to touch a piece of the victim's clothing so she could "see" the killer's face and describe it to him. He seemed genuinely disappointed when she told him that was not the way it worked.

In reflection, Vail now found herself smiling. In the middle of a brutal crime scene, she was smiling. Smiling at the stupidity of the cop, at the irony and ineptitude of her own skills at times, and how sometimes she could not see even the obvious *tangible* things right in front of her . . . let alone phantom images through a killer's eyes. Profilers don't see what the offender sees. But they do symbolically get inside his head, think like he does, imagine what he felt at the time of the murder—and why.

But that was not to say she did not get *something* from being in the same room as the killer. She did, though she had never been able to classify these feelings, be they intuition, an intense perception or understanding or identification with the offender and what she thought he'd felt at the time. But whenever possible, she spent a few moments alone with the body. It beat color photos, videotape, and written descriptions.

She shifted her attention back to the victim. To *Melanie*—Vail always felt it was better to use their names. It kept it personal, reminded her that someone out there did this horrible thing to a real, living, formerly breathing human being. It was too easy to slip into the generic "vic," or victim reference, and sometimes she wondered if the law enforcement brain did it by necessity, as a self-protection mechanism against emotional overload . . . the mind's way of forcing them to keep a distance. To stay sane.

Bledsoe's comment that the killer might have known his victim, if correct, would mean it was a relatively easy murder to have committed. The offender could get close to her without much difficulty. And if he'd gotten to know her so he could increase her comfort levels and decrease her defense mechanisms, that said a lot. It meant this killer

was smart, that he had spent considerable time planning his crime. I
that was the case, it would indicate an organized offender.

A crime scene was often a mixture of the two—elements of or
ganization blended with elements of disorganization—making th
UNSUB's identification harder. Though Vail had initially though
Dead Eyes was more disorganized than organized, she was begin
ning to have doubts.

Vail heard a noise in the hallway, followed by a loud voice: "Yo
Where's the dick that bleeds?"

"In here, Mandisa," Bledsoe called from the bathroom. H
opened the door and stepped out just as Spotsylvania County Detec
tive Mandisa Manette, one of the former Dead Eyes Task Forc
members, entered. Manette was a lanky woman with broad shoulder
and a smile that stretched across her face. Cornrows lifted off he
head and stuck out like a loose bundle of ropes that bounced whe
she walked. She always wore platform shoes, a move Vail felt wa
aimed more at power and control than fashion. With the adde
height, she hit six feet and was a good three inches taller than Vai
Vail had come to think it was Manette's way of keeping Vail on
notch below her in the pecking order.

Vail pulled herself out of the chair and tried to bring her min
back into a state capable of socializing. She reached the doorway i
time to see Manette's reaction to Melanie Hoffman's demise.

"How you doing, Mannie?" Bledsoe gave her a quick hug. Va
had not seen Manette since the task force had been suspended—an
judging by their reactions, she figured Bledsoe hadn't either.

"How's my favorite dick hanging?" Manette asked Bledsoe.

Vail cringed. She was no prude, but after a while, the sexual innu
endoes wore thin.

"Divorce is in the books," Bledsoe said. "Trying to move on."

"You deserve better, Blood. You do." She grabbed a hunk o
Bledsoe's ample cheek and squeezed. "Maybe a fine thing like m
would consider taking on a work like you."

Bledsoe turned a bit crimson and rolled his eyes.

Manette threw a hand up to her chest in mock surprise at seein

Vail. "Kari! My least favorite shrink. Still lookin' for that trapdoor that'll take you into the killer's mind?"

Vail turned away, preferring not to get into it with Manette. "I'll be back in five," she said to Bledsoe. She walked out of the house, moving beyond the crime scene tape to clear her mind and regain her concentration. The smell of death was rank, even with Mentholatum on her lip, and stealing some brisk, moist air of a misty winter day provided a needed respite.

Lacking a caffeine-laced soft drink, Vail bummed a Marlboro from a nearby technician and lit it. She had given up the awful habit when she left Deacon—considering it part of his curse—and hadn't smoked since. She tugged on the end and sucked in her fix of stimulant. After blowing a few rings in the air and snubbing out the barely smoked cigarette, she saw a car pull up across the street, behind two parked police cruisers. Acura, late model, navy blue. Too pricey for an unmarked, unless it was left over from a search and seizure.

The driver leaned forward and Vail got a clear view of the man, despite the high gray sky reflecting off the tinted glass. She stormed back into the house and sought out Bledsoe.

"What the hell is Hancock doing here?"

Bledsoe twisted away from Manette. "Hancock?"

"Chase Hancock. Arrogant, pain-in-the-ass SOB."

"Don't hold back, Kari. Tell us what you really think of him."

Vail opened her mouth to respond, but the electronic tone of Beethoven's Fifth interrupted her.

Bledsoe rooted a cell phone from his jacket pocket and answered the call. He shook his head, walked a few feet away, and appeared to put up a mild protest. Seconds later, he disconnected the call, then threw a furrowed look at Vail.

"Well, well, well. Karen Vail, Paul Bledsoe, and . . . who is this lovely creature I haven't had the pleasure of meeting?" Trim but thick, with a mound of slicked back blond hair, sky blue eyes, and a divot of a dimple in a square chin, Chase Hancock was all smiles. His extended right hand hung in the air in front of Manette.

Manette looked Hancock over and nodded her approval, but she

did not offer her hand in acknowledgment—thus making her assessment known: she did not care for anything else other than the physical package.

"Interesting name, *Hancock*," Manette mused. "Kind of sound
like—"

"What the hell are you doing here?" Vail asked.

"He's here on order of Chief Thurston."

Vail's frown shifted toward Bledsoe. "What?"

Bledsoe looked away. "Hancock's been named to the task force.
Just got the call," he said, holding up his cell phone.

With Vail's fisted hands turning white, Bledsoe led her out to the
front of the house. "Let's take a walk," he said as they stepped onto
the cement path that fed the sidewalk.

"Did you think I might hit him?"

"I never know with you sometimes."

Vail shoved her hands into her coat pockets. "Just because I hate
the guy?"

"He's got an ego the size of DC, that's pretty damn obvious. But
what'd he do to you?"

"Before he hooked on with Senator Linwood's security detail,
Hancock was a field agent for a dozen years."

"He was a fibbie?"

"Don't call us that."

"You call us dicks."

"Only because some of you are." Vail nudged Bledsoe playfully
with a shoulder. He rocked a bit onto the neighbor's front lawn before regaining his balance. "Anyway, Hancock applied for the open
position at the profiling unit same time I did. I'd worked a couple of
crossover cases with him and his work was, well, shitty. I mentioned
it to my partner, who told my ASAC. Next thing, I get the promotion, Hancock doesn't."

"You're giving yourself a lot of credit if you think the Bureau was
swayed by your opinion, Karen."

"They weren't. My ASAC swore he never said anything to anyone
about what my partner told him. But Hancock knows I thought he

work was shitty, and my field reports didn't pull any punches. I called a spade a spade, basically saying Hancock's an incompetent idiot. He thinks he got passed over because of me." She drew in a deep breath and sighed. "He threw a fit, brought a discrimination suit, left the Bureau."

"He win the case?"

"Nah, it was bullshit. Judge threw it out."

They stopped walking and looked around at the quiet residential street. Modest, well-kept one- and two-story brick houses sat like silent witnesses to the recent murder.

"How long ago was this?"

"Little over six years. Word was he found a spiffy job in the private sector doing security work for some Internet company."

Bledsoe kicked at a rock. "And now he heads up Linwood's security detail."

"Pretty boy found a new roost."

"Hey, it works for Linwood. The senator gets a relatively young guy with a dozen years in the Bureau. Asshole or not, that's good experience to have on your side."

Vail shivered and crossed her arms in front of her chest. "So why did Chief Thurston get involved? What's his stake in all this?"

"Don't know. Sounded important to him. Something important enough to pull strings."

Vail turned and started heading back. "Something? Or someone."

Bledsoe pursed his lips, then nodded.

WHEN THEY RETURNED to Melanie Hoffman's house, Hancock and Mandisa Manette were huddled over the victim's body with Bubba Sinclair, a detective from the FCPD, Fairfax City Police Department. Sinclair, head shaved bald and his face peppered with scars from childhood acne, was nodding at something Manette had said. When he saw Vail, he stood from his crouch and smiled. "Hey shrink, how goes it?"

"Good, Sin, good. Except we got us another Dead Eyes vic."

Sinclair nodded. "This one's real bad. Worse than before. Sure it's our guy?"

"Signature's right on. Vics done in their beds, their own steak knives rammed right through the eyes. Organs eviscerated. Left hand severed. Blood smeared on the walls. Afterwards, offender takes in a meal at the scene, watches the tube. Want me to go on?"

Sinclair shook his head. "Nah, enough for now."

Manette's arms were resting on her hips. "Looks just like them other vics. One and two."

Vail knew this was a slap at her opinion that victim number three was also one of Dead Eyes's jobs, even though the crime scenes looked markedly different from the previous two. Different even from Melanie Hoffman's.

"I'll need to get up to speed," Hancock said. "Review all the files. Victimologies, photos, interviews—"

"We know what's in the files, Hancock," Vail said.

Bledsoe held up a hand to keep the peace. "Task force is my responsibility. I'll make sure you get what you need."

Hancock nodded, rocked on his heels, and threw a sideways glance at Vail.

"So how'd you pull this assignment?" Manette asked.

"Simple," Hancock said. "I asked for it."

Manette's head jutted back. "Who you with?"

Vail grunted, then turned to walk away. "He's not a LEO."

"Not law enforcement?" Manette looked from Hancock to Bledsoe. "Don't you be telling me he's a reporter—"

"Agent Chase Hancock." He again extended a hand toward Manette, but again she ignored it and instead turned to Vail.

"*Agent* Hancock? He's one of yours?"

"I'm agent-in-charge of Senator Linwood's security detail," Hancock said. "The senator's appalled over this offender's boldness and is shocked by the ineptitude of local law enforcement in catching this guy." He looked at Vail. "Including the FBI."

Sinclair stepped forward. "What gives you the right—"

"I've got an idea," Bledsoe said. "How about we get back to the crime scene? In other words, do what we get paid to do. We can powwow later and lay our thoughts on the table then."

That quieted the group and, despite a grumble from Hancock, they dispersed.

Vail made her way over to Melanie Hoffman's body and stood there, letting her eyes move from the bare feet up to the head. Staring at the protruding knives . . . wondering: Was she dead when he plunged them into her brain? If she was like the other two victims, the answer would be yes. What was the significance of stabbing the eyes? Was it sexual in nature? And what was the meaning of the message the offender left on the wall?

A knock at the door interrupted the background clicks and flashes of the criminalists' cameras. "Hey everybody." In walked Roberto Enrique Umberto Hernandez, the six-foot-seven Vienna Police Department Detective whose small-town murder case gave birth to the Dead Eyes killer. Vail met him at the doorway and they hugged briefly.

"Karen, how've you been?" He looked over at Bledsoe, who tipped his head back in acknowledgment. Manette reached over and touched her fist to Robby's. "What's up?" Robby asked Manette.

"I think we should stop meeting like this. Take in dinner, a movie instead." Manette ran her hand across his thick forearm and winked at him. Even with his darker complexion, Vail could swear that Robby blushed.

Robby had gotten into law enforcement for the same reason many cops had, because of the violent death of a loved one. In his case, his uncle, who had served as a surrogate father. Robby had witnessed the killing himself, a particularly brutal job carried out by gang members. His uncle was an honest, hardworking man, and why he would be a gang target Robby never understood. But it changed Robby's life in ways he could not anticipate. Like upping in the LAPD. That turned some heads in the old 'hood, especially when he made detective and was stationed in the Pico District, LA's premier Hispanic gang neighborhood.

But even though Robby had a gentle soul, at six-seven, with a square jaw and deep-set eyes, his body language said, "Don't fuck with me." To hear Robby tell it, not many did. Vail was inclined to believe him.

Robby's eyes found Melanie Hoffman's body, and his shoulders sagged forward. He cleared his throat.

"Roll up your sleeves and dig in," Vail said.

The next half hour passed without much discussion. The crime scene unit continued their work, and the task force did theirs. Robby broke away from the trio of detectives and crouched next to Vail as she studied the congealed pool of blood beside the bed.

"I'm thinking of applying to the Academy." Robby said it near her right ear, barely above a whisper, but it snagged her full attention.

Vail's eyebrows rose. "Yeah? Had enough of Pocatello?"

"Vienna's a small town. Not a whole lot to do, you know? Counting the Dead Eyes vic, three murders in fourteen years."

"A waste of your talents?"

Robby shrugged. "I guess you could put it that way. Just so many robberies, car thefts, and dom vio's you can take before you're staring out the window, hoping for something more . . . challenging. Sounds bad, huh?"

Though Vail hadn't known him all that long, she had come to learn that Robby was very intuitive. When they first started working Dead Eyes, she found they could talk to each other without words, and often did.

"Why the Bureau? Why not apply for a slot with Bledsoe's department? Plenty of action there."

"I was thinking about profiling."

Vail gave a sideways glance at Hancock, who appeared to be listening with half an ear. She took Robby's elbow and rose from her crouch. "Let's go get some air."

They moved outside, and the chill struck her body like a slap to the face. She sunk her hands into her pants pockets and walked over to the curb. "You know, Robby, there's another option. The International Criminal Investigative Analysis Fellowship. It's a two-year understudy training program. You'd have to be sponsored by an agency, one that's big like Bledsoe's. You'd spend the last month with my unit, then take a test. You could then do profiling for the police department."

Robby shrugged, then said, "Not quite the same."

Vail nodded. "Okay, but you can't just apply for the profiling unit. You have the street experience, but you've got to be an agent for a while. You know, pay your dues, meet some pretty rigid criteria. There are a lot of candidates for very few openings."

"You don't think I have the talent."

"I didn't say that. From what I've seen, I think you've got great natural instincts. But it's a lot more than that. A good profiler is open-minded. He can see the big picture and keep his feelings and emotions in check. He needs to be able to look at a scene and instantly analyze things logically: why did the offender do *this*—or not do *that*? He has to be able to think like the offender. I haven't really assessed you in those terms. I'd need to work more cases with you before I could say you've got all the tools."

"My mom's friend thinks I do."

"Man, it's cold. Gotta walk, move the blood." She started down the sidewalk and Robby followed. "So your *mom's friend* thinks you've got the knack. That's great, Robby. But who the hell's your mom's friend?"

"Thomas Gifford."

"My ASAC?" Vail asked, referring to the Assistant Special Agent-in-Charge of the profiling unit.

"Yeah."

Vail stopped walking and turned to face Robby. "You never told me that."

"Never came up. I wasn't that close with my mom till she got sick, when I moved back here to take care of her. Gifford came around from time to time to see if she needed anything. I got the feeling they might've had a thing once. Anyway, after she died, suddenly the guy's in my life, trying to help me out with all sorts of stuff. Probably made my mom a promise."

"So you want to be a profiler. Well, you've got a good 'in,' which will definitely help."

"I don't want my mother's friend pulling strings to get me a job, Karen. I want it legit." Robby glanced up at the high sky as raindrops began to dot the pavement. "Come on, we should get back."

They turned and headed toward Melanie Hoffman's house.

"Wanting to earn it on your own is fine, but don't ever overlook inside contacts. Sometimes merit means shit. Good people, better people, get passed over all the time."

"Fine, so I'll use one of my inside contacts. Teach me, be my tutor."

Vail looked up at the man who was a foot taller than she. "It's not that easy. I mean, yeah, I could teach you stuff. But unless you have a good footing in psychology—"

"I was a psych minor at Cal State Northridge."

Vail hesitated. "Well, that's a start, I guess." She continued on another few steps as she considered his request. "I guess there's no harm. Just keep it from Hancock. Think of him as your enemy and you'll be fine."

"Hancock—that the GQ dude in there?"

"His history is short and sweet. Used to be with the Bureau, got passed over for the one vacant profiling position—which went to me—got pissed off, and left. He now heads up Senator Linwood's security detail."

"So he's got a chip on his shoulder."

"Not just a chip, the whole rock."

They shared a laugh.

"Okay. Lesson one. You ready for this?"

"Hey, I'm a dry sponge."

"Somehow that image doesn't work for me, Robby." They arrived at the house and stood by the front door, under the eave. "We were all in Melanie Hoffman's bedroom looking over the crime scene. But we were seeing different things. You, Bledsoe, Manette, and Sinclair were following the criminalists' lead, hoping to find a fingerprint, an errant hair fiber, a milligram of saliva. Something that'll identify the monster who did this. I was looking at the offender's *behavior*." She paused a second and noted Robby's furrowed brow. "A profiler isn't concerned with fingerprints and DNA. We look at the behaviors the offender leaves behind at the scene. They're crucial to helping us understand him, so we can figure out the type of person who did it."

"What do you mean by 'behaviors'?"

"Think of it this way. A sixteen year old who keeps a diary doesn't lie to herself in her diary, right?"

"There's no reason to. She's writing to herself."

"Exactly. So when you look at an offender, it's best to look at his diary, which is the crime scene. He doesn't lie to himself when he commits the crime. These behaviors, these things the offender has done *after* he's killed his victim, are all over the crime scene, and they tell us a lot about him."

"Like stabbing the eyes."

"Right. Stabbing the eyes doesn't prevent him from getting caught, and he doesn't do it to disable the victim—she's already dead."

"So then why does he do it?"

"That's the key question, Robby. Most of these offenders begin these behaviors when they're young. For Dead Eyes, stabbing the eyes is part of a fantasy that kept evolving, developing over time. What we find repulsive is normal, even comforting to him. We find out why he finds it comforting, and we're a step closer to understanding who this guy is. Understand who he is, and we can narrow the suspect pool. See, we don't catch the bad guys, we give you dicks the information that helps you look at your suspects and say, this one fits, this one doesn't." She shivered. "Let's go in, I'm freezing."

"So why would a guy stab a woman in the eyes?"

"First of all, you can't consider all the possibilities of why he did something. It'll take you in a million different directions and you'll never be able to focus. Only look at what's most probable. So for the eyes, think symbolism," she said as they walked through the hallway. "Maybe he didn't want her to see what he was doing. Or maybe he'd met her somewhere and made a pass. She rejected him, and this was his way of making her pay for not *seeing* his true value. Or piercing the eyes may be sexual in nature. Maybe he's incapable of having an erection."

"I'd say it was probably rejection."

"You can't say it was anything. Not yet, anyway. A profiler has to come into the crime scene with her eyes wide open. No preconceived notions, no trying to attach labels to things. Consider the scene one fact at a time." They stood at the doorway to the bedroom. "I've got some binders back in my office I can give you to read. Notes and research articles. They'll give you an overview of all this stuff."

"Cool."

Vail nodded. "Okay, let's go in again. And remember, you're not looking at forensics. Keep an open mind and take what's there, what the offender has given you. No biases."

"Okay."

Vail walked in and saw the other task force members standing at the foot of Melanie's bed, staring at the wall.

"Those dot painters," Hancock said.

"What?" Bledsoe asked.

"Those painters from like, a hundred years ago. They had a weird way of painting. See the wall, the paint strokes?"

Vail moved beside Bledsoe to get Hancock's perspective. "That's ridiculous," she said. "It's *blood*, not paint."

"You of all people should appreciate this, Vail." Hancock looked at her. "These walls are filled with psycho stuff. Rorschachs all over the place."

"Your mind's as twisted as the offender's."

"Hang on," Manette said, holding up a hand. She gestured to Hancock. "Tell us what you're thinking."

"The painters who used dots to paint their pictures," he said. "That's what this looks like."

Vail studied the blood patterns on the wall. "Pointillism or Impressionism?" she finally asked. "Pointillism involved dot painting. If I had to fit this into a category, I'd say this looks more like Impressionism to me."

Bledsoe eyed her curiously.

"Art history/psych double major," she explained.

Hancock tilted his chin ever so slightly toward the ceiling, as if looking down at Vail through reading glasses. "So, Miss Art History Major, still think my mind's twisted?"

"I do," Vail said, "but it's got nothing to do with this case."

"Let's get some shots," Bledsoe said to the forensic technician. "Wide angles, close-ups of all the walls." He turned to Vail and said, under his breath, "Just in case. I think the guy's onto something."

Vail frowned, but she knew Bledsoe—and Hancock—were right. The blood murals were worth reviewing. In rejecting Hancock's observation due to her prior history with him, she had broken the cardinal rule on which she had just counseled Robby: go in with an open mind and don't bring any personal biases to the scene. She would discuss it with Robby later, if he didn't bring it up himself.

Sinclair was standing at the edge of the bedroom with his forearms folded across his chest. "Anybody find the left hand?"

Everyone glanced around. Blank faces stared at each other. Bledsoe turned to the head forensic technician. "Chuck, you guys locate the severed hand?"

Chuck scanned the clipboarded list of identified and photographed items. "No left hand."

Vail thought she knew why the hand was missing, but for the moment decided to keep her theory to herself until she could be more certain. "Let us know if there are any other . . . anatomical parts missing," she said to Chuck.

"Why'd he bother to cut her hair?" Robby asked.

Vail nodded at the victim's right hand. "Goes with the fingernails. For some reason, he's trying to make her ugly. Butcher the hair, cut the nails down so short they bleed. It holds some meaning to him. Nothing can be overlooked."

VAIL REMAINED ANOTHER FIFTEEN MINUTES, then left the forensic crew and task force to finish their work and headed to her office to gather materials for a class she was teaching at the Academy. While on the interstate, she pulled out her PDA and dictated her impressions on the Melanie Hoffman crime scene. She arrived earlier than expected, so she decided to grab a coffee at Gargoyle's, the café across the road from the BAU, or Behavioral Analysis Unit, housed in the Aquia Commerce Center.

The downtime would allow her to collect her thoughts and transition between the crime scene and her office. She needed to become a person again, even if for only half an hour, before plunging back into the underworld of serial killers. Over the years, she'd found she needed that time, or risk losing herself in the dark abyss of the offenders' twisted minds. If she entered that world, it would be harder to separate herself from the killer, harder to maintain her touch with reality.

If Thomas Gifford, her boss, ever found out she needed this "downtime," he'd probably transfer her to a resident agency in a quiet town in the middle of nowhere. Because a profiler sees so much violent death—the worst offenses humanity has to offer—the Bureau has to be careful who it exposes to these atrocities on a daily basis. Gifford, the man who owned the desk where the profiling buck stopped, maintained a hawk-like vigilance over the people in his command. If there was a hint someone in the unit was not handling it well, he was gone. No questions asked and no chances for reinstatement. A suicide in the profiling unit would be a slight . . . kink in the old FBI shield of public opinion. Profilers had been known to tip the glass a bit too much, and suffer from heart disease and other stress-induced maladies, but none had committed suicide. Yet.

The commerce center was a grouping of modern two-story brick buildings in Aquia, Virginia, fifteen minutes south of the FBI Academy. The BAU, colloquially the "Profiling Unit," having undergone myriad name changes and reorganizations over the years, underwent its most sweeping transformation of all when it moved out of the Academy's subbasement. The brain trust realized that sitting sixty feet underground in an old bunker while analyzing grotesque photos of mutilated women was too much to ask the human mind to endure.

Divorcing itself from a shared existence with the BSU, or Behavioral Science Unit, its research and academic arm, the BAU moved down the road into the Aquia Commerce Center buildings. The new buildings' large windows provided the antitoxin to death's depressing cloak of subbasement bleakness: sunlight.

When Vail returned to her nine-by-nine office to retrieve her voice mail, she found a FedEx box on her desk with five pink "While you were out" messages sitting on her chair. She grabbed up the notes and sat down heavily. Her office had a cluttered feel to it, but though there were books and files and reports stacked atop every level surface, nothing was out of place. Two incandescent lights were clamped to opposite ends of her desk, reminder notes clipped to the rippled lampshades. Lining the metal bookshelves were black FBI binders with computer-printed titles peeking through the windowed spines: SEXUAL HOMICIDE, STALKING, BLOODSTAIN PATTERN INTERPRETATION, and SEXUAL SADISM. A handwritten sign taped to the shelf served as a warning: Do not "borrow" *ANY* of these binders.

Vail pressed a button on her phone and found three voice mails waiting for her. One was from the Office of Professional Responsibility about the shooting this morning at the bank. The second message was from her attorney, informing her the divorce was almost final. She closed her eyes and sighed relief.

Her euphoria lasted only until she heard the third message, which was from Jonathan, her fourteen-year-old, who was staying with his father this week. The message said he needed to talk. A teenager needing to talk is like a volcano erupting: it doesn't happen often, and when it does, one never knows which way the lava is going to flow. Vail figured the topic of conversation was going to be his father, and she had spent the better part of the past eighteen months trying to get away from that man. Like it or not, her son was doing his best to unintentionally draw them back together.

She picked up the phone. At least it would buy her another five minutes of sanity before leaving for class. She'd had enough blood and guts today. She was in no hurry to wade through more.

He moved amongst his various creations, vases and large containers, fired hard and slick. All standing on pedestals of varying heights, lit by overhead spots that showcased them as the works of art that they were. The potter's wheels and bisque kilns were in the rear of his studio, in another room and out of sight, visible only to his students. An artiste never left his tools of creation in plain view for the unindoctrinated to see. Only the finished products, the masterpieces, were worthy of display.

He stored the boxes of wet clay off to the side of his studio, behind a movable wall. Every month he loaded and unloaded a half ton of clay—literally a thousand pounds—from the distributor to his Audi's trailer and from the trailer to his studio. At first, whenever he'd go buy the stuff, the damn boxes were so heavy he'd need a student to help carry them. But after a few months of hauling the cases to and from his car and kneading the stuff with his hands, he could maneuver them around the loft pretty easily without any help.

But the best part of being a ceramicist was the feel of the cold, wet, firm clay as he squeezed it between his fingers. It kind of felt like a liver, heavy and dense. Holding someone's liver in your hands was a tremendous feeling of power.

He closed up the plastic bag so the clay would stay fresh, rinsed off his hands, and headed into the adjacent loft to change into his dark suit. After slipping on the jacket, he stepped into the old walk-in closet to pick out a tie and something—the musty smell? the darkness? the brush of clothing against his cheek? Something set off the old memories. It was dizzying, almost disorienting. He shut the door and sat down at his nearby desk, thoughts and emotions flooding into his mind. He just wanted it to stop, but realized it may be best to embrace it, confront it. Shape it.

He lifted the screen to his laptop and woke it from sleep. The words, the feelings, the memories just flowed out of him like some kind of rushing river that kept surging no matter what stood in its path.

> The hiding place smells like some musty box I once opened when I was looking for his cigarettes. It's strong and kind of burns my nose. It's small and dark, but it's mine. He doesn't know I have it, which means he can't find me here. And if he can't find me, he can't hurt me. I can think here, I can breathe here (well, except for the smell) without him yelling. I sit in the darkness, alone with myself, where no one can hurt me. Where HE can't hurt me.
>
> But I watch him. I watch everything he does through little holes in the walls. I watch him bring home the whores, I watch what he does to them before dragging them upstairs to his bedroom. Sometimes I even hear what they're saying, but most of the time I just see. I see what he does.
>
> But I really don't have to see. I already know. I know because he does the same things to me.

He shook his head, as if trying to dislodge the childhood memories from his mind. He'd have to do more of this. It was very liberating, and very . . . stimulating. He glanced at the clock on his screen and realized he was late. He closed the laptop's lid, grabbed the tie, and ran down the steps to his car. He was at the evil bitch's house pretty fast, but then again he was daydreaming about what he'd written and wasn't paying attention to the time.

He'd only been here once, a drive-by to see if the site was a suitable location for his work. An artist must survey his setting to make sure it can inspire him, bring the creative juices to boil at just the right moment. Timing was so crucial. But for this type of art, the creative part came only after the evil was purged. Only then could the brilliance be fully expressed.

He parked a block away, down a side street, and huffed it toward the house. In suit and tie, he wouldn't attract attention walking around the neighborhood. And if anyone did question him, he'd pull out his FBI shield and they'd slink away, properly silenced.

He approached the side yard, looking for signs of a security system: magnetic trips on the window sill, wire tape, or even the obnoxious "Protected by" placard stuck in the dirt by the front door. As if a stupid alarm is really going to protect them from someone who wanted to do something evil. Evil—they don't know what evil is!

He stood by the back door and knocked lightly. Listened for a barking dog. Nothing. Very good. He did another walk-around of the perimeter, then stopped at the front door, which was shielded from the street by a dense shrub that stretched ten feet high toward the eave. He gave one last knock and a ring of the doorbell, then decided no one was home. He slipped on latex gloves, removed a lockpick kit from his pocket, chose the proper tools.

A couple minutes later, he was standing in the hallway, taking in the décor. Not bad, but not as elaborate as the last bitch's place. Couple of fabric sofas with a horrid floral print, an old GE television in the corner in a melamine entertainment cabinet, and an area rug on the wood floor. House must've been about thirty, forty years old. Bad taste was a lot older than that.

He made his way into the master bedroom and looked around, in the dresser and night table drawers. No condoms, no thick, heavy watches, no *Sports Illustrated* magazines. No aftershave or musky cologne. Only women's clothing in the closet. Bottom line: no boyfriend or male figure to worry about.

On the way out of the room, he pressed on the mattress. New and firm, perfect for his work. An artist required the proper media, or the result would be unacceptable. But first things first. Purge the evil.

He moved into the kitchen and checked the drawers: four steak knives. He removed one and examined it. Sufficiently sharp. It would do nicely. He replaced it and turned his attention to the refrigerator . . . always a valuable resource. It told so much about people. Not just what's inside, but what's outside. Mounted with magnets were a series of snapshots, all showing the bitch of the house in various poses: standing with a set of snow skis in the winter, barreling through a plume of water on jet skis in the summer, and flexing with her personal trainer at a health club.

Off the main hallway that stretched the length of the house sat another two bedrooms. No furniture in one, an old twin bed and matching oak dresser that were angling for the distressed look in the other. No personal effects. In sum, no roommate.

As he headed back toward the front door, he saw an unopened bill on the credenza. Addressed to Sandra Ann Franks. The bitch's name. He was sure he already knew more about her than her gynecologist. Sandra Ann Franks. Well, it wouldn't be Franks for long. *"I'll have to be frank with you, Miss Franks. No, no, let me be blunt as I drive this knife through your eyes!"*

Sometimes you get so focused you forget to see the humor in the situation.

But evil was no laughing matter. This was serious business. And Sandra Ann Franks had passed the final test. Like moist clay right out of the box, she was ready to be molded and shaped. And cut into pieces.

He glanced at his stopwatch: he'd been in the house nearly four minutes . . . time to go. He clicked the door shut behind him, made sure it was locked. He didn't want anything happening to the bitch before he returned.

Karen Vail stood in the back of an Academy classroom waiting her turn to speak. For each new agent class, she taught an overview of behavioral analysis so the recruits didn't end up like those cops who thought she could hold a piece of the victim's clothing and describe the face of the killer.

"So without further ado, I'd like to have Special Agent Vail come to the podium."

All heads swiveled in Vail's direction, but there was no clapping. Usually, the instructor gave her such a buildup that the new agents felt compelled to stand and bow as if she were some demigod. Or at least welcome her with a warm round of applause. But this instructor was new, and he didn't seem to go into her background as much as the others had. At least, she didn't think he did. Her mind was on Melanie Hoffman, and she wasn't really listening.

She made her way to the front, opened her laptop, and gazed at the inclined classroom—at the eager faces staring at her. She remembered that look, that feeling of excitement at beginning something new. She still loved her work—in an odd sort of way given what she did—and still felt challenged. But it was no longer fresh, and like the exhilaration one feels at the start of a budding romantic relationship the magic had faded with time. The challenge, instead of only coming from the job, morphed into a struggle to keep it interesting.

"I'm Karen Vail," she started. "I know, you were probably expecting a man. I can see it in your faces." She liked to start by putting them on the defensive. Part of the new agent initiation protocol Either that or she'd done too many interrogations—after a while you started looking for the upper hand in all conversations.

"Profiling isn't an exact science, no matter what anyone tells you Now I can just assign you one of Douglas's books to read, then come back in a couple of days to answer questions, but that's not my style. I'm here to give you a perspective on the sick minds we're tracking out there. Well, that's not entirely accurate. The violence they perpetrate on others is sick, for sure, but they're not mentally ill—they know damn well what they're doing. We'll talk more about this later."

After spending a few moments outlining the organizational chart for her unit, she sensed it was time to pick up the pace. A couple of the agents in the back row were slumped over, heads resting in their hands, no doubt thinking about lunch in the dining hall.

"Let's go into some actual examples to give you an idea of how we look at things." She lifted the lid of her laptop, then pressed a button on the lectern's AV panel. The classroom lights dimmed and the rear projection screen behind her glowed with yellow and white text against a black background. "Critical Incident Response Group, Behavioral Profiling Analysis" was boldly emblazoned across the screen. She pressed the Bluetooth remote and advanced to the next PowerPoint slide. In public school, when Vail was growing up, they used real slides. They jammed, they faded if you left them under the projection light too long, and you didn't have near the creativity of the graphics she was able to produce for her FBI presentations on PowerPoint. Now her slides zipped across the screen with fancy corner-to-corner wipes, dissolves, and all sorts of neat effects. Her students still fell asleep on her. So much for technology.

"This is the case I'm currently working on," Vail said. "The Dead Eyes killer." She heard a few snickers. "This isn't a laughing matter," she barked at them. The room got very quiet very quickly. "What you're about to see is disgusting, the product of a monster. I hope none of you have to come upon a crime scene like this one. But my goal is that if you do, you'll at least know something about what you're looking at. And how to go about helping catch the bastard."

She hit the button on the remote and the first slide dissolved on the screen. A woman's bedroom beamed from the computer. Her brutalized torso lay on the bed in front of a mirror, the now-familiar sight of steak knives protruding from both eye orbits. "This was the first victim. Marci Evers. Twenty-eight, brunet. Worked as a paralegal in Vienna." She pressed another button and a second slide wiped across the screen beside the one displaying the crime scene. "Here you see the statistics and facts we know about the victim. I'm going to direct you to one thing, to illustrate a point. How many of you know what MO stands for?" This was basic "Cop 101" stuff, and she knew all their hands would be raised. But she was planning to throw them a curveball, to see who could hit it.

There were forty-some-odd new agents ready to answer. Vail looked at one of the women and nodded. "Go ahead."

"Modus operandi," she said.

"Or method of operation, in English. Yes. Now a tougher question. Does MO ever change?"

This time there were no hands raised. They were thinking, which was good. Vail waited a moment, then gave them the answer. "Research indicates that the MO of sex offenders changes every three to four months. Why?"

Again, no hands were raised. "Okay, let's take a look as to why it would change."

She pulled a laser pointer from her jacket pocket and pointed it at the screen. "Everyone see this blood on Marci Evers's cranium?" The area had been shaved and a small skin laceration was evident at the crown of her head. "Why would there be such an injury?"

"He hit her to knock her out," a new agent said.

Vail nodded. "Good answer. You might be right." She turned back to the screen. "Now let's look at Dead Eyes's second victim." She pressed the remote and another set of slides materialized "Noreen Galvan O'Regan. Twenty-six, brunet, licensed nurse practitioner. Worked in Fredericksburg, lived in Maryes Heights." She pointed at the cranium. "What do we see here?" The laser was pointed at a shaved portion of Noreen's scalp.

"Another blow to the head," a woman in the back row remarked.

"Indeed. But this one's larger, wouldn't you say? The injury is more extensive. This is Dead Eyes's MO, ladies and gentlemen. A blow to the head. But we're still not sure why the killer did this to his victims, and we can't explain why Noreen's is worse than Marci's. Let's look further." She changed the slide. "What's this—anybody?" It was a close-up of Marci's right hand, showing two broken fingernails, cuts, and bruises on the hand and forearm.

"Defensive wounds?" asked someone in the first row.

"Exactly. Defensive wounds. Let's back up a second and take a look at Noreen's hands." She hit the next slide. "No broken nails. A large bruise on the right forearm. So why are there so few defensive wounds on Noreen?"

Vail clicked a few times with the mouse and located a folder containing digital pictures. After opening one of the photos, she could tell from their faces that some of them were getting it.

"This is Melanie Hoffman, his latest victim. I was at her crime scene this morning." She clicked the mouse again and additional views of Melanie's crime scene appeared. Vail glanced at each one, then asked the class, "What do you see?"

"The back of her head is totally caved in," an agent said. "And there aren't any defensive wounds."

"Now, can we reach a conclusion as to why the offender inflicted these blows on his victims?"

"To immobilize them." The voice came from a corner in the back of the room. It was Thomas Gifford, the Assistant Special Agent-in-Charge of Special Investigations—Vail's boss. She had not seen him come in, but that was Gifford's way. Stealth.

"That's exactly right," Vail said, playing along, unsure why Gifford was sitting in on her class. His office was in the same building as hers was, fifteen minutes down the road. "The offender used the blows to immobilize his victims. The head injuries were progressively more substantial as we go from victim one to victim three because he learned from his encounter with Marci Evers. She fought back. We saw all those defensive wounds. The next time around, he was more prepared. He took out Noreen O'Regan more efficiently, with a more damaging blow to her cranium—and he succeeded. No broken nails, just a bruise on the forearm. She didn't put up much of a fight. And now, when he gets to his next victim, Melanie Hoffman, we

don't see any defensive wounds. He learned from his two prior en
counters and refined his methods. He improved his MO."

"So MO can change," ASAC Gifford said.

He was trying to help her. Vail didn't need—or want—his assis
tance. "That's right. Give Agent Gifford a gold star." The smile dis
appeared from his face. "MO can change, so that's why we don"
usually rely on it to give us *linkage*. Linkage allows us to connect on
victim to another, which gives us valuable information about the of
fender. So if we can't use MO to establish linkage, we have to use an
other convention, called *ritual*. Anyone want to venture what ritua
is? Anyone other than my boss," she said, forcing a smile.

There were no takers. "Ritual," Vail said, "is psychosexual need
based behavior. It's behavior that's unnecessary to the successfu
commission of a crime. It can be cutting the victim's hair, removing
her organs—things that have nothing do with killing the victim o
preventing us from catching him. These kinds of *behavior* speak to a
inner need the killer's not even aware of." She stopped, glanced a
Gifford, then looked away. "So we know MO changes. What abou
ritual?"

No hands raised.

"Ritual behavior does not change, primarily because, unlike MO
he's not even conscious of why he's doing it. Now," Vail said, raising
an index finger for emphasis, "*signature* is another term we need t
discuss. It's the unique combination of ritual behaviors seen at tw
or more crime scenes. This is important because we can get a signa
ture *within* MO and ritual, which is an exciting new paradigm—"

"Agent Vail."

It was Gifford, and his face, in the gray and red hue thrown of
from the projected photos, looked hard. Angry.

"Yes, Agent Gifford." She tried to treat him like one of the clas
but knew that wouldn't last long.

"Signature is signature. MO is MO. The two do not mix."

Gifford had been a profiler for a couple of years but throug
some inner political maneuverings, a death, and some unexpected–
and untimely—retirements, he moved up the chain of command ver

rapidly. His brief stint with the profiling unit made him an annoyance. He knew just enough to make skilled profilers' lives miserable, but not enough to really know what he was doing. Most ASACs in the history of the unit were pure administrators and had no on-the-job training. Vail figured it had been done that way for a reason.

Vail did not like being corrected in front of a class of new agents. She swallowed hard, then forced a smile. "Well, I can see why you think I'm wrong. However, after an offender perfects his MO, and there's no need to change it, we start to see the offender engaging in well-defined MO *behaviors*—behaviors that won't change because he doesn't *need* to change them. These behaviors become a signature *within* the MO."

"Agent Vail," Gifford said, standing and moving to the front of the small auditorium. "I think you're done here today. Why don't you wait for me in the library."

She watched him approach, shocked he would treat her like this, in this setting. She must have stood there a little too long, as he leaned into her face.

"The library, Agent Vail."

"Yes, sir." She laid the remote on the lectern, put her head down, and walked out, avoiding the gaze of all the embarrassed agents. But she knew they were more than likely shocked; she was the one who was embarrassed.

And furious.

VAIL SAT WAITING for Gifford for twenty minutes. The library was neat and orderly, quiet and grand, with floor-to-ceiling brown brick walls and wood panel insets, black granite countertops and a three-story central atrium. Against a wall stood a silent grandfather clock that, Vail noticed, was running fifteen minutes slow.

Gifford walked in with a scowl on his large face and sat down hard at the table to her right. He pulled out his PDA and began making notes with the stylus, completely ignoring Vail's presence. But she knew what was going on. With her background in psychology, it was quite clear. He was maneuvering for control, establishing who was in charge. He was telling her that he would talk to her when he was ready—and that she would have to come to him.

Vail decided to play a little control game of her own. She opened a book she had brought with her to class, which happened to be the bible of investigators worldwide—a reference text on violent crimes written by the founding FBI profilers. She had been through the *Crime Classification Manual* several times in the past and wasn't really reading it now. However, showing Gifford that she was not put off by his behavior neutralized the power he was trying to assert over her.

Vail thumbed through the pages. Gifford pecked away with his stylus. She wondered how long he was planning to keep up the charade. She knew he was reaching when he began poking at the tiny on-screen keyboard, one letter at a time. There was just so much patience someone could have with that.

"Turn to page two sixty-one."

Vail looked up, unsure if he was talking to her. "Sir?"

"Page two sixty-one. Bottom of the page, I believe."

Gifford was referring to the section on MO and signature. She closed the text and turned to face him. He was looking at her, his expression telling her he thought he had made his point. "Sir, this was written over twenty-five years ago. It was groundbreaking back then but it's outdated. Or at least incomplete."

"Karen Vail, crack profiler for six years, says that the preeminent research on the topic is outdated. Well let me tell you something, Agent Vail. Human behavior doesn't change—"

"But the way we look at it and classify it does."

"Let's get one thing straight. If you want to write a research paper filled with your personal theories, go ahead. Get it published if you can. Hell, when you retire you can follow in the paths of John Douglas and Thomas Underwood and write several goddamn books on the topic. But until your theory is generally accepted procedure, you stick with what is. I want you out there expounding *these* principles. Outdated as you may *think* they are."

"Sir—"

"I think I've made myself clear. Now, whether you're teaching new agents or out in the field giving lectures to the law enforcement community, the message has to be consistent. And right now, that means quoting chapter and verse from that manual you hold in your hands."

"Sir, in the beginning *all* of this was theory. The principles you speak about arose from a group of agents' understanding of criminology and their personal beliefs."

"Wrong. Their *principles* arose from thousands of hours of interviews with prisoners and years of painstaking research into the minds of these killers. Their principles have helped lead to the arrest and conviction of hundreds of violent offenders over the years."

"I'm well aware of that. And I have tremendous respect for them and their work—"

"But you think you've come up with something they didn't think of."

"Yes, sir, I do."

"Fine. Keep it to yourself. When you've done exhaustive research and can prove your theories, I'll be willing to listen to what you have to say. Until then, you're mute on the subject."

He rose from his chair and headed out of the library, leaving Vail at the adjacent table, chewing on her lip.

Following her acrimonious meeting with Gifford, Vail headed down I-95 to Jonathan's middle school. The sky was still overcast and the air was heavy with the smell of precipitation. As she approached the school grounds, she saw Jonathan walking along the sidewalk with an auburn-haired girl who had a shapelier figure than Vail remembered having had herself at fourteen.

Vail pulled over to the curb and rolled down the window. "Hey handsome," she said to her son, "want a ride?"

Jonathan smiled and some color filled his cheeks. Obviously, this girl meant something to him. "Mom, this is Becca."

Vail nodded. "Nice to meet you." She knew Jonathan wanted to talk, and she'd promised to meet with him around 4:30, but was now a good time, when he was with his latest heartthrob? "Becca, can I give you a ride home?"

"I'm fine," she said. "I only live across the street." Becca turned to Jonathan and took his hand, then whispered something in his ear. Vail turned away, attempting to respect her son's privacy . . . even though she really wished Jonathan was wearing a wire.

Jonathan got in the car and fastened his seat belt as Vail pulled away.

"She's cute."

"I guess."

Vail glanced over at Jonathan. "So how was school?"

"Fine."

The one- and two-word answers drove Vail crazy much of the time, but she knew it was all part of being a teenager.

"Everything okay?"

"Yeah."

"Look, I took time off work. If there's something bothering you, I think we should talk. Don't you?"

Jonathan was still staring out the window as they passed a Baskin-Robbins. "How about some ice cream?" he asked.

"It's winter. Are you serious?"

"Serious."

The smell of French vanilla hit her as she walked through the door. "See? It's empty because no one eats ice cream in the winter when it's twenty-five degrees outside."

"I do." He walked up to the counter and ordered a chocolate shake, then joined his mother at a small table across the room. It was warm inside, practically humid, and the storefront windows were fogged almost the entire way up to the ceiling. Vail pulled off her gloves and undid her scarf. Jonathan sat there, hunkered down with his coat zipped to his chin.

"When you call me and tell me you need to talk, it's usually for one of two things. Money is the second. Your father is the first."

Her son nodded but did not say anything.

"You know I'm an FBI agent, not a dentist, right? I'm not good at pulling teeth." She smiled, but his face remained a mask. "Okay, so this is serious. Your father, right? You're angry with him."

"Well, duh. How'd you guess?"

Vail resisted the urge to admonish him for his fresh mouth. "So what'd he do that made you so angry?"

Jonathan's jaw tightened, and he looked away.

Vail decided it was best to wait him out. She could tell he wanted to talk; it was a matter of him gathering the courage to open up.

The whir of the milkshake machine filled the small store. A moment later, when Jonathan turned back to her, his nostrils were flaring. "He never listens to me. He never talks to me unless he wants me to do something for him. Then he yells at me if I don't do things just the way he wants them done. Calls me a retard. A stupid retard, that he's—" Jonathan stopped and looked away again.

Vail detected a slight quiver in his lower lip. There was a glassy look to his eyes, too. "That he's what, Jonathan?"

"That he's embarrassed to have an idiot for a son."

Vail felt the anger well up inside her. It was the same bullshit Deacon had pulled with her, in the last year of their marriage. The verbal abuse. The need to feel powerful by berating others. "That must've hurt."

Jonathan's gaze was down in his lap somewhere, as if trying to hide his emotions.

The milkshake machine stopped its whine, replaced by the taps and clinks of glass and metal scoops.

Vail scooted her chair over slightly and placed a hand on Jonathan's. "I know what it's like. Your father is . . . insensitive." *An asshole* is what she wanted to say. Deacon wasn't always like that—though he was never the empathetic type, he was always good to her, and he was there for her when she needed him—until his career fell apart, until he became bitter and jealous. The slide into anger and resentment came soon after, a deepening abyss from which he never escaped.

Vail eyed Jonathan and felt sorry she couldn't have spared him the pain of a breakup, of having to leave him half-time with a bitter, downtrodden father. "But honey," she said, "you know what he said isn't true, right? You're a talented, loving, bright young man. I'm very proud to have you as my son."

Jonathan looked up and found his mother's soft, hazel eyes. Then his face flushed and he began sobbing. She leaned closer and took her son by the back of the neck and brought him against her shoulder and held him there, letting him cry. She flashed on the memory of her six-year-old boy who'd fallen off his bicycle . . . his friends laughing at him and Jonathan bursting into tears, more out of embarrassment than from injury. She stroked his hair now as she'd done then and waited until he calmed himself.

The counter clerk put the shake on top of the ice cream case and nodded at Vail. She looked down at Jonathan, who pulled away, sniffling and swiping at his nose with the back of a hand. She grabbed a napkin from the dispenser and gave it to him.

"He gets drunk just about every night. He pushes me, grabs my shirt collar, and gets in my face." He paused. "I don't want to go back there, Mom. I don't care if I never see him again."

Vail completely understood his feelings, but at the same time, it disheartened her to think that her son couldn't stand to be with his father. "He's got joint custody. It's not up to you, or even me."

"You've got to do something, Mom. I'm not going back there."

"I'll call my attorney. You may have to talk to him, probably even someone from the court, too. The judge won't listen to me. He needs to hear it from you."

"Fine. Whatever."

"In the meantime, you're going to have to stay at your father's. When he says those things to you, just ignore him. Hum a song in your head, or just think of me, telling you how terrific you are. I know it's hard. I lived through it myself."

"Yeah, but one day you decided you were leaving, and that was that."

"It wasn't that simple, Jonathan."

"Doesn't matter. You're gone and I'm still there."

His words were like arrows to her heart. It *wasn't* that simple . . . but Jonathan was right: he was stuck there and she had escaped. They sat silently for a moment, memories rushing through her mind like a bullet train. A tear rolled down her cheek, lost its hold, then dropped to her lap.

Jonathan sat there, staring at the window, and did not say a thing. Vail dabbed at her eyes with a napkin, then took the shake from the counter, and placed it in front of her son. He didn't move. Vail followed his gaze to a small droplet of water winding its way down the fogged window, leaving behind a trail of clear glass as it moved lower. She wondered if Jonathan was somehow relating to the path of the lone drop moving through a wall of murky fog. Then the image of Melanie Hoffman's blood murals popped into her mind.

She shook her head and forced her thoughts back to Jonathan. But as so often was the case, her work had intruded on her personal space.

"Go ahead and drink your shake," Vail said. She pulled out her phone. "I'll call my attorney, see about getting you out of that house as soon as possible." She punched the keys with a vicious anger. "Whatever it takes, Jonathan, I promise I'll get you out of there."

After dropping Jonathan at Deacon's house, Vail put in another call to her family law attorney and spent a nervous evening plotting out her strategy . . . making lists and organizing her thoughts to help the lawyer build a solid argument for revisiting the custody arrangement.

But with the dawning of the new morning, she had to push Jonathan's problems aside and force her attention back to her job. Robby was waiting for her to pick him up en route to an interview with Melanie Hoffman's parents. The Hoffmans lived in an older clapboard house on acreage buried in a wooded area of Bethesda. Built eighty or ninety years ago, by Vail's estimation, it was well maintained and sported a collection of flowerpots and wreaths arranged on the front porch.

She and Robby stood at the door and waited for the Hoffmans to answer the knock. A detective had already delivered the news about their daughter's death, so they were at least spared the task of having to tell parents their little girl had not only passed on, but that her death was a horrific one, one you wouldn't wish on your worst enemies.

Footsteps clapped along behind the front door. Wood flooring, Vail figured, heavy steps. Mr. Hoffman, no doubt.

"Sounds like we got the man of the house," Robby muttered to Vail.

The door swung open and revealed a man of around fifty, about thirty extra pounds piled on his midsection. Clear blue eyes, glazed over, with a head of receding dark brown hair. Delicate features. Melanie's father, for sure.

"Roberto Hernandez, Vienna PD. We spoke on the phone." Robby waited a beat, received a slight flicker in the man's eyes as ac knowledgment, then continued: "This is my partner, Karen Vail, with the FBI."

The man nodded. "Howard Hoffman. Wife's in the living room." He held the door open for them, and they entered the modest home. Wood plank floors, as Vail surmised. What she hadn't anticipated were the paintings hanging everywhere there was wall space. Paintings similar in style to those they had seen in Melanie's house.

"Melanie was very talented," Vail noted as they followed Howard into the living room.

"My wife," he said, motioning with a hand. "Cynthia."

"Ma'am," Robby said, nodding at her. He and Vail stood there awkwardly, awaiting a response from the woman. But she simply stared ahead at the window at the far end of the room.

"Can I get you anything?" Howard asked.

"Just some answers," Vail said, attempting a slight smile.

Howard sat on the couch beside Cynthia and motioned his guests to the opposing love seat.

"We're sorry for your loss," Robby said. "I can't imagine—"

"She was a very special girl."

The voice came from Cynthia, but it was so soft Vail wondered whether she had actually heard something. But Robby had heard it too, because he stopped in midsentence. They both looked at the woman. She was Howard's age, but her posture and grief made her appear older. Shoulders rolled forward, hands curled around a tissue in her lap, eyes bloodshot, and wavy chestnut hair falling loosely around the sides of a haggard face.

Vail waited for elaboration, but Cynthia did not offer anything. Her gaze did not move.

"Mr. Hoffman," Robby said softly, "we know Melanie had just started working for McGinty & Pollock. Where did she work before that?"

"A big firm in DC, I don't remember the name. Began with a 'P.'"

"Price Finnerton." From Cynthia. They looked at her, and Vail made note of the name on her pad.

"Did she have any problems there? Did anyone give her a hard time, any conflicts with her boss?"

"Nothing."

Vail and Robby waited for elaboration from Cynthia, but there was no reaction.

"Do you know why she left? Was she unhappy there?"

"She loved working there," Howard said. "I told her she was worth more than they were paying her. I kept nagging her about it and to put me off she called some company, I think they call them headhunters. Three weeks later, she got a job offer from McGinty for twenty thousand more than Price Finnerton was paying her." He paused, his head bowing down. "Maybe if she'd stayed put this wouldn't have happened. . . ."

Vail inched forward on the couch. "Mr. Hoffman, we're searching for details right now as to why this happened, but I can assure you it's got nothing to do with what you told Melanie. The man who did this has killed other women and he'll kill again. It has nothing to do with you or the advice you gave your daughter." Vail had no guarantee what she was telling Howard was true, but she hated seeing the victim's family beat themselves up with guilt over things they had said or hadn't said, done or hadn't done.

Howard nodded but kept his head down. Robby offered him a tissue, and he took it, wiped at his eyes.

"Mr. Hoffman, are you aware of anyone, family members included, who might've had a disagreement with Melanie?"

"No."

"What about friends? Did she have many?"

Howard tilted his head up, made eye contact. "A few close ones. They were all good people. Most were single, one was divorced, like Melanie."

Robby squinted. "Melanie was divorced?"

"Annulled," Cynthia said. She turned to face Robby. "Her marriage was annulled. There's a difference." Her voice was stronger, but her eyes fluttered back down to her lap.

"This guy's name?" Vail asked.

"You don't think he—"

Robby held up a hand. "We turn over a lot of rocks during the course of an investigation. Just to see what crawls out."

"Neil Kroes. We've got a number somewhere. Cynthia, hun, can you get it?" Without a word, Cynthia rose and walked out of the room.

"We'll need a list of her friends, too," Vail said. She tore a piece of paper from her notepad and handed it to Howard with a pen. While he wrote down their names, Vail continued: "Do you know if she frequented any bars or nightclubs?"

"That wasn't Melanie. She didn't drink, didn't like the nightlife. And she didn't use drugs, either, if that was going to be your next question."

Vail sensed some anger, as if it would be an insult if she had asked. The murals flashed in her mind, along with Hancock's comment. "What about her artwork? Did she have classes, formal training of any sort?"

"She took classes in college, then studied privately with a family friend in Alexandria."

"The friend's name?"

Howard's eyes narrowed. "She's seventy-nine years old, Agent Vail. I doubt she murdered my daughter."

Vail was about to tell him that often an innocent person can provide information that leads to another individual, who leads to someone else that turns out to be the killer. But Robby told him before she could open her mouth.

"Cyn, honey," Howard called into the kitchen, "we need Martha's number, too."

They continued to ask Howard questions about his daughter's habits, family background, dating habits, and the always delicate question, her sexual practices. Howard's drawn face looked ashen when Vail asked the question. But he answered it succinctly: "She wasn't promiscuous, and besides, she didn't have much time for dating."

Cynthia returned to the room, handed Robby a slip of paper, and took her place on the couch.

Vail felt they had reached their limits for this visit. If they needed more information, they could drop by again, or simply call—which might be easier on the Hoffmans.

Robby, apparently sensing what Vail was thinking, rose from the couch and extended a hand. Howard shook it but didn't make eye contact.

"Thanks for your help," Vail said. "We'll let ourselves out."

They made their way down the hall but were stopped in their tracks by Howard's voice. "When you catch this monster, I want to see him. I want some time alone with him."

Vail and Robby had no answer, other than to nod. They turned back to the door and left.

*H*er eyes stare straight ahead in rapture as I pull the bindings tighter. She doesn't cry out, which is odd, but the terror is in her face—the jaw muscles are vise-tight, the forehead crinkled with dread. She doesn't deserve to live. Because it's there, like I tell them, it's there if you'd only look. Do you see it, Agent Vail? Just like Douglas said—study the art, you'll know the artist. So study! What do you see?

I'll tell you what you see. You see nothing. Because you can't; you're blinded by what it means. You watch, frozen and helpless as I bring the knife back and stab her right eye, a nauseating squish! as the blade penetrates the surface and goes deeper into the brain—

Vail sat up, chest heaving, her throat dryer than dust, her heart bruising itself against her ribcage. *Holy shit.* That was all she could think: *Holy shit, that was intense.*

She lay in bed another hour or so, trying to fall back asleep, all the while hoping she wouldn't, fearing a return to the dream that just about took her breath away. By the time dawn began creeping around the edges of her window shades, she was finally tired enough to drift off. Her alarm clock blared an hour later, and had she not just bought the damn thing she would have thrown it through the window. But then she'd have a window to repair, and in the past year the divorce had caused enough self-inflicted hell in her life. She was enjoying the calm and hoped there wasn't a storm lurking around the bend.

When Vail got to the office, she remembered she was first up on the card to present. Twenty-five years ago, the founders of the profiling unit chose Wednesday mornings for a free-thinking roundtable discussion of current cases the agents were working. The unit still met on Wednesday mornings, and the brainstorming sessions remained a useful tool that ensured the lead profiler had not overlooked something because he had gotten too close to his case. Sometimes having some-one look over your shoulder enabled you to pull back from the needle to see the haystack.

The meetings were held in a large rectangular conference room, with the new budget-conscious Bureau crafting a fiscally intelligent setup. Instead of a long, traditional oval table that had but one pur-pose, the new look was six rectangular cherry wood tables neatly abutting each other, forming one large table around which sixteen people could sit. If needed, the tables could be separated into six-seaters for impromptu workshop sessions.

Tan wallpaper with textured vertical stripes added to the room's utilitarian feel. An LCD projector and wall-mounted screen, over-head projector, large pivoting white board, and television/VCR/DVD setup were silently placed off to the side in an alcove, like a coroner ready to pull back the sheet to expose the horrors of psy-chotic minds.

Seated around the segmented conference table were Vail's profil-ing colleagues: senior members Art Rooney, Dietrich Hutchings, Tom van Owen, Frank Del Monaco, and nine other men who'd been with the unit fewer than five years.

Vail hadn't had much time to prepare this morning's presenta-tion. She had been handed a CD with the remaining photos from Melanie Hoffman's crime scene fifteen minutes ago, and she had rushed to view them on her laptop to throw them into some sem-blance of order. But she knew the case well, at least up to the point of the latest victim, and felt confident she could wing the rest of it.

Because she was the first and only woman in the profiling unit, looking good in front of her peers was important. She always felt she was held to different standards, higher levels of scrutiny. During her first few weeks in the new position, every time she was shown a crime scene photo of a dismembered body, a female so grotesquely beaten that she no longer had a face, the others in the unit expected her to grab for the garbage pail and puke her guts out. Not that they didn't do that *their* first time around—they simply expected her to be weak because she was a woman. She was not superhuman—of course the pictures affected her—but she only wanted to be treated the same way they had treated each other.

But Vail felt that people learned who they were by placing themselves into situations and seeing how they reacted. While staring at grotesque photos of women who had been abused, she gained a tremendous amount of insight into herself. Insight that told her when it was time to leave her husband.

Vail stood at the head of the room with her expandable Dead Eyes case folder lying on the conference table in front of her. She opened the PowerPoint file and started the slide show mode.

She brushed back her hair, then took a sip of burnt coffee. It was time to start. "I've got an update on Dead Eyes," she said in a normal speaking volume. The obligatory "shushes" followed. "He's struck again, this time a young female CPA. Baseline crime scene pretty much the way he left it with vics one and two." Vail punched the remote and the first slide appeared. Someone hit the light switch in the back of the room and everything darkened except for the faces of the agents, which were illuminated by the light bouncing off the screen.

It was a wide-angle view of Melanie Hoffman's bedroom. Vail took a second to scan it, then said, "Stabbed through the eyes with ordinary steak knives taken from the vic's apartment. Eviscerated stomach, kidneys, and liver. Left hand severed but not recovered by the techs. Small intestine tied around the victim's thighs. Blood painted all over the walls." She paused for a moment to let the information sink in. "Victim was a recent addition to a DC accounting firm. Nothing stood out in the interview with the parents. Couple of things to follow up on, but that's it. The task force was reassembled, headed up by Paul Bledsoe, Fairfax County."

One of the agents leaned forward. "I haven't looked at this case in a while, but are we still thinking this guy's disorganized?"

Vail looked at the man who had asked the question. Tom van Owen, a nine-year veteran of the unit. His cuticles were red and inflamed, the skin peeling from being incessantly picked. Even now, he sat reclining in the ergonomic chair, absently scraping at the calluses around the nail bed with his other hand.

"I don't think so," Vail said. She clicked past the next few slides until she reached the ones that showed the murals. "Even though there *is* an awful lot of blood, I'm not convinced it's a sign of disorganization." Vail thought of Chase Hancock's "painter" comment. She clenched her jaw, irritated he may've been right.

"He used weapons of opportunity. Those knives," Dietrich Hutchings said. He waved at the screen with his thick-framed reading glasses. "They're the vic's, you said."

"I know that points to disorganization, but I'm thinking something else." Typically, disorganized offenders did not bring weapons with them; they used common objects found in the victim's own house. "Cause of death appears to be asphyxiation, just like the others. So the knives aren't opportunistic weapons," Vail explained. "The knife wounds are postmortem—making them part of his ritual, not his MO. The fact that he knows most women have a set of steak knives in their kitchen, which means he doesn't have to risk hauling knives with him, indicates organization. Not disorganization."

There was quiet for a moment before Art Rooney spoke up. Rooney had a crew cut and a military politeness and formality to him. He had once called the Quantico Marine Base home. "So we're adjusting our profile to indicate a mixture of organization and disorganization."

Vail hesitated. "I haven't had much time to digest this. At this point, I'd have to say yes. If not almost completely organized."

"Did the vic have defensive wounds?" Rooney's slow, Southern demeanor seemed to be out of sync with the rest of the profilers' urgent tones.

"None. Which again suggests this guy is planning his approach better, possibly using guile and disguise to comfort his vics before he takes them out. Definitely organized."

Rooney frowned and his eyes again found the screen. "But the mess, the blood. . . . "

Vail respected Rooney's profiling abilities and understood his point: typically, a crime scene like Melanie Hoffman's indicated a disorganized offender, one of lower intelligence who did less planning.

Their attacks tended to be blitzlike, creating more blood. Vail paged through the slides to the murals. "I think we're looking at a series of *paintings* here. I'm having prints of these sent over to BSU for analysis. There might be some deep-seated message in here. I've also asked for them to be examined by an expert in Impressionist art, in case the offender had art training."

"An *artiste*. That's a new one," Frank Del Monaco said, his round, saggy face contorting into a smirk. He glanced at a few of his colleagues, who shared the ridicule. "But I can't disagree. He certainly left . . . an *impression*."

Laughter erupted just before the conference room door opened and a long male shadow spilled into the room. Thomas Gifford walked in and observed the levity; a few of the agents were still guffawing. Gifford then looked at Vail, whose stern face indicated she was not sharing the joke.

Vail locked eyes with Del Monaco. "I don't want to miss anything, Frank. Thinking out of the box is supposed to be a strength here."

Gifford marched to Vail's side and stood in front of the screen. The room became silent. The blood mural covered his dark suit and face with a red pall as he spoke. "Just a heads-up. I got word late yesterday that Senator Eleanor Linwood has requested—or more like *told*—Fairfax PD's Chief Thurston to add her lead security detail agent to the Dead Eyes Task Force. His name is Chase Hancock. Ring a bell to anyone?"

Frank Del Monaco spoke. "The asshole who sued the Bureau because he didn't get one of our seats."

"That's the one," Gifford said. "Now let me warn you people. This guy is trouble. But the police chief is doing the senator a favor. Some backroom political maneuvering. She wants to look tough on crime in an election year. That democrat, Redmond, is breathing down her throat in the early polls and she thinks she can use Dead Eyes to boost her approval rating."

"So we get dragged into shoveling their political bullshit," van Owen said.

"We're thirty miles from DC," Gifford said. "They've got a list of shit shovelers there dating back two hundred years."

Rooney coughed a deep, raspy gurgling, then cleared his throat and asked, "Any chance we can do an end run around this? I've known assholes with more brains than this Hancock chump."

"Easiest way to be rid of him is to draw up the best goddamn profile you've ever done. Give the dicks a write-up that's right on the money, something they can run with. Otherwise, stay out of Hancock's way. That's how we play it. Do your jobs, and let him do his. If he gets to be a problem, let me know and I'll handle it."

"Let him hang himself," Vail said.

"Exactly." Gifford dipped his chin in her direction, handing the discussion back to Vail, and then took a seat in the back of the room.

Vail hit the next slide, a wide-angle view of the exterior of the house. "Bledsoe is checking into Melanie Hoffman's past and present accounting firms. It's possible whoever did her might have met her through the workplace. Co-workers, clients, support staff, everyone's being looked at. There's also an ex-husband. Marriage was annulled three years ago."

She hit the remote a few more times, showing the photos of what was once a beautiful young woman. Again and again slides flicked across the screen, the latest one being a close-up of Melanie's head and trunk.

"This is his fourth victim." Vail said it as if they should feel shame for not having helped catch the offender before he'd taken another young life.

"You mean third. This is his third vic," Del Monaco said. "That last one wasn't the same guy."

"You know my thoughts on that." And indeed he did. Everyone knew her opinion, because a year ago, when Dead Eyes had last struck, she made her opinion well-known.

"What does Bledsoe think?"

Vail glared at Del Monaco. "He's operating under the same assumption."

"Uh huh."

"What's your problem, Frank?"

"All we have with that other vic is a very loose connection to Dead Eyes. Vic was killed and disemboweled. That's it. No wrapping of the intestines around the thigh, no stabbing of the eyes, no severing of the hand, almost no other signature evidence. We've seen scenes like that a hundred times before. Nothing links the vic, or the offender, to Dead Eyes."

Vail scanned the faces in the room. No one seemed to be disagreeing with Del Monaco. If anything, their expressions seemed to put the onus on her to prove his opinion wrong. But her brain was foggy from the rotten night's sleep and she didn't feel like getting into it with him. She tried to focus. Before her brain had the sense to back off, her mouth was moving. "True, the eyes weren't stabbed. So what?"

"So what?" Del Monaco looked around the room, as if to garner support for his consternation. Since most gazes remained on Vail, he turned his attention back to her. "So, *Karen,* the signature is all wrong. Just about all the behaviors are missing. You've got some parallel aspects between the killings but there's no linkage."

"We've been through all this before," another profiler said.

"Copycat," Hutchings said. "That's all it was, if you could even call it that."

Vail was shaking her head in disagreement. "You're all missing the point. True, there are things the offender didn't do with this victim, but I believe it's the same guy. I mean, just look at the crime scene."

"We looked, a year ago," Rooney said. His voice was even more scratchy now. "There's no convincing linkage there."

"Art, there were only a few defensive wounds, and there was a lot of blood." She stopped, then realized she should review the photos from the scene, in case the offender had left the same murals. If she recalled, there was no blood at all on the walls. If that was correct, it would do nothing to support her linkage theory.

"Were there any Impressionist blood murals?" Del Monaco asked.

"I'll have to check—"

"And what about food? Did he eat his usual peanut butter and cream cheese ketchup sandwich at the scene, postmortem?"

"No."

"And the incapacitating blow?" Del Monaco was flipping pages as he spoke.

"Disabling skull wound. Same as vics one and two—"

"You can't say that, Karen." This from Rooney, whose eyes were fixed on a particular document. "You can't say it was the same. Vics one and two were hit from behind, the other one from the side."

"So she suddenly realized what was happening and turned her head at the last second."

"When you turn your head to duck, you throw your hands up. It would've broken a few fingers. Hell, even a nail or two." Rooney held up the file. "There were no such defensive wounds."

There was quiet. Vail felt as if she'd been cross-examined and the defense attorney had just made a case-breaking point. But even as she tried to concentrate on a reply, she felt Gifford's stare boring into her, disrupting her concentration.

She knew what he was thinking. It wasn't the same way she knew what Robby Hernandez was thinking. She knew what to expect because she'd already gone toe to toe with Gifford about linkage of this victim to the Dead Eyes killer.

With his arms folded across his wide chest, it was as if Gifford wanted Vail to put her foot in her mouth. And unfortunately, she was about to accommodate him.

"Look at the facts, Karen," Del Monaco said. It was as if he had suddenly realized Gifford was still in the room, and was now playing to him. "Just about none of the behaviors were present in the third scene that were present in the first two. Think about it logically. It's a different guy."

Telling her to think about it logically was like saying she was being irrational. At least, that's the way she saw it. But she didn't want to blow it all out of proportion and claim he'd said that because she was a woman. It pissed her off regardless. "I believe the offender was interrupted before he had a chance to finish what he'd started.

That's why the crime scene looked different." Admitting the crime scene looked different threw water on her fire, killed her entire argument. Such major variations in crime scenes often meant a different killer was involved. This wasn't lost on Gifford.

"The crime scene did look different, didn't it, Agent Vail?"

Gifford was leaning back, an attorney asking a hostile witness a damaging question to which he knew the answer.

Vail wondered how much of this was fallout from their prior altercation in the library. "Because the offender was interrupted," she said. "Otherwise, we'd be seeing the same ritualistic behavior we've seen in his other crime scenes."

"That's assuming it's the same offender."

She clenched her jaw. They were breaking all the rules of what the session was about. It was supposed to be a free-thinking exchange of ideas, not an attack.

"Pretty damn clear," Del Monaco said. "We have no reason to think it's the same guy."

Several other agents nodded their heads, and like grains of sand sliding through her fingers, she felt control slipping away.

"We had this debate a year or so ago, right?" Gifford asked. "Until we have convincing evidence to think otherwise, we need to put this to rest. It's time to move on."

Vail set the remote down and flipped her file folder shut. "That's all I have." She glanced over her shoulder at the image of a blood mural spilling over the screen's edge, the indelible picture of Melanie Hoffman's defaced torso embedded in her mind. She faced her colleagues, who were reclining in their seats, looking at her. "Thanks for all your input."

She gathered her belongings and headed out the door.

He had another burst of inspiration and found himself running to the keyboard. He sat pecking away at the keys, the words flying onto the document as if being spray painted onto the screen.

"Where the hell are you, you little runt? Come here and play with me!"

I cover my ears and close my eyes, even though it's dark in here. So dark, I'm sometimes scared. But I'm safe. I can do anything I want in here, and he can't stop me. I can stay here for hours and hours. He never wonders where I am unless he wants me. As long as I don't answer him, he thinks I'm outside, hiding somewhere on the ranch. He knows he'd never find me until I'm ready to come home. All that land is good for hiding, too. I can sleep out with the stars, I can see them all at night, it's so dark, so very dark.

But my place here is warm and secret. I've brought stuff in here with me, made it my home. Besides, I can watch him from here. I know where he is. As long as he doesn't find me—

"Son of a bitch, where the fuck are you?"

I hear the back door open and slam shut. Looking for me. He wants me again.

I hate his smell, his dirty nails, his crooked teeth, and beer breath. I hate his yellow pee-stained underwear.

I hate him.

No more of this. No more pain.

No more—

He jumped up from his chair and stood in front of his desk, the laptop screen glowing, the cursor blinking, his face damp with cold sweat. So powerful. So vivid the memories, yet so far away, so very long ago. He had to find a vehicle for these thoughts, these memories. He thought on that for a moment but nothing useful came to him, not yet, at least. He wiped his face with a sleeve, then walked over to his workbench, where he folded a soft diaper into a precise square, then huffed a cloud of fog onto the brass badge and buffed it hard. Three times. Rub, rub, rub. The smudges wiped away, leaving behind the emblem of authority. Power.

He reinserted the badge into his credentials wallet and slipped the leather case into his suit coat pocket. He reviewed the surveillance pictures he'd taken of Sandra Franks, the woman who'd caught his attention a few days ago. Yes, she was an evil one all right. As he flipped through the photos, his jaw tightened. *Definitely evil.*

"This evening's prize is a thirty-year-old dental hygienist originally from Tallahassee, Florida," he announced with game-show-host vigor. "She skis in the winter, swims in the summer, and lifts weights year-round. A fine physical specimen. Dennis, tell her what she's won."

He chuckled and began swinging his legs beneath his chair. Three times forward, followed by a clicking of his heels. Click click click. Three times; that's just the way it had to be.

He put the photos down, then slipped the pipe into the handmade holster on his belt.

"It's time! We're off to see the Wizard, the wonderful Wizard of Oz. The wizard of Oz! Ozzie, Ozzie and Harriet. Harriet, the original bitch. Bitch, bitch, that's all she does. Bitch, bitch, I'll get that bitch!"

He shrugged into his suit coat, smoothed down the lapels, then appraised his tie in the mirror. He straightened it, then tightened it. Patted down the faux mustache, checked it from all angles. Next was a wool overcoat, topped off with a black Stetson hat.

He stopped by the hall mirror and regarded his reflection. He reached into his jacket pocket and pulled the FBI credentials case. He flipped it open as he'd done a hundred times before and tilted his chin back. "FBI, ma'am. Please open the door. I need your help." *I need your soul. I need your . . . Eyes.*

The pulsed tones of her BlackBerry made Vail jump as she rounded the corner a few blocks from her house. She fished through her pocket and rooted out the device, which displayed a missed call from Robby. Alternating her gaze between the dark, rain-slick roadway and the touch pad, she phoned him back.

As it rang, the intermittent rain returned and began pelting her windshield with a fury. She fumbled for the wiper control as Robby answered.

"Got a call from Bledsoe," he said. "Neighbor found a body, 609 Herrington. He said it sounds like our guy. He's en route, at least fifteen out, asked me to call you."

"I'm only about half a mile away."

"I'm not too far myself. Meet you over there."

The house was a modest one-story brick colonial, the lawn and planters in need of a gardener. A candy apple red Hyundai Sonata was parked in the driveway, a police cruiser behind it, kissing its bumper.

Vail pulled up to the curb, her headlights catching the tear-smeared face of a woman in her fifties standing beneath the porch overhang. Her eyes were puffy, her legs dancing from the cold. A uniformed officer stood beside her.

Vail displayed her credentials as she approached the house.

"Sandy!" the woman whined. "Sandy, she's in there, she's . . . oh, God. She's—"

"Did you clear the house?" Vail asked the young cop.

"No, when I saw the victim, I left everything as it was and got the hell out. I didn't want to compromise—"

"Wait right here," Vail told the woman. "Stay with the officer."

Vail drew her Glock, holding it in a white knuckle grip as she pushed open the front door. Complete darkness. A sudden crack of thunder in the near distance sent another few cc's of adrenaline cascading into her bloodstream.

A metallic smell stung her nose as she walked into the tile entryway. Blood. Death. Slowly into the hall, her pupils large black holes. Heart thumping, sweat popping out across the back of her shoulders.

Off in the distance, above the din of pouring rain striking pavement . . . footsteps.

Rapid, like her heart. The chambering of a round. A semiautomatic . . . a large one. She pressed her back against the wall and waited in the darkness. The footfalls stopped suddenly, and she could feel the presence of a body as it moved down the carpeted hallway toward her. Breathing.

She slid into a crouch and squinted so the whites of her eyes did not reflect a light source and give away her position. A large body turned the corner a few feet away. It was Robby.

She let air escape from her lips and her shoulders slumped in relaxation. "Scared the shit out of me."

"Vic?"

"Haven't found her yet."

They walked in tandem toward what appeared to be the bedroom. But before they reached the door, Vail saw something in the darkness smeared across the walls. Blood. Murals.

"Shit."

"Yeah."

Vail pushed her right shoe against the bedroom door and swung it open. They stood in the doorway and stared at the young woman splayed out across her bed, filleted in the abdomen, and skewered through the eyes.

A flicker of lightning followed by a brilliant flash poured in through the open bedroom window. Vail's eye caught something in the yard, and she again tightened the grip on her sidearm, her head swiveling, eyes searching—

"What's the matter?"

"He's out there," she said, moving down the hallway.

"Who's out there?"

She pulled her cell and hit "9," connecting her with FBI dispatch. "This is Agent Karen Vail with CIRG. Get an air unit over to 609 Herrington. Potential sighting of Dead Eyes suspect." She dropped the phone into her pocket as she ran into the kitchen. Grabbed the knob, yanked open the door.

HE SAW HER, some woman cop, through the bedroom window. She was right there, thirty feet away in the darkness, admiring his artwork. Just what he needed, another critic.

But somehow she knew he was there. He darted through the bushes but stopped when he cut his hand on a sharp branch. He found a safe place to crouch while he licked the blood, to taste it, see what it was like.

Running his tongue across the open wound stung. He didn't think it would hurt so much. At least he tasted better than that slut Sandra did. She was satisfying, but predictably bitter with a strong aftertaste. More iron, less copper. Maybe he was a bit anemic.

He swiveled around, staying behind some bushes. Watching for movement. That bitch cop was going to be coming after him, and he had to be ready.

ROBBY'S .40-CALIBER GLOCK was out in front of him now, his back against the left door frame. Vail was facing him, pressed against the opposite side of the doorway.

"How do you know? How do you know he's here?"

"I saw something, when the lightning lit up the yard. I feel him."

In the next half second, Vail was outside, the rain pouring, another rumble of thunder crawling across the horizon. She made her way through the side yard with reckless abandon, pushing away the thick, overgrown brush with her free forearm. Robby was five feet behind her, slipping on the thick weeds and bushes that hadn't been pruned back in years.

"Karen, where the hell are you going?"

THERE SHE IS! He knew it! Running into the yard—looking for him—but going in the wrong direction. He crouched lower. Thick, woody bushes and a dark suit . . . good cover. He was fairly safe, if only for a short time. But as any good prey who wants to survive knows, you need to get a close look at the hunter. Assess his strengths and weaknesses. After all, even though he knew there'd be no way they'd find him, he still had to be vigilant in making sure he didn't give them too much. Tempting fate was not a smart thing to do.

He put his head back and sniffed. Sucked in deeply. Smelled her scent riding the breeze that carried the rain droplets against his face. Light scent, perfume, with a hint of fear and anger. Yes, she was angry. Very angry.

"KAREN, SLOW DOWN. He could be setting a trap—"

"Shh!" Vail hissed into the darkness, which was illuminated by an obscure moon hiding behind engorged rain clouds. She cut left round a tree but slipped and went down hard. "Goddamnit!"

"You okay?" Robby's voice was behind her, a dozen feet or so.

Another bolt of lightning cracked the sky and lit up the yard, which seemed to go on for a rolling acre of pines, firs, and wild shrubs. Robby was now at Vail's side, his gaze bouncing around the flora. He grasped her by the right arm and lifted her up.

"He's here," she whispered.

"You sure?"

She nodded, though she knew Robby's eyes were on the surrounding shrubs and bushes. Gun in his right hand, legs spread wide and bent slightly at the knees. He was ready, but the question was, ready for what?

"Where?" he asked.

She smelled something on the breeze. Sniffed, crinkled her nose. A scent she couldn't readily identify . . . as well as an odor she knew too well: *Blood*. She looked around, wishing she could hit a switch and turn on the sun, if only for a minute. Get a good look around. *So damn close—*

"Karen?"

"I don't know, I just feel him. Saw something in the yard when the lightning hit. I looked over, saw movement. He was watching us."

"Like an arsonist coming back to watch his handiwork."

Vail didn't answer. She stood there, her left knee throbbing something fierce and bug bite itches prickling her legs. But the most irritating itch of all was the mental one: her need to know why the offender had waited there when he could've been long gone. She had tracked these killers for years from a distance. Glossy black-and-white and color photos in a file folder, interview forms, witness statements. It was all so removed. This was more visceral, urgent, and real-time.

Up close and personal.

He never had a subconscious desire to get caught, as some killers did.

He only got a glimpse of her, but she was good, this woman cop. He could tell. Just a bitch with a badge, but still . . . she was someone he couldn't be sloppy around. She somehow knew he was there . . . as if they shared some kind of sixth sense. The thought sickened him. He hated sharing anything with bitches, let alone his mind.

After that last bolt of lightning had lit up the sky, he took off, scampering through several untended yards. He then sat in his car for a few minutes and panted hard to slow his breathing just in case the police were lurking down the street.

He started the engine and headed home, taking care to stick to the speed limit, signal properly, and make his full stops. He'd once read that a lot of criminals got caught by the police for stupid things, like having a burnt-out brake light. He couldn't imagine that— going through all the hard work and planning, executing perfectly, and then getting pulled over for some inane traffic violation.

Thirty minutes later, he was back at his loft tuning in to the eleven o'clock news. Their lead story: the murder of another bitch . . . but, of course, that's not what the reporter called her. His words were something like, "A young woman, another apparent victim of the Dead Eyes killer." Interesting name they gave him—but not far from the truth, actually.

He watched as a woman they identified as an FBI profiler ducked through the crowd of press corps. She dropped her head and threw up a hand, avoiding the camera as if it would give her skin cancer. He waited until the segment was over, then replayed the recording he'd made. He was looking for one thing in particular.

There! There it was . . . a single frame with a dark, blurry view of her beady little eyes. He hadn't seen them when she was chasing him, hunting him down. But there was something about them. The paused picture was grainy and small, most of her face was blocked, and the image jumped a little as he stared at it. But there was *something* about the eyes. . . .

The TV picture suddenly snapped back to life and the recording began playing again. He let it run and again listened to the reporter drone on, making some comment about how important the case was because a profiler had been assigned. But it didn't bother him. It really wasn't that big a deal. Because he knew they could examine his artwork and look inside his head all they wanted. They would never find him.

As soon as the press heard the calls from Fairfax County PD on their police scanners, TV news vans mobilized. They set up shop at Sandra Franks's house and telescoped their microwave antennae into the sky, as if plugging into the clouds to eavesdrop on God.

But there was no God at this crime scene, or so it seemed to those with even a rudimentary understanding of religious belief. God would not have allowed Sandra Franks to be murdered. God would not have created monsters capable of committing such heinous acts.

"Damn reporters," Vail said.

"Just doing their job," Robby said. "Cut 'em some slack."

"I don't like them blocking my way and shoving mikes in my face. I'm here to do a job, too, and they're in the way."

They stood in the back of the room, staring at the walls, at more murals. Hancock had arrived and was waiting outside with Manette and Bledsoe until the forensic unit had finished documenting the scene. Since Vail and Robby had already been in the house, they figured it was best to stay put rather than tramp through the evidence again.

"So what do you think it all means?"

"This guy is very bold, Robby. A lot of serial killers prey on prostitutes." She turned to him. "You know why?"

"Because they won't be missed."

"Exactly. No one would know they're missing for days, weeks, sometimes months. By then, the trail is cold." A technician's camera flashed. "So the question is, why is this guy picking middle-class women? What is it about them that feeds his fantasy?"

"He knows one that he hates."

"Or knew one. His fantasy goes back a long time, don't forget."

Hancock came up behind them and caught sight of the far wall, where the offender's "It's in the" message was scrawled. "I get it," he said under his breath. "I get it! It's like a puzzle you can't figure out, and then when you do, it's so damn obvious you can't believe you didn't see it before."

Vail's eyes found Robby's in a sideways glance.

"He's hidden something," Hancock continued. "The hand, he's telling us where the hand is. The left hand. He's telling us it's in the house. *It's in the* drawer, *it's in the* refrigerator, *in the* bedroom—"

"It's in *your head*," Vail said. "You can't assume it means anything."

Hancock turned away. "You're wrong. He's telling us something."

"He could also be a whacko." Vail shifted her gaze to Robby. "At this point, all we can say is that either the offender is a nut job—in which case his message means nothing—or that he's quite sane and it carries great meaning to him. The fact that he used the victim's blood tells us it was likely done postmortem. She was either badly injured or dead. And if she's dead, which is likely, then he's taking a huge risk to spend more time there. Longer he's there, more chance he gets caught. For what? If we go with the odds, he's not a whacko. So the message means a great deal to him. But it's not intended *for* him. It's meant for the victim, or for whoever discovers the body."

Vail paced a few steps back and forth, reasoning it through. "If it's a message for us, we have to ask: What's he trying to tell us? Is it something that's true? Or something that's false? Is it literal . . . do we have to start *looking* for something—the hand, like Hancock is suggesting? Or is he taunting, playing with us?"

Vail stopped, regarded Robby for a moment. "Do you see why you can't jump to conclusions about any of this?" She looked at Hancock, who was staring at the wall, attempting to appear as if he hadn't heard what she had said.

But suddenly, he turned toward her. "And sometimes you can overthink something, Detective Hernandez. That's what your friend is doing here. She knows so much, she's trying to impress you, confuse you with issues and questions and all sorts of bullshit that's got nothing to do with anything."

Vail's arms were clenched across her chest. "The only bullshit in the room, Robby, is what Hancock's dishing up. But you know what? This message could be bullshit, too. There was a case where the offender wrote 'Death to the pigs' in blood. It was so Hollywood, it was weird. It scored pretty high on the bullshit radar for me. Turned out he took the phrase from a *Life* magazine article, and he wrote it at the scene to throw us off. You know how long people spent mulling over 'Death to the pigs'? Was it meant for cops, or did he just hate pork?"

Robby laughed.

Vail placed a hand on his forearm. "Listen to me, Robby. Right now we can't make any assumptions about it. You want to help Hancock look for the missing hand, go for it. Maybe you'll find it—or you'll find something else. I don't know. But *to me,* the most significant thing to consider from that message is that the offender took the time to write it in the first place. It meant a lot to him, and it's my job to find out why."

"He didn't finish the sentence," said Sinclair, who had just walked in the door. "You're talking about the message, right? What I want to know is, why didn't the fucker finish the sentence?"

"Good question," Vail said.

"Maybe he wants us to finish it for him," Robby said.

Hancock threw up his hands. "Which is what I've been trying to do. *It's in the* kitchen, *it's in the* drawer, *it's in the* closet. . . ." He walked out of the bedroom, still muttering.

"He okay?" Sinclair asked.

"He's never been okay."

Robby asked, "So what do we do next with this message?"

"We can run it through VICAP. Bureau keeps a database of crime stats just for this reason. It'll give us a rundown of other cases where offenders have written messages in blood—in any bodily fluid, for that matter. It'll tell us what we know about those cases and those offenders. Maybe we can make some connections or establish some patterns or parallels. Offenders don't leave messages very often, so it's a pretty isolated type of activity. Database is going to be small."

"Meantime, we keep plugging away and asking questions."

"The day we stop asking questions," Vail said, "is the day we should turn in our badges."

TWO HOURS LATER, the task force members were huddled in their new base of operations, which had been haphazardly thrown together over the past two days.

It was an old brick house two miles from the latest victim's home, on a mature street with seventy-five-year-old houses. The rooms were dark, lit only by incandescent lamps standing on the floor. Long shadows loomed across the walls, and everyone's faces—being lit from below—looked like something out of a Bela Lugosi horror flick.

A couple of plastic folding tables had been opened in the middle of what had previously been a rectangular living room. There were no shades or blinds on the windows, and the continuous pelting of the glass by the wind and rain created streaks of water blown across the slick surface.

"We got a telephone here?" Mandisa Manette asked.

"Not yet," Bledsoe said. He lifted a medium-size cardboard box from a stack in the corner of the room and dropped it on one of the card tables. He leaned back and swatted at the dust that rose from the box. "I ordered five lines. Four for voice and DSL, one for fax. Be here in a day or two. Till then use your cell."

Bledsoe ripped open the box and removed a few rubber-banded markers. He looked around the room and craned his neck to catch a glimpse of the kitchen. "Who are we missing?"

"Hancock," Vail said. "I say we start without him."

Bledsoe smirked, then leaned close to Vail's ear. "Lay off, okay? The guy may be an asshole, but I'd rather not poison the pool. Let the others find out for themselves. I don't need any trouble, none of us do. Just cooperate with him."

"Yeah, yeah, fine."

"You okay, your knee? Hernandez said you twisted it."

"Went down in the vic's yard."

"You need to go? Get it taken care of?"

"I'm good. Don't worry about it."

Bledsoe nodded, then spun around. "Okay, everyone into the living room. Let's get started."

The front door swung open and in walked Chase Hancock. He closed his umbrella and shook the water onto the linoleum floors that were already slick from the detectives' muddy shoes.

Hancock glanced around, then crinkled his nose. "Who chose this rat hole?"

"We wanted to make you feel at home," Vail said, "but we can't get the stench right."

"Cute, Vail, very cute."

Bledsoe waited for everyone to situate themselves, then took his place at the head of the room. "This is going to be our home until we catch this guy. The accommodations are pretty crappy. I've got eyes, I can see. You don't have to tell me. I'm having some stuff done on the place over the next week or so, to make it functional. One thing it won't be is nice or comfortable. They don't want us getting too cozy here. Feeling is, if we like our surroundings, we won't be in any rush to solve the case." Moans erupted. Bledsoe held up a hand. "I know it's crap, but I'm just telling you how it is. Now, I know it's late—what the hell time is it?" He pulled back his sleeve to see his watch.

"Eleven-thirty," Bubba Sinclair said.

"Jesus. Okay then," Bledsoe continued. "Let's get started so we can all get home sometime before the sun comes up."

Vail thought of Jonathan and remembered she had an appointment with an attorney in the morning. She had already called in to get the time off, and she would have to pull Jonathan out of school. But it was the first step in getting him out of Deacon's reach.

"Our guy struck again this evening. Vic named Sandra Franks. Dental hygienist with a doc on the west side. Hey, Hernandez, you're tall. Why don't you write all this down on the whiteboard?" He tossed Robby the bunch of rubber-banded colored markers.

"What does being tall have to do with—"

"It's late, let's just get through this so we can go home."

Robby stepped up to the whiteboard and wrote, "Sandra Franks, dental hygienist."

"Dental hygienists are weird. They work P-T at lots of different offices," Manette said.

Bledsoe nodded. "Which means our workload just increased. Sin, find out what other docs she works for and while you're at it, round up their patient lists. Perp might be on there."

"Will they give us their patient lists? Confidentiality—"

"Come on," Manette said. "Who's gonna get bent outta shape over a freaking root canal? They give you problems, lean on 'em. They're dentists, they don't want no trouble. Besides, we're not asking for their records, just a list. You want, I'll do it."

Sinclair's bald head flushed with anger. "I can handle it."

"Good," Bledsoe said. "There's a bunch of things we're working on, so I put together a quick summary of what's going on and who's doing what. You can add Sin's assignment to the bottom."

"How do you want to handle the perp's message?" Manette asked.

Bledsoe pulled a small spiral notepad from his sport coat pocket, flipped a couple of pages. "'It's in the . . . ,'" he mumbled. He shook his head, then said, "I think we should attack this like we would any other piece of evidence. Karen, you have any new thoughts on this?"

"Nothing I'm willing to share just yet."

"Look, I know you don't like to guess, but right now we've got nothing to go on. Even a guess would send us in a direction. Might be the wrong one, but it could also be the right one."

"I've got one," Hancock said.

Vail rolled her eyes. "Here we go."

"I think it means he's playing with us, taunting us, daring us to find the severed hand."

"And?" Bledsoe asked. "Did you find it?"

"Not yet, but—"

"Look, Bledsoe, you wanted my opinion, I'll give it to you," Vail said. "Right now there are too many possibilities. So I'll tell you what my gut says. This message meant a lot to this offender. He took great risks to leave it for us. I don't think it's taunting per se, but I think he's trying to tell us something without directly telling us. He doesn't want to make it too easy. But bottom line is, there is meaning in it. Just what that meaning is, I don't have a clue and a hunch wouldn't be worth anything. Hancock's got a hunch and it means nothing."

"To hell with you, Vail," Hancock yelled. "You've been on my case since the minute I walked through the vic's door. What did I ever do to you?"

Bledsoe shook his head in disgust. "Okay, all right, enough." He turned to Vail. "He's right, Karen, lose the attitude."

"Damn straight," Hancock said.

"I'm consulting VICAP, see if we get any hits on similar cases," Vail said calmly.

"Who's got the vic's employers?" Sinclair asked.

"Hernandez," Bledsoe said, "that's yours. Check out the people the vics worked for. Then check out their customers. Anything pops up that's even possibly suspicious, let's all discuss it."

"Got it, boss."

They spent the next two hours running scenarios and making phone calls and assembling lists. The usual bone-grinding police work. As they rose to disperse, Bledsoe gave a quick whistle. "Before I forget. Expenses. Save your receipts, give 'em to me in an envelope marked with your name every Monday for the previous week. Make sure you write down what each receipt is for. I'll get them to admin at my house and they'll send it through internal review. So don't be ordering no three-course meals. Now go home and get some rest. We'll meet here every morning at eight. You can't make it, let me know. We're on flex time, but I don't want anyone taking advantage. We got us a killer to catch, and each day, each hour, each minute that passes we don't get something accomplished means some other woman is closer to being cut up. Clear?"

Everyone nodded, then dispersed. Vail walked over to Hancock, who tilted his chin back and looked down his nose at her. She said, "I think you were right, Hancock. About the artistic feel to the murals. Just wanted you to know."

Hancock regarded her for a few seconds before responding. "You know, I could've done your job, Vail. I could've been a profiler."

Vail pulled a stick of gum from her pocket and folded it into her mouth. "What do you want me to say? Wasn't my decision."

"That's what you want to think. No guilt that way. But I'm over it, I've got a good job. And I'm in charge. I don't need to take any orders from superiors. I call the shots."

"Glad it worked out." Vail turned to gather her papers, but Hancock grabbed her arm.

"I know you said some bad things about me." His voice was low, as if he didn't want anyone else to hear. "I won't forget that."

Vail's eyes narrowed. "Don't threaten me, Hancock. Nothing you say or do scares me. You come at me, I'll crush you under my heel. Don't you forget *that*."

Vail grabbed her leather messenger bag and winked at Robby, then walked out the door.

Charcoal gray thunderclouds threatened a downpour, but thus far they had held their load. Karen Vail had a ten o'clock appointment with her family law attorney but stopped at Deacon's house on the way. If there was an amicable solution to the custody issue—meaning no attorneys involved—she wanted to find it. She liked her attorney but had no desire to fund another of his five-star resort vacations.

She didn't think Deacon would go for it, but she was prepared to make a Mafia-style offer: one he couldn't refuse . . . one that would waive her rights to the house. If there was one way to get at the armored organ Deacon once called a heart, it was through his wallet.

Vail stood at the peeling steel gray wood door and felt like a trespasser. It'd only been eighteen months since she had moved out, but in that time she had become a different person. A person who couldn't stand the man who owned the house she used to call her own. She put her hands on her hips and glanced down at her feet. Did she really want to ring this bell? Did she really want to see Deacon?

She could go through her attorney, have him handle everything, and never have to see her ex's face again. But if she could appeal to the side of him she used to love, the good-natured, hard-working soul that shriveled into oblivion, maybe get him to agree—

The wood door swung open and revealed a disheveled forty-year old man, leather-grained face and wild, pepper-colored hair. A stained white T-shirt hung over faded jeans. He may have stood near five-eleven, but his large-boned frame and new paunch made him look larger than that. He stepped closer to the screen door. "The fuck you doing here?"

Vail immediately marveled at how an individual could descend so quickly, and completely, into Dante's Inferno.

"You knock? Didn't hear a knock."

"I was about to ring the bell."

"You didn't answer me. What the fuck do you want?"

"I wanted to talk to you about Jonathan."

"What about?"

"Can I come in?"

Deacon pushed the screen door open and nearly struck Vail in the face. He turned and headed into the darkness. Bargain basement furniture adorned the living room. It was the same assortment of couches and recliners Vail had wanted to throw out—Good Will and Salvation Army turned her down—but after being out of work awhile, Deacon didn't want to spend money on new pieces. "These work just fine for me," he had said at the time. As if he was the only one who lived there.

Vail glanced at the issues of *Penthouse* and *Jugs* strewn across the coffee table and cringed at the thought that Jonathan was being exposed to this on a regular basis. These were things she would mention should they end up in court, to paint a picture of the home environment Deacon provided.

Deacon bent over and turned off the television. "So?"

"Jonathan's not happy here, Deacon. From what I gather, you're not happy having him here, either."

"Don't be speaking for me. He's my boy, a man needs his boy around. A boy needs his father."

Normally, Vail wouldn't argue with that statement. But since Deacon was the father—

"So if that's all you came to talk to me about, I'd say we're about done."

But Vail didn't like being dictated to, and she despised his flippant attitude. Her heart began pounding. Anger swelled. No, not just anger. Hatred. Where had the man gone she'd loved so many years ago?

"I came to offer you something," she said. "For Jonathan. Give me full custody and I'll waive all my rights to the house."

Deacon walked over to her and stood three inches from her face. A common intimidation tactic used during interrogation was to invade someone's space. Vail had been taught the technique by a seasoned NYPD detective. For Deacon, it came naturally.

Vail was not about to yield her ground. She knew how the game was played, so she stood there and stared into the man's dark eyes, his beer breath battering her nose.

He rested his hands on his hips and looked down at her. "You have a lot of nerve, coming here, thinking you can buy my son from me."

"He's not happy, Deacon. If you want what's best for him, take my offer. Full custody for me, the house is all yours. No strings."

Deacon clenched his jaw. "I don't think you heard me, Karen. Answer's no."

"What possible reason would you have for wanting him around, if all you're going to do is put him down all the time?"

"Is that what he says?" Deacon shook his head. "Fucking kids. None of 'em tell the truth. It's like a disease."

"I believe him, Deacon. Jonathan has no reason to lie to me."

"Well, whoop-dee-do for you, Miss Perfect Parent."

"If you won't take my offer, I'm gonna go back to court, let the judge decide."

Deacon's face curled into a snarl. "You bitch. Do that and you'll be sorry."

Vail smirked and shook her head. "I don't respond to your threats anymore, Deacon. There's nothing you can do to hurt me."

With that, Vail felt something hook behind her right foot—and Deacon's right hand push against her chest. She was moving backward faster than she could react, and a second later her head struck the wood floor in an explosion of blinding pain.

I awake with a start. I realize I'd fallen asleep in my room. Shit! He's coming. Creaky floorboards. Heavy footsteps.

Before I fell asleep, he was with a whore. I know her, she's been here before. I've seen her eyes, the way she looks at him. They're mean eyes.

The door swings open and my father stands there, his overalls unbuttoned at the top, the straps dangling at his sides.

"There was someone here."

He sneers. "She was a bitch, I got rid of her."

"I didn't like her."

"Yeah, well, she didn't like you none, either. She thought you were bad. Ugly. Just like your mama saw you."

Mother. She didn't know what it meant to be a mother. She couldn't have. She was a bitch, just like the ones he brings home.

"Let me tell you something, them bitches are real bad. They see you as trash. Ugly, rotting trash. The whores always say mean things about you. They say you're ugly and you're lucky to have a father like me who takes care of you."

Lucky is not the word I use to describe my life.

He comes over to the bed and I'm waiting for the belt to come whipping at me. I shy away, waiting. . . .

"It's your mama of a whore's fault you're ugly. She made you this way."

I lift my head slowly, still waiting for the leather to snap against my skin. But I notice he's not wearing a belt.

"Time for a haircut, your hair's gettin' too long! Come on, now!"

He grabs me and pulls me off the bed—

Amazing stuff! He realized he had to do something with it, publish it somewhere. He could use someone else's name so no one would know it was him. *Or maybe I do want people to know what I endured.* Fiction or nonfiction? It's all true, but who'd believe it? They'd look at him like he was the bad one, because who wants to be associated with someone who'd been treated like that?

But there *were* people who would be interested in this stuff. People who'd eat it up, consider it downright brilliant. They'd read it and read it again, show it to other people, scrutinize it until they broke it down by word choice, grade level, and whatever other silly metrics they'd designed to evaluate writing.

And the cops would analyze it, too.

Let them comb through it, they'll never get anywhere with it. Of course it meant he'd have to cover his tracks. So be it. Put it out there and see what reaction his readers had. If it came off well, maybe he'd go for a bigger audience.

He closed the laptop and yawned hard, but a jolt of pain made him wince. His face was killing him. The last bitch got in a cheap shot, a roundhouse punch that landed square and stunned him for a second. After letting him in the house, something must've tipped her off, because she took the first swing. But he wanted her dead a little bit more than she wanted to be alive, because after hitting him she started to run. He grabbed her arm, spun her around, and punched her back, a left and right combination, real fast. All he knew was that it hurt his knuckles. But she went down and then he got his pipe out and that was that.

He'd been on the receiving end of a beating too many times, so if you wanted to go toe to toe with him, fine, he was ready to rumble. He knew all the moves because he lived through them.

He shoved an ice pack against the lump on his forehead. The swelling had drained a bit into the side of his face and jaw, but fortunately the discoloration was easily covered by makeup. An FBI agent with a large purple and black bruise on his face would attract attention, and that was something he needed to avoid.

But if there was one thing this bitch taught him, it was that he

needed to handle these encounters better, find a way of knockin
them out faster, before they had a chance to swing at him. Next tim
it could be a knife or a broken bottle.

He made a list of possible solutions, but they all involved risk—
the biggest of which was being seen in public buying a weapon. Bu
the Internet, on the other hand, allowed him to go anywhere and d
anything he wanted, without anyone scrutinizing his face or ques
tioning his motives.

He could buy whatever he needed, within reason. A simple searc
brought him to numerous websites that sold stun guns, which coul
incapacitate a bitch for minutes at a time. All he'd have to do is touc
the probe to her body—hell, even her clothing. The longer the con
tact, the longer the period of incapacitation.

He clicked on the Frequently Asked Questions link, and read
"Using a high pulse frequency, stun guns scramble the nervous sys
tem and make the muscles work so rapidly their source of energ
converts immediately into lactic acid, exhausting and disabling th
muscles. At the same time, the pulse interrupts the brain's nerve im
pulses, causing the stunned individual to lose muscle control and be
come disoriented. This incapacitated and confused state will last tw
to five minutes or longer depending on body mass and. . . . "

Minutes! He only needed a few seconds, really. A few seconds t
get his hands around her neck, a few seconds to squeeze the life fron
her body. Two hands, two eyes. Two bugged out eyes, the capillarie
bursting from the pressure. . . .

He quickly paged through the website, entered the credit car
number, then logged off. He'd have the package tomorrow.

It seemed almost too good to be true.

The room spun for a second before coming back into focus. Vail blinked a few times and realized she was staring at the light fixture on her ceiling. No, not her ceiling, not anymore. Deacon's ceiling. Deacon's house.

The television was on, the unmistakable sound of cars racing around a track blaring from the speakers. A cigarette was burning down near the filter in an ashtray beside Deacon's recliner. And—what the hell?—her pants were unzipped.

What time is it?

Why am I on the floor?

Why does my head hurt so much?

Vail rolled onto her side and saw Deacon's empty Lazy Boy. *Where the hell is he?*

She felt like a hammer had crushed her skull. She reached back and felt a bruise, as if her head were a piece of damaged fruit. Whatever had happened, it involved Deacon. And that meant it wasn't good.

Vail pulled herself up and stood in the middle of the living room, which tilted back and forth like a seesaw. She swayed, dizzy and wobbly, bending her knees and holding her arms out like a surfer for balance. After steadying herself, she stumbled out to her car.

She rooted around her pocket for the keys, opened the door, and drove away. Her mind was still a blur, and she was more or less driving on autopilot. She knew the way to her office without thinking—which was good, because at the moment thinking was more than her shaken brain could handle.

As she headed back toward the interstate, she struggled to recall what had transpired after arriving at Deacon's. The dashboard clock read 10:36. Ten-thirty-six . . . she had been there an hour and a half.

Whatever she had done, whatever had happened, had taken a considerable amount of time.

She remembered going there to discuss a change in Jonathan's custody—and Deacon had been less than cooperative. Things were coming back to her, but she was still drawing blanks.

Ten-thirty. There was something she was supposed to have done at ten. What was it?

She stopped at a light and looked around. Was it something for work? Was she supposed to meet the task force somewhere? She yawned and her jaw hurt. She looked in the mirror and fought back dizziness to see half-mast eyes and frazzled hair. What the hell had happened?

Come on, Karen, think! The light turned green—and her thoughts cleared a bit. She took what she knew and mixed in a little inference . . . and figured she and Deacon had gotten into it over Jonathan's custody. The end result she knew—an unexpected nap on Deacon's floor, some dizziness, and one hell of a headache. He must've clocked her good, because she still didn't remember it. But there was no bruising on her face.

However it went down, she only hoped she'd gotten him good, too. But judging by the fact that the TV was on and a smoke was burning in the ashtray, she probably did not get the best of the encounter.

A sprinkling drizzle began dotting her windshield. As she reached to turn on the wipers, her forearm brushed up against her holster, and oh, shit—

She slammed on the brakes and skidded to a stop on the rain-slick roadway, a portfolio of papers and files stacked in the backseat flying to the floor.

Though she didn't remember what had happened at Deacon's, her weapon was missing, and that was something she did not want to have to explain—to anyone, let alone Gifford or the policy freaks at OPR.

Vail swung the car around and headed back to Deacon's, taking care to obey the traffic ordinances of the local jurisdiction—actually, she was doing about eighty and swerving all over the road on the wet asphalt. Jesus Christ . . . she had to get there before he left with her Glock. Knowing him, he'd make sure the sidearm was found somewhere embarrassing . . . or he'd put it in the hands of a junkie in the bad part of DC so it would be used in a crime. That wouldn't go over well with the Bureau. It'd be in all the papers, make national news. She'd be disgraced. And if it was used in a murder . . . how could she live with that?

Vail made it back to his house in a little over five minutes. His car was still in the driveway. She ran to the front door, yanked it open. Deacon was somewhere in the house, singing. *Singing? Why the hell is he singing?*

Her eyes scanned the room. Didn't see her Glock anywhere. Knelt down, searched beneath the couch and coffee table when suddenly she heard—

"Looking for this?"

She spun, still on her knees. Deacon was standing there, ten feet away, her Glock in his hand, holding it up as if showing it to her.

"Give it—"

He lowered the pistol and pointed it at her. "Now just a minute, Karen. I don't think I like your tone. See, I'm holding the goddamn gun here. Understand what that means?"

Oh, she understood all right. She understood that she hated this man. She hated him so much that she envisioned taking her own serrated knife and ramming it through *his* eyes.

"Stay where you are. On your knees." He raised his eyebrows in mock excitement. "Hmm. How appropriate."

No, how infuriating. What to do? Rush him? Too risky. Not yet. She'd give it a bit longer to unfold before acting. It couldn't get any worse than it was right now, so she had nothing to lose by waiting for, perhaps, a better opportunity.

He unzipped his pants with his left hand and extended his right elbow, the one holding the weapon.

She forced a laugh. "Keep dreaming, Deacon. No fucking way."

"Funny you should use that vulgar term. You know those pink slips they use in offices that say, 'While You Were Out'?" He chuckled. "Well, while *you* were out, I mean, 'out cold,' I had some fun."

He raped me? No—couldn't be. Could it? She wanted to put her hand on her crotch, feel to see if she was wet. But she wouldn't give him that. From what she could tell, she didn't feel any soreness or irritation. "Nice try, asshole. I'd know if you raped me."

"Rape? Such a strong word, don't you think? We *are* married—"

"Only in your warped mind. Divorce is just about done."

"So maybe I did *rape* you. And maybe I didn't."

She shook her head in disgust. "When did you become such a vile human being?"

"You're being kind of harsh, Karen. I mean, don't you deal with a lot worse?"

"It's just a matter of degree. And believe me, the dividing line between you and those scumbags isn't that wide. You're a lot closer to those monsters than you think."

He stepped closer, wiggled the handgun at her. "How's your head feel? I hit you pretty hard."

Is that how I ended up on the floor? He hit me? But she hadn't seen a bruise on her face—which she would have by now if he'd punched her. Still, her jaw did hurt. She looked up at him. "I'm getting up now, Deacon, and you're going to hand over my gun."

"Well, you can get up. Let's start with that."

She rose—and in one motion, pivoted on her back heel and swung her leg wide, her left foot side-slamming the Glock and sending it across the room.

She scrambled after it—but so did Deacon—and they both dove

forward onto the hardwood like linebackers pursuing a fumble, their bodies colliding and Vail scooping up the weapon with her right hand. She swung it around, and, while on her side, slammed the barrel up against Deacon's nose. "You goddamn son of a bitch. Were you going to pull the trigger? Huh?"

His eyes crossed as he focused on the Glock.

"I should blow your goddamn brains out, you useless piece of shit!"

"Go ahead, Karen," he said, unfazed. "Pull the trigger." He shifted his gaze back to her face. "Throw away your career. Leave Jonathan without parents. Come on, I dare you."

Her breath was coming in spasms, her heart pounding so forcefully she felt it in her ears. *Calm down. Think.* She looked into his eyes, seeing the malevolence she often saw in the killers she interviewed in prison. She wasn't sure what it was, only that she knew it when she saw it: a cold depth, an emotional void.

Vail got to her feet but kept the weapon pointed at Deacon. Her hand was shaking—not out of fear but out of concern she'd lose her nerve and pull the trigger. He was right—she had more at stake than he did. Given his shambles of a life, he would probably embrace suicide if he had the guts to do it.

Vail backed out of the house and didn't holster the Glock until she sat down in her car. She pulled away from the house and stopped at a light. She felt dirty, poisoned. *He didn't rape me,* she told herself. *He was just screwing with my head.*

Overwhelming unease pulled at her thoughts. The light turned green and she drove on, in the direction of the task force headquarters. She needed to get her head back into the Dead Eyes investigation, to do something useful and productive. To get her mind off Deacon, off what had happened.

When she arrived at the house, a Verizon Communications van was parked out front, no doubt installing the phone lines Bledsoe ordered. Still in a semifog, Vail nearly ran into the technician, who was on his way back to his truck.

As soon as Bledsoe caught sight of her, he opened his mouth to ask the obvious question. She had been so absorbed in her anger she had forgotten to brush her hair or throw on some makeup. *I probably look like shit.* Bledsoe placed a hand around her shoulders and led her into the room that had once passed as a rudimentary kitchen. He sat her down and stood there looking at her, clearly at a loss about what to do.

A moment passed before he finally grabbed a seat in front of her. She realized he was in cop mode, which would explain why he was keeping his distance.

"What's wrong?" he asked.

She didn't know how to start. "Anyone else around? Manette, Hancock—"

"Came and went. No one else is here. Just us." Bledsoe gave her a second, but she still didn't say anything.

She noticed his eyes brighten—she figured the light had come on. Having worked with Vail so closely during the task force's first tour of duty, Bledsoe knew the garbage she had to navigate during her custody battle with Deacon.

"Your ex, something happen with him?"

Vail nodded.

"Did he touch you?" Bledsoe waited a beat, got no response, and then was out of his chair, hands on his hips, pacing. "You going to file a report? I can write it up, assault, and have him brought in. Scare the shit out of him."

She thought about it, then shook her head. "Truth is, I don't know what happened. I went there to talk to him about changing our custody arrangement, and about an hour later I woke up on the floor of his living room." She hesitated, unsure if she wanted to go any further.

He stopped pacing and pulled his chair beside Vail. He rested his elbows on his knees and looked into her eyes. "You know what happened. It's enough to file a report. Get it on record."

"Bledsoe, I *don't* know what happened. I can piece things together, make inferences . . . but it's not the same as *knowing*. Besides, it doesn't look good for me to have gone to his place. He'll just say I started the argument."

Bledsoe sat there staring at her, then finally asked, "You think he raped you?"

"No." Bledsoe was a good cop; she knew that—but she had never been on the receiving end of his investigative sensibilities. He had put it all together, perhaps seen something in her body language. He'd been around the block with enough victims to know what had transpired.

"But if you don't remember what happened, how can you be so sure?"

She tilted her head and gave him a stern look. "I would know if he—if something penetrated me."

Bledsoe stood up and faced the wall, as if he were studying the accumulated stains and layers of paint drips. Finally, he turned to her. "We gotta nail this guy, Karen. Just file the damn report."

"Yeah, that'll go over real well, especially when the investigating dick pulls out his pad and says, 'So, Agent Vail, tell me what happened.' And I say, 'Gee, detective, I don't know what happened. I can't remember.' Even if he goes the extra mile for the uniform and runs Deacon, how's it going to look in court? The defense attorney will tear me apart: 'Are you saying, Agent Vail, that you reported being assaulted, even though you can't remember actually being struck? Maybe you tripped and fell and hit your head. In fact, you can't remember anything about what happened, isn't that true?'" *To say nothing about leaving my Glock in his house, then threatening to blow his brains out.* She waved a hand. "There's no case."

And that's when it hit her. "The *case,* shit. That's what I was supposed to do at ten. Meet with my attorney about Jonathan." Vail pulled out her cell phone and rescheduled the missed appointment, then called the school to get a message to Jonathan explaining why she hadn't come for him.

When she hung up, Bledsoe's face was still crumpled in concentration. "We can bring him in, I can lean on him, get a confession. I know I can, Karen. And even if I don't, it'll be worth it just to see him squirm."

Vail slumped back in her chair. "I'll deal with this in my own way. Thanks, though. I appreciate the offer."

Bledsoe regarded her for a moment. "Just don't do anything you'll regret later."

"I'll let my attorney handle it, okay?" She managed a thin smile. "I'll only regret it when I get his bill."

After talking with Bledsoe about Deacon's attack, Vail settled down at the long folding table set up in the living room and began thumbing through the Dead Eyes file. She knew there was something in there she had missed. More than that, however, there was information she had not yet had time to adequately analyze.

Around one thirty, Mandisa Manette arrived with a shoulder bag slung across her back stuffed with files and supplies. She claimed her space in a far corner of the living room, stretched a piece of masking tape marked with her name across a filing cabinet drawer, then began setting out her paperwork and materials. Yellow pushpins held a couple of photos of a young girl to the wall. Other than a nod when she arrived, Vail did not even exchange a glance with her.

Bubba Sinclair was next to arrive, half an hour later. He chatted with Bledsoe for a bit about the Chicago Bears—his hometown team—and then took a spot at the table near the dining room. He set out a couple of picture frames that were facing away from Vail, and an autographed basketball.

Sinclair looked up and said, "We lock this place at night, right?"

"Locked and alarmed," Bledsoe said. "They installed the system after you left this morning."

"What's up with that ball?" Manette asked.

"I helped some on Michael Jordan's dad's murder case. Did some legwork for Carolina PD. MJ appreciated the work I done, gave me a signed ball."

"What's it for, good luck?"

"Why not? We could use some. If this helps. . . . "

"Hey, rabbit's feet, lucky charms, no problem," Manette said. "Just don't be chanting any incantations, okay? That's where I draw the line."

"How about this?" Sinclair pulled a large necklace from beneath his shirt.

"Dare I ask what that is?"

"My lucky hunting necklace." He fingered the various animal teeth of disparate sizes and shapes strung together on the leather lanyard. "Took out each one of these. Bear, deer, even an elk. That was a tough one." He found the bear tooth and held it up. "I don't want to tell you what we had to do to take this one down."

"Put that thing away," Manette said. "I like animals."

"Hey, I like animals, too," Sinclair said.

Vail sat back and ignored the banter; she was formulating an opinion and needed her concentration.

Within the hour, Robby and Chase Hancock had arrived. They each carved out their own work spaces, with Robby predictably choosing one beside Vail, and Hancock taking a spot in the other room, facing away from her.

"I've got something worth looking into," Vail said once everyone had settled in. They each turned their bodies, or at least their attention, in her direction. "I've been trying to understand the significance of stabbing the eyes. It holds a lot of importance to the offender. It's comforting to him, serves a deep-seated purpose. The fact that he does this as part of his ritual and not his MO tells me it could hold the key to understanding who this guy is."

"Why's that?" Bledsoe asked.

"Because he doesn't have to do it to subdue his victim. She's already dead," Hancock said.

Bledsoe turned to Vail for confirmation. She reluctantly nodded.

"So why would this guy stab the eyes?"

"That's the question. My unit floated some theories last year on vics one and two, but nothing anyone could agree on. But I've got this feeling—I mean, theory—that he does it because he has a physical deformity. Scarring on his face, an old wound, acne, harelip, don't know exactly, but it's worth looking into."

"I'll do a search," Sinclair said. "Ex-cons released in the past few years with a history of violent offenses who had a facial disfigure ment. We can cross match it against anything we pick up on the blood angle."

"It's just a theory," Vail cautioned.

Bledsoe frowned. "All we've got are theories right now."

Vail dipped her chin in conciliatory agreement.

"While we're on the topic of symbolism," Bledsoe said, "what's up with the hands, what's that all about?"

"Symbolism ain't gonna catch us a killer or find us a suspect." Manette tilted her head toward Vail. "No offense, *Kari*, but why waste our time with this psycho stuff?"

"Behavioral analysis," Robby corrected.

"Whatever you wanna call it, it's like looking into a crystal ball. And we all know there aren't no crystal balls."

"The key is narrowing the suspect pool," Robby said. "To give us a place to focus. With no eyewitnesses or smoking gun forensics, profiling can at least give us a direction. Tell us what kind of guy we're looking for."

Bledsoe leaned back in his chair and it let out an ear-piercing squeak. "Right now, we got nothing." He turned to Vail. "The hands?"

Vail sighed, grateful Robby and Bledsoe had stepped in. She wasn't in the mood to deal with another confrontation. Her headache had been dulled by Excedrin, but her thoughts still felt a bit fuzzy. She looked over at Manette, who appeared mollified for the moment. "He takes the hand with him as a trophy," Vail said, "so he can relive the murder in his mind. Relive his fantasy. My guess is he's probably got pictures, too. Of the vics after he's done with them, maybe even of the walls, which I think he considers to be works of art."

"So if these hands fulfill his fantasy, why does he need to kill again?" Sinclair asked.

"For serial killers, the act of killing their victims never lives up to their best fantasies. So they're constantly refining and perfecting the fantasy. With Dead Eyes, when the hands or photos no longer bring him the excitement or satisfaction of the original act, the urges build and become overwhelming."

"And that's when he kills again," Robby said.

"Exactly. Almost like an addict. Maybe more like a child who wants instant gratification and does whatever he needs to do to satisfy himself. Even if society feels it's morally wrong."

"Does he know it's wrong?"

"On some level, absolutely. But he doesn't feel any guilt. If he did, he'd cover their faces or bodies. He doesn't. He leaves them on display, right there in their bed. He doesn't even bother to move them to the bathtub when he eviscerates them. Doing it in bed has to have special meaning to him."

"But a hand?" Manette asked. "How's that a trophy?"

"Like the eyes, the hands have relevance to him. Maybe he had an abusive father who beat him all the time."

"A left hand from each victim," Sinclair said. "So to get to him, we find an abusive left-handed father."

Manette rolled her eyes. "You can't be serious, Sin. You believe this shit?"

Sinclair ignored her. "Let's get back to the hand. These whackos really get off on severed hands? I've seen whips and chains and shit like that, but a whacked-off hand?"

"Dahmer used to skin the flesh off his victims and preserve their skeletons," Vail said matter-of-factly. "When looking at the skulls and spines, he saw the victims—as if they were still alive, still there with him. He'd actually masturbate over the skeleton."

"Jesus," Robby said.

"And you know this, how?" Manette asked.

"He told us."

Manette raised her eyebrows. "So naturally we just believed him. After all, he's an upstanding citizen and all. . . . "

"Okay, let's keep to the matter at hand," Bledsoe said. He drew a dirty look from Robby for the pun.

"Sorry, didn't mean it." He sat up straight in his chair. "Karen, obviously you've got enough now to give us something. Right?" He seemed to be pleading, or at least hoping, that Vail would produce.

Vail looked down at her makeshift desk. A file was open and notes were scrawled on yellow lined paper. "The guy we're looking for is a

Caucasian about thirty to forty years old. Medium build, and according to forensics about five-eight. He works a blue-collar job but may be in business for himself. My bet is he puts a lot of time into stalking his victims because they're all somewhat similar in age, marital status, and appearance. It's likely his job gives him a flexible schedule to get all this stuff done. The job might also give him access to either photos or descriptions of the women he chooses. It's possible he gets their addresses from a database, or he goes out hunting. When he finds one who fits his fantasy, he follows them home. I don't know enough just yet to say which way he does it. We need to keep working the employee angle.

"He's bright, above average intelligence. This is a guy who's into power, so he probably drives a power car. An older German make. Porsche maybe, or Mercedes, red if it's a Porsche and a dark color if it's a Mercedes. It'll be older because he can't afford a newer one. But age doesn't matter to him. It's the illusion."

"Kind of like sleight of hand, like this hocus-pocus profiling shit," Manette muttered.

"Go on," Bledsoe said.

Vail glanced down at her notes. "He's got some deep-seated issues, as we've discussed. First on the list is an abusive childhood. I'm guessing the father since that's the case ninety percent of the time. The father's probably left-handed—" she shot a look at Manette— "and he probably beat the offender with his hand. There's something with his face—maybe a facial deformity, as I mentioned. Maybe even caused by the father during one of the beatings. The eyes are a bit tougher. Could be symbolic, too. Like the father put him down all the time by telling him everyone *sees* him as a fuck-up."

Vail looked down at her pad. "There might be something with the blood murals. It's unlike anything I've personally seen before, and VICAP should have a printout for us soon. There's something here, I know it. Just a gut feeling . . . but we have to keep on that angle. Either this guy had formal art training, or he works in the art field. He might even be a frustrated artist. Painter is the most obvious. But I wouldn't rule out jobs involving manual labor, where he

could tap his creative side. Sculptor, carpenter . . . hell, even poet
musician, or massage therapist." She stopped for a moment, turned
to Bledsoe. "We're checking out habits common to all the vics
right? Maybe see if they all visited the same massage therapist."

"Manny and I got that," Sinclair said. "So far, the only thing
we've come up with is that two of 'em shopped at the same super
market chain. Different stores, though. We're still working on it
there's a lot of ground to cover." He flipped the page on his yellow
pad and made a note. "We'll add massage therapists."

Robby asked, "Make any sense to create a list of people in the
fields you mentioned above—sculptors, painters, that type of thing?"

"We'll end up with a huge database if we don't narrow it," Bled
soe said. "Go for it, but don't give me grief when the computer spit
out five thousand names."

"We can cross-reference it against the other lists."

"Fine. Do it."

Sinclair asked Vail, "You said this guy had above average intelli
gence. How do you know that?"

"First, he gains access to the vic's houses with relative ease. He ei
ther knows them or has found some slick way of disarming them ver
bally. Typically, offenders who tend toward organization are socially
adept; they'll use slick talk to approach and calm the vic. He migh
role-play with them, impersonating a cop or security guard to earn
their confidence. I'd expect him to be well groomed and in the uni
form of the role he takes on."

"We should continue talking with the vics' neighbors," Robby
said. "Maybe they've seen a stranger in some kind of uniform."

"So tell me, Kari, what set him off? What happened a year and
half ago to put this guy on the map?"

"Could've been a lot of things. Most likely, there was some stres
sor in his life prior to Marci Evers's murder. A job change, a relation
ship gone sour. Some other type of situational stress that happened
right before the first murder that set him off. Whatever it was, he
reached maximum capacity and popped."

"You said he was organized," Sinclair said.

Vail nodded. "He's what we call an organized offender. There's thought and premeditation to everything he does. There's no evidence of a struggle and only minimal defensive wounds, if any. That indicates he did a significant amount of planning. If we look at each of the victim's houses, we see that the front door has sufficient cover from the street. That allows him to interact with the vic without anyone seeing him, just in case a neighbor is passing by at the time. Or, could be it's a safety net in case she denies him admittance and he has to force his way in. Either way, there's planning involved.

"At the other end of the spectrum are lower IQ killers. They're usually *disorganized*. The killing is more impulsive, they use weapons of opportunity, or those already in the victim's apartment, and they make a great deal of mess by mutilating the victim and smearing her blood around the crime scene."

"Hold it a second," Hancock said. "Your profile indicates organization but the crime scenes show the opposite."

Vail sighed. She was tired and didn't feel like justifying her opinions to Hancock. But his confusion was understandable, and she figured that if he hadn't asked the question, someone else would have.

"There's a lot of blood, I know. That usually points to disorganization. But if we look at the blood not by volume but by what he does with it, the painting, the artistic nature of the images, then I think we have to consider it to be purposeful. Purpose indicates organization."

"What about weapons of opportunity—"

"Every person has steak knives of some sort in their kitchen. Fact that he didn't bring the knives to the vics tells me he's smart. Why risk getting caught with knives that can be traced to other victims? He uses what's there because he knows it's likely going to be there. To me, that's another sign of organization. But beyond that, stabbing the eyes is not how he kills these women, asphyxiation is. The knives are merely used for his postmortem behaviors."

"What about the evisceration? That's mutilation, disorganization for sure, even going by your own definition."

Vail tapped her foot and hesitated before answering. "I don't know. I can't explain it, except to say that maybe this guy is a mix. Elements of organization blended with some disorganization. More often than not, that's the case anyway." Vail rubbed at her painful brow. "Wish I could give you more. I might be able to refine it a bit once I have time to go through it again, run it by my unit."

"A lot of mights and maybes," Manette said.

Vail closed the file on her desk. "Hey, a profile is just a tool, like an alternative light source or a compound microscope. It's not going to give you a suspect's name and number. You think you can do better, have at it."

There was silence for a moment before Robby spoke. "I heard one of the forensics guys saying they found some dirt in Sandra Franks's house."

"Loose dirt in the hallway and bedroom. One tread mark that matched your shoe," Bledsoe said. "So that's of no help. As for the other dirt, they're running it through the chromatograph and spectrometer. I don't have the results yet."

"We didn't put booties on till after we chased him through the yard," Vail said. "Ten to one that dirt comes back a dead end."

Bledsoe shrugged. "We'll know soon enough. Also looking over hair and fibers. Some latent prints were found, but no hits on AFIS. Except . . . one good latent was lifted from the murals. Judging by the commonly used items in the house as a reference source for Sandra's fingerprints, seems he used the vic's severed left hand to paint."

"That's just gross," Manette said.

"All this shit is gross," Bledsoe said. "Now, as for the other prints . . . Sin, what've you got?"

Sinclair stood up and stretched. "I'm checking into Franks's friends and family, just in case the prints are theirs. Some of the latents have probably been there awhile. But I doubt we'll find anything: with all the blood at the scene, if the fucker wasn't wearing gloves, he'd have left bloody prints all over the damn place. There weren't any, so I think the latents are also gonna be a dead end."

"And that puts us back to where we were. To hocus-pocus psychosymbolism," Manette said.

A tiny watch alarm started beeping, and Sinclair glanced at his wrist with trepidation. "Got an appointment with one of the vic's employer's personnel administrators. This guy's a real prick." He pushed out of his chair and gathered up his weathered brown leather shoulder bag.

Bledsoe stood as well. "Okay, let's get back out there. You know your assignments. Let's dig a little deeper, see if we can come up with something."

"DETECTIVE," HANCOCK SAID, crowding Bledsoe's space, "you got a minute?"

The other detectives were filing out the front door. Bledsoe shrugged, took a step backward. "Yeah, what's on your mind?"

Hancock danced a bit, checked over his shoulder, and watched Vail leave with Robby. "I gotta talk to you." He leaned close again, lowered his voice. "About Vail, I think it could be something."

Bledsoe's eyes narrowed a bit, then he turned and led the way into the kitchen. They waited until the front door closed, then he brought his eyes up to Hancock's. "We're alone, what's on your mind?"

"I was reading the files you put together for me. Thanks, by the way, I appreciate it."

"No problem. Is that what you had to tell me?"

"No, no. I found something in the crime scene manifest for vic number two." He opened a file he had tucked beneath his arm. "Here, under fiber analysis." He handed Bledsoe the report.

"Yeah, so? A red hair. What's the problem?"

"Vail has red hair. The conclusion is that the comparison microscope study matched it to comps on Vail." He paused, the corners of his mouth sinking, as if Bledsoe should've caught on by now. "Vail's hair was found at the second vic's crime scene. Why wasn't anything done about it?"

"Done?" Bledsoe asked. He folded his arms across his chest and stared at Hancock. "What would you have wanted us to do?"

"Did you investigate her?"

"Karen Vail? Special Agent Karen Vail? The woman who has trouble sleeping because this killer is still out on the street?"

Hancock shifted his feet again. "You don't know her like I know her. She's devious, ruthless—"

Bledsoe held up a hand. "Okay, Hancock. Thanks for the tip—"

"You need to investigate her. She could be our killer."

The statement left them both quiet. Bledsoe sighed, then settled into a chair. "That's a very serious allegation you're making, you realize that? Based on a strand of hair found at a crime scene?"

Hancock did not answer.

Bledsoe continued: "When an investigator steps into a crime scene, it's possible his or her fibers, fingerprints, DNA—hell, any trace evidence could be deposited there. That's one of the challenges we face when our guys answer a call. That's why we rope off and secure the area—"

"Don't talk down to me, Detective."

"I'm explaining why Karen's hair was at the vic's house."

"And you're *sure* that's the reason."

Bledsoe shook his head in disgust.

"Vail was an art history major. We've got these blood murals all over the vics' walls that look like the work of someone with a background in art. Still not convinced?"

Bledsoe pushed out of his chair and stepped up to Hancock, toe to toe. "Look, Vail told me you were a prick. I've tried to keep an open mind, because both of you have biases against each other. If this is a cheap shot to discredit her, to get back at her for your problems with the Bureau several years ago—"

"This has nothing to do with that."

Bledsoe's head was tilted back, his gaze fixed on Hancock's eyes. Neither of them blinked. "You want to investigate Karen Vail on your own time, go for it. Have a picnic. Just don't poison my investigation." Bledsoe pushed past Hancock and headed out of the kitchen.

"You'll see," Hancock called after him. "You'll see that I'm right."

Robby walked Vail to her car and stood there a bit longer than necessary after she'd said good-bye and closed the door.

She opened the window and looked up at him, shielding her eyes from the sky's dreary glare. "Something wrong?"

"I, well . . . no." He looked down at the ground, then gazed at the houses on the street.

"Robby?"

"How would you like to grab some lunch. Or dinner. I've got some more questions. Profiling questions."

Vail sat there staring at him, wondering if he was, in fact, asking her out. This wasn't the best timing, after what had happened with Deacon—

"You agreed to tutor me, remember?"

But maybe it was exactly what she needed. Take her mind off all the negatives, bring some happiness into her life. Everyone needs balance; it was a lesson she'd learned many years ago. She spoke before allowing herself to think the situation to death. "Lunch or dinner, huh?"

"Or coffee. Whatever."

"You know, a sharp profiler might conclude she's being asked out on a date."

His gaze drifted off to the surrounding houses again. "But a plain old small-town detective might just think it's two colleagues getting together to talk about a case. Theories and methods."

"Theories and methods. . . ." A smile crept across her lips. "Okay. I like theories and methods. Reminds me of my favorite course at the Academy. Dinner tonight, six o'clock?"

"Great."

"Something casual. Meet me at the office, we'll go from there."

"Sure, great."

"Oh, and Art Rooney, another profiler, may want to join us. That okay?"

Robby's face drooped a bit, though he seemed to try to keep it propped up. He shrugged an indifferent shoulder. "Yeah."

Vail smiled, squinted against the sun that had poked through the clouds. "You know what, forget Rooney; he's probably got other plans. Can't discuss theories and methods with more than just a couple of people anyway, right?"

Robby winked. "Exactly. Pick you up at six."

ROBBY POURED A GLASS of chardonnay for each of them and set the bottle back on the table. "So you never told me how a nice detective like you got stuck in a gross profession like profiling."

"It was one of the safest jobs in the Bureau. I had a scare about seven years ago when I was caught in the cross fire during a botched bank robbery." Her mind flashed back to Alvin in the bank a few days ago. Different scenario, but the setting was all too familiar. "It was just the way things went down. We were following a tip, moving on these guys fast, and I got there first. While I was waiting for backup, the perps came out of the bank. Another couple agents arrived on scene and didn't know what hit them. The scumbags took out one agent and put the other down with a shot to the chest. I was pinned down but eventually got out of it."

Robby's eyes were narrow with interest. "How?"

She took a gulp of wine. "I thought we were going to discuss theories and methods."

Robby's eyebrows rose. "We are. Karen Vail's theories on getting out of a tough spot with only her brains and bare hands—"

"Try a Glock and a spare magazine. And they had MAC-10s. Sprayed the shit out of my car. Windows were blowing out all over the place. We were hunkered down returning fire." She shook her head. "It was war, right there on the street in the middle of suburbia. . . . "

Robby edged forward on his seat. "And? What happened?"

She took another drink of chardonnay, then looked up and found Robby's eyes. "What?"

"How'd you get out of it?"

"I got down low, under the car, and shot the perp in the ankle. He went down, the other agent survived, all the scumbags died, and everything turned out okay." She let the words linger in the air for a moment, staring at her nearly empty wine glass.

"So, the safest job in the Bureau," Robby prompted.

"After that lovely episode, I realized it wasn't something I should be doing while trying to raise a child. Jonathan was seven at the time. The thought of him growing up without a mother made me think long and hard about what I was doing with my life." She laughed a hollow chuckle. "I make it sound as if it was a rational, one-night decision. It wasn't. It took me weeks to decide what I was going to do. I even thought of leaving the Bureau."

"Instead you ended up in the profiling unit?"

"While OPR investigated, my ASAC felt it was best to give me a break from my usual surroundings. He loaned me out to nearby police departments to help them solve a few dormant cases. The trails were so cold you could get frostbite just by handling the case folders."

Robby leaned back in his chair. "Ouch. You think he did that on purpose, to kill your career?"

"Nah, he was a good guy. Besides, if that was what he had in mind, I screwed up his plans big time. I solved almost every one of the cases. Word traveled fast. Got a rep around the Bureau."

"I can see why."

"My ASAC sent a memo to the Division Two unit chief at BSU, and next thing I knew I was the profiling unit's Eastern District liaison. A month later, I was competing with Chase Hancock for the one vacant spot in the unit. Rest is history."

Robby's head was tilted and his gaze was fixed on Vail's face.

She finished off her glass of wine and waited for a response. "You okay?" she finally asked.

"Fine," he said, breaking his daze and sitting up straight.

"Theories and methods," she said with a smile.

"Right. And here's my theory: you're a special person, Karen Vail, and I'd like to get to know you better."

"Told you this smelled of a date."

"Guess a small-town detective can't put one over on a sharp FBI agent."

The waiter delivered their food: Oriental chicken salad for Vail, well-done chili burger for Robby. Vail watched him dump globs of ketchup onto his fries. She flashed on the image of herself as a child. The thought seemed to emphasize the age difference between the two of them. She lifted her fork and felt Robby's gaze on her face. He had put his foot forward and was patiently waiting for her to take the next step. She let her wrist go limp, lowering her fork back to the plate, and said, "You're what, twenty-nine, thirty?"

"Thirty."

"I'm . . . a little older. Why don't you pick on someone your own age?"

Robby's hamburger sat in front of him, untouched. He leaned toward her; she was now his total focus. "Karen, I've seen things, lived things most kids never should have to live through. I could've ended up on the street like the thugs we haul in—but that's not what I'm about." He paused to read her face, but she did not react. He popped a ketchup-dripping french fry in his mouth. She took another sip of wine. He finally swallowed, then shrugged. "I may not be thirty-two, like you," he said with a wry smile, "but I've been around the block. A couple hundred times."

She nodded slowly, then held up her glass. He filled it and topped off his own.

Her eyes moved from the wine to his face. "So then the *method* would be *one step at a time,* see how things turn out."

Robby smiled. "A methodical approach. Like any good investigation."

"Move too fast and you can screw things up, make mistakes."

Robby lifted his glass. "To theories and methods."

Vail raised her glass and touched it against Robby's. "And methodical approaches."

*A*nother victim lies in the next room, tied up and waiting for me to return. And there's nothing you can do about it. You're like a quadriplegic, watching things happen around you but physically unable to participate. You see the deaths, the murder, the devastation of their lives, and you're powerless to stop me.

Look—look at the victim. Open your eyes, do you see her? I said look! In the bed, tied down. Look at her face, look at her eyes, watch as I climb atop, straddle her, then stab her left eye. I draw the knife back, bring it forward fast and hard and whack! The blade sinks into the socket. Blood and fluid spatter on me, on my chest, on my chin. I withdraw the knife, agonizingly slowly as if it were some playful act of sex, then lean back and shift my weight so I can stab the right eye.

Don't you see it yet? I stab the eyes because you can't see what needs to be seen. You can't see me. Look! Look in the mirror above the bed. That's it—come on, raise your head!

As she tilts her chin back, she sees the mirror's reflection. And staring back at her, in vivid Technicolor, is a redhead.

You see it now, don't you. You see it!

She looks at the killer's face but can't see anything—no eyes, no mouth, just a blurred out image as if a television censor had altered it, the way they obscure a woman's bare breast. But just as she is about to turn away, it comes into focus—and staring back at her from the mirror is someone she knows.

She's looking at her own face—

Vail awoke with a gasp. She'd seen the face of the Dead Eyes killer. And it was hers. She dragged a clammy hand across her eyes, as if wiping them would make the image disappear. What did it mean? She didn't have much time to ponder it—and even if she did, what good would it do? It was just a dream, something that no doubt stemmed from her frustration with being unable to get a handle on the case. Still, it hovered like a storm cloud, following her throughout the day.

She got out of bed and showered, then drove to work. The call from the unit secretary came through at 8:03 A.M., two minutes after she had sat down at her desk: "Mr. Gifford wants to see you in his office ASAP."

Vail dropped her leather satchel on the chair and headed into Gifford's office.

The meeting was short and to the point: the Office of Professional Responsibility had reviewed her report on the Virginia Commonwealth Savings Bank incident and concluded she needed to complete a refresher course at the Bureau's training facility, Hogan's Alley. The mock-up town had been created to hone an agent's real-world skills: because when you were in Hogan's "town," in the bank, in the drugstore or movie theater, motel or photo lab, anything could happen. You never knew who or what was part of the exercise . . . you had to play it as it came, and as you saw fit. As Gifford had explained it, after the episode in the bank, the bureaucrats felt she needed "some work" on her tactical skills.

"It's a small price to pay," Gifford had told her, "and a light sentence."

The vivid image of this morning's nightmare crept into her thoughts. She pushed it aside and forced herself to focus on Gifford's comment. He seemed to be waiting for her to respond. "In the middle of Dead Eyes? Can't it wait?"

"You're one member of a task force, Agent Vail. You're not even one of the investigators. You're just support."

"Gee, thanks."

"Report to the Academy immediately. Your contact is Agent Paul Ortega."

That was an hour ago, and she was now standing outside the Hogan Bank and Trust, gun drawn—blanks in the chamber—but her pulse jumping just the same. *Fucking OPR. Why'd they have to make it a bank?*

"We've got three armed Caucasian males inside," the voice cracked over her radio.

*No, we've got a serial killer on the loose in our own damn backyard.
And I'm playing games.*

She peered around the brick wall into the front window, then
lifted the radio from her belt and depressed the talk button. "Suspects visible."

"Two units on their way. Hold your position. ETA one minute,
then we're going in."

Her heart continued to pound. Adrenaline was in her veins,
speeding her pulse, dilating her pupils. Brain as sharp as a pinpoint.
I'm ready.

She tightened the grip on her gun and she flashed on Alvin
cradling the hostage in his arms, his eyes bouncing back and forth,
his feet shuffling—

And her cell rang. *What the hell?*

Anything goes in the town of Hogan's Alley. Anything. But a
phone call in the middle of a bank robbery? It could happen. It *is*
happening. *Answer it? Was this part of the exercise?*

Low roar of a car engine in the distance . . . she would have to
storm the bank in a matter of seconds. *Phone ringing.*

Shit. Pulled the BlackBerry from her belt, looked at the display.
Blocked number. Of course. They were not going to make it easy.
Hit the button, glanced down the street for the approaching vehi-
cles. "Vail."

"Karen, get your fucking ass over here. Jonathan forgot his
school book and wants you to pick it up—"

"Deacon?"

"Jonathan says the teacher needs the book today. Come get it."

Her eyes swept the street. This wasn't supposed to happen. Training exercise or not, she didn't want to blow this, especially since the
report would be going straight to OPR.

Back to Deacon: "Why can't you bring it over?"

"'Cause I can't. I'm busy."

Shit. "Fine, I'll be there as soon as I can get away."

"Only gonna be here another hour—"

She hit the End button as the first vehicle pulled up to the curb. Two agents poured out and made eye contact with her. The second unmarked car then screeched to a stop, followed by the voice over the radio: "All units, Charlie Delta Echo. *Go go go!*"

Vail grabbed the door handle, swung her body around, and stormed the bank.

THE CAR KEYS were in Deacon's hand as he stared at Vail through the screen. "Didn't think you were gonna make it. I'm out the door."

"Just give me the damn book, Deacon." Vail had handled the bank situation just fine, but the exercise left her jittery, the residual adrenaline still sloshing around her bloodstream. She was in no mood for Deacon's bullshit.

He snarled, then walked back toward the living room. She entered and stood in the entryway, tapping her foot. Being in the house gave her the willies. She had the overwhelming urge to take the butt of her gun and crack him good across the noggin. Just for old times' sake. And for what he'd been doing to Jonathan. Most of all, for what he'd done to her yesterday.

"So," Deacon called from the kitchen, "did you enjoy our last rendezvous, Karen?"

She squeezed her left arm against her body and felt her Glock shoved into its holster. Deacon suddenly appeared around the bend with Jonathan's book in hand.

He was wearing a shit-eating grin as he danced into the living room. Did a spin in front of Vail. "Here ya go, darlin'." Held the book in front of him.

As she reached for it, he pulled it away and hid it behind his back. Rage. *Crack him across the head. Right between his mud brown eyes.*

"Deacon, I'm not in the mood. Give me the damn book."

Her face was inches from his. She leaned forward, he leaned back. "You shoulda pulled the trigger yesterday, Karen. Because I'm still

round, and as long as I'm still around I'm gonna make your life
miserable. Then there's Jonathan, and I'm already making his
fe miserable—"

Her blood pressure had risen beyond safe limits and if she didn't let
ff some steam or get the hell out of there fast, she was going to do
something she would regret. She clenched her jaw, then spun around.
ook or not, she was leaving. Jonathan would have to understand.

But as she turned away
Deacon grabbed her arm
And the tap opened and anger poured out like water from a
aucet—

she swung hard, bone on bone
and he fell backwards
knees crumpling

And he hit the floor with a loud *thump!*

She looked down at her fallen ex, who was shaking his head, try-
ng to regain some sense of self. "You deserve that you son of a
itch," she spat. "Don't you ever touch me again!"

She located the textbook, which had skittered beneath the sofa,
nd bent down to retrieve it. After straightening up, Vail heard
movement behind her and started to turn—

But Deacon grabbed her ankles and twisted and she fell back,
nding sideways on the couch.

Looking at him, his eyes still distant and vacant: she yanked her
ght leg free and kicked him in the face, a swift shot intensified by
he heel of her shoe. A moan escaped from Deacon's bloody lips and
e fell back to the floor.

Vail pushed herself off the couch and stood over her stunned ex-
usband. Then kicked him in the ribs, for good measure. "I mean it,
eacon. You come near me again, I'll kill you."

OUTSIDE, VAIL SAT IN HER CAR, her heart pounding, her strength
one, her mind racing, on the verge of tears. The squeal of brakes
om a nearby delivery truck put her back on track. She found her

keys, tossed the book onto the seat beside her, and started the engine.

She thought of the last time she drove down this road . . . beaten, dazed, and frazzled. A victim.

But at the moment, Deacon was the one beaten and dazed. And she had to admit, it felt much better this way.

He sent off his message but had not yet received a response. He ended up having to do some thinking, let alone a lot of research, to make it work. He could've just haphazardly thrown his writings out there, but what's the sense in that? No, he had to do it just right. The proper tool is key to honing your work. A painter could no more create a finely detailed landscape with a wide brush than a photographer could capture the close-up beauty of a flower with a box camera. The right tools for the right jobs.

Which got him to thinking . . . tools weren't the only things that mattered. Presentation was critical. Would an artiste display his most precious work in a basement somewhere, where no one could see it? Or would he look for the right stand, the proper lighting to emphasize its attributes, the best setting for his piece? A writer must do the same. What good would his work do sitting on a hard drive locked away in a computer? So he spent the time to do it right . . . such things can't be rushed. After all, patience is a virtue. *Who said that? Who cares? Somebody did, and it happens to be true. And that's really all that matters to me.*

They'll react. They have to.

The neighbor's dog was barking and that made it hard to concentrate. He sat at the computer and nothing came out. Was this writer's block? He'd read about that, where you stare at the blank screen and can't write anything. He was no writer, at least he never thought he was, but that goddamn cocker spaniel had been hitting the same pitch and rhythm for the past fifteen minutes. *Bark-bark-bark. Bark-bark-bark. Bark-bark-bark.* Same monotonous tone that wore on him. Who can write with this noise? Can Stephen King? Definitely not!

He had the urge to go next door and drive a knife through i fucking brain, end the incessant noise.

Yet annoying as it was, it was something he was able to contro He could stop himself from killing the dog because it was a low form of life—and therefore worthy of some mercy. It knows ne what it does.

But when it came to the bitch-whores, he couldn't help himsel He finally realized he didn't want to, because it defined the ver essence of who he was. It took him a while to understand tha Once he did, he knew how to satisfy the desire, the need for more For satisfaction.

No, it was more than that. It was an uncontrollable urge. . *hunger.*

It was something only he understood. He'd never tried to mal others feel what he felt, because he knew they wouldn't, or couldn' He accepted that. He accepted that he was different—and that eve his inner self would never accept him for who he was.

So be it. He'd gotten comfortable with who he'd become. N longer would someone control his life, dictate when he could do th things he wanted to do. He'd learned how to free himself. Freedor was one of the most valued rights of our great country, and it toc him years to learn how to find it. So much more the reason to savor i

But perhaps the best freedom of all is that no one has stoppe him from fulfilling his needs. Because they couldn't. No one coul find him. He had the perfect hiding place, the perfect disguise. An no matter how hard they searched, no matter what places the looked, he wasn't there.

They will never find me.

The dog's bark quickened for a moment, the change in rhythm breaking the monotony. Someone strange was near. If there was or thing he looked for in a potential target, it was the absence of a dog He could kill the dog, that wasn't the problem—first time he di that he was about thirteen, maybe fourteen. The problem was th the damn thing would bark and he didn't need the noise. Or the has sle of possibly getting bitten. It was just easier to avoid them.

He walked to his door in time to see the FedEx delivery person heading toward his stoop, a box wedged beneath her arm. As the woman was reaching for the buzzer, he pulled the door open. Ms. FedEx jumped backward.

He sniffed deeply, smelled fear. A dense odor, putrid almost, and moist . . . a familiar scent he'd sampled far too many times to count . . and it was oozing from this slut's pores like sweat. Must've scared the crap out of her.

He signed for the package, and as he was taking it, Ms. FedEx squinted a bit when looking at him. He hated when people did that. It's just damned rude. He dismissed the delivery person—she didn't realize how lucky she was—and grabbed a pair of scissors, then took to the box with the excitement of a child descending the stairs on Christmas morning.

After clearing away the packing, he saw his new tool . . . lying in the box, propped up and ready for use. He removed the stun gun and read the advertising panels. Some guys get excited over drills and power saws and screwdrivers. For him, a useful tool has to do more. It has to help him define his freedom. That's the way he looked at it. This was his freedom tool.

He glanced at the instruction manual. Not as precise a resource as he'd like it to have been. There was more mumbo jumbo lawyer junk to head off liability claims if the unit was used improperly than about the operation of the damn thing.

Downstairs, the cocker spaniel barked again.

He looked down at the stun gun in his hands and instantly felt the spark of excitement inside his chest. He would try out his new tool on the dog. Lower species or not, it was going to get the jolt of its life.

He felt the balance of the precisely machined device and realized the power harnessed in its small, black rectangular body.

The right tool for the right job.

State Senator Eleanor Linwood sat behind her massive, highly po
ished mahogany desk. Her auburn hair had been colored and re
cut this morning, then gelled and sprayed into place. A man, bent a
her side, swiped a makeup brush across the gentle folds of her neck
attempting to lessen their prominence for the TV cameras. With gol
reading glasses perched on the tip of her nose, she read aloud th
lines her speechwriter had prepared. "And let me state right here an
now—"

"Senator." Chief-of-staff Levar Wilson was standing in the door
way, sheaves of dog-eared papers clutched in both hands. "What ar
you doing?"

She waved off the man applying the makeup. "What does it loo
like I'm doing? I'm practicing, for the press conference."

"Senator, with all due respect, this is an extremely importan
speech. The public is going to see you like they've never seen you be
fore; you need to make the most of this situation, seize th
moment—"

"I've delivered hundreds of speeches over the years, Levar—"

"This isn't a stump speech where you're angling for votes. You'r
telling your constituents they're safe. That you're doing everythin
humanly possible to catch this killer. All the mothers out there ar
putting the safety of their daughters in your hands. You have to sho
them you're strong and in control, that you're up to the task."

"Your point?"

"Let's give it a run-through in the conference room. I need to g
over some details with you."

"Do you really think that's necessary? I've only got thirty-fiv
minutes before—"

"Yes. Please come with me."

She frowned, then gathered her papers and followed Wilson down the hall. The conference room was rectangular, twice as deep as it was wide, and large enough to accommodate a small army of press people packed a bit more loosely than sardines. A wooden podium stood alone on a raised platform against a brown curtained backdrop.

"There'll be a cup of water on the podium. Do not touch it. You have to tell the viewers you're working to the exclusion of everything else to keep them safe. You're not even going to stop for a glass of water."

"That's a bit over the top, Levar."

"Now," he said, ignoring her objection, "set the papers down and grasp both edges of the podium. I hope you don't mind borrowing a bit from the Democrats, but Bill Clinton had this down to a science. He has these large hands and he curled them around the edges of the podium, caressing it, symbolizing that he had a full grasp of the situation."

"Levar—"

"Go with me on this, Senator. It'll work."

She sighed her consternation, then dropped her papers on the podium and took hold of its edges.

"No, no—stand at ease, the podium is merely a prop. Here, picture it this way. The edges of the podium are a woman's shoulders. Pretend it's your daughter—"

"I don't have a daughter," she said firmly.

"Pretend, Senator. Please."

"Very well."

"Hold her shoulders gently, but with authority. She's upset about something, and you're about to give her some comforting advice. Look into her eyes. In this case, the camera. Tilt your head," he said, doing the same with his and waiting for her to follow. "That's it, now pause for a second. You're thoughtful, but deliberate. Explain to your daughter that she's safe and that you're going to do everything possible to look after her safety."

Linwood's eyes softened a bit. Wilson nodded his approval. "Good, perfect. Now, back to your papers. Pick up with the sentence, "And I promise. . . . ""

THE TELEVISION ZOOMED IN on the senator's face; this was true drama, in primetime. And it was all because of him. How flattering. Not his intention, but what the hell. We all got our fifteen minutes of fame sooner or later.

"And I promise to do my best to make sure no woman has to worry about being safe in her own home. My representatives and I are working hand-in-hand with the police to catch this madman. And I assure you, we *will* catch him."

"Shut up, shut up, shut up!" He pressed the mute button and she had no choice but to listen to him. "Now, wouldn't that be something . . . a remote control to make all the bitch-whores shut up on my command!"

Madman, she called me a madman. I'm not mad! I may be angry, but I'm not mad. Only a dog can be mad, not a person! Stupid bitch.

He hit the remote and her voice came alive again.

"The police and the FBI are poised to act on several leads. I expect we'll see a major break in the case any time now."

"Several leads . . . major break. . . ." Why can't people tell the truth? They got *jack*. "Admit it! You don't know who you're dealing with! You'll never find me!"

VAIL WALKED INTO the task force's operations center and heard the measured drone of a television emanating from the kitchen. She was jumpy yet exhausted, remnants of her latest run-in with Deacon. She had dropped off the book at Jonathan's school and gone home to straighten herself up before heading to the op center.

She laid her purse atop her makeshift desk and picked up a note clipped to a folder. As she started to read it, someone tapped her shoulder. She turned, saw Bledsoe, and winced as pain cut through her left leg. When Deacon had grabbed her ankles, he'd twisted the knee she had injured in Sandra Franks's yard. It had been killing her since leaving Deacon's a couple of hours ago.

"You okay?"

"I'm fine. Knee's a little sore. What's up?"

"Linwood's on TV. Dead Eyes press conference."

"What press conference?"

"You already know as much as I do. Far as I know, she's doing this on her own."

Bledsoe followed Vail into the kitchen. Manette and Robby were huddled around a scarred, faux wood–encased Sony television with fuzzy reception.

Vail moved in beside them to get a clear view of the screen, which showed Linwood standing behind a podium.

". . . and to the Dead Eyes killer, I say your days are numbered. We're on your trail, and we will persevere until we find you. You will rot in hell, your soul hung out to dry in front of everyone, for society to see who and what you are—"

"Oh, that's just great," Vail said, grabbing the back of her neck. "Incite him." She turned to Bledsoe. "How can she do this—shouldn't she need clearance from us to go on TV?"

"Politics," Robby said. "That's what this is about."

Vail looked around the room and noticed someone was missing. "Where's Hancock?"

"I texted him," Bledsoe said. "Haven't heard back."

"I bet he's behind this," Vail said. "Doesn't she realize what'll happen if the offender sees this?" Vail asked. "We can't have loose cannons—"

"She challenged him," Manette said. "Right on network TV. It'll be shown in sound bites on every major channel for the next several days."

"Not to be cynical, but I bet that's exactly what she's counting on," Robby said. "Prime-time exposure, for free. Leading up to an election, getting in the offender's face, and showing him who's boss is a powerful political statement. Brilliant strategy, really."

"She won't look so smart when he uses it as an excuse to kill again," Bledsoe said.

Manette rose slowly from her chair. "As if he needed an excuse."

"Whether he did or not," Vail said, "she's just given him one."

I KNOW THOSE EYES. He paused the recording and stared at Linwood's face. *Oh, yes . . . evil, evil eyes.* His gaze remained fixed on the image until it suddenly sputtered back to life.

"You will rot in hell, your soul hung out to dry in front of everyone, for society to see who and what you are: a monster. A wart, a sin on the face of God."

He grabbed a gob of clay and hurled it at the TV. It stuck to the screen as if clinging for its life. "I'll rot in hell, huh?" He threw his tools off the table. Pulled at his collar. Hard to breathe. *Fucking bitch.* "Whore!"

The clay suddenly lost its grip and fell with a light thud to the floor.

"Rot in hell? *I'll* rot in hell? How dare she talk to me like that? How dare she, how dare she? If I'm a wart on the face of God, she's a fucking boil!"

He laughed. Laughed so hard he couldn't stop. He bent down on one knee and gathered himself. He felt the blood rushing to his head, pounding, pounding, pounding. Finally it eased and he sat on the floor, leaned against the wall.

But this was not a laughing matter. He wasn't laughing because it was *funny.* He grabbed his new tool, got his keys, and headed out. Someone was going to pay.

MANETTE left the op center shortly after Linwood's speech had ended. Robby walked Vail to her car and watched as she searched her purse for her keys.

"I had a good time last night," he said.

She pulled her empty hand from her purse and looked toward the house. "Me too." She was not in the mood for flirting, not with

Deacon's sneering face still branded in her mind—and on the bottom of her shoe.

"What's wrong?"

"Left my keys in the house."

"That's not what I mean."

"Is it that obvious?"

"To me it is."

She studied his face for a moment, then turned and leaned back against her car. "Problems with my ex," she said, then gave him an abbreviated version of her last two encounters with Deacon.

Robby's gaze was fixed on the ground, his foot tapping furiously. "I've never met this guy. But I'd like to, just to talk to him, you know?" His fists were clenched and his shoulder muscles were bunched in anger.

Vail placed a reassuring hand on his taut forearm. "I've got it handled, Robby. I don't think he'll bother me again."

"And what about your son? This asshole is gonna take out his beating on Jonathan. Do you have him tonight or does Deacon?"

"Deacon."

"Then I suggest you go by his school and pick him up. You want, I'll call Deacon and tell him you've got him, after the fact. He won't give me any grief. Better yet, I'll go with you."

Vail shook her head. "He wouldn't hurt Jonathan. He did, I'd kill him. He knows that. And after today, he knows I'm capable of it."

"Probably true. But I still think it's best to err on the side of caution. Pick him up, keep him at your place till Deacon cools off."

Vail nodded slowly. "What day is today?"

"Twenty-third." Robby's cell phone began to ring. He fished it out of his pocket.

Vail's eyebrows crumpled, then she consulted her watch. Four thirty. Jonathan had a chess club meeting today, which meant he would be out at five.

Robby flipped his phone shut. "I've gotta go, something came up on one of my old cases. Break-and-enter on this rich guy's condo. I know the perp they like for it, busted him a couple of times before. He's holed up in a house, took a kid hostage. EST's on the scene, but the perp's asking for me." He dropped the phone in his pocket and started to back away. "You want me to get someone to go with you, I can arrange it. Hell, ask Bledsoe."

"Not necessary."

"I'll catch up with you later. You need any help, let me know."

While Robby got into his car, Vail ran back into the house to retrieve her keys. She waved to Bledsoe, who was in the kitchen with the phone handset tucked beneath his chin. She grabbed her keys and ran outside, where a Fairfax County police cruiser was pulling up behind her Dodge Stratus. She nodded at the officer as he got out of his car.

"Karen Vail?"

Vail glanced at him over her shoulder. "Yeah." She unlocked the door and opened it, tossed her purse on the passenger seat.

"Ma'am, I'm Officer Greenwich, County Police. I need a moment of your time."

"Wish I could help you, Officer, but I've got an appointment. Detective Paul Bledsoe is in the house—"

"Ma'am, he won't be able to help me. I need to talk to *you*."

"I really do have to run. If this is about Dead Eyes, Bledsoe heads up the task force." She sat down in her seat and started to pull the door closed, but the cop grabbed it and held it open.

"Excuse me?" she said. "Let go of my door."

The cop removed his hands. "Ma'am, I really need your assistance. Police business."

Vail squinted at the cop, forgot his name. Glanced at his name tag. "Look, Officer Greenwich, if this is some kind of joke—"

"It's not, ma'am. I've got some questions. Can you step out of the car? I just need a minute of your time."

As Vail got out, another cruiser pulled up to the curb across the street. She stood and faced Greenwich, who couldn't have been more than twenty-five or so. African American, head shaved bald, and large eyes, he exuded confidence. Maybe he was all jacked up about hassling an FBI agent. "Ask away, just make it quick."

The other officer, gelled brown hair and medium build, took a position ten feet away, to Greenwich's left. He hooked both thumbs in his utility belt but did not say a word. Vail did not like the look of this.

"Ma'am, mind telling me where you were at noon today?"

Then it hit her. This was about Deacon. "Why, what's the problem?"

"It'd be easier if I ask the questions. Now, noon today. . . . "

She folded her arms across her chest. "At my ex-husband's house. Deacon Tucker. I was picking up a school book for my son."

"Can you tell me what happened while you were there?"

"Look, Officer. This all goes back—" and then she stopped herself and realized she should just shut her mouth and say as little as possible. "Has he sworn a complaint against me?"

"Yes, ma'am," the young officer said, his posture erect and confident. "I just came from the hospital. He's being treated for two fractured ribs and a broken nose. Did you strike Mr. Tucker, ma'am?"

Jesus. This rookie is going to run me in. Goddamn you, Deacon. She bit her lip, then shook her head out of disbelief. Time was ticking. She needed to get to Jonathan's school. "Yes, in self-defense."

He tilted his head from side to side, looking her over. "I don't see any bruising on your person. Do you have any bruises, ma'am?"

"No, Officer, I don't have any bruises."

"Self-defense, but you don't have any bruising?"

Was it self-defense? He taunted me, grabbed my arm, but I took the first swing. I took the only swing. Goddamn you, Deacon.

"Can you show me any evidence that he injured you?"

Through a tightened jaw, she said, "No."

"You said it was in self-defense. What exactly did he do that made you feel as if you needed to defend yourself?"

"He grabbed my arm."

"Mind rolling up your sleeve?"

Vail thought of the bump on the back of her head, but with her dense hair, what was he going to see? Besides, that was hardly proof Deacon had hit her. In truth, she didn't even know how it happened. She noticed Greenwich was waiting, so she did as requested and pulled back the loose sleeve of her sport coat. "He grabbed my forearm, right here." She pointed; the officer stepped closer, tilted his head and examined the area. "I don't see anything."

"I told you. No bruising."

Greenwich glanced at his colleague, then back at Vail. "Ma'am, are you carrying a weapon?"

"Of course I am—"

"Where is it located?"

Vail moved her suit coat back, about to expose the shoulder harness—

And Greenwich held out a hand. "No, no. That's okay, just tell me where it is."

"In my shoulder holster."

"Any other weapons on your person?"

"No, that's it."

"Protocol, ma'am. Have to follow protocol," he said as if she would immediately understand.

In fact, she did understand. But it didn't make it any easier.

Greenwich removed her Glock from its holster, then handed it to his partner. "Ma'am, according to eighteen-two-fifty-seven point two of the Virginia Code, in a domestic violence case I'm compelled by law to make an arrest."

"The bastard knocked me unconscious and took my handgun! I wasn't going to let him do it to me again—"

"Hang on a second," he said, holding out a hand. "Now you're saying he knocked you unconscious? Your story seems to be changing—"

"No—it's not. Look, Officer, let me explain—"

"I think at this point I've got to advise you of your right to remain silent—"

"No, no. Listen to me. You don't have to do this—"

"In fact, ma'am, I do have to do this. You'll have your say, I promise you that, but I'm going to need to take you in. I'll be as discreet about it as I can." He pulled a set of cuffs from his belt and held it out in front of him long enough for her to see what was going to have to happen. He cocked his head, waiting for her to turn around. "You have the right to remain silent—"

"I'm a fucking FBI agent, I know my rights!"

But he continued on nonetheless.

"Bledsoe!" she shouted at the closed door to the house. Would he hear her? What could he do, anyway? She felt the cold metal touch her wrists and the deputy's voice disappeared in her mind. Tears filled her eyes. *This can't be happening.* "I need to get my son. I need to—*ow!*" The hard cuffs bit into her skin. "You don't need to make the damn things so tight. Didn't they teach you anything at the academy?"

Greenwich swung the cruiser door open and nudged Vail toward the backseat. She more or less fell in as he guided her head past the door frame.

"Can I at least make a phone call?"

He looked down at her. "After you're processed, I'll make sure you get access to a phone."

And then the door slammed shut.

She looked at the front door to the house, willing Bledsoe to walk out and save her from this nightmare. "Bledsoe!" she screamed.

But the cruiser windows were closed. She glanced at the clock: it was ten minutes to five. Even if she was able to reach Robby—who was in the middle of a crisis of his own—he wouldn't be able to get someone to the school in time.

The other officer headed back toward his squad car as Greenwich opened the door, got in, then slammed it shut. "Four-ten Baker," he said into his radio.

"Go ahead Four-ten Baker."

"Heading toward ADC, prisoner in custody."

As the car pulled away from the curb, Vail closed her eyes and let her head fall back against the seat. *This can't be happening.*

Goddamn you, Deacon.

He was so pissed at the moment, he had the urge to do some*thing*, to do some*one*. Right now. Like that dog that wouldn't stop barking, this was monopolizing his thoughts. He stunned the dog to shut him up. But he couldn't shut off the anger inside him. He couldn't make it go away. He paced, then kneaded some clay, but none of it helped. He sat down and began to write.

> I want to stab him, hurt him like he hurts those whores he
> brings home. I want to kill him. How would I do it? Shooting him
> would be the easiest and least risky way, but I don't have a gun.
> I'd hit him with a baseball bat, but I don't know if I could hit
> him hard enough before he turned it on me.
> But a knife . . . a knife in the face would stun him. In the eye
> and he wouldn't be able to come back at me. A fast attack. I could
> do that.
> Stab and run. No, stab and stab and stab.
> Yes, I could do that. I could do that. I could.

He liked what he'd written, but it didn't cool his anger, his urge, which felt like a ravenous hunger eating away at his stomach. If anything, the rage, the fury he felt toward the prick was driving him to take action sooner rather than later. He wasn't prepared for this, and for a few seconds wondered if he was behaving irrationally, allowing his emotions to control his actions. He had a plan, and he should stick with it. It's when you cut corners that you end up making mistakes.

But he couldn't help himself.

He found himself sitting outside the nearest Food & More about twenty minutes from his house. Supermarkets, bars, and malls were the best places to find a bitch when you were desperate, that much he'd thought through. And the stun gun was tucked away in his glove box, just in case he got pulled over. So many details, so many things to keep straight.

It was four o'clock and the sky was darkening, meaning he had maybe forty-five minutes of light left. He got out and walked into the market, his overcoat flapping in the brisk breeze, the hat threatening to lift off his head.

He angled for the deli counter. Women standing around, nowhere to go while they waited for their orders. He stayed there for ten, fifteen minutes watching them chitchat, watching them peer into the display cases. Watching their eyes. But none of them intrigued him. On to the dairy section . . . another place where the bitches seem to always linger while they scanned the ever-expanding varieties of cheese.

He hurried there, the heat of the hunt making his neck sweaty. He was close, he could feel it. He turned left down an aisle and slammed into a bitch coming right at him. They'd both been moving at a good clip and were thrown back a bit. Her purse went flying and opened, scattering all sorts of shit across the aisle.

Her hands flew into the air, then came to rest on her sunken cheeks. "You okay?" she asked.

"I'm fine," he said. *You bitch-whore. Next time watch where you're going.* He forced a smile. "Guess we were both in a hurry."

She bent down to collect her fallen items. He knelt, too, and they were nose to nose. Crows feet hidden below caked foundation, dirty blond hair. And her eyes: hollow, nearly lifeless. This one was dead already. She just didn't know it. Definitely not the one. He had to disguise his lingering gaze, so he grabbed a lipstick, makeup case, and a pack of Wrigley's off the floor. He handed them to her and she took them with cold hands and a crooked smile.

But then, a high-pitched voice: "Oh, here. Let me help."

His head whipped to the right. Brunet twenty-something kneeling beside him, wire-rimmed glasses magnifying her golden tiger eyes. What incredible detail. He'd never seen so many swirling colors before. Golds and browns and tans with a hint of black. He couldn't move. *Yes, yes, yes.* Pretty but *evil.* Like camouflage, you had to look carefully to find it. But once you saw it, it stood out like a green tomato.

You, you're the one.

The brunet gathered up a handful of the remaining items and handed them to the blond-haired bitch, who held her purse open. "Thanks for your help, both of you."

He fought back a smile and couldn't help but think, *No, no . . . thank* you.

TWENTY-NINE MINUTES LATER, the tiger-eyed brunet came slinking out of the Food & More. He sat back and watched from about thirty yards away. She quickly loaded the groceries into the trunk and got into her car. He started his Audi and drove toward her, timing his arrival with her exit.

He'd taken a quick inventory of her before they'd parted company: a bare ring finger; a smattering of items in her cart: veggies, spices, herbal tea, fresh salmon. No beer or frozen pizza, steaks or pork chops. Not as foolproof as checking the house for large tennis shoes or men's clothing, but he felt reasonably sure she did not have a male significant other waiting for her at home.

They left the parking lot together and headed home. *Her home,* where they'd soon be face-to-face. And eye-to-eye.

The drive to the Adult Detention Center was a long one, slowed by rush hour traffic. The deputy moved through the lines of cars using his overhead light bar whenever possible, but even driving the shoulders made the hour-long ride seem twice as long.

Vail kept her head turned away from the window, hoping no one she knew would see her. With her arms drawn back behind her shoulders, she had to sit forward in the seat—and after the first fifteen minutes, her hands had gone numb and her back ached something terrible. But her ego and emotions were in far worse shape. Humiliation was much too weak a word to describe how she felt: the anger, the embarrassment ran much deeper.

For a fleeting moment, she wondered how the arrest would affect her position with the Bureau. She had heard of agents getting into domestic disputes, but it hadn't happened to anyone she knew or anyone who'd worked out of her field office, so she never learned the agents' final disposition.

For a fleeting moment, she wondered how her unit would relate to her now. She'd always had difficulty fitting in, even with six years under her belt. Now, having been accused of assaulting her ex-husband, it would feed the stereotype every law enforcement professional had of a female agent: that she had to be buff and butch and aggressive to succeed. She wanted to think it wasn't true, but another part of her conceded that to some extent, it might just be the case.

For a fleeting moment, she thought of putting a gun to Deacon's head.

For a fleeting moment, tears began to pool in her eyes.

And it was then that the cruiser pulled up to the sprawling Adult Detention Center on Judicial Drive. Populated with multistory buildings and encompassing several square blocks, the campus housed the booking center, the male and female prisons, the sheriff's department, Juvenile and Domestic Relations, magistrate offices, and the courthouse. Vail had visited the ADC a number of times while meeting deputies in court, visiting prisoners she needed to interview for her research papers, and consulting on the department's new LiveScan fingerprint identification database. But there were thousands of employees, and she knew only a handful. Doubtful she would run into any of them, particularly now, since the day shift had long since ended. Doubtful they could do anything to help her, anyway.

The squad car pulled down the long ramp leading to the Sally Port and waited for the guard, who was watching them on a monitor inside the building, to open the mammoth electronic steel doors. Vail had never come in this way before, and as the large entryway slammed shut behind them and darkness descended on the garage, she decided once was enough.

After parking the cruiser beside an unmarked cherry red Ford Mustang, the deputy placed his handgun and her Glock into the weapons locker, then led her through the Sally Port's double set of electronic security doors into the central booking area. The last time Vail had been here was when she'd been given a tour of the new facility a few days before it had opened a few years ago. It was then a cavernous, deserted room, computers and equipment blanketed with clear covers, white ceramic tile, and freshly painted cinder block walls. Her nose had stung from recently varnished oak trim and countertops. It was almost too spiffy to be a jail, she'd thought at the time.

But she didn't feel that way now. Deputies manned the expansive booking desk, where papers stuck to clipboards and files were stacked on end, memos and rosters were taped to walls. Phones rang, keys clanged, printers spat out documents . . . movement was everywhere as prisoners were being processed.

She was led to a counter-mounted camera, positioned in front of a wall with measured hash marks, and handed a metal identification sign that she held in front of her chest. The flash flickered, her face flushed out of embarrassment, and she was ushered over to a fixed cement stool. "Wait here," Officer Greenwich instructed. He handed some paperwork to another deputy, who was operating the free-standing electronic fingerprint unit.

"It'll be a while, I've got a line ahead of her," the deputy said.

Greenwich leaned forward, turned his body slightly, and spoke into his colleague's ear. The deputy glanced at Vail, said something to Greenwich, who nodded, then walked back over to Vail.

"He's going to move you up a bit," Greenwich said. "Professional courtesy."

Forty-five minutes later she was standing in front of the LiveScan fingerprint scanner, where her ridges and whorls were recorded electronically. She knew this system intimately. The thought of being on the receiving—rather than the demonstrating end—depressed her. And she had plenty of time to be alone with her thoughts, as she waited again, this time for over an hour, before being led to a row of intake booths, a line of four-by-four semiprivate cubicles outfitted with bulletproof glass, a built-in microphone, and a pass-through slot. This was where she would meet with a magistrate, where she would finally have her chance to say something in her defense.

Greenwich slid the signed statement of facts through the narrow opening in the glass. The magistrate—Nicholas Harrison, according to the nameplate on the desk—was a broad, round-faced man with black-rimmed bifocals. He pushed a file aside and picked up the deputy's form. He glanced at Vail, then nodded to Greenwich, who was standing behind her and off to the right.

"Good evening, Your Honor. I've got an eighteen-two-fifty-seven point two, Dom Vio. Complainant is Deacon Tucker. Suspect is Karen Vail, a special agent with the FBI. Mr. Tucker alleges that Ms. Vail presented to his house, and when he asked her to leave, she became violent and kicked him in the face—"

Vail stepped forward. "That's not the way it happened—"

"Just a moment, Agent Vail," Harrison instructed through the glass. His voice was tinny through the speaker, but his wrinkled brow and extended index finger were quite clear. "You'll have an opportunity to give your version in a moment." He turned back to Greenwich. "Continue."

"After getting kicked in the face, Mr. Tucker fell. He alleges that Agent Vail then delivered two kicks to his torso. She left the scene and complainant was taken by ambulance to Virginia Presbyterian with multiple broken ribs. He was treated and released four hours later."

The magistrate reclined in his high-backed chair. "Anything else?"

"Computer picked up a PD forty-two in the file from eighteen months ago."

"Same complainant?"

"Yes, sir."

"What's a PD forty-two?" Vail asked.

Harrison removed his glasses and leaned forward. "It's what's called a suspicious event. If there's a violent altercation between spouses but insufficient evidence to make an arrest, the incident is logged and held inactive in the file." He replaced his glasses and opened a folder, then rifled through some papers. He pulled a document and looked it over.

Vail shifted her feet. Eighteen months ago. That was when Deacon hit her with his fist and she hit him back with an iron skillet, opening a gash on his forehead. He called the police and attempted to have her arrested. But because she had also had physical signs of an injury—a swollen and bloody lip—and no eyewitnesses, the officers were unable to identify the primary aggressor and could not take any action.

"Well," the magistrate said without lifting his eyes from the sheet, "there seems to be a pattern of violence here, Agent Vail." He slowly met her gaze. "Do you have anything to say?"

"I do, Your Honor. The incident eighteen months ago was perpetrated by my ex-husband. He hit me and I hit him back with a pan. I took my son with me and we left that night. I filed for divorce the next morning. Today's incident was an extension of something that happened a few days ago. Deacon Tucker assaulted me—"

The magistrate's eyebrows rose. "Oh. Is there a report on file with FPD?"

"No, Your Honor. I didn't report it. I should have, but he'd knocked me unconscious and I wasn't thinking straight. But I told Detective Paul Bledsoe about it right after that and he'll corroborate my story."

Harrison looked away, which Vail interpreted as a bad sign. "Paul Bledsoe is a fine detective, but he didn't directly witness anything. I'm sure you understand, Agent Vail."

Of course I understand, but understanding won't end this nightmare. "As to the incident this morning, Deacon summoned me to his house to pick up a book for my son. He refused to bring it to school—"

"Cut to the chase, please."

He was getting impatient, another bad sign. "We got into an argument, Your Honor, and tempers flared. He was gloating—"

"According to Officer Greenwich's statement here," he said, searching for the right document, "you claimed it was self-defense. Did he ever take a swing at you?"

"When I saw he wasn't going to give me the book, I turned to leave. I didn't want to get into it again with him. He grabbed my arm and pulled and . . . I swung at him."

Harrison sighed. "I'm not a trial judge, and this isn't a trial, Agent Vail. My purpose here is only to determine probable cause, and I believe I've got more than enough for that. You're in a tough spot. I hope it gets resolved to your satisfaction."

Vail bristled while watching the magistrate scribble his signature on a document, then pass it through the slot. "Officer, you've got your warrant."

Greenwich took the paper and signed it, then handed it to Vail. "Your Honor, I'm required to request an EPO on behalf of the complainant."

"An Emergency Protective Order? Against *me?*"

Harrison stared back at Vail. "Agent Vail, when you make bond and are out roaming the streets, I need some assurance that you're

not going to go over to your ex-hubby's house and blow h
brains out."

That was exactly what she felt like doing. But voicing her desire
would surely land her in a heap of trouble. "I'm not going to do any
thing of the sort. I'm going to steer clear of him."

Vail's hesitation was not lost on Harrison, apparently, as he shoo
his head. "You waited just a tad too long for me there, Agent Vai
I'm reasonably sure you're not going to do anything foolish, but yo
own a gun, you're skilled in using it, there's substantial bad bloo
between the two of you, and you've already demonstrated to me yo
have the potential for violence if the situation presents itself. I'm go
ing to help you out here, Agent, though I doubt you're going to se
it that way."

Harrison pulled another form from his desk, signed it, an
handed it through the slot to Greenwich. "Fill it out, Officer. She'
got a seventy-two-hour EPO slapped on her." He looked at Vail. "
cooling off period, to think about your actions. Guilty of the charge
or not, you're better off staying away from Deacon Tucker."

Vail sighed through pursed lips and shook her head. Could thi
day get any worse?

"One other note, Agent. Consider it another favor. Get yourse
the very best defense attorney you can afford. Misdemeanor Domes
tic Violence/Assault is not something to fool around with. You ge
convicted, it's not just a measly misdemeanor. Under the new law
it's taken very seriously. You'll lose the ability to carry a weapor
That's Federal law, not Virginia code. You'll lose your job. Plain a
that."

Vail closed her eyes. Her day had, in fact, just gotten worse.

"As to the issue of bond," Harrison said, "I already know you
occupation, which gives me your income level, lack of prior crimina
history, and your flight risk, which I deem to be minimal. Not if yo
have hopes of keeping your job." He wrote something on a docu
ment, signed it, and lifted the glasses off his face. He closed the file
"Five hundred dollar secured bond is hereby granted. Thank you
Officer."

Greenwich turned to Vail, who was still staring at the glass window in disbelief. "I left my purse in the car. I don't have any money with me."

"Then that phone call I promised you earlier will come in pretty handy." He forced a smile, then led her out of the intake booth.

"The jail cell was six-by-eight, Robby. A cinderblock room with a tiny window."

Robby took his eyes off the road to glance at Vail. "I know, I've seen them."

It was a few minutes past two in the morning and they were on I-395, headed toward the task force op center to pick up her car—and her purse. The winding, tree-canopied road was nature at its best during the day, but eerie on a winter night, when the headlights caught the barren, low-lying branches as the car sped beneath them.

"If I didn't have claustrophobia before, I probably have it now." Vail shivered, then pulled her seat belt away from her chest, as if it had renewed the confining sensation of the jail cell. "What a horrible experience. It took them three hours to get a phone over to me."

"Three hours?"

"There were a shitload of prisoners all waiting their turn on two phones. They cut me some slack here and there, gave me the red carpet treatment—if there is such a thing in the slammer—but even with that it took forever to get a line."

"Sorry it took me so long to get here."

She waved a tired hand. "Hey, I appreciate you laying out the cash." She leaned back against the headrest. "Hopefully the trial will go my way and I'll be able to put it all behind me."

"It will, Karen, everything'll turn out."

"It better, or I'll need to find a new line of work." She shut her eyes, tried to force the thoughts of disaster from her mind. "Tomorrow I have to find a good lawyer. Magistrate said I should hire the best I can afford. I feel like vomiting over the thought of having to hire a defense attorney. They're vermin."

"Just keep things in perspective. Focus your energy. There are more important things to deal with right now."

Robby was right, there were more important things. "I hope Jonathan's okay," she mumbled. "I never did get to his school." She was about to reflect on the frailty of life when her BlackBerry went off, followed a second later by Robby's cell phone. Vail looked down at the display, then at Robby, who was struggling to read his in the dark while keeping the car steady.

They glanced at each other, the dread of having to view another mutilated body written on Robby's face. He tightened his grip on the wheel and shook his head. "Here we go again."

"Two in the morning," she said. "Doesn't Dead Eyes know I just got out of the slammer?"

THIRTY MINUTES LATER, they were pulling up to the curb in front of a small, square brick house in Alexandria. Rattan furniture adorned its porch and an American flag hung from a column that supported the second-story overhang.

Bledsoe's Crown Victoria was parked in front, behind Hancock's Acura and Manette's Volkswagen Jetta. Crime scene tape had already been strung across the trees at the sidewalk, extending all the way over to the neighbor's side yard—a wide swath of land to protect the crime scene and guard against disturbance of potential ingress and egress footprints made by the Dead Eyes killer. Halogen lamps on tripods lit the front of the house as a criminalist scoured the exterior. To those who were awakened by the activity, it had the surreal circus atmosphere that accompanied a Hollywood movie production. But there were no cameras, no fake extras. This was, unfortunately, the real thing.

As they got out of Robby's car, Sinclair pulled behind them in his 1969 Chevy pickup. They nodded at Sinclair and the three of them walked in together. By the time they hit the bedroom, there was no doubt this was one of their cases. Murals across the walls, message written above the bed.

"No defensive wounds," Bledsoe said. "Same drill. Ate his usual meal at the scene. No dental impressions. Looking for saliva, but I doubt we'll find any." The woman had been treated to the same filet job, and the left hand had once again been amputated. "Vic is Denise Cranston. No business card, but we found a pay stub. Works for Lamplighter Design Gallery in Old Town. Sales manager."

"What is she, vic six? Or five?" Sinclair asked. "I've lost count."

Vail couldn't help but stare at the eviscerated body. "Unofficially, she's number six."

"Whatever number we give her, it's too many, far as I'm concerned," Bledsoe said.

Manette craned her neck as she took in the room's interior. "Did you say she worked at a design gallery?"

"High-end furniture," Bledsoe said.

"Judging by her digs," Manette quipped, "she shoulda brought some of that stuff home with her."

Robby sighed deeply. "She doesn't seem to fit the pattern, career wise. Sales manager, accountant, dental hygienist—"

"Unless there is no pattern and it was all our imagination," Bledsoe said.

Hancock was studying the walls. "There's something to these paintings, I'm sure of it," he said.

Vail yawned. "Keep looking, maybe you'll find it. Like the hand."

Hancock shot her a look. "I'm still working on that."

Sinclair slipped on a pair of latex gloves. The others followed suit. "Guess we just dig in."

Vail walked over to Robby and told him she was going outside to check her messages, in case Jonathan had called her.

She stood out front, beyond the crime scene tape, as the phone connected. Her answering machine started, and she entered her security code. Her lone message began playing: it was left earlier in the evening by a nurse at Fairfax Hospital, informing her that Jonathan had had an accident. Her heart fell a few feet into her stomach as she fumbled with the keypad to dial the number left by the nurse. It was the main line, and after searching the registry, the operator put her on hold.

Vail walked inside the house, pulled Robby aside, and got his car keys. After waiting on hold far too long while trying to negotiate the dark streets with a nervous hand, on unfamiliar streets in the middle of the night, the call was dropped. "Damnit!" she yelled, then tossed the BlackBerry onto the seat beside her.

Twenty minutes later, she was running toward the nurse's station at the intensive care unit. "They told me downstairs my son is here. Jonathan Tucker, he was brought here last night. I'm Karen Vail, I just got the message."

The nurse was in her early sixties, gray hair pulled up into a bun. She looked condescendingly at Vail, then consulted her paperwork. "A message was left at nine-forty-nine—"

"Yes, I know. I was—I wasn't home last night. Where's my son?"

"Follow me," she said and maneuvered her wide body out from behind the counter. She led Vail to a room in which Jonathan was lying, IV lines running into his arms.

"Oh, my God. Jonathan. . . ." She stood by his side, placed a hand on her son's shoulder. "What happened?"

"I wasn't on, but according to the records the boy was brought in with the history of having fallen down the basement stairs." She glanced at the file, flipped a page. "Ambulance was called by his father at nine-fifteen and your son arrived at the hospital at nine-thirty-one—"

"What's wrong with him? Can I talk with the doctor?"

"I'll go get him." And the nurse waddled out of the room.

Vail pulled up a chair and sat beside her son, stroked his hair. "Oh, Jonathan, I'm so sorry. I'm so sorry. . . ."

FIVE MINUTES LATER, a tall, thin black man in his late thirties walked into the room. "I'm David Altman," he said in a deep, hoarse voice. "You're the boy's mother?"

"Karen Vail."

The doctor nodded. "Ms. Vail, your son apparently fell down a flight of stairs and struck his head. The trauma rendered him unconscious and we've put IV lines in, as you can see, to feed him. He's breathing on his own. An MRI scan revealed brain swelling—"

Vail held up a hand. The other was pressed against her lips to stifle an outburst of emotion. "In short, Doctor. Please."

"He's got a closed head injury/concussion with traumatic cerebral hemorrhage. He's in a coma, Ms. Vail. My initial prognosis is guarded, but if pressed I'd say poor to fair. There are a few signs of responsiveness, but there are complicating factors. Good news is there's no need for advanced life support. My prognosis will improve if I see more signs of responsiveness and purposeful movement."

Vail took a deep, uneven breath, fearing she was losing the battle to keep from crying. But she had to be strong at the moment, she had to keep her mind clear to ask the right questions. She knew Deacon had done this, she knew it. "When he wakes up, will he remember what happened to him?"

"He'll probably have retrograde memory loss for the events immediately preceding the precipitating event. In this case, the fall. But it will come back to him. How long, it's hard to say. Could be hours, could be weeks."

She bit her lip, felt it quivering. Took a deep breath through her nose, exhaled slowly and unevenly. She felt weak and stuck out a hand behind her to feel for the chair.

"I know this is a lot to absorb all at once. I wish I could give you more information, or at least a better prognosis. At the moment, I've told you all I know. We have to give the body a chance to heal itself. Meantime, if you want to talk to him, read to him, I can't tell you for sure he can hear you, but there are some studies that suggest the comatose brain can receive such stimuli."

She forced herself to look at the doctor. "Will there be any permanent damage? Give it to me straight, Doc."

He hesitated a moment, seemed to size her up. "Right now, I can't even tell you if he's going to regain consciousness. Why don't we take it one step at a time?"

"You're not answering my question."

"There's a chance he'll be fine when he awakens, but there's also chance there'll be some residual deficits. It's too soon to tell, and hat's the truth."

Vail nodded and thanked the doctor, who excused himself. She at there, placed a clammy hand atop Jonathan's, and rested her face n his arm. As the door clicked shut, she felt a tremendous release, hen burst into tears.

Vail was thinking about happier times . . . Jonathan on a swing in the park in Queens, Deacon away on a business trip, working for a new package delivery company in a management-level position. His career prospects bright, hers likewise poised to bloom. She had just put in her application to the FBI Academy, a chance to not only move up in the law enforcement ranks, but an opportunity for a safe work environment. Jonathan swung back and forth, gently, the three year old laughing as he flew through the air. "Higher!" he said between giggles. "Higher, Mommy!"

She pushed the swing higher, the temperature a sweltering ninety-five, the humidity approaching pretty much the same figure. She swatted some air at her neck, wishing she'd brought a sun hat with her. Good old New York weather.

She thought of her promotion from the Academy, which was followed three years later by Deacon's layoff from his job because of accounting irregularities. He maintained it was an honest mistake, claim Vail believed and defended. But true or not, it began his downward spiral, a freefall that would last the next four years. He stopped taking his bipolar medication, started drinking, and lost motivation to find a new job. He drifted from one low-paying position to another, each one of lesser prestige than the last. He seemed defeated and though Vail did everything she could to help pull him out of his doldrums, he struck bottom when she was promoted to the profiling unit. His teetering male ego couldn't take another hit, and he only appeared to garner an intensified resentment toward her.

Vail took to raising Jonathan on her own, arranging for her son to go to after-school programs and day care until she could pick him up on her way home from work. Busy with her new career, she saw less and less of Deacon, who'd taken what was supposed to be a temporary job as a long-haul trucker. Like an ice cube in a refrigerator, their love slowly melted away, until there was nothing remaining of what had drawn them together so many years ago. The thought of divorce crossed her mind many times, but she could never pull the trigger. Karen Vail, expert marksman, daring NYPD detective, and crack FBI agent, couldn't hit the most significant target of her life.

When Deacon was relieved of his job because of repeated incidents of road rage, it was the final brick in the wall. He sat at home and drank beer, his anger slowly turning toward his wife in the form of verbal abuse, which built over six months to the one and only time he struck her. She walked out the door with a swollen lip and a deep sense of sadness she never imagined possible.

She served Deacon with her application for divorce five days later.

Vail shook her head. The fuse had been lit, and now this. Her son lay in a hospital bed in a coma. How could this have happened?

The rhythmic vibration of her BlackBerry invaded her thoughts and woke her from her semisleep. She lifted her head and realized she had drooled on Jonathan's forearm. She wiped it away, then looked at her watch. It was seven thirty in the morning.

The text was from a private line at the Behavioral Analysis Unit. She dialed in and was routed to Thomas Gifford's office. Her boss had no doubt just learned of the arrest. With all that had gone on, she had forgotten to call him. *Shit. Got any more kerosene for the fire?*

"Mr. Gifford wants to see you in his office ASAP," the secretary said.

"Tell him I'm on my way, be there in about forty-five minutes."

She gave Jonathan a kiss on the forehead, knowing there was nothing she could do sitting by his side. "I love you," she said, then left.

VAIL ARRIVED at the commerce center and parked. She looked in the rearview mirror and tried to fix herself up, but she had to admit, she looked like hell. She still had Robby's car, no purse, no makeup, and she still had not been home to shower and change.

She took the elevator up to the second floor, punched in her ID code, and wandered down the hallway toward Gifford's office. It was three times the size of her own cubicle, with a huge picture window view of the surrounding Aquian foliage.

Vail knocked on the open door. Gifford looked up and motioned her in. A phone was stuck to his ear and he was nodding. "I know, but that's just the way I want it. I don't care if he thinks he's the fall guy. . . . You know what? Fine, then he is. Tell him whatever you want to tell him." He grunted, then hung up.

"If this isn't a good time—" Vail started.

"No, no. Sit down. Any time's a good time to meet with one of my agents who's been—how should I put it . . . *arrested*? Any time's a good time to sit and chat about how one of my agents beat the living crap out of her husband, landed in jail, and didn't even bother to call her superior to give him a heads-up. I've gotta get a fucking call from the Fairfax County PD. Some grunt lieutenant tells me he's got some bad news for me."

"Sir, I'm sorry. I'm sorry for the embarrassment to you, to the Bureau—"

"You're supposed to be working on a task force. Dead Eyes, remember him?"

"Sir, I was going to call you when I got out of jail. Things dragged on, and I didn't get out till almost two this morning. I was on my way to the task force op center to get my car and my purse, and to leave a message on your voice mail. We got texted en route by Paul Bledsoe. There's another vic."

Gifford sat back in his leather chair. "Another Dead Eyes vic?"

Vail nodded.

"Shit." His eyes roamed his desk for a moment before coming to rest again on Vail's face. "You look like crap."

"I know, sir. Haven't been home yet. While at the vic's house, I got word my son was in the hospital—" She felt the urge to cry again, but fought it back into her throat. Took a deep breath. "His father pushed him down the stairs. He's in a coma." She turned away, wiped at the tears beneath her eyes.

"I'm sorry. I didn't know."

She nodded. "I will beat these charges against me, sir."

He picked up a pen from his desk and stared at it. Vail knew what was coming. The fact he didn't make eye contact with her made it all the more inevitable.

"I hope you realize that I'm truly sorry about what I have to do. But I've got to place you on paid administrative leave, effective immediately. You can keep your creds and gun. But you need to stay away from work. I spoke with OPR a little while ago. They'll be here at eleven to interview you. Cooperate with them. Remember, they're on your side in this. Internal review is a formality. At the moment, this is obviously a personal matter. Once they've opened their file, they monitor the situation. They'll only act if the charges stick."

Vail was looking at the floor. "I understand, sir."

"Why don't you go wait in your office, get your desk straightened up. When OPR is ready for you, I'll let you know."

She stood from her chair and headed for the door. "Thanks," she said, without turning to face him. Then she walked out.

Straighten up her desk, that was what Gifford had told her to do. But her desk was neat. She looked around her office, wondering just how serious this OPR review would be. She was, after all, arrested for assaulting her ex-husband. How would that play out? She was innocent, but was it merely a matter of giving Gifford an excuse to let her go? Did he want her gone? He was sometimes hard to read. Vail challenged him, sure, but she was damn good at what she did. That counted for a lot, didn't it? She knew the answer to that was, *not necessarily*.

Vail needed to clear her mind, stop stressing over what might happen. She opened Outlook and downloaded her email, not knowing if they'd allow her to keep accessing her Academy mail while on leave. She paged through the unimportant messages, dashed off a quick reply to a prosecutor on another case that was going to trial, and was about to close down when she saw one that caught her attention. The subject read "It's in the"—and sent a shiver through her body.

She glanced down at the preview pane, where the text hit her like a brick across the forehead. She opened the message and read:

> The hiding place smells like some musty box I once opened when I was looking for his cigarettes. It's strong and kind of burns my nose. And it's small and dark, but it's mine. He doesn't know I have it, which means he can't find me here. And if he can't find me, he can't hurt me. I can think here, I can breathe here (well, except for the smell) without him yelling. I sit in the darkness, alone with myself, where no one can hurt me. Where he can't hurt me.
>
> But I watch him. I watch everything he does through little

holes in the walls. I watch him bring home the whores, I watch what he does to them before dragging them upstairs to his bedroom. Sometimes I even hear what they're saying, but most of the time I just see. I see what he does.

But I really don't have to see. I already know. I know because he does the same things to me.

Holy shit. He's communicating with me. Dead Eyes sent me a message. Had there ever been a serial offender who sent the cops an email? A letter, yes, but an email? Not that she'd ever seen. Emails are inherently easier to trace—

She looked at the sender's name: G. G. Condon. She knew that would be a dead end, that it was easy to obtain an email account with fake information. She tried forwarding the message to the lab, but nothing happened. She clicked File/Print, yet the page came out blank.

"What the hell?"

She pressed the PrtScn key to take a "picture" of the screen—everything that was displayed on her computer desktop—and pasted the image into a Word document.

Vail lifted the phone and dialed CART, the Computer Analysis Response Team, and informed the technician, Cynthia Arnot, of what she had. While she was on the line, the email vanished from her inbox.

"It's gone?" Cynthia asked.

"Gone," Vail said, furiously scrolling through her Outlook inbox. "Like it was never there. All my other messages are there, but this one just . . . disappeared."

"Check your Deleted Items folder. Maybe you accidentally deleted it."

"I didn't delete it, Cynthia." Nonetheless, Vail clicked to the folder. "Not there."

If she'd been able to retain the email, they could've gone into the originating server, tracked the routing information, and traced it using digital clues largely unknown or poorly understood by the average computer user. The offender may think he's smart; the Bureau's experts were often smarter. But without the message. . . .

"I did get a screen shot of it."

"Very good, Karen. Send it over, let us take a look at it."

"I'm not losing my mind. I didn't delete it. Could it be some kind of virus?"

"Not likely. But there is some interesting stuff out there that can make messages unprintable, make them self-destruct, allow them to spy on your movements and passwords—"

"This isn't just spyware, Cynthia. I'm working Dead Eyes. I've got reason to believe this message was from the offender. This could be huge."

"We'll do our best. Meantime, shut it down and unplug the PC. I'll send someone over to get it, we'll need to go through the hard drive. Just because a message is deleted doesn't mean we can't pull traces of it off the disk. But it'll take a while."

Vail glanced at the clock and realized OPR would be arriving soon. "Would it help to tell you we don't have a while?"

"Nope."

Vail leaned back in her chair and sighed. "Didn't think so."

"OKAY, LISTEN UP," Bledsoe said as they walked through the door to the op center. "I hope everyone made good use of the hour off, because we've got more work to do. More legwork and more brainwork. I know you're all tired. So am I." He ripped open a box of Danish and set them on the table in front of him. "Before we get started on the new vic, I want an update on all our loose ends. This thing is threatening to get away from us real fast, and I want to make sure that doesn't happen."

The detectives and Hancock took their seats. Vail's chair was conspicuously empty.

"What about Karen?" Sinclair asked.

Bledsoe stood in front of the whiteboard at the short end of the living room. "We go on without her. I'll brief her later." He pulled the cap off a marker and wrote "Dental patient lists."

"Sin, you're first up."

"Right. Vic worked for three dentists. I've gotten patient lists from each of them and have someone at my office crunching the names. No correlations so far, but they're not done yet. I had them start with the most recent two years."

Bledsoe made a couple of notes on the board. "Good. Hernandez, you were doing the employee lists."

"Still gathering info. But I've got a few things I'm working on. Hits on three registered sex offenders. I'm running their sheets and talking to co-workers. I've got appointments with the personnel managers to correlate work shifts, days off, days called in sick, and so on."

"Interviews with victim families, friends, neighbors . . . we're all doing that. Anybody still have open appointments?"

"I've got one parent to follow up with," Manette said. "Parents are divorced, father's out of town."

Bledsoe made some notes on the whiteboard, then recapped the marker. "Ex-cons with facial disfigurements? Who's got that?"

"Mine," Sinclair said. "Had thirty-five to choose from. I've still got a dozen to get through, but so far it's a dead end. A few are dead, six or seven are in the slammer again, and the rest had solid alibis."

"Anything on the massage therapy angle?"

"Nothing," Sinclair said.

"I got myself a free massage from a major hunk," Manette said.

"I'm happy for you," Bledsoe said. "I owe all of you the soil analysis on Sandra Franks's place. Lab said it was all native to the area, mainly from the vic's backyard." He tossed his marker on the desk in front of him. "Make sure Vail gets your VICAP forms so she can correlate all the victimologies. Maybe there's something in there."

Manette snorted. "That'd be real helpful, seeing as we got dick right now."

"Oh," Bledsoe said. "Something else on Franks. Autopsy and x-rays showed antemortem bruising on her right cheek as well as a broken nose. Appears the UNSUB punched her."

Robby leaned forward. "That's new. Maybe something tipped her off and she and the UNSUB got into it. She was into working out, maybe she fought back and landed a good shot. Any defensive wounds?"

Bledsoe consulted a pad in front of him. "No, but the left hand is missing. If she punched him with her left hand, there's no way to know." He turned the page. "And she is—*was* lefty."

"So maybe our offender has a big, ugly bruise on his face," Sinclair said.

Bledsoe pursed his lips. "Without any suspects, I'm not sure that helps us. Makeup can hide shit like that, and in a few days it'll be gone." He tossed down the pad. "Okay, keep your same assignments for today's vic, Denise Cranston. Anything else?" With everyone remaining silent, Bledsoe said, "Let's get back at it."

. . . twenty-eight

He stood beside the potter's wheel, watching the blonde place her hands on the wet clay. The last of the other students had just left, the door clicking shut behind him. The studio was quiet, except for the hum of fluorescent lights.

The blonde looked up at him with round, sapphire blue eyes. "Can you help me with this?"

He hesitated for a second. *If only you knew, bitch, if only you knew.* He put on his best smile, the one he used for his students, and said, "Sure."

She was new; this was only her second class, and he'd already covered the nuts and bolts of modeling, painting, and firing . . . the usual beginner's course. He liked to hit the basics as fast as he could, then let them get their hands on the clay, because there was simply no substitute for feeling the slippery stuff slither between your fingers. He always tried to gauge his students' artistic abilities by their reaction to the consistency of the clay. What they did with it once they got their hands on it told him a great deal about them.

This one liked the clay's cold wetness; he could tell that. But as to her ability . . . he didn't think there was much promise. But she wanted to stay after class to try the wheel, which surprised him.

It's amazing, really, how trusting some people are. Especially the bitches. They think they're immune to all the bad things that can happen. They go places alone at night, the supermarket or the ATM, thinking they're safe. Thinking that nothing will happen to them. Are they just dumb, or so convinced of their immortality that they can't allow themselves to believe they could be the next victim?

Oh, some are, indeed, afraid to go out. He'd seen the news reports, read the papers. Experts advising single women to go places in groups. To avoid high-risk areas—as if he preyed in high-risk areas!—and to be aware of their surroundings. Yeah, that sage advice would do them a lot of good when he's standing at their front door in a suit holding up his FBI badge and asking for assistance.

He stood behind the blonde bitch, the sweet peppermint scent of her shampoo whispering across his nostrils. He sniffed deeply, enjoying the smell. He looked at her left hand, at the diamond ring on her finger. Such an unimaginative setting. Plain vanilla. Probably what she would produce with the clay. Not *art*, but something only marginally better than a gaudy, imperfect piece later tossed in the garbage—or the equivalent, sold in a garage sale for fifty cents. His impressions about her creative ability were suddenly reinforced.

But more important than the horrid design of the ring was the fact that she was married. And blonde. With blue eyes. Clear eyes that reminded him of the sky.

He leaned into her, his arms extending out alongside hers, then took her hands in his. The wheel was spinning, the clay a lump of formless material. He asked her if she realized the power she held in her hands. "To transform this hunk of clay into a work of art, to be able to shape it, to be able to create, is something you mustn't take for granted."

She didn't get it, but she evidently found it funny and giggled, her shoulders jumping a bit. If he didn't know any better, he'd think she was flirting with him. But maybe it was just him and his skewed view of things. If only she knew.

If only she was brunet, if only she had evil eyes. He could take her right here and now. If only.

The office of P. Jackson Parker, attorney-at-law, was sparse, with worn industrial carpet, metal-framed reproductions of Monet and Manet on the walls, and molded white plastic lawn chairs in the waiting room. The seats were surprisingly comfortable, but strangely out of place in an indoor environment. The reception area consisted of a museum-piece PC that could not even run Windows, and a two-line phone that had seen better days . . . ten years ago.

His office was on the outskirts of Washington, in a not-so-desirable patch of real estate near Union Station. Vail had gone up against Parker on two occasions, with one being most notable. She was called to testify as an expert witness, having been the agent who profiled his client. He proceeded to ridicule the work of the profiling unit, calling it a blanket of suppositions and assumptions woven together in a veil of crystal ball psychology. The case against serial killer Bobby Joe Dunning was largely circumstantial, but Vail knew the accused was the offender. There was not an ounce of doubt as far as she was concerned. But you couldn't base a case solely on a profiler's analysis because there could be thousands of people who fit the profile, and thus no compelling reason for the jury to believe the accused man the police were parading before them was the guilty party.

Parker had done a magnificent job of injecting doubt into the jury's bloodstream . . . but the prosecution prevailed. Regardless of the positive outcome, Vail never forgot how masterful Parker had been in picking apart the district attorney's case. It was largely responsible for her ending up in the man's waiting room today.

P. Jackson Parker poked his head through the beat-up wood door and caught Vail's attention. "Agent Vail, come on back."

Vail nodded at the empty receptionist chair. "A one man show? I wouldn't have thought it."

"I sent my receptionist for coffee. Our coffee maker's on the fritz, and I can't work without my java. Opens the arteries, helps me think."

She followed him down a short hallway, passing a couple of rooms with equally beat up doors. They entered Parker's office, and he meandered around piles of overstuffed files and clipped groupings of papers. Vail's head turned, panning the surroundings, her trained eyes taking everything in.

She realized she was still standing, looking at the room's disarray, while Parker was seated, his long, delicate fingers pressed together in a triangle in front of his lips.

"Please, take a seat."

Vail sat. She was on the edge of the chair, her back rigid, her eyes still moving.

"You know, I took some courses in body language many years ago. The courses taught me how to read juries, to evaluate what they were thinking. And it proved to be as important as any courses I took in law school. Maybe more so. But it had an added side benefit, Agent Vail." Her eyes met his at the mention of her name. "It also taught me how to read my clients. And in criminal defense, it's nice to know when your client is lying and when he's telling the truth. We don't always get the straight scoop, if you know what I mean."

"I think I can gather the meaning."

"You're uncomfortable, apprehensive."

"The attorney profiling the profiler."

"Sometimes we wear many hats. I've been a counselor, a psychologist, a tax advisor, a conscience. I do what it takes."

Vail nodded.

"You've got something on your mind. Why don't you say it?"

"What's there to say?"

"That you don't like me."

Vail squirmed a bit, then moved her buttocks back into the chair to cover her apparent fidgeting. "I don't think that's a fair statement. I don't like criminal defense attorneys. You just happen to be one."

"I see. I guess that's a common malady amongst your kind."

Vail conceded that point with a nod. "You might say we perceive 'your kind' as the enemy." She forced a smile.

"We're not the enemy, Agent Vail. We're purveyors of justice. We try to make sure the laws of our land are enforced. Our constitution provides for protection of the accused, to make sure the 'innocent until proven guilty' get a fair trial."

"I don't have a problem with fair trials. I have a problem when your kind manipulates facts into false truths, manipulates our statements, our witnesses, into making it appear as something completely different from what it really is."

"I see. And you're telling me the police, the prosecutors never do that? Planted evidence, hidden documents that surface years later—"

"I can't sit here and tell you it doesn't happen. But it's rare. You people do it all the time."

Parker's eyebrows rose. "By 'you people,' do you mean people of color? African-Americans?"

Vail looked away in anger. When her eyes met Parker's again, they were on fire. "You know exactly what I meant. But there you go, illustrating my point. Twisting what I said into meaning something I had no intention of saying."

Parker burst out laughing.

Vail's anger only rose with his response. "What's so funny?"

"I baited you. But you know, showing is always better than telling. I just showed you how good I am at what I do. I knew I couldn't win our disagreement, so I changed the rules. Smooth as silk. Just like that"—he snapped his fingers—"you were on the defensive." He smiled, tilted his head.

Vail chewed the inside of her lip, unsure of what to make of this man. "I'm here not because I want to be here, but because I have to—"

"Let's get something straight, Agent Vail. None of the people who come through my doors are here because they want to be here. They don't want to stand accused of a crime facing a jury of their peers. They don't want to be getting bills from me. They're here because they've got a problem. As I assume you do."

"A problem. Yeah, you could call it that." She proceeded to give him the details of what had happened. He encouraged her to be completely forthcoming, even if there was something she felt was irrelevant.

"Tell me everything and let me make the call."

So she told him everything. She realized, as she sat back in the chair, that the bloodletting had been cathartic, and she felt better.

He rocked a bit in his chair, hands again posed in a triangle in front of his mouth. "Let me tell you a little about me. I would imagine you've checked me out, beyond what you already know, but I'll assume nothing. When I'm not defending murderers, I like to dip into the family courts. Domestic violence is an interest of mine. Don't ask why, I don't feel like discussing it. Suffice it to say that I'm well respected by the judges and the Commonwealth attorneys. You'll need that. Dare I say you've made a wise choice in coming here."

Vail nodded, but she suspected her body language said otherwise as her gaze bounced around the room again.

"Don't let the surroundings color your opinion of my skills. I live in Great Falls and my home is worth two million dollars. I drive a brand new Jag. But I keep my business overhead low because in criminal defense, fancy furniture and spacious conference rooms don't do anything for the clientele I represent. It doesn't ensure them of a *not guilty* verdict. And anything that doesn't work for my client I get rid of. My sole focus is getting you off."

She looked away again.

"I know that language is disagreeable to you, because you're frequently on the other side of the table. But understand something. When you walk into that courtroom, you're not Supervisory Special Agent Karen Vail, sworn FBI agent who devotes her life to catching bad guys and keeping society safe. You're a woman accused of brutally assaulting your ex-husband, breaking his ribs and putting him in the hospital. They're going to portray you as a tough, mean-spirited cop who's trained in the use of deadly force, who has a short fuse and a chip on her shoulder. It'll be my job to show the jury that's not what you're about. I'll be painting a different picture. Point is, you need me. As of this moment, I'm your friend. Your best buddy. You'll tell me everything and hold back nothing. Because when the dust settles, I won't just be your best friend, I'll be your only friend."

Vail didn't see any need to discuss the matter further. If he made his case in front of the judge as well as he had just made it to her, she was, truly, in good hands. She read through, and then signed, his fee agreement.

And it was suddenly evident how he was able to afford his two million dollar home and brand new Jaguar.

thirty

"I waited for OPR for forty minutes." Vail stood on the porch talking to Robby, smoking a Chesterfield she had bummed off Sinclair. "Enough time to sit in my office and think. Think about how screwed up everything is, what Gifford said. Then I got that email, and, well, that's all I could think about till OPR showed up."

Robby tilted his head. "What email?"

"Didn't Bledsoe show it to you guys? I forwarded a screen shot of it to him."

"Nah, he didn't mention it. Who was it from?"

"Dead Eyes."

"He sent you an email? You sure?"

"Pretty sure. I've got the lab working it, some sort of self-destructing message. It vanished right before my eyes. But I got a hard copy of it. Subject line read 'It's in the.' Who else could know of that? We haven't released that to the press, and if it was leaked we'd see it somewhere in some paper, not some obscure email outlining child abuse."

"Child abuse?"

Vail stuck the cigarette between her lips, reached into her coat pocket, and handed Robby a folded copy of the message. "I thought Bledsoe would show it to everyone, but I should've made sure he got it. I've been a little . . . preoccupied. My follow-up's been pretty shitty."

Robby read through it, studied it a bit, then pursed his lips and nodded. "Okay, so this guy's real fucked up."

"I'm hoping for a more substantial analysis from BSU."

He handed her back the email, which she folded into her pocket. "Any news on Jonathan?"

"Nothing. I wanted to go back there again, but I'm scared. I don't think I could handle seeing him. I just. . . ." She tossed the butt to the ground and crushed it against the pavement with her heel. Swiped at a tear. "There's just too much shit going on right now, Robby."

He reached out and pulled her close. She didn't resist. "I know."

"I feel like I should be there, by his side, holding his hand, twenty-four/seven. But with everything on my plate, I'm afraid it would all come crashing down. That I'd fall apart. I need to stay busy, take my mind off things."

"You can only do what you can do, Karen. My aunt used to say we have an emotional gas tank. When that tank fills up, it starts running out and spilling over. All it would take is a spark to make everything go up in flames. She said we should always try to keep the tank from getting full."

"Emotional gas tank, huh? I guess these days I should be wearing a warning sticker on my back: Danger: highly combustible." She sighed. "I've got to find a way of getting through this."

"One day at a time, one issue at a time." He tipped her chin back with a finger. "And I'll be there every step of the way to help you through it."

She smiled. "Thanks." She pulled her overcoat around her body to ward off a chill. "I hired an attorney today. Jackson Parker. Excuse me. P. Jackson Parker."

"I've heard of him. Good things, if you're a skel."

"That's what he told me."

"What's the 'P' stand for?"

"Pompous."

He laughed.

She sighed long and loud. "I need to get away, Robby, get re-energized." He looked at her and she immediately knew what he was thinking. "Yes, I'm running away. But I know myself, and I know when I've reached my stress point. Getting out of town for a day will help."

"Want some company?"

She sniffled. "Thanks, but I need to be alone with my thoughts for a while."

"Where you gonna go?"

"Old Westbury."

"As in Long Island?"

Vail looked out across the early afternoon sky. It was hazy and overcast, unsure if it should rain or shine. "It's my mom's place, where I grew up. I haven't seen her in . . . well, too long. Our last couple conversations she seemed distracted and I've been meaning to pay her a visit, but. . . ." She waved a hand. "It's about a five-hour drive. I can have a late dinner with her, stay the night, and get back here noonish."

Robby looked down at her, thought about it a long moment. "Sure you don't want some company? I could use a change of scenery myself. I'll give you your space, I promise."

"Really, I'll be fine."

"I know you will. But after all you've been through, that knock on the head, then being up all night, sure you want to make a five-hour drive alone?"

"Bledsoe will never let you go."

"Does Bledsoe know? About the suspension?"

She shook her head. "I better go get it over with."

BLEDSOE WENT THROUGH A STORM of emotions in a matter of minutes: from anger over Vail's suspension and having gotten caught by Deacon's lies to fury over what Deacon had done to Jonathan, to frustration over her request to leave town when they were in the middle of an active time-sensitive investigation. But when Vail gave Bledsoe her reasons, he reluctantly agreed.

Before leaving, she asked him if he'd seen the message she'd sent him, but he said he hadn't read his email in days. She handed him the folded copy of Dead Eyes's missive, then gave him a quick rundown of how it self-destructed. Bledsoe wanted his people working on it, too, but he knew there was nothing they could do at this point. He checked in with his department, and, sure enough, without the coded routing information, they had to wait for the results of the data recovery efforts the Bureau was conducting on the hard drive.

"What if he sends you another one while you're gone?"

"The lab is screening my unit's email before they release it to us. Anything comes through, we'll know about it. They've got instructions to notify you immediately."

He gently squeezed her shoulder. "See you when you get back."

Vail glanced at Robby, then walked out.

As the door closed, Bledsoe looked up from a file he'd started reading and noticed Robby was still standing in front of him. "You need something, Hernandez?"

"I was thinking I should go with her, make sure she's all right."

"Karen's a tough cookie. She doesn't need a bodyguard, believe me."

"Normally, I'd agree, but—"

"I'm already one guy short." He lifted the file back to his face. "I'd have to have my head examined if I let two of you go."

Robby cleared his throat but did not move. Bledsoe lowered the folder. "What?"

"She's been through a lot of stuff the past few days, assaulted, arrested, thrown in jail—"

"I know the story, Hernandez."

"And she didn't sleep much last night. You really want her driving five hours alone? We'd be back tomorrow around noon. Not a big deal."

"I'll decide what's a big deal and what's not. Of course I don't want Karen driving herself. Hell, I don't want her going because I need her." He dropped his eyes to the report. "But that's just the way it is."

"Well, then this is the way this is: I'm taking some personal time. You don't like it, take it up with my sergeant."

Bledsoe felt the blood rushing to his head as Robby turned and walked out. Tossed the file across the room, took a deep breath, then leaned on the table. "Beautiful."

———

Robby joined Vail outside by her car. "Well?"

"We're good," Robby said. "Let's go."

She hiked her brow. "Bledsoe is full of surprises."

"We'll be back tomorrow at noon. Not a big deal."

They took Robby's car and headed up I-95 before switching onto I-495 toward Baltimore. They drove in silence for the first couple hours, which was fine by Vail, since she needed the quiet, and Robby was determined to keep his promise of giving her space. Finally, she fell asleep with her head against the side window and slept until they neared the Queens Midtown Tunnel.

Vail sat up and rubbed her eyes, then looked around. "How long have I been out?" It was dark and the lights of nearby Manhattan twinkled in the early evening haze.

"Couple of hours. We're making good time."

"Sorry I abandoned you. The lull of the highway put me out."

"Figured you needed it."

She pulled down the visor and peered into the mirror. "I look awful."

"You never did get back to your place, did you?"

"I'm looking forward to a long shower at my mom's."

The traffic slowed a bit as they approached the tunnel. Getting through the city wasn't as bad as they had thought, and half an hour later they were driving down the street where Emma Vail lived. Vail thought of how long it'd been since she had last been here. Too long. Worst of all, her mother hadn't visited her, either, meaning they hadn't seen each other in over a year. *Shame on me.*

"There," she said, pointing to a house sunken below street level. "My best friend lived there. Andrea. We used to play together all the time. Drove our parents crazy."

Robby slowed the car. "Eight nineteen, you said?"

"Yeah, right here."

He pulled the car into the driveway and killed the lights. "Looks pretty dark," he said, craning his neck. "Did you give her an idea of what time we'd be here?"

Vail opened the door and took in a lungful of the fresh night air. "I never called."

Robby got out of the car and looked at her across the roof. "Your mom doesn't know we're coming?"

She strained to see the house in the dark. Partially obscured by the tree-canopied setting she associated with Old Westbury, the two-story Craftsman style house fit in perfectly amongst the tall pines and cedars. Vail walked up the path, stepping on each flagstone square as she went, just like she did when she was a kid. One step, one stone. "You can't put two feet on one square or it's bad luck," she told Robby. "At least, that's what I thought when I was a kid." *Funny how old habits stick with you.*

She stepped onto the last flagstone and found herself at the front door. The tarnished brass knocker was still there, along with the rusted black metal mailbox.

She knocked a couple times and waited. Brushed a few hairs into place and curled a wisp behind her right ear. Lifted the brass weight and struck the door again, waited, then consulted her watch.

"Should've called," Robby said.

The porch light suddenly popped on and the curtain to their right parted. The door opened a crack and an older woman with gray hair and a rumpled face appeared. "Yes?"

"Mom, it's me." Still no response. "Kari."

The door opened halfway and Emma squinted at her daughter. "Kari," she said. "Did you forget something?"

Vail looked at Robby, who merely shrugged. *I should've warned Robby about the Alzheimer's.* "No, Mom. I needed to get away and I thought you could use some company. Should've called, I'm sorry."

Emma's eyes flicked over to Robby.

"Oh, this is my friend, Robby Hernandez."

Robby bowed his head. "Glad to meet you, ma'am."

"Ma'am? Please, call me Emma. And come in out of the cold. I need to close the door, we're letting the heat out."

They walked through the barren entryway toward the living room.

Emma turned on a couple of lamps and sat down stiffly on the edge of a plush gold chair. The house was half a century old and looked it: worn cocoa-rust carpet, tan walls, and threadbare furniture.

Vail sat on the sofa beside Robby. Her mother looked thin, the kind of unhealthy thin that accompanied a debilitating disease, like cancer. Her face had more wrinkles and the skin on her neck hung as if it had finally given up the decades-long fight against gravity's pull.

"Do you work in my daughter's office? The FBI? She works for the FBI, you know."

Robby smiled. "I'm a detective, with the police department. I'm working with Karen on a case."

"Well, I've got a case for you right here. A real who-done-it. Someone keeps stealing things from me. First it was a book I was reading, then it was my glasses. I have a good mind to call the police. Stupid neighborhood kids."

Vail glanced around. Everything appeared to be in order, from what she could tell in the dim lighting. "Did you leave the door open? Do you think someone's been in the house?"

"I hear noises," Emma said, her hands fumbling in her lap, "but I've never seen anyone."

Vail looked at Robby. "We'll take a look around, make sure all the locks work, okay?"

"Well, enough about me. Tell me, how's Deacon?"

Vail swallowed hard. "We're getting divorced, Ma."

"Divorced? What happened?"

Vail's face was stone. The progression of her mother's Alzheimer's had been far more pronounced than she had thought. During their last couple conversations, Emma had been distant and harried. But clearly it was more serious.

"Ma," Vail said, "we've talked about the divorce. Don't you remember?"

Emma's face flickered for a moment, then she turned to Robby. "Oh, I've been a terrible hostess. I don't think we've met. I'm Emma Vail."

Robby forced a smile. "Robby Hernandez."

"Are you a friend of Kari's?"

"Yes, ma'am."

"Ma'am?" She waved a hand. "Oh, please. Call me Emma." She turned to Vail, whose eyes were tearing. "What's wrong, Kari?"

"Nothing, Mom. Nothing." She stood and took Robby's hand. "I'm going to show Robby around, okay?"

"Whatever you'd like, dear," Emma said.

Vail flipped on the large backyard spots and low-voltage path lights. "I knew this day was coming, I just hoped it'd be later rather than sooner. I figured she had a few years before it got this bad." She took a deep breath of the pine-scented air, then swung her head around and looked inside to see her mother still sitting on the couch, just as they had left her. "I need to get her some help, or move her out. I don't know what would be best."

Robby took her hand and led her through the wooded yard. While the house was small—cozy, Emma had once called it—the land was not: two full acres of mature pines. They walked for a moment in silence.

"I remember the brown needles crunching under my sneakers when I was a teenager. I used to come back here to clear my mind. Sometimes I'd find a bed of needles and take a nap. If they weren't so damp, I'd lie down right now and fall asleep. Dream of happier times." She bent down and scooped up a handful. "My mom taught me to appreciate the beauty of nature. She once told me you never knew when life would deal you an unplanned twist of fate. Enjoy things while you can, she said, because you just never knew." She sighed. "Little did I know she was talking about herself."

Robby took a deep breath. "It's beautiful here. A private forest."

"When Jonathan turned eight, I brought him here to visit. He went shopping with grandma and I spent an entire day out here, whittling away with my knife, making a walking stick. It was as close to a perfect day as I can remember. I wanted to seal the image away in my mind forever. But it wilted real fast once I got back to the office and started staring at grisly crime scene photos. Looking at things like that, the beauty of nature seems to fade pretty damn quickly. You find yourself knee deep in the blood and guts, and the crunch of pine needles beneath your feet is a million miles away."

They started walking again. "Didn't help that the day after I got back I caught a new case, one of the first I profiled on my own. Vic's body was dumped on a forest floor just like this one. Kind of killed the image for me. Haven't been able to look at pine trees the same way since." She opened her hand and let the needles fall to the ground.

Robby reached into his pocket and produced a Swiss Army knife, then bent down and chose a short, thick branch. Vail reluctantly took the knife and immediately began clearing the nubs from the stick.

"I didn't know you liked to carve."

"Since I was about ten. See these?" She lifted her left hand and showed him several thin, short, barely visible scars on her fingers. "Cut myself lots of times. My father even took me to the ER for stitches once. It was a nasty bleeder."

"I take it your father passed on."

"Long time ago. I was twelve. Came home from school and my mom told me he'd had a heart attack. Died in the ambulance." She stopped carving and stared at the dark landscape ahead of her. "I wonder how Jonathan is."

"Want to call the hospital?"

She shook her head. "I gave them my cell number. I told them, anything happens, I want to know." She tossed the stick to the ground and closed the knife, handed it to Robby. "Let's go in."

They got back to the house and found Emma seated in front of the television, watching the blank screen intently. Vail took her by the hand. "Come on, Ma. Let's go make dinner."

THE KITCHEN APPLIANCES were the same ones installed when the house had been built. With the exception of the countertop microwave, they were all from the aluminum and Bakelite era. An old pink Frigidaire hummed against the far wall.

Vail found a large pot in the cabinet, where her mom had always kept it. She placed it in the sink and turned on the faucet. "Do you still see Aunt Faye?"

"Yes, of course. She comes by and we have tea."

"When was the last time you saw her?"

"Oh, it's been a while, I guess. You know how it is with three kids. She's busy, busy, busy."

Vail figured she would call her aunt after dinner, see about making temporary arrangements to have Emma stay with her until she could get her mother situated in an assisted care facility. Faye was her father's sister, but the two women had remained close even after he had passed away.

The shifting in and out of lucidity was frustrating, and Vail felt an urgency to ask important questions while her mother was able to answer them. But under pressure, nothing came to mind.

Dinner was a conglomeration of spaghetti with Ragu sauce doctored with whatever Emma had in her pantry . . . which wasn't much: stewed tomatoes, canned mushrooms, and a dash of garlic salt. After eating, Vail took Robby on a tour of the house. "Things are pretty much unchanged, if you can believe that," she said. They walked into a small room on the second floor.

"Let me guess. Your room."

A large, horizontal glass-faced cabinet was mounted on the far side of the room, which sported sunflower-yellow walls with pink trim.

"Obviously," Robby said, surveying the dolls behind the glass, "you're a collector."

"I can tell you where I got each one." She walked over to the cabinet and let her eyes roam over them—they ranged from tall to petite, porcelain to plastic—with the world's ethnicities well represented. "Figured I'd give them to my daughter one day."

"Until your girl came out a boy."

A smile flitted across her lips. "Didn't think Jonathan would appreciate them."

Robby laughed. "I think you're right."

Vail slid the wall closet door aside and found a rolled poster on the top shelf. "It's still here," she said. She pulled off the rubber band and unfurled the yellow-aged paper across her bed. "You'll never believe who my teen heartthrob was."

Robby looked at the large smiling face staring back at him. "Kind of looks familiar."

"Shaun Cassidy. Every girl I knew fell for him." She noticed the reference was lost on him. "*The Hardy Boys.*"

"Oh, yeah."

She let go of the poster and it rolled back on itself. Robby pointed to the white dresser with gold trim. "Anything left in the drawers?"

"Doubt it." She pulled one open and peered inside. "Hmm. Must be stuff my mom put in here." She removed a box, which contained a photo album. They sat on the bed together and thumbed through the photos. "I don't remember ever seeing these."

"Who are these people?"

"Haven't the slightest. Relatives and friends, I guess." The black-and-white snapshots were held in place on dark paper with scalloped corner mounts. She turned a page and pointed to one of the photos. "Oh. That's Aunt Faye with my dad. I guess I'm the little one on his lap." Robby bent forward to get a close look. "You were cute. You were, what, a year old there?"

Vail nodded. "About." Turned the page. "Here's my mom again."

"She was beautiful," he said, studying the photo. "Who's that next to her?"

"I don't know. Kind of looks like Mom, though, doesn't it?" She carefully pulled the picture out of the corner mounts and turned it over. Written in scripted pen were the words, "Me and Nellie."

"Obviously," Robby said, "that's Nellie."

Vail nudged a shoulder into his. "Guess that's why you're the detective, Detective."

"Your room is just as you left it." Emma was standing in the doorway, a knit shawl draped around her shoulders.

"Except for this," Vail said, holding up the album. "Found it in my dresser drawer."

Emma smiled. "Haven't seen that in years. I'd forgotten where I put it."

"Who are these people?" She opened the album to the first page and handed the book to Emma.

"That's Uncle Charlie—my Uncle Charlie—and his father, Nate. Nate was from Ireland. Nate O'Toole. Half the people on his side had red hair. Probably where you got yours from." She pointed to another photo. "And that's Mary Ellen, she used to live next door to us in Brooklyn, before Gramps moved us all out here."

A teapot whistled in the distance. "Oh. Do either of you want some tea?"

Robby nodded. "Sure."

"I'll go tend to it, then." She handed the album back to Vail, then disappeared down the hall.

"She's very sweet," Robby said.

"She was a good mother." Vail studied the photo she still held in her hand. "When she loses her memory completely, she'll take a good part of our family history with her."

"I've got a buddy I work with, an investigator who's been with VPD for fifteen years. He's got this software to make your own family tree. Works on it every day. Traced his roots all the way back to the Native Americans who lived in Virginia. Pretty cool. Maybe you should do one. Before it's too late."

"I hardly know anything about my family. Would've been good to get all this info together before they started dying off." Vail suddenly became aware of the teapot's building whistle. She looked at Robby. "She should've poured the tea by now, don't you think?"

They headed downstairs and found Emma sitting in the living room on the edge of the easy chair, staring at the blank television.

"I'll get it," Robby said above the shrill noise.

"Ma," Vail said, kneeling beside Emma. "Ma, what are you doing? You went to pour us some tea."

Emma's face turned hard. "You're always yelling at me. Wh
can't you just leave me alone!"

"Ma, I'm not yelling at you." But she knew that trying to reaso
with a person afflicted with Alzheimer's was futile. "I'm sorry," Va
said. "I won't yell anymore."

"I can't find my glasses," Emma said. She grabbed the arms c
the chair. "I can't find my glasses." She looked at Vail, then reache
out to touch her face. "Nellie, is that you?" She smiled. "Can yo
help me find my glasses?"

Tears pooled in Vail's eyes as she looked at Emma. She set the ol
photo on the coffee table, knelt at Emma's feet, and took her han
in hers. She had been so wrapped up with her own affairs the pas
year she hardly had any quality contact with her mother. Now, as sh
looked at Emma's wrinkled face and felt her knobbed, arthritic hand
guilt crept into her thoughts. After so many years of dealing with vic
tims' families, the phrase "I should have" was ingrained in her brai
like acid on stone. Now she felt herself uttering the same words. *
should've spent more time with her. I should've made her move closer t
me. I should've brought Jonathan here more often.*

"Did you find Papa's watch? He's going to be angry with us if w
lost it," Emma said. She took her daughter's cheeks in her hands an
looked at Vail's face as if she hadn't seen it in years, studying ever
square inch.

Then, as if someone had waved a wand over her head, Emma'
eyes changed. Vail struggled to define what had happened. A nar
rowing, maybe, or perhaps it was something more. The sharpnes
had returned. "Ma?"

"What's wrong?" Emma asked. "Why are you kneeling in front c
me, Kari? Did I faint?"

"Ma, who's Nellie?"

Emma's gaze rose above Vail's shoulder. Vail thought she had los
her again, but Emma spoke: "Nellie?"

"You were just talking about her. And I found this." She reache
beside her and scooped up the old picture. "It says 'Me and Nellie
on the back. She looks a lot like you."

Robby appeared in the doorway. Vail's gaze met his and told him not to come any closer. He set the tea cups down and hovered in the background.

"Ma, is Nellie a relative of ours?"

Emma's eyes teared. "My sister."

Vail waited for her to elaborate, but she remained silent. Emma pulled her hand from Vail's and interlocked her fingers in her lap.

"Ma, you don't have a sister."

Emma's eyes met Vail's. "I don't feel like talking about it."

Vail leaned forward. She felt pressured to elicit the story before her mother drifted back into another Alzheimer-induced fog. "Please, tell me. About Nellie."

Emma must have sensed Robby's presence, because she turned suddenly, rose from her chair, and pointed an arthritic finger. "Who are you! What are you doing in my house?"

Robby looked at Vail, who wore a look of chagrin.

"Ma, calm down, that's my friend Robby. You met him before. He's a detective, a police officer." She helped Emma sit back in her seat.

Robby reached into his shirt pocket and handed Vail a pair of glasses. "They were in the freezer, in the ice cube tray."

Vail handed them to Emma. "Look, Ma, Robby found your glasses."

"I told you the police would find them." She looked up at Robby. "Thank you, Officer."

He smiled. "Just call me Robby."

Then Emma's eyes teared up and she held a hand to her mouth. "I'm sorry, I'm sorry. I'm so sorry."

Vail sat on the adjacent couch and rested a reassuring hand on her mother's shoulder. "It's okay, Ma. I understand." She knew this was not a good time to press the issue, but as had always been the case, she had a difficult time controlling her curiosity. "Ma," she said softly, "you were going to tell me about Nellie."

"Nellie? Your mother?"

Vail's brow furrowed. She picked up the photo she had dropped on the floor and showed Emma. "No. Nellie, your sister. I want to know about Nellie."

Emma's eyes again dropped to her lap. Her hands rolled into fist and she shook one at Vail. "How could you do that to me? You asked me to watch her for a couple of hours! What kind of a mother abandons her baby?"

Vail stared at Emma, trying to understand what she was talking about. She looked up at Robby, as if he could provide some answer. He sat down slowly beside Vail on the couch.

"She thinks I'm Nellie," she whispered to him.

"You can't just show up now and expect to take her back," Emma said, her voice firm. "Ward and I raised her, she's ours."

Vail's hand slid off Emma's shoulder. She was silent for a moment, staring at Emma's reddened face.

"Talk to her as if you're Nellie," Robby said softly by Vail's ear.

"Emma," Vail said, "I'm not here to take her from you. I'd never do that. I just came by to see you. I've missed you."

"I've missed you too, Nell." She reached out and gently touched Vail's face.

"Oh, my god," Vail whispered. She swallowed hard, then turned away from Emma and found Robby's eyes. "Emma is my *aunt*. Nellie is my *mother*." Vail shook her head, as if this was a bad dream and denying it would make it go away. "No. This is just an Alzheimer's fantasy. She's confused—"

"Karen . . . Emma is still your mother. She raised you, just like my aunt raised me."

"But my biological mother is Nellie." Vail turned to Emma, who was crying silently, a hand draped across her eyes. Vail pulled her close, letting Emma cry on her shoulder.

"I'm so sorry, Kari," she said.

"It's okay, Ma," Vail said, then felt her own tears trickle down her cheek. "It's okay."

He was in a rhythm, words tumbling from his mind like rocks in a landslide. He couldn't type as fast as he was thinking, which made it frustrating. But he continued, nevertheless, figuring he'd go back and fix the typos when he was done, before he'd send these sections off for "publication."

My needs are outgrwing my home. I can do jsut so much with a space barely larger than a tiny closet. And as I've gotten older and taller, the space has gotten even smller. I even took in a pet. A mouse I call Charlie. He doesn't take up much space, other than a little cage. I take him out while I'm in there, let him roam around. He's my only friend.

But then I started thinking that I really need more room. I knocked on one of the walls, and it sounded hollow. So I bought a saw with money I made at the slaughterhose down the road. It's my job to feed the cattle and clean up after them as they get ready to be sliced and diced. It's not a great job, but it's money under the table, and if you have money you can do things.

Then I borrowed a book from the library. I didn't really borrow it, I more like stole it. But tht's okay, because it has exactly what I need. I do my sawing in the afternoon, right after I get home from school—or on days when I stay home and skip. I don't have any friends at school, so it's not like I'm missing anyhting. To me, school is a lot like being with the prick. It's all about control. Teeachers tell you where you can and can't go, what you can and can't do. They don't hit you like a father does, but it's not a whole lot different. One day I'm going to stab the pretty little whore teacher right in the stomach and watch her twist in pain.

She yelled at me the other day, and I yelled back. Almost got suspended. As if I care.

She should know I'm different from most twelve year olds. The
prick shouldv'e told her that.

I like the way my place is turning out. I ran some wire in and
now have a bare bulb light. Charlie likes it better too. I still have
to put up a littel plywood, but I can finish that tomorrow if I can
find a way of getting the plywood home. I can get my hands on a
shopping cart and load it in, then push it home. It's a few miles,
but if you want somehting bad enough, you find a way.

I also need some things to decorate the space, but that'll
come. I have a Playboy centerfold I plan to hang. I can hang it
with pushpins, right through her eyes. Yeah, that'll be good.
Through the eyes. Like most whores, she's got evil eyes—

It had never come out so fast. What does that mean? It probably
means something, because expanding his hideaway marked the beginning of his escape, another step on the road to freedom. Maybe
he should've celebrated at the time, because it turned out to be so
significant. Damn, he wished he could write like that all the time.
Maybe this was one he'd keep to himself. At least for now. Too much
information to give Super Agent Vail and her cohort, Paul Bledsoe.
But what a name for a detective! How perfect that he'd be assigned
to this case. "Gee, I'm really sorry she died, Detective, but she just
bled so! What can you do?"

He took one more look at the passage he wrote and realized he'd
have to go back and fix the spelling errors. But not now—he was too
riled up. He opened the freezer door and the cold air hit his bare feet
like a pail of water. He shivered. The fog crawled around his ankles.

He reached into the freezer and removed two Tupperware containers, the special ones he'd bought just for this purpose.

He pulled open the lid on the first one and removed the Ziploc
freezer bag. Inside, rolled in gauze, were his prizes. Slight ice crystals
had formed and the cotton stuck a little as he peeled it away.

He set the hands on the table in front of him. He was amassing quite a collection. But was it too much? Was this getting out of hand? Ha! Out of hand, that was a good one. He looked over each of them, marveling at his work. He'd had to cauterize the veins and arteries to prevent the blood from draining out completely. Then the hand would shrivel and wouldn't be the same. They needed to look as close to the way they looked when he'd harvested them.

But he couldn't move the fingers. They were curled, frozen in place, except for the index fingers, which he'd used for painting his masterpieces on the bitches' walls. It was the same finger his father used to point at him when he was young. The prick would curl it and wiggle it forward and back, his sign to come to him.

But the fingers were his now. He had control over them.

Each hand looked similar to the other: blood thick on the index finger's tip, dried and frozen to the print's ridges. But even though they looked alike, he knew which bitch-whore contributed which hand, just like a mother can tell her children's baby pictures apart.

He stuck one of the hands in the microwave, just to see if he could soften up the fingers. He chose number four, since hers were the thinnest and would probably nuke the fastest. He entered fifteen seconds, then hit start. The little tray turned slowly as it cooked. Kind of reminded him of his potter's wheel. Now that would be something.

Ideas were flying through his mind. The microwave beeped and the rotating tray came to a stop. He opened the door and heard a slight sizzle, but the skin appeared to be intact. He took it out and set it on the table. It was still frozen, but the sizzling bothered him. He didn't want to risk thawing it too fast and burning the delicate hair or skin. Perhaps a slow defrost in the refrigerator would work better. Then maybe a formaldehyde solution, brushed onto the skin and injected into the muscle. He didn't want to soak it, because that might make it tough and leathery.

He unwrapped the other hands and sat down at the table. He'd missed the third one, and he could kick himself for that. But he learned something. That was the most important thing, right? To learn from your mistakes?

Another lesson he needed to learn was to be grateful for what he had and not to lament over what he didn't have. At least he had these hands. They helped him remember each bitch, each killing, in detail. He felt his pulse quicken, and he suddenly got hot. He had to unbutton his collar. His breath had gotten shallow, just like it did whenever he sliced the bitches open.

But something was missing. *The eyes.* He needed some more eyes.

He grabbed the TV remote, and started the recording of Eleanor Linwood. "You will rot in hell, your soul hung out to dry in front of everyone, for society to see who and what you are: a monster. . . . "

Yes, he'd found the eyes he wanted next.

He looked back at the hands, undid his pants, and reached inside.

Vail was in bed, wearing a nightgown borrowed from her mother. She had taken her long overdue shower, then called Aunt Faye, who agreed to come by in the morning to help pack Emma for a temporary stay until Vail found a care facility in Virginia.

Robby had stayed awake with Vail until one in the morning, talking with her about the revelation that her mother was really her aunt, and the fact that her biological mother was nowhere to be found. Finally, she told Robby to get some sleep, and he settled himself onto the downstairs couch.

Now, as the clock hit 2 A.M., Vail was glad she was having a hard time falling asleep—no chance of lapsing into one of her nightmares, which might wake Robby. She'd then have to tell him about the dreams, and that was something she wasn't prepared to do just yet. She needed to get her own mind around them before she tried to explain them to others.

She turned onto her side and faced her closet door, where the old Shaun Cassidy poster once hung. She remembered sitting in her room listening to his records on a beat-up, secondhand Panasonic phonograph, wondering if Corey Andrews, a boy in her class, would notice her. It seemed so terribly important at the time. Totally focused on him, smiling his way, brushing up against his arm, hoping he would talk to her.

When he didn't, and the school year ended, Emma had comforted her and told her that she was beautiful and smart, and that eventually boys would be lining up to ask her out. It happened, of course, the next year in seventh grade, but that summer was miserable. Miserable because a boy hadn't asked her out.

She flashed on her memory of sitting in the six-by-eight jail cell, waiting her turn for the portable phone to be wheeled to her. Her thoughts turned to Jonathan, again, as they had done every other minute since she had visited him at the hospital. Her BlackBerry remained silent, which meant there was nothing significant to report.

Nothing significant to report.

She certainly had something significant to report. Things that really meant something, not a preteen infatuation that failed to develop. But that was the way life went. Problems seemed to weigh on you until you realized there were far worse issues, far worse situations, that would make your current concerns instantly seem petty. Her son was lying in a coma, her mother, who's really her aunt, was losing her mind, and she was on suspension because she had beaten up her ex-husband, who had assaulted her—and held her at gunpoint. And there were young women being murdered because she couldn't help catch the killer. Those were real problems. Too much for one person to handle.

She rolled out of bed and walked downstairs to Robby, who was sound asleep on the couch. She nudged him over and curled up against his body. She was close to falling off the edge, which she found hilariously ironic. How symbolic of her life at the moment.

She reached up and pulled his arm across her, feeling his warmth, the firmness of his body, and felt better. His fingers closed around her hand. He stirred, then lifted his head. "Karen?"

"I couldn't sleep. I needed some company."

"Okay." The next words he mumbled were unintelligible as he drifted back asleep.

She lay there awake, thinking and lamenting. And worrying.

The ride back to Virginia brought reflection. Robby again gave Vail her space, and after thirty minutes of highway driving, she lapsed into another nap. Not having slept much the past two days, the mounting fatigue and stress were wreaking havoc on her body.

As the car lurched out of the toll booth on I-95 near the Maryland border, Vail's head popped up. Her hands flailed in front of her, as she fought to orient herself.

"Welcome back to Earth," Robby said.

She squinted against the bright sunlight. "Where are we?"

"About to cross into Maryland."

"I think I just figured out how to link victim three to Dead Eyes. Where's your file?"

"You figured that out while you were sleeping?"

"My mind's pretty much 'on' twenty-four/seven these days. The file?"

He glanced over his shoulder. "Backseat."

Vail grabbed his leather shoulder bag, reached inside, and pulled out the thick Dead Eyes folder. She paged to victim number three, Angelina Sarducci, and found the crime scene manifest. Her finger stabbed at one of the entries. "A package," she said, curling a lock of hair behind her right ear.

She dug out her phone and dialed UPS. She entered the tracking number listed on the crime scene manifest, then waited while the automated system processed her request. She pressed "end" and handed the phone back to Robby.

"It was delivered at 6:30 P.M." She turned some more pages.

"So what?"

Her finger traced the lines of another document. "ME estimated time of death to be between 6 and 7 P.M." She looked over at Robby whose eyes were still on the road.

"I don't get it. What's the big deal?"

"Here's the scenario: vic lets offender in, he kills her, then starts to do his thing with the body. But at six-thirty, the UPS guy comes to the front door and rings the bell. Offender freaks, goes out the back door. Leaves vic as is. He never had a chance to engage in his postmortem behavior, like severing the left hand and stabbing the eyes."

"Okay, I see where you're headed." He chewed on this for a moment, then shrugged. "Works for me."

Vail nodded slowly. "Me, too."

AT 12:15 P.M., Robby pulled behind Vail's Dodge at the task force op center.

"You coming in?" he asked.

"Going right to the hospital, check in on Jonathan. Then I'll shoot over to the office, run this victim three theory by my unit. Tell Bledsoe I'll talk to him later." She placed a hand on his arm, squeezed. "Thanks."

As she got in her car, the memory of Officer Greenwich standing beside her door moved through her mind. Though it was barely two days ago, it seemed like another lifetime. She arrived at Fairfax Hospital at one o'clock, with no memory of having driven there.

She walked into Jonathan's room, where Dr. Altman and a nurse were hunched over a machine. They turned when she entered. "Ms. Vail," Altman said.

"How's Jonathan?"

"Well, he's showing incremental improvement. Some slight opening of the eyes. It's nothing dramatic, which is why I didn't have them call you. But it's definitely encouraging."

I told them to notify me of any changes. She couldn't fault them however. To her, that Jonathan had made progress was significant. But medically, it was merely "incremental improvement." Vail stepped up to her son and took his hand. "Is that all you can tell me?"

"Unfortunately, that's all I can say now. We just have to wait—"

"Wait and see. Yeah, I know." She sighed. "Sorry, Doctor. It's been a rough week." Or two.

"I understand. We'll keep you posted of any substantial changes."

"Has—I'm just curious . . . has my—has Jonathan's father been by to see him? Deacon Tucker."

Altman deferred to the nurse, who answered. "You're the only visitor he's had."

The doctor tilted his head, considering her comment. "Seems like that's important to you. Do you want to know if he comes by?"

"If my suspicions are right, he pushed Jonathan down the stairs. But I've got no proof, so I can't get a restraining order. So, yeah, I'd like to know if he shows up. The minute he checks in at the nurse's station."

Altman leaned his head back. "Okay. I'll make sure the entire nursing staff knows."

Vail thanked Altman and he left with the nurse. She pulled up a chair and stroked her son's cheek, ran her fingers through his hair, and talked to him. She told him she loved him, and that she was planning a big camping trip to Yellowstone, for when he got out of the hospital.

Vail felt foolish talking to someone who was unconscious and unable to respond. But she did it anyway, because according to Altman there was a possibility her son could hear her voice. And since no one knew how active a comatose mind was, there was also a chance Jonathan might be feeling scared and alone. Both were emotions with which she herself had suddenly become familiar. She was fortunate her friendship with Robby was strong, and that he'd made it clear he would be there to help her through things.

Jonathan, however, had only her.

Vail arrived at the BAU at five o'clock. She scanned her ID card, then moved through the heavy maple doors and down the narrow hallways toward Thomas Gifford's office. She could feel her colleagues' gazes following her, but she kept her eyes focused ahead and didn't acknowledge anyone. She was there for a reason and didn't feel like chatting with any of them about her suspension, which would be the likely topic of conversation.

She stood in front of the secretary's desk and waited for Lenka to hang up the phone. "Can you ask the boss if he's got a moment for me?"

"Sure thing." Lenka punched a button, explained into her headset that Vail was in the anteroom, and hung up. "Go on in."

Vail thanked her, then entered Gifford's office. The chief honcho was behind his desk, Frank Del Monaco reclining in the guest chair to Vail's right; Del Monaco's legs were spread apart, his pudgy fingers splayed and resting comfortably on his thighs. The two men were laughing, as if they'd shared a joke.

"Agent Vail," Gifford said, forcing the smile from his lips. "I thought you were supposed to remain at home pending the investigation."

"I have something to discuss with you, sir. Just came up." She glanced over at Del Monaco, who was biting his lip . . . as if he was still thinking about the joke. Unless the joke was about her.

Gifford bent his head down and ruffled some papers, no doubt to keep himself from looking at Del Monaco and losing his composure. "Agent Del Monaco," he said, "a moment please."

"Yes, sir." Del Monaco stood and turned to walk past Vail, a grin widening his face.

The door slipped shut behind her, and Vail stepped forward. "I was thinking—"

"How's your son?"

She hesitated a second, changing gears in her brain from business to personal. "Not much change. Some slight improvement."

"Good. That's good. Slight improvement is better than no improvement."

She twisted her lips, confounded by his awkward attempt to show concern. "Sir, I had a thought about victim number three. The one everyone doubts was done by Dead Eyes—"

He held up a hand. "If I'm not mistaken, you're on suspension."

"Yes, sir," she said. She wanted to tell him that even though she draws her paycheck from the government, she really works for the victims—and they haven't taken her off the job. Instead, Vail chose the less confrontational thought that flittered into her brain. "But being on suspension doesn't mean my mind turns off. I'm still working the case in my head."

"Just make sure it stays in your head. I don't want any media hounds ramming mikes up my ass asking about your involvement. Bureau's in for enough embarrassment once they find out you beat up your husband."

"Ex-husband. And I'm certainly not going to talk to any reporters."

"They have ways of finding these things out, you know that. That's if your ex doesn't make the call himself."

Vail sighed. The last thing she needed was the newsies invading her privacy. "Sir, about vic three. I can explain why the scene's different, why the Dead Eyes behaviors are absent."

Gifford rubbed at his eyes, then swiveled his chair to face the large window and his second-story view. "We've been through this so many times—"

"I didn't have proof before. Now I do."

"Fine. Tell it to Del Monaco, he'll present it to the unit."

"Why Del Monaco?"

"He's been assigned the file until further notice."

Vail looked away. It was like a slap to the face, but in the instant it took her to process the comment, she realized it was a likely development. Someone had to take it over. "I'd like to be the one to present it. It's my theory, it's already . . . a volatile topic. I think I should be there to stand behind it, to give it the attention it deserves."

Gifford leaned back in his chair a bit and rocked, as if mulling over her request. "I really think it's in your best interest to distance yourself from the Dead Eyes case—"

"You mean from the Bureau." She felt her blood pressure going up, the line of mercury rising in the narrow glass tube.

He spun his chair around to face her. "I mean from both. Look," he said, lowering his voice, "you've got enough trouble without Linwood and the police chief on your back, too."

"Linwood and the police chief?"

"There's only so much I can do to protect you."

"With all due respect, I don't need your protection."

"Yes, you do." He looked away. "I've already gotten calls. Pressure from all levels. I'm standing behind you, Karen, because I think you're a damn good profiler. One of the best I've got. Now I'm asking you, don't blow your career over this. Focus your energies on beating this rap. Then we'll worry about Dead Eyes. If he's still at large, you'll get the case back."

"I guess I should thank you, for helping out. I appreciate it." She sat down in the chair. "But please let me address the unit. Just this once."

Gifford held her gaze for a long moment, then buzzed an extension. "Frank, can you come in here for a minute?" He hit the button again. "Run your theory by the two of us. If it passes our smell test, you can talk to everyone else."

Vail nodded and waited the thirty seconds it took Del Monaco to return to the ASAC's office. He walked in carrying a file folder and sat down in the chair beside Vail.

Gifford nodded at Vail. "Talk."

"I have some proof to back my theory with victim three—"

Del Monaco rolled his eyes. "Not this again—"

"Listen to what she has to say, Frank. Then we'll assess."

Del Monaco crossed his legs, then reluctantly tilted his head toward Vail. His body language said "Don't bother me with this shit." But verbally, he was a bit more polite. "Go ahead, I'm listening."

Vail resented having to justify herself to Del Monaco before being permitted to go in front of the unit. But since these were the ground rules Gifford set forth, she had no choice but to take her best shot. "There's a crime scene unit manifest for a UPS package discovered at Angelina Sarducci's front door. I called UPS and tracked it. It was delivered at 6:30 P.M. ME said time of death was between 6 and 7 P.M."

"So you think the delivery guy rang the vic's doorbell and scared off the offender," Gifford said.

"Which is why he didn't engage in most of the postmortem behaviors we've seen with the other vics."

"But this is nothing new," Del Monaco said. "A year ago you said the same thing, that someone had interrupted him."

"Yeah, but now I've got proof." Vail sat back and waited for a response. Both men were staring ahead, musing on her remarks.

After a moment of reflection, Del Monaco spoke. "Karen, I know this linkage thing is important to you. And in the end you may be right. But here's the thing: our job is to look at the behaviors left by an offender at a crime scene and make inferences based on what we see. What you're doing is looking at an *absence* of behaviors and trying to create a relationship. If we later find out this is a Dead Eyes case, we can then say your UPS package theory was right on the money."

"It's possible you're right," Gifford added, "but we can't deal in possibilities or we'd be all over the damn map."

Vail was probing the inside of her teeth with her tongue, doing her best to keep her mouth shut. Now was not the time for a confrontation. Besides, she didn't really know what she would say. They had a point.

Del Monaco opened the file he was holding. "How about we take theory, opinion, and emotion out of the equation. Look at the numbers. For all the Dead Eyes vics, both the Safarik HIS scale and the ISS show a point nine-five correlation. Victim three doesn't even make the cut—"

"Of course the severity of injury to vic three is less. You can't use those numbers—"

"Hold it a second," Gifford said. "What numbers are these?"

Del Monaco seemed annoyed his boss had interrupted. "The Safarik Homicide Injury Scale measures the degree of injury suffered by the victim. It's a new variable for analyzing offender behavior. ISS stands for Injury Severity Score—"

"ISS is used by CDC for categorizing triage results from automobile accidents," Vail said.

Del Monaco nodded animatedly. "And I've seen it used for homicide victims, too."

Vail looked away.

"Bottom line," Gifford said, "is no matter how you look at it, you can't say it's a Dead Eyes vic because behavior is *absent*. Your theory accounts for the lack of additional behavioral evidence, but it doesn't necessarily point to Dead Eyes."

Vail kept her head down. She had anticipated resistance, but cursed herself for not thinking things through more thoroughly. Del Monaco and Gifford were right: though her theory might be correct, they can't abandon their conventions because of something that's not there. She sighed frustration.

"I did get something you'll find interesting, though," Del Monaco said, handing her a printout from the file. "VICAP results. They were handed to me on the way over here. Haven't even looked at them yet."

Vail took the report and scanned it. "I knew the number of hits would be small, but this is amazing." She took another few seconds to look over the data, flipped a couple of pages, then looked at Del Monaco. "I did a search of murders, attempted murders, and unidentified human remains, to see how many offenders had written something in blood at the scene. Of the twenty-three thousand VICAP cases, we got a hit on only twenty-one cases."

Del Monaco sat up straight. "Jesus. Twenty-one out of twenty-three *thousand*. That's small."

Vail thumbed back and forth. "Smaller than that, actually." She spent a moment with the data, then continued: "If we eliminate two cases where blood was smeared, and only include the cases that contained writing, we're down to nineteen cases. Those cases involved twenty-six victims. If we extrapolate out the male vics, which were gay, we're left with nine female victims."

"Out of twenty-three thousand cases."

She flipped a page. "Looking at it from the perspective of the blood murals," Vail continued, "if we eliminate the crime scenes that contained offender writing, we're looking at only two cases. *Two*."

They were silent for a moment. "Okay," Gifford finally said, "what does this mean?"

Del Monaco said, "On the surface, that it's extremely rare to find blood-based writing or painting at a scene."

"Yeah, but what does it tell us about the offender?"

Vail considered this before speaking. "Well, only one of the VICAP cases is still unsolved, and that's in Vegas. Way out of this guy's geographic range. Besides, other than the writing, the ritual behavior is very different." She handed him back the report. "Not only does this tell us that none of these other cases are related to Dead Eyes, I think we can reasonably assume that Marci Evers is, in fact, Dead Eyes's first vic." Establishing the first victim of a serial killer often provided important clues because the offender was not as sophisticated when he started killing, and thus was more likely to have made mistakes.

"You'll be getting a call from Kim Rossmo," Vail said. "I sent him the case, asked him to work up a geographic profile for us."

Del Monaco nodded. "I'll look for it."

Vail stood and glanced at Gifford. "Thanks for hearing me out."

"Use the time off wisely, Karen. Clear your head of Dead Eyes, even if it's only for a few days. Get your house in order, and then get your ass back in here. We sure could use you."

Vail forced a half-smile, then walked out. She wanted to think Gifford was being genuine, but she could never be sure with him. She took one last peek at her empty office, then headed to the elevator.

A light drizzle fell as Vail showed her credentials then drove through the checkpoint leading to the FBI Academy. Gifford's idea of getting Dead Eyes out of her thoughts for a while had merits. Besides, it would allow her some time to focus on the other mystery in her life, the identity of her biological mother.

On the way out of the commerce center, she had given the front desk receptionist the photo of Emma and Nellie, and asked her to place it in intra-agency mail for immediate shipping to a buddy of Vail's, Tim Meadows, at the FBI lab.

Once in the car, she had called Meadows to explain the package he would be receiving. "I need a huge favor, Tim. I want a computerized aging of the woman on the right. It's personal, not for a case."

"That's bigger than a huge favor. We're not supposed to—"

"I know, Tim. I wouldn't ask if it wasn't important. The woman is my mother. I need to find her."

There was a few seconds of silence. Vail figured Meadows was mulling over her request. "Okay," he finally said. "I'll do it, but it'll have to wait till eight o'clock, when I clock out. At least if I get caught I won't be doing it on taxpayer time."

She thanked him, then left a voice mail message for Bledsoe, relaying and explaining the VICAP findings so he could share them with the task force. She told him she would call him soon.

Vail chose a spot in the main parking lot and made her way toward the administration building. The Academy was laid out like a campus, with multistory earth-toned structures connected by nearly identical windowed corridors, or tubes. If you weren't careful, you could find yourself wandering down one of the hallways without the slightest hint of where you were. Directory maps, mounted on the

walls and lettered in white against a milk chocolate background, provided three-dimensional renditions of the campus. Labeled plaques
above each map used oversized arrows to point you in the proper direction. The directories were especially helpful to senior law enforcement supervisors who attended the eleven-week National Academy
certification program to improve their management, administrative,
and investigative abilities. Without the maps, or a personal guide to
take them through the labyrinthine hallways, the attendees might
never find their way to class.

Vail walked into the administration building, signed in at the receptionist desk, and passed the x-ray machine en route to the glass
doors. With the darkness outside and the windowed corridors well
lit, she felt like a rodent on display in a maze.

She walked into the library's rotunda and looked up at the second
and third stories, marveling at the beauty of the large room. The ar-
chitects who created the Academy were not typical government designers. This complex was functional, but like a high-end home it
had a majestic flair, a feeling of grandeur and self-importance.

She sat down at one of the computers and logged onto the system. Huddling over the keyboard, she organized the information in
her mind. Emma's maiden name was Irwin, and she had been born
in Brooklyn. While Vail didn't know anything about Nellie Irwin,
she made the initial assumption she had also been born in New York.
If her searches came up empty, she could then widen the parameters.

She curled some hair behind her right ear, then attacked the keyboard. Like a fisherman, she would first troll the waters where information would be most likely to yield results: birth and death records,
then real estate holdings, criminal databases, and so on until she got
a tug at her line . . . something that would make her stop the boat
and weigh anchor.

The next three hours passed without thought of food. People
came and went, the overcast darkness had dissipated into a rural star-
lit sky, and her stomach finally let her know it was beyond late. She
made her way into the closed dining hall, picked out a ready-made
turkey sandwich, and devoured it in a matter of minutes. She had

been checking her cell throughout the evening, hoping it would bring news of Jonathan's improvement.

But like a criminal facing a murder charge, the BlackBerry remained silent.

Vail returned to the library and reviewed her notes. She had located Nellie Irwin's place and date of birth: Rutland Road in Brooklyn, February 16, 1947. She did not have a criminal record, but had worked two jobs, from 1964 through 1967. She worked one week into 1968.

Vail had been searching by social security number, so even if she had gotten married, she still would have been able to trace her. But there was nothing . . . not even a tax return had been filed. She widened her search to the entire United States, then waited as the computer sifted through records.

As she reached for her cell phone to dial in to the hospital, the vibration of a text message startled her. *Jonathan—*

She pulled the device from her belt and looked at the display. Not the hospital. A number in DC. Headquarters. Tim Meadows.

AT 9:45 P.M., the drive from Quantico to the Hoover Building took forty-five minutes. She was checked against a clipboarded list of expected guests and given clearance by the FBI Police sentry standing at the mouth to the underground garage. She parked and continued up the elevator to the lab, where all was quiet except for the plucking of Andreas Vollenweider's New Age electracoustic harp. She followed the music to a back room lit with subdued fluorescents, where Tim Meadows sat at a twenty-four-inch flat panel screen, moving his mouse across an image.

"Don't look," he shouted at Vail as she neared.

"What, this is a surprise?"

"I would think so," he said.

She glanced around the room. She had only been in the back room once, about three years ago. They'd added some equipment since then, but it was nevertheless the same: a techie's dream. Floor to ceiling electronics were mounted in steel racks that resembled bookshelves. Wires and cables snaked up and down, side to side, feeding one device and sucking from another. Reel-to-reel tape decks stood beside TV screens, VCRs, DVD players and burners; stacks of VHS tapes and jewel cases, labeled with case numbers and dates, littered the Formica desk that sat like an audience inside a three-sided stage, facing the digital and analog devices . . . the performers who put on the show.

Vail remained ten feet behind Meadows, who had angled his body to block the screen. Her eye caught an LED clock that hung on the wall above Meadows's head: it was 10:40 P.M. but she felt wide awake, as if she had just gotten out of the shower.

"I really appreciate you doing this, Tim. I owe you."

"Yes, you do. How 'bout dinner at McCormick & Schmick's?"

"Whoa, that'll place a strain on the wallet. This photo that good?"

"Yes, ma'am." He struck a couple keys, then said, "Okay, come on over." Onscreen was the original photo Vail had sent to Meadows. Seeing it again—seeing Emma—sent a pang of emotion coursing through her gut. In that split second, she felt sympathy, anger, frustration, love. And distance.

"Okee dokie. That's the original. Now, you didn't give me any parameters to work from, that being what year the photo was taken, so I had to do a little extra work."

"Sorry about that."

"Not a problem. Consider it the appetizer. How about clams on the half-shell?"

"How about I've got a kid to clothe and feed?"

Meadows winked at her. "But they're soooo good."

"How would you know?"

"Read a review." He indicated the screen, zoomed in on the photo. "I determined, through a little chemical analysis of the paper and the approximate age of the automobile fender in the background, that this was taken around 1959 or '60."

Vail looked up at the ceiling and did the math. "That's probably about right."

"Thought so." A self-satisfied smile thinned his lips. "So, working on that assumption, I first enlarged your mother's face to this," he said, then clicked the mouse. "Then I began aging it. Here's about age twenty." The computer morphed the facial features and a mature woman stared back at her. "Then, if I keep going, we can see her age through the years." He struck another series of keys and the image subtly shifted, changed, evolved.

"What a horrible thing to see. Bad enough watching the aging process in the mirror. At least it happens gradually. This thing makes it happen in a matter of seconds."

He looked at her. "Happens to all of us. Wrinkle here, sagging there, some age spots thrown in for flavor."

She frowned. "See this one?" Her finger found the exact spot on her cheek without having to look in a mirror. "This isn't flavor, Tim. It's aggravation."

The computer beeped and they turned to look at the screen. "Ah, very good. There she is. That's your mother, aged to about sixty."

Vail stared at the screen. She immediately recognized the face. "Holy shit. . . ." She pried her eyes away and rested them on Meadows, who was smiling at her.

She swallowed hard. Her eyes were pulled back to the image as if drawn by an unseen force. "Can you make a print of that?"

"You betcha." He clicked with his mouse. "It'll take a few minutes."

"I'll wait."

"Thought you might."

"How accurate is this thing?"

"You questioning my work?"

She didn't answer.

"Pretty accurate. But not a hundred percent. Things happen to people, stress and other environmental factors come into play that influence the result. I'd use it as a guide."

But Vail knew the answer before he'd responded. It was a very accurate result.

"By the way you're looking at the screen, I take it you recognize her. Shit, *I* recognize her."

Vail nodded, but couldn't pull her gaze from the screen.

"Whatcha gonna do?"

The Andreas Vollenweider CD ended just as she was about to answer, and an eerie silence permeated the room. "I'm not sure."

VAIL'S FIRST COURSE OF ACTION had been to return to the FBI Academy. It was now approaching midnight, but she still felt no signs of fatigue. She was a bloodhound, nose to the ground, sniffing her trail. Her prey was near, so near she'd actually seen it. Now it was a matter of gathering information before going in for the kill.

There was no one around this time of night, other than a few new agents sitting in the commemorative hall, telling stories of their days as a beat cop or detective or attorney . . . now in training to become one of the elite law enforcers in the world.

Vail found the maintenance engineer and sweet-talked him into letting her into the library for a while. She told him the truth about locating the mother who had abandoned her, and being the sap that he was, he felt sorry for her and pulled out his ring of keys. That was forty-five minutes ago, and rather than stopping to read through the results popping up across the screen, she printed the pages to make the most efficient use of her time. Even at that, it was taking longer than she had anticipated.

While waiting for the computer to finish the last search, she pulled her cell phone and dialed the hospital. Nothing new to report, she was told by the desk nurse. Jonathan had continued to open his eyes, and had moved them a bit—more "incremental improvement"—but that was all she could tell her. Vail thanked the nurse and watched the last of the search results flicker across the monitor.

She hit PRINT, then waited by the mammoth HP LaserJet for the document. As the papers emerged, a wide yawn spread her lips. Fatigue had finally set in. She would go home, get some sleep, and review the paperwork in the morning.

There was nothing else demanding her time at the moment.

G o ahead, grab her hair and stab the eyes. Stab, stab, stab! Do it!
    Grasp a handful of straw dry hair, lift the head, then plunge the knife down into the eye. Squish!

Look at yourself, don't be blind. Look up, into the window, and see. See for yourself.

After letting go of the knife, the slime from blood and eye juice spatter trailed off the fingertips like saliva from a hungry wolf salivating over its prey. Straightened up . . . looked into the dark window across the room. It was her. Again. Karen Vail in the reflection.

You killed your mother. How does it feel?

Vail craned her head down and tried to look beyond the knife protruding from the right socket, but she couldn't see the face. She moved closer for a better angle. She killed her mother?

Yes, the bitch had to die. You did it, you did it, you did it. . . .

THE MORNING SUN burned away the clouds that had been hovering over the region the past couple weeks. Vail couldn't help but think the lingering haze had become a symbol of her misfortune. Perhaps the break would bring the promise of new opportunities, of a reversal of her bad luck.

Of course, first she had to get past the image of having murdered her mother. She needed to do something, talk to someone about it. These dreams had to stop.

While driving to the hospital, she called her Aunt Faye, who had taken on the task of finding an assisted care facility in the Alexandria region. Based on Emma's long-term care coverage, Faye had narrowed the list of possibilities to three, and it was now in Vail's hands to investigate each one to determine which would best accommodate her mother's needs. In the meantime, rather than move Emma out of her familiar surroundings, Faye's three daughters were taking turns staying at the house to make sure Emma ate regularly and did not wander off. With a backyard as large and wooded as hers, she could get turned around fifty feet from her house and forget how to get home.

Vail arrived at Fairfax Hospital and carried in with her a sampling of Jonathan's favorite childhood books: *The Hobbit, Old Yeller, The Phantom Tollbooth,* and one he had been in the middle of when he was hospitalized: the seventh *Harry Potter* tale. She brought a thermos of coffee and sat beside him, at first just looking at him, his eyes opening and closing, tracking back and forth, as if his brain was taking in the surroundings but not processing what it saw.

She read to him for an hour, then took a break and dove into the task of making screening calls to the three assisted care facilities. Based on the attitude of the staff and level of service provided, she immediately eliminated one of them. The other two would work, subject to a records search for pending complaints and violations.

She gave Jonathan a kiss, told him she loved him, and headed out for lunch with Bledsoe. They met at a Subway restaurant a mile from the op center. His face was long, but when she walked in his expression brightened. He stood as she approached the table.

"Whatever you want, it's on me," he said.

"Tuna on wheat, everything on it."

He nodded, turned to the counter person and put in the order. Bledsoe watched through the display case glass as the woman slapped on tomatoes and sprinkled oil. "How was your visit with your mother?"

"She's got Alzheimer's. It's bad, I've got to move her to an assisted care facility."

Bledsoe sighed. "Sorry."

"Me, too. I wasn't prepared."

"Must've been tough."

"Add it to the list." She considered telling him about Nellie and Emma, then thought better of it. "I thought I needed some time by myself, but given everything that happened, I'm glad Robby was there. Thanks for letting him go."

Bledsoe eyed her obliquely. "I didn't."

"You—"

"We didn't quite see eye-to-eye on the matter. He told me he was taking some personal time and walked out."

Vail chewed on that one. Robby had led her to believe Bledsoe gave his blessing.

"Don't worry about it," he said. "He and I had a chat. It won't be a thing between us. We've got bigger issues to tackle."

"Yeah, about that . . . sorry I didn't show up this morning," Vail said.

He turned his head to face hers. "You're on leave."

"From the Bureau, not from the task force."

Bledsoe moved a few steps down, paid for the sandwiches, and loaded them on a tray. "Linwood and the police chief wanted you off the case."

Vail slid into a booth and sat down. "Guess I'm bad publicity. Beating up your husband doesn't play well in the papers. Too much fallout."

Bledsoe unwrapped his sandwich and pulled off the pickles. "I told her no pickles. You heard me say that, right?" He shook his head.

"You have to close this case," Vail said. "I make your job easier—and probably faster. And a faster resolution means fewer women die. You need me." Vail bit into her sandwich and let her comment ride on the wind for a moment.

"They made it pretty clear they want you to stay away."

"Do you want me to stay away?" She had stopped chewing and focused on his eyes.

"No."

"I work for the victim, Bledsoe. Not the government, not you, not the police chief."

"I know that."

"Then to hell with 'em all. Let me work the case. I'll do it at home. Get me a copy of the file, we'll work it together."

Bledsoe took a bite and looked at Vail as he chewed. She returned the gaze. Pleading without speaking. He finished off his sandwich a few bites later, then took a long pull from his Coke.

"Okay," he said.

"You'll get me a copy of the file?"

"I'll bring it by your place myself."

She nodded. "Keep me up on what the task force does."

He wiped his mouth, then got up. "Thanks for meeting me for lunch."

"Thanks for paying. And for sticking with me."

Vail watched Bledsoe walk away, knowing she had done the right thing for the victims. But she couldn't help wondering if it was the wrong thing for her career.

... thirty-seven

There was a sunset for the first time in weeks, and Vail pulled over to the side of the road to watch the reds burn into oranges, then fade into an expansive horizon of pale pink, as if God had blown brilliantly colored chalk dust off the palette. She pulled down on the gear shift and yanked it into drive, then got on I-495 toward 193 and Great Falls, Virginia.

She turned on the radio, not bothering to change the station—it didn't matter what was playing, because she wasn't listening. It merely served as background noise to take her mind off where she was headed, and what she would say when she got there. As dusk descended, she turned on her headlights and exited at Georgetown Pike. The area of Great Falls was a sprawling community set amongst rolling hills, forests of mature oak and helm, and million dollar homes.

As Vail drove down Potomac River Road, darkness's arrival seemed to accelerate, the remaining light filtered by the dense blind of branches and leaves. She hung a right onto a shoulderless single-lane residential road and flicked on her dome light to check the directions she had scribbled on a piece of paper. The house on the left was an Early American three-story brick mansion. Vail squinted at the lamppost, which lit an address sign surrounded by well-manicured hedges. She turned onto the gravel driveway that cut through an expansive lawn and led straight to the entrance of the home.

Security lights popped on as her car approached the circular turnaround. She parked and got out, walked up to the door, and pressed the bell. A hearty chime sounded up and down the scale. Ten seconds passed, but it seemed like minutes before the hand-tooled oak door finally swung open.

Chase Hancock stood there, eyebrows raised slightly. "Vail, what are you doing here? Come to beg your way back onto the task force? Or did you come here to kick my butt?"

"That's funny, Hancock. I'd prefer the latter, but it's none of your business why I'm here. Is Senator Linwood in?"

Hancock squinted. "Are you here on official business? Otherwise, call ahead and make an appointment."

Vail forced a smile. "Thanks so much for that thoughtful bit of advice, but I'm not in the mood for your bullshit. My *business* is with the senator, not with you. Now move aside or I'll move you myself."

Hancock stepped forward and threw his chest out. "You're trespassing, Vail. I suggest you turn around and leave with your tail between your legs before I arrest you. Citizen's arrest, I can still do that."

"That won't be necessary." The voice came from behind Hancock. Vail craned her neck around his wide body and saw Eleanor Linwood standing there, still dressed in her business suit.

"I'm sorry we made so much noise, Senator," Hancock said. "I'll take care of this. Agent Vail was just leaving."

But Linwood continued to move forward and was now standing beside her head security agent. "That's okay, Chase, I'll take it from here."

"But—"

She turned her head to face his. "I've got it, thank you."

Though it was a moment Vail wanted to savor—she hadn't had many of those lately—she struggled to contain her smile.

As soon as Hancock walked off, Linwood's face hardened. "You wanted to see me, Agent Vail."

"Yes, Senator. I wanted to speak to you about . . . a private matter. Can we go somewhere to talk?"

Without comment, Linwood turned and walked down the wood plank hallway, her heels clicking as they struck the floor. Vail followed, her head rubbernecking in all directions as she took in the décor: the high ceilings and ten-foot windows of the formal dining room, rough-hewn beams, stone fireplace, and lace curtains of the

ving room. They turned left into a smaller room with a paisley sofa
nd hardwood plantation shutters. Linwood sat on the edge of the
ouch and motioned Vail to do the same. Vail reached over and shut
he door, an action Linwood found suspicious, judging by the squint
f her eyes.

"What can I do for you, Agent Vail? Or is it your policy to drop in
n elected officials' homes unannounced?"

She put Vail on the defensive with practiced ease. "I apologize,
enator. I didn't think you'd see me if I called ahead."

"Perhaps you're correct." She glanced at her watch. "And unless
ou provide me with a compelling reason for this visit in the next
hirty seconds, I'll have my very efficient security agent show you the
oor."

Vail bit the inside of her cheek. She didn't care for the senator's
mug attitude, but at the moment, she tried to see it from her point
f view. Vail hadn't yet given her an explanation.

"If this is about being removed from the task force, I'm afraid
hat's something you'll have to take up with the police department.
Contrary to what you may've heard, I have no influence over the
nachinations of the Fairfax County PD."

"With all due respect, I don't believe that for one moment. How-
ver, that's not why I'm here." Linwood started to object, but Vail
eld up a hand. "I want to tell you a story about two women born—"

"I don't have time for bedtime stories, Agent Vail. I've got—"

"You'll want to hear this one, Senator." Vail had leaned forward,
er eyebrows hunched downward. "It's a story about two sisters
orn in Brooklyn. One of them, nine years older, always seemed to
e the one who made the correct decisions in life. The younger one
vent out of her way to be different and often got into trouble."

Linwood rose from the couch. "I don't see what this has to do
vith anything—"

"I'll get to the point," Vail said, then began speaking faster. "The
ounger sister—we'll call her *Nellie*—got herself pregnant. This an-
ered her parents, a good Catholic family who didn't believe in pre-
narital sex. They disowned her. Depressed and unprepared for

dealing with a newborn, Nellie showed up at her older sister's house
She asked her sister to watch the baby for a couple of hours while sh
went to a movie. Nellie never returned, and the baby was raised b
the aunt and uncle."

Vail detected tears in Linwood's eyes. The senator sunk down i
the couch and Vail continued: "Nellie, out on her own, got a cou
ple of low-paying jobs before realizing she needed to straighten
herself up. She met someone, an up-and-coming heir to a boomin;
family business that supplied shipping containers to internationa
transportation companies. Having just graduated from Harvar
with his MBA, the man met Nellie and fell in love. Now here's th
interesting part," Vail said, leaning forward. "Her knight in shinin;
armor helped her get a new social security number, new name, nev
background, new identity. Nellie ceased to exist." Vail reached int
her shoulder-slung portfolio case and removed a hunk of papers
She dropped them on the couch beside Linwood. "It's all i
there."

Linwood's eyes fell to the stack of documents, atop which was
copy of the picture of Emma and Nellie Irwin. Linwood gently re
moved the photo and looked at it for a long moment. She then no
ticed the computer-enhanced image, and raised an eyebrow. He
gaze drifted away, coming to rest on the turn-of-the-century woo
floor. Finally, she spoke. "Nellie needed to start a new life. When sh
met Richard, it was like a dream come true. His father had the con
nections to make her past go away. And to give her a new future. I
was much easier to do in those days." After a moment, her eye
found Vail's. "You'll never prove any of it. I don't care what's i
those papers. You go to the media, I'll deny it all."

Vail's chin shot backward. "The media? Who cares about th
media?"

"Why else would you dig into my past? To force me into helpin;
you get back on the task force? To discredit me in my campaign—"

"This has nothing to do with your campaign, and it's got nothin
to do with the task force." She paused, hoping Linwood would catc]

n. But she didn't. Finally, Vail forged ahead. "Senator, I'm that ewborn you left at Emma's house thirty-eight years ago."

A tear meandered down Linwood's cheek, then dropped to her lap.

"I'm your daughter."

Linwood rose again, turned her back to Vail, appeared to swipe at er tears. Still trying to appear composed and in control. Trying to igest this information with as much dignity as she could garner and ill absorb the shock of the revelation. "What do you want from ae?" she finally asked.

What do I want from her? Vail thought for a second. She had been focused on putting together the pieces of the puzzle that she adn't allowed her mind enough time to analyze her feelings. She ad a task, one that piqued her curiosity, one that helped ease the nawing concern over Jonathan's condition. But now she needed an nswer. The first thought left her lips before she could consider it. "I ant to know who my biological parents are. Or were." She rubbed er eyes. "I just found out I wasn't Emma's child. I went to visit her esterday. She's got Alzheimer's and thought I was you."

Linwood was silent.

"You might want to go see her. Make amends—"

"Thank you, Agent Vail, for your concern."

"At least call me Karen."

Linwood bowed her head, rested a hand against the wall, steady-ag herself. Symbolic support for what she was about to say. But as ae seconds passed, Linwood did not talk. Did not move.

"Tell me about my father."

Linwood's head lifted and she stared at the ceiling. "I think it's est you leave now."

Vail should have anticipated such a response. If Linwood had, in ct, worked to bury her past—and Vail now had confirmation of that—aen that would be the last topic Linwood would want to discuss.

"You abandoned your child. How could you do that?"

"There's more to it than you know, or should ever know." The enator was quiet a long moment, then her shoulders rolled forward.

As if realizing she needed to explain further, she said, "It was th
best thing for both of us at the time. I had my own survival to worr
about. Believe me, it was a good thing Emma was there."

Though Vail had seen druggie teenagers with babies—wome
who didn't know what responsibility was, or what it meant to be
mother—she had a hard time seeing the regal Eleanor Linwood i
the same light. But Vail had not come there to understand why he
mother had abandoned her. Or perhaps she had. Perhaps it wa
something she *should* ask about, if nothing else to understand. Bu
either Linwood was a closed individual, or the thought of havin
abandoned her daughter was too painful to relive, even harder to dis
cuss. For the moment, Vail would focus on finding her father. I
might be easier for a man to talk about the past he had left behind.

"Senator, I need to know about my father. You have that infor
mation. I can find it out by other means, but the attention I'd draw
would probably be something you'd want to avoid."

"It was another lifetime. One I'd rather forget."

"Am I that much of a disappointment to you?"

Linwood spun to face her. Her eyes were swollen and red. "Thi
has nothing to do with you." Her gaze was fixed on Vail, as if ther
was more she wanted to say. But she hesitated, then finally shook he
head.

"I'm sorry to have brought this anguish to the surface. I would'v
thought you'd be glad to see me. But obviously you're not. Fine, I'
deal with that. Give me the info I want and I'll be out of your life."

Linwood looked away. "Even if I tell you who your father i
nothing good will come of it."

"You don't know that."

Her eyes narrowed. "In fact, I do."

"Maybe he's not the same person he was forty years ago."

"Someone like that doesn't change."

"Senator, your secret is safe with me. I won't tell him who yo
are or where you live."

"It's more complicated than that."

Vail began to feel the same frustration she'd felt hundreds of times in the past, sitting in an interview room opposite a skel she knew was guilty, but who refused to give it up. There was one case where a kidnapper would not divulge the location of his victim. Vail never could elicit the information, and they never found the woman. She felt that frustration now, swelling in her throat, threatening to choke her.

Vail took a cleansing breath and slipped into interrogation mode, using techniques she taught at the Academy. "You're worried he'll find you, that my poking around will somehow compromise your secret. Or even make him resurface, bring him back into your life. I can understand that. But I won't let it happen. You have my word."

"It would destroy my political career. I'm gearing up for reelection. My opponent would take me to task in the media if he found out about my association with your father. And if it ever got out I'd changed my identity—"

"No one would be able to piece it together. I'll make sure of that."

Linwood swallowed hard. "Agent Vail . . . Karen. . . ." She sat back down on the edge of the sofa. "It was a long time ago. I was young and stupid and didn't know any better. As soon as I realized the kind of person he was, I left him. It took me longer than it should've, but I was scared."

Vail thought of herself, and her marriage to Deacon. She, too, should've seen the warning signs months sooner than she had. She looked up and realized the two of them were sitting there in silence, each absorbed in her own thoughts. "At least you were able to get away," Vail managed. "A lot of women don't have the fortitude to make the break." She said it for her own validation as much as Linwood's.

The senator was staring ahead, oblivious to Vail's comments. "There's nothing to be gained by making contact with him."

"With all due respect, that's not for you to decide."

Linwood stood up and straightened her skirt. "I'm glad you came by, Agent Vail. It's been nice visiting with you." She turned the knob and held the door open. The universal sign for the end to an acrimonious meeting.

Vail remained seated. "'It's been nice visiting with you'? I'm your daughter, Senator, not one of your campaign donors." Her voice was louder than she'd intended it to be—but she was tired, and angry, and her dreams of finding her mother had deteriorated into a nightmare. "Like it or not, *Mother,* I'm a part of you, always will be. Whether or not you want to admit it."

"I think it's time you left." Linwood's voice was firm, its volume matching Vail's.

"Don't you have any maternal instincts?" Vail's hand found the outer pocket of her leather shoulder case. She pulled a photo and held it in front of Linwood's face. "You've got a grandson, too—but that probably doesn't mean anything to you, does it?"

Linwood looked past the picture and glared at Vail, her eyes cold and fierce. "Make sure you keep this information confidential. Or I'll see to it you never work for any law enforcement agency again." She turned and walked out of the room. Vail started to follow, but Hancock stepped in front of her, his arms spread like an eagle's wings.

"I believe the senator asked you to leave." He raised his eyebrows, expecting a sharp retort. But Vail was empty and numb. And sickened by the thought that Hancock was standing outside the door, listening to their conversation.

Vail shoved Hancock aside with a stiff forearm, then walked out of the house.

He'd had the hardest time concentrating during class. All he could think about was his next bitch. And her eyes. He had bought a pair of night-vision binoculars at the local camping supply chain store and spent the last evening in surveillance of his new victim. It was a bit of a challenge, but what's life without challenges?

First, however, he had to get rid of his last student. She wanted to finish her stinking vase. Jesus, she had to get it just right. He certainly understood the need for perfection, but he had more important things to deal with. He had to work extra hard to keep himself from doing something he'd regret later, because if she hadn't left when she finally did, he would've had to take care of her. But she wasn't the one, and killing her would've aroused suspicion. Others no doubt knew she had been at his class, and no one would've seen her leave. It was traceable back to him. So he had to keep his focus, keep thinking about his target.

Focus, challenges . . . nothing new in any of that. The rest of the evening—that was where things would be different. But he thought the thrill, the kill, and the aftermath would be well worth the uncharted waters. He'd know in a day whether or not he was right. But he suspected he would be. Because this was the one, the ultimate prize. Unlike the others, she knows what she does. And what she did.

He waited patiently for the right time, then felt the excitement. He was jittery. It was tough to get a full breath.

"It's time! It's time! It's time!" He wanted to roll down the window and scream, but was able to control himself long enough to get out of the car and focus on his stealth approach to the house.

He moved through the forested cover and remained behind a row of hedges across the narrow road. Peered through his binoculars. Everything was quiet until one of the garage doors rolled up.

He moved quickly through the brush, remaining low and scampering toward the house. The car backed out, then drove onto the long driveway. Front yard lights snapped on, illuminating the front of the garage with bright halogen spots. He sprinted along a row of bushes, using their cover to keep from tripping the side yard motion sensors. He clutched the cold, moist brick siding of the house and waited for the sectional wood garage door to begin closing.

As soon as it started lowering, the car drove off, its tires crunching on the rough gravel. He stepped over the sensors mounted along the floor of the garage's threshold, then knelt down, a large black ball hidden in the corner shadows. The weak light from the small incandescent bulb barely lit the empty garage. The door thumped closed and he was alone. Just him and his stun gun.

And the bitch.

After leaving Linwood's house, Vail drove aimlessly, moving along the winding Georgetown Pike before getting back onto 495. Though it wasn't a conscious decision, she was headed home.

When she walked into her house, her head was throbbing and her left knee was stiff from driving. She threw her keys on the table and trudged toward the bath. She felt dirty and wanted to strip down and relax in a tub of hot water with bubbles and a glass of cabernet. The perpetual stress over the past several days had reached a pinnacle, and she needed to find the release valve before the pressure cooker burst.

She started the water and heard a clunk in the bedroom. Her heart dropped. She shut the water and listened, but there was only silence. She moved toward her armoire, lifted her holster, and removed the Glock, then noticed her BlackBerry on the floor, its red light blinking. She picked it up and clicked through to the message: Bledsoe. The Dead Eyes code.

"Shit." She reached him at home.

"Just got word," he answered, not needing to ask who it was. The luxury of caller ID. "Thought you should know."

"What's the address? I'll meet you—"

"Too risky—it's one thing to work behind the scenes, but to show up at—"

"You only get one chance to see a fresh crime scene, Bledsoe. I need to see it, experience it. We'll deal with the details later. And the fallout."

"This one's different, Karen."

"If it's different, it may not be Dead Eyes. That's why I need to see it."

"No, it's different because of the MO, not the signature. He didn't hit a middle-class professional. He hit a senator. State Senator Eleanor Linwood."

Vail felt a swirl of dizziness shake her. She reached out, grabbed the edge of the armoire, and somehow hung on to the phone. Her vision was gray snow, her body spinning faster than a merry-go-round. Her headache was instantly worse, pounding at her temples like a pair of anvils.

"Karen, you there?"

"Here. I'm . . . here. I'm just, give me a minute."

"I've gotta go, get over there. You want, I'll call you from my car—"

"No, I'm coming," she said, her head clearing. "I'm coming. I have to come."

"Jesus Christ, Karen." He paused a moment, then said, "Look, I don't have time to debate this anymore. You wanna come, fine."

"Was everyone notified?"

"Everyone, including Hancock, who's probably at the scene anyway, and Del Monaco, who's now on the task force. Chief's going to be there, and probably the media—"

"I'll worry about all that when I get there."

"House is off Georgetown Pike—"

"I know where she lives. I'll see you there." Vail hung up, steadied herself again, and hit the number for Robby. "You heard?"

"Karen. Yeah, I'm out the door."

"Pick me up on the way."

There was a long silence. "You sure?"

"Dead sure. I've got something to tell you. I'll be waiting out front."

BARELY TEN MINUTES HAD PASSED when Robby stopped at the curb in front of her house. She got in and he pulled away in a hurry, barely waiting for her to close the door.

"So what's so important that it's worth committing professional suicide?" he asked.

"Eleanor Linwood is my mother. Was my mother."

"What?" Robby's eyes locked with hers.

"Watch the road, please," she said evenly.

"When'd you find this out?"

"I confirmed it two or three hours ago. That photo we took from Mom's—from Emma's? I had it age-enhanced at the lab. It was her, it was Linwood."

"That software isn't always accurate—"

"I went to Linwood's. I met with her, showed her the photo, told her what I'd found out from digging through records."

"She 'fessed up?"

"Pretty much. Filled in some of the blanks, how she had the muscle to change identity. Refused to tell me who my father was, though. Afraid it'd ruin her career."

"And now she's dead."

Vail glanced out the side window, watching the dark residences fly by beneath the occasional streetlight. "Now she's dead."

"Coincidence?" Robby asked.

She turned to him. "What's that supposed to mean?"

"I don't know. Just seems funny. You find out she's your mother and three hours later she's a Dead Eyes vic."

Vail sighed. "Don't know. What would the connection be?" She flashed on the chase through Sandra Franks's backyard, the feeling the offender was there . . . that he had been waiting there for them. For her?

"We've got to tell the task force," Robby said.

"Hancock probably knows. I think he was eavesdropping."

"Prick." Robby drove on for a moment, then asked, "Any news on Jonathan?"

She shrugged. "Some improvement. Small steps, you know?"

"Some improvement is better than no improvement."

Vail frowned. It was the same thing Gifford had said . . . but somehow, it sounded more genuine coming from Robby.

He accelerated and entered the interstate.

POLICE CRUISERS, their light bars swirling in a rhythmic pulse, we blocking the entrance to the senator's street. Robby badged the p trol officer and drove around the barricade. They pulled off to th side and approached Bledsoe, who was talking to a uniform near th rim of the circular driveway.

In the harsh halogen security lighting bearing down on them Bledsoe's face looked weary and defeated. He nodded at Vail an Robby, then turned to Sinclair and Manette, who were approachin from his left. "Anything?"

"We got some shoe prints in the dirt over by the south end of th house," Sinclair said, motioning with his Mag-Lite. "Looks like the come from the woods. I sent a tech out to track them, get a plast casting."

Manette said, "Means this guy came in on foot. Tells me he kne what he was doing, who lived here. That she'd have some kind security."

Sinclair shook his head. "Not *who* so much as *what*. Look at th neighborhood. The person who lived here had money."

"Either way," Bledsoe said, "he didn't know about the securi lights. Or he took a big chance no one would see him as he got clos Our guy's a planner, he'd know about the lights."

Vail looked toward the side of the house. "I was him, I'd ap proach along that line of bushes. Motion sensors would be blocke Lights would never come on."

"That's exactly where the footprints are," Sinclair said, "rig along the bushes."

"They have cameras?" Bledsoe asked.

Manette shook her head. "Hancock said the senator didn't wa to live like Big Brother was watching her. Didn't think anything li this'd ever happen. Especially in this neighborhood."

"Get anything back on that email?" Sinclair asked.

Vail's gaze was still off in the general area of the house. "Nothir yet."

"We really could use some help on that—"

"I know, Sin," Vail said. "I know. I can't make them work faster. I
ried."

Bledsoe held up a hand. "Keep it down. Let's at least look like we
ll get along, okay?" He nodded toward the house. "Sin, why don't
ou go check on Hancock."

Sinclair frowned, then mumbled something under his breath as
e headed off down the gravel path.

"Hancock's pretty shaken up," Manette said, "so I wouldn't ex-
ect too much from him."

Vail chuckled. "I never expect anything from him, so it's not like
his'll be any different."

"I meant in terms of helping us construct a time line for the sena-
or's movements tonight."

"I can help with that," Vail said. She glanced at Robby, then con-
inued. "I came by earlier—"

"Detective!" Approaching on the run were Gifford, Del Monaco,
nd Police Chief Lee Thurston.

Bledsoe turned and opened a space in the huddle to accommo-
ate the three men, who were dressed in nearly identical black wool
vercoats.

"Agent Vail, what are you doing here?" Gifford asked. His eyes
arrowed as his arms folded across his chest.

"I called her," Bledsoe said. "Given the identity of our victim, I
anted my best people on it."

Gifford looked at Vail. "Agent Vail is under orders not to partake
n any Bureau business."

"This isn't Bureau business," Bledsoe said. "It's a multijurisdic-
ional task force, which I'm heading—"

"But I gave you a direct order to remove her," Thurston said to
ledsoe.

"With all due respect, sir, the idea is to catch this fucker. Karen
ail is a vital member of my team. The faster we catch him, the less
eople he'll kill. And with the senator's murder, the heat just got
urned up. Media's gonna be all over us."

As if on cue, the downdraft of thumping helicopter rotor blades began whipping nearby treetops. The task force members craned their necks to the patch of illuminated sky . . . where a chopper emblazoned with the WSAW-TV logo—a bird with a magnifying glass—swung into view.

"Speak of the devil," Robby said.

Bledsoe held out a hand, palm up, as if pleading his case. "Look, Vail's the best. I need her help with this. Right now, I gotta catch a killer. I don't care about politics."

Thurston reached up and caught his fedora that had been lifted off his bald head by a gust of chilled wind. "Apparently, you don't care about following orders, either."

Gifford leaned in close and said something in Thurston's ear. Thurston, a hand pressing down on his hat, bent his head forward, listening.

Bledsoe grabbed the radio from his pocket and yelled to the uniform on the other end to do whatever was necessary to get the chopper out of the area. As Bledsoe shoved the handset into his pocket, Thurston turned to him.

"Vail's in, but we both have real problems with this. Next time you think you know better than me, you come to me first so I can knock some sense up your ass."

"Yes, sir."

Gifford pointed an index finger in Vail's face. "I don't want you showing up at any more Dead Eyes scenes."

"Let's hope this'll be his last," Vail said. Gifford threw an angry look at Bledsoe, then turned away. Vail had thoughts about telling them Linwood was her mother, but that would open a door to a room she didn't want to enter, at least not yet. With the tightrope she had been walking lately, she knew it was best to be completely forthcoming, because in a very short time Hancock would come out of his funk and tell everyone who had ears that Vail had gotten into an argument with the senator. But if she spoke up now, they would never let her view the crime scene, as she would immediately become a suspect.

As Vail watched Gifford and Thurston walk off, Bledsoe rubbed his hands together. "Okay everyone, let's go in and take a look round."

Del Monaco moved beside Vail and matched her strides. "You've got a set of balls, showing up here."

Vail brushed him aside with a forearm. "At least one of us does."

Manette, bringing up the rear, started laughing. "Good one, Kari."

Del Monaco, his fair skin reddened from the blistering cold, nevertheless displayed a blush of embarrassment. "Who the hell are you?"

"Mandisa Manette, a dick with Spotsylvania County SD. And I've got a set of balls, too."

Del Monaco gave her an evil eye and moved into the house. Manette held up a hand and Vail palmed it. They shared a smile and entered the residence.

VAIL FELT A TIGHTENING in her chest as she walked down the hall. Only a few hours ago she had made her way down this very corridor, Linwood leading the way. Was it a coincidence, as Robby had noted, that a short time after their meeting Linwood became a Dead Eyes victim? Was the episode at the Franks house related? Had the killer even been there, or had she been seeing things? Or was this all the product of Linwood's ill-advised news conference?

And in the back of her mind, the nightmares. Seeing the killer's face—her face—in the mirror. . . . *No. They're just dreams.*

Everything was so confusing. She never felt so uncertain of things on the job. Her personal life was another story . . . a book full of uncertainty, each chapter building toward a divorce, climaxing with her son lying in ICU and herself sitting in a jail cell, arrested on an assault charge. No, not confusing. Fucked up.

But until Dead Eyes came along, she always could grab the gun by the handle and drill the target. No uncertainty, no second thoughts. When had her life taken a left turn?

She stepped around Del Monaco and Sinclair and grabbed Bledsoe's arm. She pulled him aside, into the living room. "There's something you should know." She then proceeded to outline the details of her discovery of her relationship to Linwood, including the conversation she'd had with her earlier in the evening.

Bledsoe brought both hands to his face and rubbed, as if he could scrub away the fatigue—and his mounting problems. He sat down heavily on the couch. "You realize this makes you a suspect."

"That's why I didn't say anything to Gifford and Thurston. For sure they would've sent me home."

He looked up at her with bloodshot eyes. "Where were you tonight after leaving here?"

"I went for a drive, by myself. I ended up at home around nine thirty. I was about to take a bath when you texted me."

Bledsoe nodded, looked away, his eyes roaming the tall drapes and window. Finally, his eyes came to rest on Vail's. "Did you kill Eleanor Linwood?"

Vail held his gaze. "No, Bledsoe, I didn't."

He didn't look away, at least not for a long moment. Then, he rose from the couch. "Okay. Let's go join the others."

She was surprised he took her word at face value . . . or, perhaps he had enough confidence in his abilities that he could tell when someone was lying to him. Whatever the reason, she was relieved he had let the issue drop so easily.

They walked toward the senator's bedroom. "There's blood spatter in the foyer, near the garage," Robby said as he joined them. "Looks like he bludgeoned her with a blunt object, maybe to the point of death, then dragged her into the bedroom."

"That doesn't fit," Vail said.

Del Monaco was kneeling in the wide hall, examining the trail of blood they had all been careful to avoid. "No, it doesn't."

They walked into the cavernous master bedroom and immediately saw the studied gazes of Manette and Sinclair. The scene laid out before them was more horrific than they had previously seen. Eleanor Linwood's body was mutilated in the same grotesque manner as Dead Eyes's other victims—with two notable exceptions: both her breasts had been severed, and her face was disfigured. More than just disfigured, it had been burned or peeled away, the remaining flesh and blood vessels and nerves exposed in a mess resembling raw meat.

Bledsoe quickly turned, clutching a vomit bag to his mouth, and barfed. Whether it was the smell, or Vail's relationship to this victim, or simply the fact that it had finally gotten to her as well, she had to cup her mouth and use her tongue to close down her throat and force down the bile that had risen.

"Oh, man," Robby said, looking away. "That's bad. That's bad. Worse than the others. Shit." He walked out of the room.

"This guy was pissed off, big time," Del Monaco managed. "Very personal attack."

Manette shook her head. "Yeah, that press conference was a real good idea. I want to meet the guy who signed off on that one."

"She wanted to do it and Gifford didn't see any harm at the time," Del Monaco said. "I mean, he knew there was a risk it'd incite him, but he thought it could also scare him enough to slow him down, buy us some time." He rubbed at his neck. "He never thought he'd come after her. She doesn't fit the victimology at all."

Bledsoe wiped his mouth and turned his body strategically to avoid having to look at Linwood. "Okay, so he was pissed off. Does that explain . . . all this?" He took a sideways glance at the body and motioned in the air with a hand.

Vail took a deep breath and forced herself to evaluate the scene. "It might. She really got in his face, challenged him big time on TV. But there could be more going on here. He might've known her. Or, at least, there might've been some connection we're not aware of."

Manette shook her head. "There we go again, 'might've this, might've that.' Ain't nothing you sure about?"

"I'm sure this guy is escalating. For whatever reason, we've got a problem on our hands."

"We've had a problem," Robby said. "Now it's a nightmare."

Vail's gaze settled on what remained of Linwood's face. "I think this vic could be the key. Trauma to the face and head generally means a relationship between the offender and victim. Like Del

Monaco said, this was a personal attack. And he didn't merely disable her, like the others, he bludgeoned her before bringing her into the bedroom."

"Detective Bledsoe." A forensic technician walked in wearing latex gloves. "You should see this."

Bledsoe led the entourage into the master bathroom. The technician pointed to a small drinking glass filled with blood.

"Is that what I think it is?"

"As near as I can tell," the tech said, "it's blood. We'll run it and see if it's the vic's. Could be animal."

Robby knelt beside the glass. "Has it been dusted and photographed yet?"

"Yeah, we're done with it."

Robby held his hand out and the tech passed him a pair of latex gloves. He slapped them on and carefully lifted the glass up to the light. "Looks like he drank from it."

"Hard to say," the tech said. "There's a smudge where the lip print would be, and there's a coating of blood on the inside of the glass. We still have to luminol the bathroom, but it may be he poured blood out of the glass into the sink."

"Or he drank from it and wiped it afterwards to smudge the print."

"Pretty smart offender if he did that," Sinclair said.

Vail moved closer to examine the glass. "We already know the guy is smart."

Bledsoe held a hand against his stomach. He looked a bit ashen and was heading toward the door. "Let's move out of here, discuss this in the other room."

As they walked back into the bedroom, Manette scrunched her face. "I'm afraid to ask, but what does it mean, if the guy drank her blood? That's beyond gross."

Vail sighed. "Drinking the victim's blood, which our killer's never done before, is stimulating, even exciting for him; it heightens his fantasy."

Manette shook her head. "Damn."

Everyone was quiet, alone with his or her own thoughts. Murder scenes like this one often prompted such a response. Pondering how someone could do such a thing to a human being. But they had seen plenty of murders during the course of their careers and most detectives reached a point where they became numb to stabbings and shooting deaths. But this went beyond what most of them were accustomed to dealing with. Even Vail and Del Monaco, though having seen some of this before, were nevertheless scratching their heads.

"Okay, so let's look at what we've got," Robby said. "Footprints from outside the property leading along a row of hedges that gives him cover from either the front of the house or the security lights. He gets in, how?"

"Only entry on that side of the house is through the garage," Sinclair said.

Del Monaco rubbed at his jiggly chin. "Okay, so he waits for someone to leave out of the garage, and he slips in. Linwood hears something, or she's standing near the garage anyway, and he bludgeons her with a blunt object. Beats her, where?"

"Possibly on the face, but definitely above the left ear," Sinclair said, kneeling beside the bed and examining the corpse.

"Defensive wounds?"

Robby crouched by Linwood's right side. "Abrasion right forearm, possibly a couple of fingers, too. Need an x-ray to see if there're any fractures."

"So this guy has totally changed his MO," Vail added. "He's not interested in talking to this woman. Usually, we figure he enters through the front door, sweet talks them into letting him in. Once in, he hits them and knocks them unconscious. We've never found blood near any of the front doors, so it's just a disabling blow. But with this one, he hits her hard. And she's facing him when he attacks. Tells me he's angry at her, or at something she said or did."

"MO's can change, right?" Robby asked. "If the offender thinks something might work better, he refines his methods."

Vail smiled internally. Robby had been reading the materials she had given him. "That's right."

"Or, it could've been the press conference," Bledsoe said. "Linwood went after him pretty good, probably pissed him off big time."

Del Monaco looked away, rested his hands on his hips. "Or, could be we're dealing with a different offender altogether."

"Whoa," Vail said, holding up a hand. "How do you get that?"

"MO's very different. Yes, it can change when an offender refines his skills to be more successful. But that's not the case here. He was pretty damn successful before. Very few defensive wounds. He disabled them fairly efficiently. Why change what works?" He shrugged. "Besides, signature's way different, too. Much more violent. Major damage to face and head. Severing the breasts suggests a sexual component. Was she raped?"

"Chuck," Bledsoe called, "any signs of sexual assault?"

A technician appeared in the doorway. "Sodomized. Smooth object. Damage to the surrounding tissue. Best guess, postmortem. Don't know yet if there's any semen. ME will be able to tell you more." Bledsoe gave him a nod and the tech returned to his work in the bathroom.

"Also a first," Del Monaco said. "And now he might be drinking the vic's blood. These are all very significant variants."

Vail held up a hand. "Unless this vic holds special significance to him, like we said before. That still makes the most sense to me, Frank. As to the change in MO, he had a different situation here." She turned to the others, focusing mostly on Robby, to explain: "Some offenders will case the place to see if there are any boyfriends or husbands or roommates they have to worry about. If there are, and the offender still wants this victim, he'll take out the male first and then go after the intended target. We saw that with Danny Rolling in Gainesville. If Dead Eyes scoped the place, and I bet he did, then he'd know Linwood wouldn't answer her own door like the other vics did."

Quiet settled on the room for a moment. Sinclair asked, "She's married, right? That shipping guy?"

"Yeah," Bledsoe said. "He's been overseas. Chief was going to notify him."

"Maid lives in the servant's quarters out back," Manette said. "She's had the flu past few days. She ordered take-out for Linwood, it was delivered around five. She went back to her place and passed out. Didn't hear or see nothing. I gotta follow up with the delivery guy, run his sheet, see if he's got any priors. And get proof of his whereabouts after he left."

"Where's Hancock?" Vail asked.

"Office in the back, it's his base of operations," Sinclair said. "Didn't want to talk. Couldn't get him to say shit."

Manette turned to Bledsoe. "You want me to go get him, Blood?" She winked. "I think he'll listen to me."

Bledsoe nodded. "We need him to talk to us. Let's do it out in the living room, let the crime scene guys finish up in here. We've . . . seen enough."

"Got that right," Sinclair said, following Bledsoe out of the room.

HANCOCK SAT DOWN heavily on the couch, his tie pulled loose to one side and his hair a frazzled mess. His eyes were glazed and his movements heavy, as if he had been drinking. Manette brought up the rear and tipped back a phantom cup, confirming that their compadre had, in fact, been dipping into the sauce.

"Well, lookee what we got here. A fuckin' party. Well, fuck me. So glad y'all could make it."

"We need to ask you a few questions," Sinclair said.

"Cops already asked me some questions." His bloodshot eyes wandered around the room.

Manette, who sat opposite Hancock on an identical sofa separated by a coffee table with espresso-swirl granite, said, "We know you're pretty upset about the senator."

His head whipped over to her. "Shouldn't I be? She was good to me. And I just lost my fucking job."

Vail frowned, stretched her neck up toward Robby's ear. "That's why he's all bent out of shape. Two hundred K and benees down the drain."

"Yeah, and look at all the protection it got her."

Manette threw Vail an angry glance, then turned back to Hancock. "Look, you're the security guy here. It was your job to look after the senator's well-being. Where were you when—where were you tonight after six o'clock?"

Hancock's eyes found Vail. "It's all your fault. You got her all upset and she wanted to be left alone." He turned back to Manette. "I went out for a drive."

Vail felt everyone's gaze shift to her face, awaiting an explanation. "I was here earlier," she said, "around six. I'd just found out that the senator was my—my biological mother." She glanced over at Robby, hoping to find a sympathetic face. "I came by to talk to her about it."

Del Monaco snorted. "You're kidding, right?"

"How'd the conversation go?" Sinclair asked.

"She was a rock. She didn't say a whole lot—"

"They argued," Hancock shouted. "Vail wanted to know who her father was, but the senator wouldn't tell her. Vail was pissed off."

Vail banded her arms across her chest. "I left around six-thirty, I think. I was upset, I went for a drive. When I got home, Bledsoe texted me." She waited for more questions, a grilling, an interrogation. But everyone was quiet.

Bledsoe's Motorola sung Beethoven's Fifth. He fumbled with the handset and walked off.

"I'll leave you all alone for a few minutes," Vail said, "so you can talk." She spun and followed Bledsoe out of the house.

THE FRONT DOOR CLICKED CLOSED. The silence continued, except for the shuffling movements of crime scene technicians who continued to move about, taking photos and transporting evidence from the bedroom to their vehicle. Finally, Hancock spoke. "Vail's got no alibi."

"But Karen Vail's not a killer," Robby said.

Hancock reached into his sport jacket and pulled out a brown cigarette.

"Not one of them stinkers," Manette whined.

Sinclair touched Manette's arm and leaned close to her ear. "Let him go. May help calm him down, sober him up."

"But it's some Turkish herbal shit in there. It'll stink this place up, I won't be able to breathe."

Hancock's hands were trembling slightly. Robby watched as he maneuvered the lighter in front of his lips, the flame missing the tip. Hancock put his left hand in front of the right, as if one tremor would cancel the other and get the cigarette lit. He finally succeeded.

Sinclair pulled a crumpled handkerchief from his pocket and offered it to Manette. "Here's a filter."

She pushed his hand away. "No thanks." She waved her hands in the air to disperse the smoke. "What else you got on Vail?" she asked Hancock.

Hancock sucked in a long drag, blew it out his nostrils. "She beat up her husband, put him in the hospital. She's got a violent streak." He flicked the ashes into a baby blue and opal colored porcelain vase on the coffee table. "Here's how it went down. Vail is depressed. She's got problems with her ex, and her son is in a coma. She finds out her mother isn't her mother after all, and she starts snooping around. Somehow she discovers the senator is her real mother. She comes here to confront her, to find out why she pawned her off like an old TV. Vail gets on her case, so the senator asks her to leave. Vail throws a fit, a loud one. I'm worried she may assault the senator, just like she did to her ex. So I step in and show Vail the door. She storms out, drives away, and parks. She comes back on foot and waits nearby."

Hancock took another puff and rubbed at his right temple, the trail of smoke zigzagging as his hand moved back and forth over his skin. He blew a haze into the air and continued. "The senator's very upset and wants to be alone. I try to help, but she tells me to leave. Vail waits till I drive away, then comes back in and whacks her. Makes it look like a Dead Eyes kill, which isn't hard to do because she knows this shit so well she could recite it in her sleep." He leaned back on the couch, his gaze resting somewhere on the floor.

After a moment of silence during which everyone seemed to be digesting Hancock's theory, Del Monaco spoke up. "But it doesn't exactly match Dead Eyes. If she was staging the scene, she'd want to follow it to the letter. So there'd be no doubt."

Hancock blew a plume out the side of his mouth. "She can't control herself. Rage takes over. Overkill, because of the personal connection."

Del Monaco bobbed his head about, as if to say he couldn't completely rule out Hancock's assertions. Robby remembered reading about overkill in the binders Vail had given him: it was a term used to describe excessive violence found at a crime scene, usually as a result of a soured personal relationship between the assailant and his victim.

"And she's got no alibi," Hancock added.

Robby stepped forward, stopping a few strides from Hancock's feet. He rested his hands on his hips and looked down at Hancock. "Neither do you. And you could've staged the scene just as well as Karen could've."

"Yeah, but here's the thing, Mr. Roberto Enrique *Humper*to Hernandez, or whatever the hell your names are." He looked up and blew some smoke in Robby's face. "I don't have a motive."

Robby swatted it away and looked at Sinclair. It was a look that begged him to intervene before Robby slugged him in the face and caved in his skull.

"Robby, honey," Manette said, taking the hint. "Let's chat over here for a moment." She stepped forward and grabbed him by the crook of his elbow. She pulled him close and he reluctantly craned his neck down to her level. "We don't know what happened yet. So he may be a suspect, but he's our only witness, too. Let's not piss him off before we get a chance to ask him some questions."

Robby knew she was right, but his hand was still curled into a fist. And he was ready to use it. "Fine. Ask your questions. I'm going out for some air."

ROBBY JOINED BLEDSOE in the middle of the circular drive. Bledsoe hung up his phone and stood there, nodding his head slowly.

Vail, coming up from behind him, acknowledged Robby. "So are they raking me over the coals?"

"Just Hancock."

"Well," Bledsoe said, "I think we've got something on Mr. GQ."

Robby and Vail looked at him, anticipation raising their brows.

"That was the chief. Gave me something he thought we could use. Seems that Linwood was helping herself to some dessert on the side."

"An affair?" Vail asked. "With Hancock?"

Robby turned toward the front door. "Now *that* I can use."

"Hold on," Bledsoe said. "We have to decide *how* to use this. We need to poke around a little bit, get our ducks in a row."

"Asshole is trying to pin this on Karen, smug on account that she had a motive and he didn't. Now we know he might have one. Scorned lover. She wants to call it off, he refuses."

"Husband needs to be looked at," Vail said. "We sure he's overseas?"

"It's being checked, but they reached him at his hotel in Hong Kong, so I think his alibi is pretty damn strong."

"Unless it was a contract job," Robby said. "Hubby wants her out of the picture, hires someone to take her out."

Vail shook her head. "Contract jobs are impersonal. Bullet to the head and it's over. None of this bloody mess to the face and breasts." She turned to Bledsoe. "Maybe forensics will give us something. I say we wait on nailing Hancock to the chair until at least tomorrow. We might get something else to use on him."

Bledsoe nodded. "I'll ask the lab to put a rush on trace. Meantime, we wait. Okay?"

Robby curled his mouth into a frown. "Yeah. Fine."

"Go home, get some rest. I'll post a uniform, make sure no one goes in or out of the place when we leave. Including Hancock."

"Especially Hancock," Robby said.

BLEDSOE WALKED BACK IN, Vail at his side. His brow was furrowed and his hands were shoved into the pockets of his overcoat. He stopped beside Hancock, took a seat on the couch. "I know this is a tough time for you. I'm sorry you had to be the one to discover the body."

Hancock leaned back on the couch.

"You said the senator had asked you to leave the house. What time was that?"

He squinted as if blinding sunlight was bathing his eyes. "I don't know," he whined. "Around seven. Maybe a few minutes after. I wasn't looking at the clock."

"And when did you get back?"

Hancock shrugged, looked across the room at the grandfather clock, as if he were calculating the time by working backwards. "Around eight-thirty."

Manette consulted her notepad. "Nine-one-one was placed around eight-forty-five."

"Then it was closer to eight-forty-five," Hancock said, his hands turning palm up. "Look, if you don't mind, I'd like to be left alone. I've had a really crappy night."

Vail glanced at the bloody trail in the hallway and thought, *Eleanor Linwood could say the same thing.*

*T*he doctor stood between Karen Vail's legs, which were spread wide and resting in stirrups on the birthing table. She had been in labor for six hours, the hospital gown matted down to her slick skin with so much perspiration it appeared as if she had just stepped out of the shower.

Deacon stood by her side, wiping her forehead with a cold, wet cloth, occasionally feeding ice chips into her mouth.

"Ahhh!" Vail bore down, grabbed the edge of the table, and swore under her breath.

"You can do this, honey," Deacon said by her ear. "I know it hurts. Try to breathe through it, like we practiced."

"Ahhh!" Vail winced, then gasped and said, breathless, "Fuck the damn breathing." She brought her right hand up to her large, contracted abdomen, then winced again.

"It won't be long," the doctor said calmly. "The head is crowning. In a minute I'm going to have you push. Not until then. Okay?"

All Vail could manage between clenched teeth was a groan.

Deacon wiped her forehead, leaned close to her ear. "Hang on another few minutes, just another few minutes. Our son's almost here."

"Okay, Karen, here he comes," the doctor said. He pushed his rolling stool away with a flick of his foot, then reached out and placed his fingers atop the baby's crowning head. A nurse came up alongside and pressed a button on the adjacent monitor. "Go ahead and push," the doctor said. "We'll have him out in a jiffy."

Vail bore down, the strain lifting her torso off the bed. "Ahhh! It burns, it burns!"

"He's just about through. That's it, that's it . . . all right!" The doctor guided the baby's shoulder through, then straightened up, his face a wide grin. "Congratulations." He handed the baby to the nurse, who *wrapped the child in a small towel and placed him on Vail's chest. "Do you have a name?"*

"Jonathan Taylor," Deacon said, stroking his baby's soft cheek.

"Jonathan Taylor Tucker, I like it. . . . "

VAIL'S EYES OPENED, locks of hair pasted to her face, thoughts of Jonathan tickling her mind. Her alarm clock glowed 4:35. She looked around, oriented herself, then began crying. Reliving Jonathan's birth, she agonized over the life she'd had, the good-natured man Deacon once was, the joy of bringing her son into the world. How different things were now. As tears rolled onto her pillow, Vail scolded herself for never taking the time to appreciate what she had, when she had it.

She made her way into the family room and picked up a photo of Jonathan as an infant. She touched his face, then held the frame to her chest, hugging it, as if the warmth and love could somehow move through the still photo and invigorate his spirit.

"Please wake up," she whispered.

Vail sat in the family room, sipping hot chocolate and waiting for the sun to rise. The *Today Show* droned from the television. She watched the small digital clock in the corner of the screen tick away, figuring she would go to the hospital as soon as visiting hours began.

Go there and do what? What could she possibly accomplish by sitting at Jonathan's bedside? To talk to him, in case he could hear her? For someone whose work revolved around analytic logic, the concept of talking to a comatose mind seemed designed to comfort those who needed something to cling to. But she realized she was now one of those people. She had to believe Jonathan could hear her, that he could know she was near . . . because if it was true, then there was hope. And as long as there was hope, she could get through the day.

At seven thirty, she walked into the kitchen to refill her mug. Before she could pour the hot chocolate, her doorbell rang. She squinted at the clock and wondered who it would be this time of morning. She walked to the door and saw a large, dark figure standing on her porch. Robby.

"You're here early."

Robby walked in and gave her the once over. "You look like you didn't sleep last night."

"Not true. I slept about four hours."

Robby smirked, then reached out and touched her hair, pushed it off her face and behind her ear. A gentle brush, a tentative, non-threatening gesture to test the waters. "You doing okay?"

She shrugged. "I've had better years." She wanted him to reach out and take her in his arms, to hold her and tell her it's all going to be all right. She needed his company, his strength, his support. They stared at each other, her mind willing him to reach out to her. Instead, he stood there, seemingly reading her face like a closed book. *You usually know what I'm thinking. Why can't you sense my thoughts now?*

As if she had spoken aloud, he reached behind the small of her back and drew her close. She melted into his body, squeezed him tightly. Seconds dissolved into minutes. She didn't want to move, to lose the feeling. It had been too long since she had felt the extreme desire for a male body, for someone she truly wanted to touch and feel and explore and become totally absorbed in.

He bent his head down and with his index finger, tilted her chin back. His full lips met hers, two pillows coming to rest against one another. He pulled back and she slowly opened her eyes. She didn't want the moment to end. She looked at him, desire gripping at the sleeves of his sport coat.

"I can't stay."

"I know." She released him and straightened her nightshirt. "Come by later?"

"If you want."

"I want."

He was silent a few seconds, then said, "Okay." He brought his hand out from behind her back. He was clutching a thick envelope.

"Oh, almost forgot. I brought you a present," he said, handing her the package.

She tore it open and pulled out an overstuffed file folder. "What is this?"

"Copy of everything the task force has in its Dead Eyes file. Copies of the photos are not as good as the real pictures, but at least you've got something to work on."

Vail, still standing with Robby in the entryway, quickly thumbed through the file. She smiled, again feeling part of a team. "Tell Bledsoe I said thanks."

"Will do. We're going to lean on Hancock this morning. Bledsoe called in some favors, got a couple of techs to work through the night. They found some interesting stuff back at Linwood's place that might help us turn him."

"For Linwood or Dead Eyes?"

Robby shrugged. "You tell me."

Vail put a hand on her hip and walked down the hall. She turned and came back, looked up at Robby. "For Linwood, it's possible. Affair gone sour. He's pissed, takes her out. Does a Dead Eyes copycat to throw attention in a totally different direction. As for him being Dead Eyes, I'd have to give it more thought. In some ways he fits the profile, in some ways not. He's bright and organized, right age range and ethnic background, drives the right type of power car. I don't know about his art background, family history, or upbringing. Some of that we can get through his Bureau application.

"But one thing that stands out is that he's injected himself into the investigation by having Linwood place him on the task force. That's common with organized offenders. It's a means of control, of checking in on where the investigation is. Can't get a better finger on the pulse than being named to our team." She nodded slowly. "Be good to see if he was even in the area and alibied at the times of the murders."

"Sin's on it. I'll see about either getting his personnel file from Gifford or ask him to have a look around inside himself."

"Good. Why don't—" The phone's electronic bleat sent her into the kitchen to answer it; it was Cynthia from CART with the lab's analysis of Vail's hard drive.

"I've got good news and bad news," Cynthia said. "First, I've got a guy working on the sender's name, G. G. Condon. But we both know that's going to be a dead end. However, because the offender sent the message to you at work, it was stored on the Academy server. That's the good news. From what we've been able to determine, the way this self-destructing email works is that it sends its message with a tracking number embedded in its source code. Unbeknownst to you, he sent another message simultaneously to our mail server, which also got downloaded into your inbox; it looked like an identical copy of message number one, so you probably ignored it. But its source code was different. The effect was like a ticking time bomb; message two contained simple instructions that identified the tracking code on message one, which triggered a self-destruct countdown as soon as you read it. At the predetermined time, message one "dissolved," to use an inaccurate but descriptive term, into its digital components— ones and zeroes. The message literally vanished."

"Great."

"Actually, it is. We were able to recover the message and routing information, including the second message that erased the first."

"Let's cut to the chase. What'd we learn from all this digital skulking?"

"Your message originated from a cybercafé in Arlington."

"Arlington." She wondered if Kim Rossmo had finished the geographic profile yet. Would Arlington fall within the offender's geographic range? "If we have the time stamp on it, we can check their security cameras to see who was in the café at that time. They do have security cameras, don't they?"

"That would be too easy," Cynthia said. "Either the offender got lucky or he's smart."

"He's smart. Very smart."

"Then I'm afraid the only thing you can do is stake out the place, see if he comes back." Vail's shoulders slumped. "We don't even know what the guy looks like."

"Even if you did, there's no guarantee he'll use the same cybercafé."

"He won't," Vail said with resignation in her voice. "We need to find some other way of tracking him."

"That's your neck of the woods. We decrypt and unlock secrets, report the info to you. You guys get to have all the fun."

Vail had another word for it but thanked Cynthia and hung up. After relaying the information to Robby, she said, "Why don't you go find out what forensics came up with. Meantime, I'll spend some time with the file."

He placed a hand on her cheek, then turned and walked out.

"He's coming up the path," Robby said. Everyone scattered, as if a pebble had been dropped in a pond. Robby pretended to have just arrived and started removing his jacket as Hancock walked through the door. He nodded casually at Hancock, then took his seat.

Bledsoe sauntered in, tossed a few papers onto Sinclair's desk, and stopped in front of Hancock. "You doing okay?"

Hancock shrugged a shoulder. "I wouldn't be here if you hadn't called me."

"We had some stuff to go over. Lab findings. I thought you'd want to get back in the saddle and help us out. We sure could use it."

Del Monaco, sitting at Vail's desk, reclined in his chair, observing Hancock's demeanor, body language, and speech patterns. Sinclair, Manette, and Robby all tried to busy themselves with paperwork, though they each kept an eye on Hancock's movements.

"Yeah, sure. Help any way I can."

"Good. Get me a copy of your CV, I'll circulate it at the station, see if anyone knows somebody who needs a security chief."

Hancock's eyes narrowed. "You'd do that for me?"

"Why not? You've been very helpful with this investigation. You're the one who came up with the artist interpretation of the blood murals. I think that's going to turn out to be significant. Even Karen didn't think of that."

Hancock frowned. Perhaps mentioning Vail's name was a mistake. But a second later, he reached into his leather attaché and removed a stapled document. "It's up to date," Hancock said.

Bledsoe took the papers, then mumbled, "You're definitely prepared."

"Hey Blood," Manette interrupted, "I got a theory on Linwood. Don't know if it's got anything to do with Dead Eyes, because it could just be a copycat, but I was thinking."

"Spill it," Bledsoe said. It was an invitation for everyone to join the discussion.

"Well, I figure that if the husband's alibi holds up, the first thing we should look at is the senator's private life. You know, was she doing a stud on the side."

Bledsoe turned to Hancock. This was Bledsoe's interrogation. He would ask most of the questions directed at their prime suspect. "What do you think, Hancock? You were her security chief. Did she have anything going with anyone?"

Hancock twisted his neck a bit, freeing it from his tight collar. "Senator Linwood having an affair? Absolutely not. She was happily married, far as I could tell."

"Yeah, but hubby wasn't around much. Maybe that presented an opportunity. Or a need."

Hancock shook his head. "Not that I saw. She had her reputation to protect."

He had made a good point. Why would Linwood risk it? "What if someone had something on her, some deep secret, and this was her way of keeping him quiet."

Hancock shrugged, looked away. "I wouldn't know anything about that. Guess it's possible."

Bledsoe nodded slowly. "So nothing happened between the two of you."

"Me?" Hancock leaned back in his chair, as if he were trying to fend off the accusation by putting distance between himself and Bledsoe. "Absolutely not. My job was to guard her, not bone her."

"Well, you failed, then, didn't you? I mean, your job was to guard her, but she ended up dead. And you happened to leave just when she needed you the most."

Hancock sat up straight. "What the hell is this about? What are you saying?"

"We're just talking. It's not about anything." Bledsoe shrugged. "Just trying to get at what happened last night."

"Some deranged maniac killed her, that's what happened."

"You said she and Vail had had an argument, and that the senator was upset afterwards. She told you she needed some space, and you just drove off and left her alone."

Hancock relaxed a bit, pulled out a cigarette. "That's right."

"Well, you're her security guard. Was that a smart thing to do? You could've just gone outside for a smoke. But you left, drove away."

"I drove away. And if I hadn't. . . ." He looked away and shook his head. "She'd probably still be alive." He reached into his pocket and pulled out a lighter. Manette winced as the cigarette ignited.

"You know," Robby said, "the lab faxed us a report this morning." Hancock puffed on his cigarette and seemed to ignore the comment. "The techs are pretty good. We had the best of the best combing Linwood's place. And they found something interesting." Still no response from Hancock.

"What'd they find?" Sinclair asked.

"Something I've never seen. Some Turkish cigarette tobacco in the senator's bedroom." Robby paused, looked at Hancock. The others turned to him as well.

Hancock lifted his head and noticed their gazes. "Look, you want to lean on someone, what about Vail? She had big time motive, means, and opportunity. Not to mention a violent history."

Everyone was silent.

"I'd rather talk about the tobacco," Bledsoe said. He kept his voice calm, his eyes riveted on Hancock.

"There's nothing to talk about. I spent a lot of time around the house. I smoked here and there. Hell, you'll probably even find clothing fibers and DNA around the place, too. I worked there, for Christ's sake."

"You're right," Robby said, looking at the report. "There were hair and fibers there, too."

"See?"

Robby nodded. "Simple transfer."

"Exactly."

"Except that the tobacco fibers were found embedded in the bed sheets. Linwood's bed sheets." Robby tilted his head back and waited for a response.

"Like you said, simple transfer."

"I want to accept that," Bledsoe said, standing and starting to pace, circling Hancock. "I really do, because the thought of one of us doing the senator in such a grotesque way . . . turns my stomach." He stopped in front of Hancock and looked down at him. "We also found dried semen on the bed sheets. Her husband had been in Asia for nearly two weeks. I bet if we run the semen, it won't be his."

"Fine, then run it."

Bledsoe leaned forward, rested his hands on the armrests of Hancock's chair. "Come on, Hancock. We know about the affair."

"What affair?"

"Don't insult us any more than you already have. We have a very reliable source who'll be more than willing to testify."

Pushing Bledsoe's large, unyielding frame out of his way, Hancock struggled to stand. "I don't have to sit here and take this. If you had something, you'd have cuffed me by now." He shook his head, his lips bent into a frown. Shaming them. "You people have a viable suspect—Karen Vail—but you're not interested. You think you hold all the cards? Wait till I let the media know Lee Thurston's finest is dodging the investigation, overlooking the one person who's quite possibly the Dead Eyes killer, all because they're protecting one of their own."

"Gather your things and get the hell out of here," Bledsoe said. "In case you're wondering, you're off the task force. There's no senator to pull strings for you. And the police chief won't touch you with a ten foot pole."

Hancock snatched up his attaché, threw assorted papers inside, and grabbed his coat.

Robby rose from his chair and rested his hands on his hips. "Talk to the media, and you'll only bring more heat on yourself."

Hancock stormed to the front door, stopped, and turned around. "You people are imbeciles."

"At least we've got jobs," Sinclair said. "You're an *unemployed* imbecile."

The door slammed and Hancock was gone.

I usually take some cheese into my secret room for Charlie to munch on. He's getting a little fat, probably because I feed him too much. But whenever I go there, it's like I've come home and he comes over to say hi. He climbs into my lap and sniffs around. Probably looking for more food. Damn parasite, that's all he is. Give me, give me, give me.

I'm not in the mood today. The prick's latest whore saw me last night and made fun of me. I didn't need that, I get enough of it from him. I'd like to make him feel the way he makes me feel for once.

Charlie climbs up on my chest and looks at me, his tiny nose wiggling and his whiskers shaking accusingly at me.

"What the hell is your problem?" I shout, then stop to think if anyone is home. I can't let this little rodent ruin things. He looks at me with those eyes, evil eyes. "Don't look at me that way! I hate you!"

I grab him by the neck and reach to my right, where there are some nails left over from the construction I'd done to expand the room. I pick one up and jam it right through his eye socket. He stiffens, then goes limp in my hand.

My heart is beating rapidly, and I feel high, like I'm floating. What a feeling! I'm wired, I can't get a deep breath.

I throw Charlie's body down on the shelf mounted on the wall and pull out my pocket knife. I wonder what he'd look like if I just make a slice right here. I pant like a dog, unable to control myself. A dog. Now that would be something. Do this to a dog—

He remembered that day quite well. Certain memories just stick in your mind like a piece of chewing gum on the bottom of a shoe. You pull and twist and stretch and the damn gum just won't let go.

He shut down the laptop and put it aside. He had a little less than an hour before students started arriving for his advanced pottery class and he needed to decompress, turn his thoughts away from his childhood. He grabbed an unfinished sandwich from the small refrigerator and switched on the television. But of course he wouldn't be able to escape it altogether. After all, he'd made the news. Literally made it. The Dead Eyes killer was a nightly story, if only as a feature piece on public safety. But he was always mentioned.

Yet somehow, the police had managed to keep a tight lid on the Linwood murder. Guess it would kind of freak people out if they heard that the Dead Eyes killer had gotten to a state senator. If he could get to a senator, no bitch-whore would be safe. "You hear that? None of you are safe!"

He finished the sandwich, then sat in front of the TV kneading a hunk of clay. Kneading clay relaxed him, kept his hands and arms strong.

The six o'clock news logo swirled onto the screen with a building crescendo of music and a photo array of its anchors. Such drama. Just report the goddamn news and cut the fat.

"Good evening," the anchor said. *Yes, it was indeed a good evening, thank you very much.* He felt satisfied, the way you feel after eating a well-cooked meal.

". . . the murder of Senator Eleanor Linwood has stunned members of the legislature and caused an outpouring of support across bipartisan lines. The senator's husband, Richard Linwood, heir to the Linwood Shipping empire, was reportedly returning home from a business trip. Police are not releasing many details about the murder, except to say leads are being pursued. For more complete coverage on Senator Linwood's long career, we go to Steve Schneiderman, standing by live. . . . "

He switched off the television, went to his freezer, and took out the container holding the beloved senator's hand. He set the severed appendage on the table beside him and looked at it, observing it from multiple angles. "You were a very naughty bitch, *Senator*. Would anyone have voted for you if they knew the type of person you really were? Of course not. Of course not. Of course not."

Well, he hoped she enjoyed their time together. He sure did. It was the most satisfying event of his life. He felt free again. Free . . . free to do whatever he wanted to, because she wasn't there to stop him.

Almost free. Because there were a few loose ends that needed to be tied up. But there was time for that. If there was one thing he could be sure of, it was that time was on his side.

Vail had spent the afternoon at the hospital, holding Jonathan's hand, stroking his hair, talking to him. Just in case. She told him she loved him about a hundred times, or maybe it was more. It didn't matter. He was still comatose, and although previously his eyes only opened and closed, they now moved side to side and tracked moving objects. As time passed, it was increasingly difficult for her to get excited over "incremental improvement."

But the doctor continued to be encouraging: "He's taking small steps. No matter how small, they *are* small steps. We have to remain hopeful."

Vail shook her head. It sounded similar to what Gifford and Robby had said. Maybe she needed to start taking their words to heart.

After returning to her house, she grabbed the Dead Eyes file and spread the paperwork out on the floor in her study. The profile and supporting information went in one pile, the crime scene photos in another, VICAP reports on each victim grouped with victimology analyses. Interview notes with family members, employers, and acquaintances were placed in another spot. Medical examiner, forensic, and lab reports were separated out and laid across the floor.

Vail stood up and looked at it all, neatly organized. Like the offender.

She sat on the futon couch beside the long wall of the eight-by-ten room and let everything flow through her mind, not stopping to analyze any particular item. The blood murals, the messages left at each scene after the disputed third victim, the severed left hand, the knives through the eyes. Disemboweled vics, easily disabled. Substantial planning involved. Intelligent offender. *Organized*. Her thoughts had come full circle.

The doorbell rang. She pulled herself off the futon and meandered to the front door. Robby was standing there with a bouquet of
flowers. "Good afternoon, Miss, care to make a contribution to the
Police Officer's Foundation?"

Vail pushed opened the screen door and said, "Sure, Officer.
Here's my donation." She reached out, grabbed his lapel, and pulled
him down to her height. Planted a hard kiss on his lips. She leaned
back and studied his face.

"I'll make sure you get a receipt. For tax purposes."

He bent over and lifted her off her feet, carrying her in his arms
into the family room, where they kissed again. They fell onto the
couch, tongues probing, hands exploring—

Suddenly, Vail stopped. She rested her head on Robby's chest, a
hand on his shoulder.

"What's the matter?"

"I don't want anything to ruin the moment. Can we just lie here
for a few minutes?"

"Of course."

Seconds passed. She asked, "Do you mind if we slow it down a
bit? I just need some time. I'm not sure what I want. I mean, I know
what I want. It's just that with so much going on right now, maybe
it's best to wait—"

Robby pressed fingers to her lips. "You want to wait, we'll wait. I
think I can withstand a few more cold showers." They smiled.

"Thanks."

"We'll grab some dinner. A movie, too, while we're out. I think
we could both use a good escape."

She nodded against his chest. "In a little while. For the moment,
I just want to stay right where I am."

"So teach me more." Robby grabbed his rolled burrito and held an end of it in front of his mouth. "About profiling."

Vail unwrapped the foil that cocooned her food. "Not exactly the sort of conversation made for dinner. But if it doesn't bother you, I'm game." She sighed, eyes down, searching the table between them but seeing nothing. "Typing the offender is an important consideration. With Dead Eyes, it's a question I've grappled with over and over again. What type of offender is this guy?"

"I thought he was organized."

"He is, yes. But there's more to it than just organized or disorganized. Kim Rossmo—the guy who I asked to do a geographic profile, talks about classifying offenders by the way they search for their victims, and the way they go about attacking them. He classifies them as *hunters, poachers, trollers,* and *trappers.* I'm fairly sure Dead Eyes is either a hunter or poacher. A hunter uses his home as a focal point and goes out in search of a victim. A poacher also goes in search of a victim but chooses a different place as his focal point. Could be where he works or some other place he's comfortable around—even if he has to travel to get there."

"Okay, so he's an organized hunter or poacher."

She held up a hand. "It's not quite that simple."

"Somehow I knew it wouldn't be."

Vail smiled. "If it was simple, you guys wouldn't need people like us." She took a sip of her ice tea, then continued: "There are three victim attack methods. A *raptor* attacks a victim as soon as he sees her. A *stalker* finds his victim, then follows her for a while before attacking her. An *ambusher* behaves like a spider, luring her to his safe place, where he can be in total control, and then attacks. Based on the fact that Dead Eyes attacks them in their own home, and appears to be of high intelligence, I'd think he spends some amount of time casing out the house and the neighborhood before going in for the kill. That's why he only chooses front doors that are hidden from the street."

Robby swallowed. "Then he's an organized hunting or poaching stalker. How does this help us?"

"First of all, it's another tool in establishing linkage. Linkage is an issue for vic three—we know that—but also with Linwood. At first glance, she appears to be the work of the same offender, but in some respects not. Aside from linkage, a geographic profile uses the search and attack classifications to create a distribution of where the offender has already struck, and where he might strike next. If we overlay this analysis on top of a map, we can make certain inferences. And if he's not a poacher, it might even give us an idea where he lives."

"When will this geographic profile be done?"

"Hopefully soon."

Robby took another bite of his burrito, then nodded.

THE CLOUDS HAD RETURNED. Gray skies and the threat of rain hovered like salt in sea air. After dinner, Robby and Vail went to a movie and made out like pimply-faced high school kids. Their next stop was Davina's Creamery for dessert, before ending up at Robby's place. They fell asleep on the couch in each other's arms, their empty dishes of ice cream resting on the coffee table. The next morning, Robby drove her home on his way to the task force op center.

Upon pulling up to the curb by Vail's house, he nodded at the open front door. "Please tell me you're expecting someone."

She followed his gaze. "What?" Her eyes narrowed as they found the door. She reached for her Glock and got out of the car in one motion.

Robby drew his weapon and followed her oblique path across the lawn. Using hand signals, Vail indicated she'd go right and he should go left. She rested her back against the brick; Robby ducked below eye level and scrambled across the front of the house.

She nodded to him, then turned the screen door's knob and

pulled it open. He held it in place with the toe of his shoe as she entered in a crouch, gun tip out in front of her. She moved through the hallway, Robby at her heels.

She motioned him into the kitchen, while she went left, into the living room. They converged in the hallway and continued on toward the bedrooms.

Vail toed open the door to her study and peered in. She cleared the room, then took in the mess of documents scattered across the floor. Her copy of the Dead Eyes file, rifled through. At first glance, with such a blizzard of papers, it was impossible to determine what was missing.

They finished clearing the house, then returned to Vail's study. She sat on the futon, her face resting in her hands.

Robby sat beside her. "Looks like you had a visitor."

Without looking up, she nodded. "He got my profile. All my notes."

"Who did?"

Vail turned her head slightly, nodded at the wall behind them. Written in lipstick were the words they'd seen so many times before: "It's in the."

"**H**oly shit."

Robby couldn't help himself; the words just tumbled from his lips. "He was here, in your place. He went through your stuff—"

"And saw the profile. He now knows everything we know about him."

"Holy shit."

"So you said."

"I gotta call Bledsoe," he murmured, then rooted out his cell phone. "We gotta get crime scene here, have them comb through this place."

"Call Bledsoe, but we can't have any techies here. I wasn't supposed to have the file. We'd all be canned faster than the Jolly Green Giant."

"Just don't touch anything. Let's get out of here, wait out front."

She followed him out of the house, the Glock still in her right hand, dangling at her side. She was off in another dimension, thoughts swimming in her head, gurgling up to the surface before she could push them back down.

Robby pressed END and dropped the phone back in his pocket. "He's on his way. Should be here in fifteen, he's at the op center."

"He'll make it in ten." Her voice was flat, her mind numb. She sat down on the cement steps of the porch and cradled her head in her hands. The hard, rough surface of the Glock dug into her face. She didn't care.

"I can't believe it. He was in my goddamn house. Why me?"

"That's the question, Karen. Why you?"

Vail shook her head. "I don't know."

Robby started walking away toward his car.

"Where you going?"

"I've got a kit in my trunk. We can at least document the scene, dust for prints."

"Yeah," she said beneath her breath, "and tighten the nooses around our necks another notch."

Robby walked in with a medium-size toolbox. He set it on the kitchen table and removed the fingerprinting kit. "It's been a good three years since I did this."

"You don't want to know how many years it's been for me."

He removed the two-ounce vial of black dust and handed Vail the stiff brush. "Be careful. These bristles cut the print if you're not careful."

"Lovely." She headed down the hall. "I assume we start with the study because we know for sure he was in there."

"Makes the most sense. Honestly, I doubt we'll find anything. Guy's been real careful up to now. Not one stray print in six crime scenes. No reason to think he'd take his gloves off for this one."

"Maybe he doesn't see this as a crime scene. Breaking and entering's nothing compared to serial murder."

Robby started at the doorway. He took the brush from Vail, swirled it between his fingers to fluff out the bristles, then dipped the tip into the vial. He deposited the dust around the frame, taking care to brush lightly. "If you've got a camera, I'd snap some pictures. Let's do it right."

Vail fished out her HP 8-megapixel point-and-shoot from the closet and began documenting the scene. Using the standard protocol for crime scene photography, she shot the study from various angles, including close-ups of the message on the wall and the layout of the papers on the floor.

"Why don't you take the ninhydrin," he said. "Start spraying the papers on the floor. We know he went through them. If he wasn't wearing gloves, the most likely place we'll find a print is on those papers."

They worked for the next fifteen minutes when Vail heard a "Hello!" through the screen door. Bledsoe. They walked to the porch and stepped out, each holding their tools of the trade.

"What the hell are you two doing?"

"Checking for prints."

"This may be news to you, but we've got *trained* personnel for shit like that."

"We were trained in evidence collection," Vail said. "It's just been a while."

"Yeah, a long while." Bledsoe looked around them, through the screen door. "So fill me in."

Vail pulled off her latex gloves with a snap. "I had the papers spread out across the floor of my study, the ones Robby brought by yesterday. The Dead Eyes file. I went out for dinner and a movie last night and . . . got back this morning, about half an hour ago."

Bledsoe's eyebrows lifted and he gave a sideways glance at Robby. Adding it up. Vail was sure he hadn't known there was something between them. But now he was probably patching it all together in his head. The overnight to Westbury, the rapport they seemed to share.

"So you think Dead Eyes was in your house sometime between last night and this morning?"

"Don't you?"

"It seems to be the obvious conclusion," Bledsoe said. "He's trying to scare you. Trying to get inside your head."

"Yeah, well, it worked."

"Okay, I think some conclusions are in order," Bledsoe continued. "One, the offender knows where you live. Second, he obviously found out your email address. For whatever reason, he feels the need to play head games with you. That's good. If we can bait him, we can eventually catch him."

"And it also places Karen at risk. I don't think there's anything good in that."

Bledsoe looked away. "It's the element we deal with. We're always at risk."

"It also tells us that he went to considerable effort to find your home address," Robby said.

Vail nodded. "You're adding to the profile."

"Nothing we don't already know. His approach indicates planning, which means intelligence. Organization."

"Do we know what he did while he was here?"

"He rifled through the labs, forensic reports . . . and my profile. He now knows everything we know about him. Ed Kemper all over again."

"Kemper," Bledsoe said, snapping his fingers. "Kemper—I've heard that name."

"Serial killer who hung out with cops at their favorite watering hole. He knew all the moves the dicks were making, all the evidence they had, because they would tell him. They never suspected he was the killer."

They stood there staring at each other. Vail could tell the impact of this was beginning to hit them.

"So it's possible this guy will alter his MO," Robby said, "now that he knows our analysis of him—and his crime scenes?"

"Yes. He could alter his MO. But his ritual behavior would remain the same." Vail shrugged. "Then again, I've never seen something like this happen before. And Kemper was before my time."

Bledsoe asked, "What about getting Del Monaco's take? He said he's been in your unit the longest. Maybe he's had a case where the profile's been compromised."

"We can't ask Del Monaco." Vail looked down at the cracked cement. "In order to ask him, we'd have to tell him that I had all these documents here. The next question he'd ask is—"

"How you got all this stuff if you're suspended and off the case," Bledsoe finished.

Robby held up a hand. "Let's back up a second. We can't be sure the offender actually saw the profile. We haven't inventoried all the papers to see if he's taken anything."

Without a word, Vail turned and headed into the study, her compatriots following behind. She pulled on another pair of latex gloves, got down on her hands and knees, and started searching. Since it wasn't the actual file, but loose papers she had organized into piles, it was more difficult to arrive at an accurate accounting.

"Well?" Bledsoe asked. "Is it here or not?"

Vail kept pushing papers aside, moving to another section of the floor and sifting through other piles. Finally, she sat cross-legged on the floor and slumped back against the futon. "It's gone, along with the victimology analyses, VICAP forms, and. . . . "

"And what?" Bledsoe asked.

Vail swallowed hard. "The crime scene photos."

There was silence. Finally, Robby spoke. "Karen, we really need to report this."

She sat up suddenly. "Are you out of your mind? You'll destroy two careers, and mine is already on the edge of the cliff."

Robby sat down on the floor next to her. In a soft voice, he said, "Karen, this is bad. Very bad. It'll affect this entire investigation."

"The only one conducting this investigation is the task force," Bledsoe bellowed. "The three of us here makes half the group. Besides, I run the damn thing and I already know what happened. Tell anyone, Bureau or PD, and it'll be a lynching. With Thurston's nose in everything, he'll suspend me, for Christ's sake. My guess, Robby, is that you won't stand a rat's chance in a pool of cyanide of escaping the purge. And then the whole investigation will hit the brakes. No, I say we keep this little . . . situation between the three of us."

Vail looked at her ethical colleague, he looked at her, and then they both looked at Bledsoe.

Everyone nodded and the contract was sealed.

The agreement having been reached, the question begging for an answer was Vail's connection to the offender. They stood there, hands on hips, the issue riding on the air between them.

"Whatever the answer is, I don't think it's safe for you to stay here. He knows where you live, where to find you."

Vail clenched her jaw. "I'm not leaving. I'm not letting him run me out of my house." She turned and walked away. "I won't do it."

Bledsoe shared a look with Robby.

"She can stay at my place," Robby said. "I've got an extra room."

The corners of Vail's mouth curled upwards, but she turned slightly so Bledsoe wouldn't see. *That was funny, Robby.* She knew Bledsoe was too good a cop not to suspect there was something between them.

"Yeah, good, whatever," Bledsoe said.

"Okay," Robby said. "Go pack some things and I'll—"

"No." Vail said it firmly, as if it was the final word on the topic.

But Bledsoe was not to be denied his say. "We made a pact on this break-in. But the deal's off if you're going to put your life in danger without good reason. And this isn't a good reason."

Robby nodded. "I agree. Draw your line in the sand with this guy some other way."

Vail let her arms fall to her sides. "Fine," she sighed. "I'll stay at your place. For a few days."

"And I'll get someone in civvies posted near Jonathan's room. Not sure how I'll explain it, but I'll find a way."

"Then we're back to the main question," Robby said. "Your connection to the offender."

Vail shrugged and headed down the hall to the study. Most of the papers had been sprayed with ninhydrin and carefully stacked. "Can you get these processed?"

Bledsoe shook open a plastic bag. "I'll have a guy at the lab do it for me. He owes me some favors for a private job I did for him. Helped him out big time in his divorce settlement. He'll run them, no questions, no strings." He placed the stack of papers in the bag, along with the memory card from her camera.

"Cool," Robby said.

Vail was leaning against her desk, staring at the wall above the futon, where the offender's message was scrawled. "It's in the," she mumbled.

Robby rolled his head from side to side. "He didn't write it in blood this time." He leaned closer. With his height, he was almost looking directly at it. "Looks like lipstick—"

"That's it," Vail said, moving to Robby's side.

Bledsoe set the bag on the desk and joined them. "That's what?"

Vail shared a look with Robby. "I can't believe we didn't see it before," he said.

She shook her head, disbelief knitting her brows together. "It was right there."

"What was?"

Vail half smiled. "It's in the *blood*, every message he's left was written in blood." Vail crossed her arms and leaned her right shoulder against the wall. "Offender could be a disgruntled lover, someone who got HIV or hepatitis or some other viral infection from a woman. It would fit the pattern of offenders who displace their anger against a particular woman to all women in general—or against specific women who remind him of the one who infected him. The familiarity could be a scent, a touch, a look. For all we know, that woman had brown eyes, like our vics. But again, this is all just a possibility and if we look at possibilities, the field is very wide. I'm not sure that would really be helping us."

Bledsoe paced for a moment, then pulled his cell phone. "Let's meet at the op center in thirty minutes. I'll get everyone over there."

"You want me there?"

"For this, yes. I'll take the heat."

FRANK DEL MONACO greeted Vail as she entered the front door to the operations center. "Not a good idea for you to be here, Karen."

"I'm a big girl, Frank. You don't need to be my parent. I'll deal with Gifford."

Del Monaco unfurled the front page of the *Washington Herald* and held it in front of Vail's face. The bold headline was like a kick to her gut:

IS FBI AGENT DEAD EYES KILLER?
POSSIBLE TIES TO SENATOR'S DEATH

A large photo of Vail, taken several years ago during an FBI-DEA drug bust in New York City, accompanied the article. She had always liked the picture—she was cuffing the suspect, straddling his legs, her hair tousled and a serious look on her face. The photo documented one of the biggest cases she had ever broken. It had been framed by the *New York Post* and now hung on a wall in her office.

"What the hell is this?" She snatched the paper from his hands and began reading. Bledsoe and Robby read over her shoulder:

Sources close to the FBI charged today that the identity of the Dead Eyes killer is known to the Bureau, but that the Bureau has been reluctant to move against the killer because she is one of their own, Special Agent Karen Vail. Vail, the profiler assigned to the Dead Eyes case for the Behavioral Analysis Unit, is currently serving a suspension for brutally assaulting her ex-husband—an attack that sent him to the hospital with fractured bones. . . .

"Son of a bitch."

Informed sources also state that Senator Eleanor Linwood— whose death has been kept under tight seal by the Vienna Police

Department—was murdered by the Dead Eyes killer. In a
bizarre, though related twist, it appears that the senator was
Agent Vail's biological mother, though the senator abandoned her
as an infant. . . .

Vail leaned back against the entryway wall and slid her butt to the
floor. Her legs were weak and she was light-headed. Bledsoe and
Robby knelt at her side.

"Karen, you okay?"

"Del Monaco," Bledsoe said, making no attempt to temper his
anger, "make yourself useful and get her some water."

The voices were off in the distance. She was aware of Robby
kneeling in front of her, holding her arm. His touch was warm, his
hands moist. A glass was pressed against her lips, and she drank
reflexively.

She could sense Manette off to her left. Robby was peering into
her eyes. She set the glass down and asked him to help her over to a
chair. He guided her to the nearest desk and remained by her side.
She could feel her senses returning, her mind clearing. Everyone was
staring at her.

"I'm sorry," she mumbled.

"You don't have to apologize," Bledsoe said. "Hancock threatened to go to the media unless we moved on you. It's all bullshit.
Don't worry about it."

"We're behind you, Kari," Manette said. "You'll get through
this."

Vail wet her parched lips. "Gifford. I've gotta talk to Gifford."

"He's on his way," Del Monaco said, setting the phone handset
on the desk. He was standing in the kitchen doorway.

"You told him she's here?" Robby asked, his face contorting into
a snarl. He started toward Del Monaco, but Bledsoe grabbed his
thick arm. Robby shrugged it off and in two strides was in front of
Del Monaco, his large hands gathered around the profiler's suit
lapels. "What were you thinking?"

"I was thinking about my job, Hernandez. My boss called me and said he'd tried reaching her. If I don't tell him she's here, it's my ass that's going to get whooped." He shrugged against Robby's grip. "Now, let go of me or I'll have a chat with your sergeant."

Bledsoe was behind Robby, his five-eight frame barely putting him up to Robby's shoulders. "C'mon, Hernandez. We're all upset by this. Let's just get a grip on things." He reached forward and pried Robby's hands off Del Monaco's jacket. Del Monaco looked up at Robby and then smoothed out his wrinkled lapels.

Robby turned toward Vail, who gave him a tight nod. Bledsoe was right, and she knew Robby knew it. She took another gulp of water, wishing it was something stronger, like scotch or gin—neither of which she drank. But at least it would deaden her anxiety.

The front door to the op center swung open and in walked Sinclair. He seemed to notice the quiet, the tension on everyone's faces. "Another vic?" His face went down to his cell, as if he'd somehow missed the code.

"No," Bledsoe said, then motioned him aside to fill him in.

Vail rested her head in her hands, trying to absorb the impact of what was about to happen. The implications were plentiful and threatened to overwhelm her.

She felt Robby's hand on her shoulder, just resting there, no doubt his way of telling her she had his support. She knew there was nothing he could say or do to ease the pain of being the focus of a national media lynching. How convenient to have a suspect, a name and face on which anger and outrage could be pinned. All delivered in a front page article that was soon going to be picked up by the international press.

She took a deep, uneven breath and looked up. Everyone was looking away, avoiding the situation. "We've got work to do," she said, her voice hoarse and raspy. She tipped her chin at Bledsoe, who was still leaning against a wall chatting with Sinclair.

He pushed back from the wall. "Yeah. Let's get to it." He moved to the front of the living room. "Karen's got a new theory on what the messages mean. They were all written in blood, so 'It's in the' could mean 'It's in the blood.'" He paused, noticed a few raised eyebrows.

"HIV," Manette said.

Robby remained beside Vail. The warmth of his body, of his presence, made her feel more confident. She couldn't recall the last time she had relied on anyone else for self-assurance.

"That's the first thing to look at," Robby said. "HIV, AIDS, Hepatitis C."

"Let's dole out some assignments and get on it," Bledsoe said. "Manny, get us a list of all area blood banks, and a roster of the organizations and medical facilities they supply. We'll have to go through each of their databases and cross-reference them with the FBI's national database to see if we get any hits. We're looking for males who've received donated blood that was tainted."

"That's like fishing with a little pole in a big lake," Manette said. "And I can tell you as a woman, that ain't no fun, if you get my drift." A seductive smile spread her lips and she winked at a blushing Bledsoe. "How about we start with the vics? Were any of them infected with HIV or hepatitis?"

"Sexual innuendoes aside, Manette's right," Vail said. "I say we look for a connection to the blood through the vics."

Bledsoe considered this a moment, then nodded. "That would help narrow our suspect pool, wouldn't it?" He shook his head, as if embarrassed he hadn't thought of that. "I'll look into it."

"He could be finding the women through the blood bank," Manette said. "Maybe our guy works there and the vics donated regularly. I'd get a list of their female donors. See if any of our vics donated within the past couple of years."

Vail mulled this over, then realized those parameters would be too limiting. "What about other blood sources? He could've been in a hospital and gotten a bad pint. If that's the case, and for some reason he thinks a woman was responsible, bingo—that's all it would take to get him going."

"Then we should also check out the labs. Hospital and private,"

Robby said. "Employees, suppliers, subcontractors. Anyone with a record or history of mental illness."

"Do we want to go regional?" Del Monaco asked. "Or even national?"

"First start locally," Vail said. "If we look at all the possible labs in the country, we'll be doing paperwork for the next year while our killer continues to do his thing. I say if the local angle comes up empty, then we expand to regional. Then national."

Del Monaco's right foot was dancing, tapping the floor with anger. "I disagree. Regional first. Split it up, we should get it done in a few days."

"Serial killers start close to home because it's familiar territory to them," Vail said.

Del Monaco's ample face shaded red. "I don't need you to tell me that, Karen—"

"Start locally," Bledsoe said firmly. "Focus our efforts within a fifty mile radius. We need to, we can always look further."

"The geographic profile would help narrow it down," Vail said. Let Bledsoe pressure Del Monaco.

Bledsoe cocked his head to one side, his eyes coming to rest on Del Monaco, who was pretending to read some papers. He must have felt Bledsoe's glare, because he spoke without lifting his head. "Kim Rossmo's associate was preparing it. I'll look into it."

"Good," Bledsoe said. "Much better when we all cooperate with each other, isn't it? We're on the same side, working toward a common goal: to catch this fucker. Let's not forget that." He waited a beat, then told them to get started on their new assignments.

GIFFORD ARRIVED AT THE OP CENTER thirty-five minutes later, moments after everyone had left. Vail had just finished running another copy of the case file when the door swung open and Gifford walked in. His black raincoat was open, his hands shoved deep into the pockets. He had a direct line of sight of Vail, who stood with her hands on the lid of the copier. The case file was splayed open. She turned and headed toward him, hoping he would not see what she had been duplicating. It would require an explanation, and what she needed were answers, not more questions.

"Sir," she said, meeting him ten feet from the copier. "Frank said you wanted to see me."

"I texted you. Never got a response."

She pulled the BlackBerry from her belt and inspected the display. "Never came through."

He stood there, looking down at her. "Uh huh." He turned and looked around the converted living room/dining room and nodded approvingly. "Nice setup."

"Bledsoe's a pro. He runs a tight ship."

"Evidently not tight enough." Boom. Direct hit.

Vail stood there awkwardly, wondering if she should sit or keep standing. She had never felt intimidated by Gifford before, but now was different. He came here to talk with her, the revelation about Linwood fresh in his mind. The *Herald's* allegations, for which he had to answer, no doubt at the forefront of his thoughts. For the moment, she would let him call the shots.

He took a seat at the closest desk, which was Sinclair's. He lifted the basketball, which stood on a small stand, and rolled it around with his fingertips. "Signed by Jordan?"

Vail nodded. "Bubba Sinclair's. He keeps it here for good luck."

"Hmph."

Just that, an indirect swipe at the task force, as if to say "a lot of good it's done you." But he kept his comment to himself, which was fine with her. She didn't need any overt sarcasm to piss her off. In her current state, she didn't know how she would react, and the last thing she needed was to fly off the handle at her boss.

Still holding the ball, rolling it with his fingertips, his eyes watching it spin, he leaned back in the chair and said simply, "So, was it true, that Linwood was your mother?"

"Yes." Short answer, to the point. Less trouble that way.

"Hmph." He stopped rolling the ball and peered over the top at Vail. "Was it true, that you had an argument with her the night she was murdered?"

"Yes."

Gifford nodded. "And you didn't see fit to mention this when we were standing in front of her house?"

"No, sir."

"Why the hell not?" His voice was loud, his brow bunched.

Vail cleared her throat. "Because if I told you about it, you would never have let me view the crime scene. And, because it's irrelevant. I didn't kill her."

He leaned forward in the chair, the springs squeaking with the shift in his weight. "Agent Vail, that has to rank with one of the stupidest things you've ever done in your career."

"Yes, sir. I told Bledsoe and Hernandez—"

"Oh, do they outrank me now? I'm your boss, Vail, and you seem to have a knack for forgetting that lately."

"Sir, I only meant to help."

He rolled the ball some more. "Help. Well, I sure need that now, don't I? Director Knox is on my case. The goddamn director called me this morning and set a meeting for this afternoon. You know what that means? It means my ass is in the sling. My job is on the line."

"I didn't mean to involve you. It's Hancock—"

"Hancock! Yes, it is Hancock who's the problem, isn't it? The same guy I told you to back off of, to leave alone and let hang himself."

"Sir, he went to the media to deflect attention off himself. The task force leaned on him, he'd had an affair—"

"I know all about the affair. When Thurston mentioned it in the car after we left you, I was the one who pushed him to call Bledsoe and tell him." Gifford put the basketball back down on the stand, stood up, and faced the wall. "We issued an official denial to the story, of course." He buried his hands in his pockets again. "I don't know where this is going to lead, but I can tell you one thing: it's not going to be fun. For any of us." He turned to face her. "I got seventeen calls from the media this morning. After the *Herald* broke the story, everyone in the country picked it up. A buddy of mine at

New Scotland Yard even heard about it. What's bigger than the FBI covering up the fact that one of its profilers is a serial killer?"

"With all due respect, sir, you're not the only injured party here." She suddenly felt empowered, fed up by the fact that the entire focus was on him. "I'm the one they're saying brutally murdered seven innocent women. How do you think that makes me feel?"

Gifford did not say anything. He looked away, kicked at an exposed power cord that ran along the carpet to the computer on Bledsoe's desk. "There's only one way to solve this problem." He looked up at her.

"Find the killer," she said.

Gifford walked past her and grabbed the doorknob. "Find the killer."

Vail watched him walk out and stood there wondering if that was his unofficial way of telling her to pull out all the stops . . . or merely a self-affirmation that they needed to find the person responsible for making his life a living hell.

As she stood there, she realized it did not matter. Dead Eyes had targeted her, broken into her house, and violated her space. Now he was helping dismantle her career. She needed to find this guy soon, before he killed her—from within.

Now it was personal.

The weather turned for the worse in the space of an hour, with dark storm clouds and high winds moving in as temperatures plummeted. After having spent the past three hours with Jonathan, Vail sat in her study, fingerprint powder still splashed across the door frame. Though she did not plan on staying at her house long, her presence there was enough to satisfy her need to show the killer she would not be driven from her home. Nevertheless, her Glock sat on her lap, ready for action.

The phone had not stopped ringing. News stations and reporters from all over the country, all wanting her take on the accusations made by the unnamed source. She wanted to tell them everything, tell them they were chasing lies, pursuing bad news, being led astray by a manipulator whose only intent was to deflect attention off himself.

But she would not dare say any of that. Her life was in a precarious place right now, and the best course to follow was to keep her mouth shut. In situations like hers, no one got into trouble by saying nothing.

The phone rang again and the machine snapped on. She had turned the volume up so she could listen from the study, screening the calls in case it was one she needed to take. But it was another reporter, this one from southern California. She sighed and turned back to the Dead Eyes file. This copy she would carry with her wherever she went. But she knew it was a ridiculous precaution: too little, too late. The damage had already been done.

As she sat there, she began thinking the connection between her and the UNSUB had to go back to her relationship with Eleanor Linwood, Dead Eyes' seventh victim. Her biological mother was the focal point of the killer's rage, it seemed. That much had been evident by the violence imparted to Linwood's face and body. Assuming Hancock was not involved. And as much as she wanted to believe he was the one responsible, something told her deep down that he was incapable of such fury. She had pushed him quite hard, challenged him and his abilities many times over. And not once had it caused him to come after her. Overtly or covertly. There was the threat, recently, at the op center, but she wrote that off as merely a tangle of testosterone and ego. Not nearly the same motivator as a love affair gone sour with all the emotions—anger, betrayal, rejection—that accompanied it.

But he had blamed Vail for destroying his career. Again, not as strong as breaking off an affair . . . yet it did seem to have caused him significant embarrassment. And it did have over six years to fester. . . .

She rubbed at her eyes, then consulted her watch. Time to get back to Robby's. As she gathered the papers together, her phone rang again. This time it was a fax signal. On cue, her OfficeJet woke up and began receiving the transmission. She looked at the display and recognized the station identifier as one belonging to the profiling unit.

Finally, the cover page emerged: there was a handwritten note from Del Monaco indicating the geographic profile was to follow. Her heart seemed to thump faster as the pages rolled out. She struggled to read the text as the paper exited the printer.

Realizing it would be a long document, she walked out of the room to grab a Scharffen Berger mocha bar. Dark chocolate settled her nerves or at least seemed to mollify her agitated state whenever something was bothering her. *These days, I should keep a box of these things in my car.*

She heard the fax beep, signaling the end of transmission, and ran into the study. She pulled the stack of pages from the OfficeJet and called Bledsoe. "I've got the geographic profile," she said. "Can we get everyone together in a couple of hours to discuss it?"

He said he would, and like a kid who's just returned from trick or treating with a full bag of candy, she dove into the report.

The task force op center was blanketed in snow. It had been falling for the past two hours, the white powder sticking to the asphalt and making driving a challenge. Rather, the challenge was driving without skidding into a tree or another car.

Vail grabbed her leather satchel, then got out of the car, shooing the falling snowflakes from her face. She stepped onto the snow-packed cement, but slipped on a slick of ice and caught herself before going down. A sharp, electric shock shot through her left knee. *Just what I need.* She took the next several steps to the front door slowly, then gingerly wiped her shoes on the bristle mat—each slight movement intensifying the pain—and entered the house.

Del Monaco was already there, standing beside Bledsoe, pointing to a page of the report. His copy was in full color, which made the 3D diagrams and maps easier to evaluate. Vail's fax was a third-generation copy, the colors translated into dark and darker gray tones. She limped in and walked over to Bledsoe.

"What happened?"

"Slipped on the ice." She pointed to the report. "Helpful, huh?"

Bledsoe shrugged. "Don't know yet. Just got it." He looked past her at everyone in the living room and seemed to take roll. His eyes settled back on Vail. "How about you take us through it?"

"Wait a minute," Del Monaco said. "I thought I'd do that—"

"I know, but I'd rather Karen do it. No offense."

Del Monaco frowned and walked away, his shoulder giving Vail a light nudge as he passed. Bledsoe winked at her, then took his seat.

Vail asked to borrow the color copy from Del Monaco, who picked up the report and held it above his head. You want it, come get it, he was saying.

Vail took the power struggle in stride and moved across the room as gracefully as possible with a bum knee. She took the papers from Del Monaco and decided to remain there to discuss the report. She stood in front of him, her back to his face. He emitted a noise that sounded like a growl, then scooted his rolling chair a few feet to the side, away from his desk.

"I asked Kim Rossmo at Texas State to put together a profile for us," Vail started. "I've worked with Rossmo on a number of cases and have been super impressed with the work he's done. This one was prepared by William Broussard, his associate." She flipped to the front page of the report.

"I'm not familiar with geographic profiling," Sinclair said.

Manette reclined in her seat. "Probably more *might haves* and *might have nots*," she said.

"I think you'll find this a bit more palatable, Mandisa," Vail said. "It's a computer algorithm that focuses on an offender's projected spatial behavior using the locations of, and the spatial relationships between, that serial offender's crime sites. A geographic profile works real well with a behavioral assessment, because how an offender chooses the areas he preys in is influenced by who he is and what motivates him."

"So this is an objective measurement?" Bledsoe asked.

"Yes and no. It's got both quantitative and qualitative components. The quantitative part uses objective measurements to analyze what Rossmo calls 'point patterns' created from the locations of the victim target sites. The qualitative part comes from an interpretation of the offender's 'mental map.'"

"I wanna hear more about the computer stuff," Manette said. "I got enough theories. Gimme something concrete."

"Rossmo developed something called criminal geographic targeting that takes the locations of the offender's crime scenes and produces a three-dimensional probability distribution of where the offender's home or workplace would be. The greater the height of the point indicates a greater probability that this is where the offender would live or work. This 3D distribution, which he calls a 'Jeopardy Surface,' is then superimposed over a map of the region.

giving us a 'geoprofile' of the offender. Rossmo says the geoprofile is a fingerprint of the offender's cognitive map."

"This shit actually work?" Sinclair asked.

"Indeed, this *shit* does work," Vail said.

Del Monaco, still fuming over having been rebuffed by Bledsoe, craned his neck to be seen around Vail's body. "I've worked with this guy. I can personally vouch for him."

Vail turned slightly and gave Del Monaco a sharp look, wanting to tell him that neither she nor Rossmo needed his endorsement. "What this does," Vail said, "is help us focus the investigation. And when we finally come up with some suspects, we can prioritize who to pursue first, based on where they live and work."

"We can also then put patrols on alert in the more statistically probable areas of offender activity," Robby said.

"I like it," Bledsoe said.

"That concrete enough for you?" Vail asked Manette.

She bobbed her head, chewing on her lip. "I like it, too. But I'll wait to give you my opinion till after we catch this bastard."

"So what's it show?" Bledsoe asked.

Vail looked to Del Monaco. "You have copies?"

He opened a brown manila routing envelope and pulled out a stack of stapled packets. They were passed around the room.

"Turn to page eight," Vail said, finding the spot herself. The splash of colors hit her like a sunset on a cloudy day. A huge difference from the black-and-blacker fax.

"Looks like we've got some areas to focus on," Robby said.

Sinclair's face was buried in the document. "That's an understatement. Looks like, what, three or four hundred square miles? That's a lot of ground to cover."

"Yeah, but the areas are prioritized. Look at the key, it's called out by color and by height of the three-dimensional drawing." There was quiet again as everyone studied the map.

Manette leaned back in her chair. "Still a lot of ground to cover. There's no guarantee he'll stick to one particular area just because we think he will. And if we take patrols away from one area because we're banking on him hitting another—"

"Helluva gamble," Sinclair said. He winked at Vail. "And I know about gambling."

Bledsoe straightened up. "Yeah, well, everything we do involves a certain amount of risk. Sometimes it's just guesswork. This at least gives us some statistical analysis and a focus. And last I heard, we're out of sure bets. I'll get the info over to the involved PDs, let them decide how to use it."

A cell phone started ringing and Robby and Sinclair checked their pockets. It was Sinclair's.

"Give the PDs my number," Del Monaco said to Bledsoe. "They may not know what they're looking at or what significance to give it."

Bledsoe nodded. "We'll make the calls together."

Sinclair flipped his phone shut and tossed it on his desk. "Bit of news. On Hancock. I say we plug the asshole's info into that geoprofile, see if his house falls in the highly probable areas. We already know his workplace did. That was a buddy of mine. Hancock's not alibied for any of the Dead Eyes kills. He was in town and off duty for each of them."

Robby's eyebrows rose. "I say we lean on him again. At least for Linwood, maybe all of them."

"I've got someone on him," Bledsoe said. "Discreet tail, recording his movements. So far he's been pretty mobile, putting in applications at all sorts of security firms, even a few law offices. Nothing suspicious."

"Not with us watching him," Vail said. "He may be an asshole, but given his law enforcement experience, he'd be extremely sensitive to a surveillance team."

Bledsoe grabbed the cordless phone from the kitchen wall. "I think we got enough for a warrant. Hernandez, it's your jurisdiction." He tossed the handset across the room to Robby. "I'll get with the lab at my station, get a forensics team out to his house. We'll want to go over that place with a vacuum cleaner. Literally."

Sinclair laughed. "Guess that's one way of seeing if he's clean."

He looked at the newspaper article they'd written on the bitch Linwood. State senator, big deal. Didn't they know she was as corrupt as most politicians? All they care about is themselves. *How can I raise more money? How can I get reelected?*

All politicians have their dark secrets. Affairs, trysts, backroom deals. Buried tax dodges. And other secrets, the kind this bitch Linwood kept. The kind of secrets worth killing for.

He wondered how long it would be till they found it. If they were good, it shouldn't be much longer. If they were as incompetent as it seemed they were—look how long it was taking them to catch him—they might never find it. It then hit him. Maybe he should've made it more obvious.

But what's life without challenges? If he made it so easy, served it up on a plate for them, what would that say about him? He's better than them, he'd proved it. There was nothing they could do to find him, as he had suspected all along. But he only had a couple more things to accomplish, and then he'd be done. What if he finished and they never figured out who was responsible? How much fun would that be?

Who would know? No one. How disappointing.

He didn't *have* to stop. He didn't want to stop. He didn't want to, so maybe he wouldn't. The thrill of the kill was so exhilarating, so . . . filling. When the feeling struck, it had to be satisfied. Which got him to thinking: maybe he wasn't as in control of things as he'd like to have thought. Maybe it's not that he'd *want* to continue killing, but that he would *need* to continue.

The thought suddenly excited him. He opened the freezer door and pulled out his growing collection of hands. Each one a memory, each one special in its own right.

He set them out on the table, in a circle around some papers he'd recently obtained. Pretty funny reading through this stuff . . . a profile prepared by Supervisory Special Agent Karen Vail. Very impressive. They had a supervisory agent on his case, not just a special agent. They were all special, weren't they? *They* seemed to think so.

Oh, here's a good one: "'He's bright, above average intelligence. He may have a background in art, either in practice or in school. He might even be a frustrated artist. . . .'" *A frustrated artist*? "Bitch! I'm not frustrated, I AM an artist! Come look at my studio, see my work. Talk to my students. How dare you doubt my talents!"

He found his spot in the document and continued reading. "'He's got some deep-seated issues . . . an abusive childhood'. . . Jesus, is it that obvious? Yes! *An abusive childhood*. Are you incredibly stupid, or just incredibly unenlightened? I told you that in my writings. I couldn't have said it any plainer. Did it take an FBI profiler to figure that one out?"

He skipped to the next paragraph. "'Fixation on eyes could be symbolic . . . perhaps the father put him down by telling him everyone *sees* him as a failure . . .'" Now that's perceptive. He hadn't thought of it that way. Very interesting. And he had to admit, pretty damn accurate. She nailed that one. Gotta give credit where it's due. He was fair in that respect.

She can't explain the evisceration. Think anger, Supervisory Special Agent Vail. Think the utmost in humiliation, in power. Of what it represents.

He turned the page and read some more. Digesting all this would take a while. But judging by what little they had on him, he had the time.

Chase Hancock's home was a well-groomed one-story, renovated in recent years with built-in teak furniture, flat-panel television with surround sound system and frilly window coverings that screamed women's touch. But Hancock was not married and never had been. One might assume he had hired a decorator.

One might have also assumed he had done quite well for himself since leaving the FBI. "So why did he have such a hard time with Karen?" Robby asked.

"Male ego," Bledsoe answered. "She got something he wanted. Those types of wounds take a long time to heal."

Bledsoe stood in the living room and ran a hand along one of the leather sofas. "Pricey stuff. Feels like a lambskin coat my father wore." He directed one of the forensic technicians into the house. "We're looking for anything and everything pertaining to a murder. Hair and clothing fibers to match against what we've got on our vics. Blood. Blunt objects used as weapons. You know the drill."

"We're going to vacuum first," the head tech said. "As we clear each room, you'll be allowed in."

Robby thanked the tech, then headed out of the house to wait. "He's had time to clean up," he said to Bledsoe. "You think we'll find anything? Hancock knows the drill, he's been on our end of things."

Bledsoe shrugged. "I've never seen the perfect murder, Hernandez. Even if he's Mr. Clean, there's bound to be something he left behind." They stepped outside into the blustery winter air, where Chase Hancock stood ten feet away, buttocks leaning against his Acura, arms folded against his chest.

Robby turned to Bledsoe. "Whatever that *something* is, I just hope we find it."

Vail checked her voice mail from her cell phone on the way to visit Jonathan. Thirty messages were logged when her machine started refusing additional calls. As she started to go through them, she realized they were all requests from media outlets across the country, including a couple from overseas. She thought about deleting the messages, then realized she had better review them in case any were regarding Emma or Jonathan—or herself: OPR, Gifford, and Jackson Parker were all possibilities.

She inserted her Bluetooth headset and listened as she drove, fast-forwarding to the next message as soon as she ascertained the source of the caller. She finally deleted all of them when she had reached the end. Nothing important.

She arrived at the hospital and made her way up to ICU. As soon as she headed down the hall, she was accosted by a man in his thirties wearing a pair of khakis and an oxford dress shirt cuffed at the sleeves. A microcassette recorder, held tightly in one hand, hovered near Vail's face as he asked her a question: "Agent Vail, how do you feel about being targeted as the Dead Eyes killer?"

She knocked the recorder out of her face and continued walking, but did not say anything.

"I personally don't believe you're the killer," he continued, "but how does it make you feel to have your picture pasted all over the front page?"

Vail stopped and turned to face him. He was younger than she had originally thought when she had looked at him peripherally. "How long have you been on the beat, kid? You're the only one of the press corps bright enough to find a way up to this floor, and you come up with lame questions like those? Even if I felt like talking, which I don't, you didn't earn an answer from me."

The reporter was stunned into silence. His arm, holding the recorder, dropped to his side in defeat. Vail turned away and continued walking.

"How about giving me another chance?" he shouted down the hall. "We could meet for lunch—on me. . . . "

Vail noted a man in his midtwenties dressed in scrubs hovering down the hall near Jonathan's room. Her instincts told her it was Bledsoe's undercover man, and when she made eye contact, he dipped his chin at her. Obviously, he had been well briefed and knew who she was on sight . . . or he'd heard enough of the exchange with the reporter to make the connection.

She stopped at the nurse's station and asked her to page Dr. Altman. The woman gave Vail a cautious look, then backed away slightly and reached for the phone. She didn't take her eyes off Vail as she dialed.

"Unbelievable," Vail muttered, then walked away and pushed through the door to Jonathan's room. She stood by her son's side, waiting for Dr. Altman. She had the feeling neurologists dreaded cases like these, where there was little for them to do but make their rounds—that is, go through the motions—look over the patient's vitals and talk with the concerned parents . . . having nothing of value to tell them. Certainly there were those victorious moments when the child regained consciousness. Perhaps those were the ones that kept the doctors sane, that allowed them to deal with the ones who didn't recover. A few successes and happy endings made the intolerable failures more palatable. Sometimes. At least in theory.

Vail pressed her lips to Jonathan's forehead, then took his hand. A tear trailed down her face and dropped onto his cheek. She gently wiped it away, then stood there watching him breathe. She talked to him and let him know she was there. Beyond that, she felt as helpless as she imagined Dr. Altman felt. The doctor poked his head in the door and smiled when he saw Vail. He stepped in, shook her hand, and picked up Jonathan's chart to scan the nurse's notes.

"I suppose you want to know how your son is doing," he said absentmindedly.

"I'm not here selling Girl Scout cookies."

Altman looked at her, his face conveying the realization he had asked a stupid question. "No, of course not," he said, setting the metal chart on the table beside the bed.

"I'm sorry," Vail said.

Altman shrugged. "No need to apologize. I've seen the papers, I know the stress you must be under. But I do have some good news. Watch." He leaned close to Jonathan and clapped his hands in front of the boy's eyes. Jonathan blinked. Altman looked at Vail for confirmation, as if he had just revealed something wondrous. "Did you see?"

"See what? He blinked."

"Exactly. He wasn't doing that before. He's recovering mental function. His brain is regaining consciousness, so to speak."

Vail's eyebrows elevated, then she blew some air through pursed lips. "This really is a case of small steps."

"That's the nature of the condition. A small step translates into a huge advancement. I'm very encouraged by his progress."

"This is what you live for, isn't it? I mean, I guess it's a lot like an investigation, tracking a killer. Small pieces of evidence at each crime scene add up over time to help us get a full picture. The small steps make a difference."

Altman smiled. "They sure do. The day-to-day improvement may be painstakingly slow for some, but I look at it like doing a jigsaw puzzle: I'll search for the next piece, and the one after that, and the one after that. Piece by piece, until I finally complete the puzzle. Because to answer your question, 'what I live for' is the completed puzzle."

Vail nodded, buoyed by the new perspective.

The law enforcement analogy was one she could grasp. As long as the evidence kept coming, as long as the clues were adding up, she would break the case. If the same principles applied to Jonathan, she could deal with the slow but steady progress.

She thanked the doctor, who nodded and then left the room.

Little by little, she thought. Vail kissed her son's cheek and whispered in his ear. "Come on, Jonathan. Just like when you were a baby learning how to walk. One foot in front of the other, one step at a time. You'll pull through this. You're gonna make it. You hear me, sweetheart?" She waited for a blink, a twitch of his mouth . . . but got nothing.

Wiping away the tears, she walked out of his room and left the hospital, moving past a few members of the press who had camped out near the exit, "no commenting" as she pushed by them.

What she needed now was slow, steady progress on Dead Eyes. As if in response to her thoughts, her cell phone rang: someone at BSU, the Behavioral Science Unit, had information for her.

Wayne Rudnick of BSU was cagey about what he had discovered regarding the Dead Eyes case but told her he couldn't wait around for her to drive to the Academy. He had an exploding toothache and was heading out to an emergency dental appointment. He suggested they meet tomorrow morning instead.

Vail went back to Robby's place and found him with an apron on, mixing a pot of tomato sauce. Boiling water sat on the stove beside it, awaiting the introduction of a handful of stiff spaghetti noodles. As he dropped in the pasta, the water calmed like antacid on a queasy stomach.

"Smells good," she said as she approached the kitchen. Robby's house, inherited from his mother several years ago when she passed away, showed its age. Nails, tape, and other items permanently embedded in the plaster walls' surfaces had been covered over by repeated coats of paint. The old casement windows were drafty and needed to be replaced. New carpet had been installed, and it looked as if Robby had made an attempt at home decorating. But it still lacked warmth.

Vail stepped up to the pot and sniffed. "Smells better than it looks. Is that Ragu or Prego?"

"Hey," Robby said, wooden spoon in hand. "Are you insulting me?"

She looked into the pot again. "Just stating my observations. But if I'm wrong—"

"It's Prego."

"I see. Guess I'll have to help out a bit. Do some of the cooking."

"You're definitely insulting me."

Vail moved into the living room and sat down heavily on the couch. "Jonathan's showing some more improvement."

Robby lowered the flames beneath the pots, then settled onto the sofa beside her. "That's great," he said, taking her hand in his own. "What'd the doctor say?"

"He's encouraged, feels it's all going the way he'd expected. Small steps." She kicked her shoes off and brought her feet up onto the couch, rested her head in Robby's lap. "Raising a kid is tough. It's easy to see how things go wrong, you know?"

"How do you mean?"

"On the drive over, I was thinking about Deacon, and how bad an influence he's been on Jonathan the past year or so. It's the kind of stuff that leads to the development of the twisted personalities the offenders develop."

"Oh, come on. A child of yours becoming a killer?"

"Sounds silly, huh? But I worry about it sometimes. If it wasn't for Deacon, it'd be the furthest thing from my mind. But he's such a bad influence. When you're in a relationship for so many years, and you know he's going through tough times and you're trying to help him through it. . . ." She shook her head. "I overlooked a lot of things. It took me months to step back and see there was nothing I could do, that he was beyond help. I realize that now. But what if he did things I never knew about, when Jonathan was younger. . . ." Her body tensed. "It's not unusual with killers, in their youth, to withdraw into themselves. They'd never talk about things that happened to them when they were young. It hurts me just to think about the possibility." She let the words hang in the air, then continued: "I keep playing things back in my mind, memories, things I saw in Jonathan's behavior. Searching my memory for the warning signs."

"What kind of warning signs?"

"Behaviors that show a lack of regard and caring for others." She sat up and pulled her legs beneath her, winced in pain from her knee, then straightened it out. "When the early profilers interviewed convicted serial killers in prison, they found that the killer's internal world was filled with thoughts of dominance over others. Cruelty to other kids, to animals. They set fires, stole things, destroyed property. I had a problem with Jonathan at one point where he was getting into fights at school. Third grade. He was bullying other kids. I tried talking to him, and he seemed to stop. But it bothered me he didn't have any close friends. I worked with him on developing his social skills, and I thought I'd gotten through. But he started having problems again when Deacon and I started having problems."

"That could be considered normal."

"That's what I kept telling myself. But that type of behavior, unless checked, can lead to other things. Things I'd never find out about. If he killed a cat or a dog, or a squirrel, I'd never know. During the interviews, the killers almost always described times when they'd killed an animal. It allowed them to express their rage and use it as an outlet because there were no consequences. No one knew they'd done it. That only isolated them more from family members or other kids their age. They eventually realized they were different, and that just made them retreat further into themselves. They never learned empathy, or how to control their impulses. They thought they were entitled to act the way they did because no one was there to tell them otherwise."

"You know what I think?"

Vail looked at him, inviting him to continue.

"I think you've been in the minds of serial killers so much, twenty-four/seven, three-sixty-five, that you begin to look for things that aren't there. You live the life, deep in the trenches, and it consumes you. I think you need some time off." He paused a moment, then said, "Maybe permanently."

She looked at him, in a fleeting second realizing he was right, but not wanting to acknowledge it. She rose from the couch, banded her arms across her chest, and began to pace in her nyloned feet. "Quitting is not my style. But you're right, I'll take some time. Once we catch Dead Eyes, I'll take a month assuming I can work it out with the timing of my trial. I'll need the time to get my mom's stuff settled and the house sold."

"I think it'll do you some good. Get away for a while. I'll come visit you on weekends."

She bit the inside of her lip. "And if I don't win this case? If Deacon succeeds? I'm out of the Bureau. I'll never carry a badge again."

Robby stood and stopped her from pacing. "He won't. But if by some strange twist of fate he is successful, then I'll be there with you, by your side. We'll get through it together."

Vail forced a smile. "I could do consulting, right? Write a few books."

"Yeah, like that guy, one of your BSU pioneers, Thomas Underwood."

"I could fly all over the world, developing profiles, helping out the locals, visiting exotic places."

"Doesn't sound so bad, does it?"

She stood there for a moment, pondering such a future. "I want my job back, Robby. At the Bureau. Staring at grisly photos and dealing with male chauvinists."

Robby looked at her a long moment, then nodded. "Then that's the goal."

She nodded back.

"Let's go eat," he said as he took her hand. "Take it from me, Prego is best served hot."

Vail and Robby parked in the Academy's main lot and entered through Jefferson Hall. They signed in at the security station and navigated the maze of glass hallways, Vail playing tour guide and pointing out notable areas and rooms. They made their way through the armory and indoor shooting range, caught the elevator, and took it down into the Behavioral Science Unit's basement offices.

BSU's Investigative Support Unit gained attention because of a handful of agents whose profiling work in the seventies and eighties proved invaluable in cracking several high-profile serial offender cases. It was made famous by its appearance in the movie *The Silence of the Lambs,* followed by mentions in numerous novels.

When the BSU was divided (though not conquered), the Investigative Support Unit was renamed and carted down the road. The profilers gained windows and a more cheerful working environment. The BSU criminologists who remained in the subbasement gained . . . more office space.

Vail led Robby through the cream-colored cinderblock corridor to Wayne Rudnick's office, an eight-by-ten room lit with four incandescent fixtures standing on surfaces of varied heights. The attempt to brighten a dull, depressing environment had fallen somewhat short, Vail thought, but it was an improvement nonetheless.

"Kind of creepy down here," Robby said.

"You get used to it. It's a kick to visit, because of all the history and legends who've worked here."

Rudnick, a sixteen-year veteran, had spent every moment of his tenure in the now-famous subbasement. On his door was a sign scrawled in black magic marker that read:

Welcome to BSU—
sixty feet underground
ten times deeper than dead people

Vail knocked on Rudnick's partially open door and waited but did not get a response. She gave it a slight nudge and it swung open with a squeal.

Rudnick was sitting behind his desk tossing a gel-filled stress-relief ball in the air. He had been doing it for years, claiming it helped him clear his mind. He had once organized a unit-wide challenge to see who could come closest to the ceiling without hitting it. Rudnick had won, but someone had monkeyed with his office chair, and much to the delight of everyone who was in on the prank, Rudnick complained the arc and force of his toss were impaired by the change in the "feel" of his chair. He remained pissed for days when he discovered the conspiracy had been organized by his special agent-in-charge.

"Well, if it's not the Redhead Express." Rudnick jumped out of his chair, arms up and extended for a hug.

She obliged him and then introduced Robby.

Rudnick brushed back his wild Albert Einstein hair, then shook Robby's hand. "You're here on a case, aren't you?" He turned back to his desk, lifting various papers and files, as if looking for something.

"Dead Eyes," Robby said. "Karen sent the case over to you for input." He looked to Vail for confirmation. "How long ago was that?"

"Dead Eyes, Dead Eyes. That rings a bell." Rudnick continued searching his desk, the movement of papers becoming a bit more frantic.

Vail crossed her arms over her chest and, with a slight smirk, shook her head.

"Is there a problem?" Robby asked.

"He's pulling your leg," Vail said. "He knows where the file is."

Rudnick suddenly reached out and poked a folder from atop a pile. "Here it is."

"See? He does this all the time. He thinks it's funny."

"I love playing with new agents' heads."

Robby took a step forward, his thick thighs stopped by the edge of the desk. He looked down at the diminutive Rudnick. "I'm not a new agent."

Rudnick looked up at Robby, over the tops of his thick-rimmed eyeglasses. "But you're someone of authority, I can see that."

"Investigator with Vienna PD."

"Vienna! The poke and plumb town over on the northwest side. Poke your head in and you're plumb out of town."

"We're small, yes. Kind of like you."

"Ooh. Okay. I think that's enough horsing around. Time to get down to business." Rudnick sat and opened the file folder.

"How's your tooth?" Vail asked.

"Need a root canal. Tell ya, I think we should start including dentists routinely in our suspect pool. They're sadists, every one of 'em, I swear."

"Dead Eyes," Robby reminded.

"Yes, okay. Okay. Dead Eyes . . . the serial offender who's plugged into the information superhighway."

"Information superhighway?" Vail asked. "Who uses that term anymore?"

Rudnick glanced at her over the tops of his glasses. "I do, apparently." He opened the file and consulted a page on the left side of the flap. "So as I was saying, this guy is tech savvy, or at least knows how to access the information necessary in constructing the parameters by which he can make it appear that he's tech savvy." Rudnick looked from Vail to Robby and apparently sensed their impatience. "Let me explain. According to our cyber geeks, he—"

"You got something back from the lab?"

Rudnick's eyebrows rose. "Didn't you?"

Vail frowned. "Go on."

"Yes, well, as I was saying, the geek cops said our offender used technique that allows the email message to dissolve into its core constituents—ones and zeroes, the digital equivalent of blood and guts—to prevent us from tracking the email back to him. There're a few things interesting about that. First, they said the info on how to do that's available on the superhigh—excuse me, the Internet—so it's not clear whether he possessed this knowledge or if he just followed the instructions online. But given what other information you've submitted, I'd have to say it's the latter. Kind of like a fanatic who cooks up a bomb from a recipe posted on some militia webpage."

"I agree," Vail said. "Our offender's no technogeek. But he's bright and can certainly find out how to do it."

"Second, and perhaps this goes to the point of it all, is that this vanishing act he's playing with us means he only wants one way communication—a monologue, if you will. Either he's not interested in what you have to say about it, or he's more interested in what you'll do about it."

Vail nodded slowly, as if she were absorbing the meaning into her skin, filtering it as she mulled it through her mind.

"And the content?" Robby asked.

"Yes, yes, the content. Flesch-Kincaid Index scores it at a sixth grade level, though I'm not sure that's worth much to us because he's writing in a voice consistent with a child. More significantly, I'd say his writing appears to emanate from a different part of his brain than his 'blood murals,' which I'll get to in a minute. Unlike the murals, which likely come from some subconscious expression of his feelings, these writings are very consciously constructed. He's gone to considerable effort to send them to you in an untraceable form. He doesn't want to get caught, but he's compelled to share these experiences with you people. His use of the first person is significant—he chose it for a reason, the reason being that they're personal accounts of actual events in this offender's life."

"How can we rule out the possibility he's merely writing fiction?"

"With his flare for creativity, that's certainly an option. But I believe there's more going on here than just a frustrated writer at work. I think this stuff is deeply personal to him. That's why he's showing it to you. It's his outlet for whatever happened to him as a youth. And I believe these writings are very closely related to what we're seeing play out when he's with the bodies. He abuses them, much like he was abused as a child. He's telling you what his childhood was like, the events that made him who he is today. Maybe it's his way of explaining his actions so you won't think badly of him."

Robby squinted. "You think the killer cares what we think of him?"

"I think he definitely cares how he's perceived. Not in the same way we care about the way other people see us, you understand." Rudnick shook his head, started to say something, then stopped.

"What is it?" Vail asked.

"There's something more going on here." He switched to reading glasses and looked down at the file. "I just haven't been able to put my finger on it."

After a long moment of watching Rudnick stare at the page and shake his head in frustration, Vail asked, "What about the blood murals?"

Rudnick's face brightened. "Ah, okay, that's a bit easier to explain. Let's talk for a moment in generalities. There was a question about Impressionism." He got a nod from Vail and continued. "Well, Impressionism is an artistic movement that was born in France and lasted from the 1860s to about 1886. It consisted of a group of artists who shared a set of related approaches and techniques—"

"I was an art history major, Wayne. I know all about its origins."

"For your very intimidating colleague, then, since odds are good that both of you weren't art history majors."

"That's correct," Robby said.

Rudnick winked at Vail, glanced down at his notes, then continued. "Impressionism was considered an extreme departure from the previous major art movement of the Renaissance. These painters rejected the concept of perspective, idealized figures, and chiaroscuro—the use of dark and light in a stylistic manner—"

Vail held up a hand. "I wonder if Dead Eyes is using Impressionism as a symbol, consciously or unconsciously. His rejection of something in society, his way of making a statement."

Rudnick nodded. "That's certainly a possibility. I'd thought of that, but haven't had time to run it through the old gears," he said, pointing to his brain. He turned back to Robby. "The Impressionist painter's focus was on capturing the effect of light on the colors of a landscape. Up close, their paintings look like splashes of color. They don't look like much of a picture until you view them from a bit of a distance." He looked at Vail. "I'm only getting this stuff second-hand, so if you have anything to offer, cut in."

"Nothing to offer. But I think you—and your expert—are missing the point. I said the offender's blood murals reminded me of an Impressionism era painting. Mostly because of the strokes, the way the blood was laid out. It wasn't merely blood spattered on a wall, like a disorganized offender would leave it. It was . . . applied in a very specific pattern. Like a painting, as if the offender looked at these murals as an art form in and of itself."

Rudnick was nodding animatedly. "Yes, yes, that's my point. But again, you're jumping the gun. You on speed today, Karen, or what? Too much coffee?"

"You take forever to get to the point sometimes, Wayne."

"Fine. Here's the point: I checked with an expert on offender and inmate artwork. She analyzes their doodlings as well as the more elaborate sketches, including pictures drawn pre-arrest and during incarceration. It took her a while to come up with something. She took it to an art historian, who saw what you were talking about, the possible influence of Impressionist painters, but since it was 'painted' with fingertips and not a brush, she couldn't analyze brush strokes, which seems to be a key indicator when trying to evaluate artistic trends. There was a suggestion of Impressionist influence, but she wasn't willing to commit to anything more than that. It didn't really follow the conventions of Impressionism, particularly the technique of light and color. There's no light source and no color because there are no pigments. It's just blood. She said it's like trying to paint an entire rainbow with only blue or red on your palette.

"So it fell back on the desk of the offender artwork expert, whose best guess was that there was a method to the brush strokes. Very organized and planned, with an inherent order. There was a repetition in the strokes, but she was unsure it meant anything other than to make it distinguishable and unique. She couldn't discern any hidden meaning to the murals but was sure it was the work of the same 'artist.'" He flipped a page of the report and concluded: "She did say the suggestion of Impressionistic influence was likely not coincidental or accidental."

"Meaning?"

"Meaning that it's likely our offender does have a background in art history, or is an artist of some sort."

Robby looked at Vail. "You'd already figured that out."

"Oh, don't tell her that," Rudnick said. "It'll just go to her head."

Vail rose from her seat. "Confirmation is always nice to have," she said. "The way things have been going, it's good to have someone like Wayne at my back."

"I'd much rather be at your front." He winked. "Oh, excuse me, I'm not supposed to make those kinds of remarks. Workplace etiquette. Sexual harassment laws and such."

"Did your expert say anything about what the murals said about the offender?"

"The fact that he paints in blood is sick."

"Yes, Wayne. Something useful."

Rudnick's face hardened, as if he suddenly realized the gravity of her question. "We both feel the blood is deeply arousing to him. It follows closely with the intense relationship he has with the body. He spends an incredibly long time with the victim. First he eviscerates them, then he grooms them to match some skewed image he has of women, making them ugly, almost repulsive. Then he takes their blood and paints on the wall. In a very deliberate fashion

There is definitely artistic talent there, but it's abstract. No one I showed the photos to could ascertain anything useful from the patterns and shapes. And despite this repetitive 'internal order,' overall they're different from crime scene to crime scene. So whatever he's painting isn't a consistent image, which makes me think it's not borne of a fantasy. The act of painting on the wall may be, but what he's painting . . . no one seems to know." Rudnick grabbed his gel ball and began squeezing it. "In sum, your guy is consistent with what we'd expect to see in this type of offender: the themes of dominance, revenge, violence, power, control, mutilation . . . they're all there."

Vail took a second to absorb this, then nodded. "Thanks for the help, Wayne. Stay sane."

His face brightened again into a mischievous smirk. "Hard to do around here. I sometimes think they've buried us down here for a reason, like it's some secret insane asylum. Like we're the inmates, but in telling us we work for the FBI, they've calmed our murderous instincts."

"Uh huh. Take care, Wayne. And thanks again." Vail led the way out, Robby fast on her heels. As soon as the door clicked shut, he asked, "Stay sane? That implies he's sane to begin with."

Vail tilted her head and nodded. "Guess you're right. Down here, such assumptions might be a bit of a stretch."

WHEN THE ELEVATOR DOORS spread open on the main floor, Vail handed Robby her keys and told him to wait for her in the car; she forgot to ask Rudnick something on a prior case of hers and had to run back down. She appeared in the doorway to Rudnick's office a couple minutes later, and there was the bushy haired analyst, reclining in his chair tossing the ball at the ceiling.

Vail cleared her throat and the ball skittered off his fingertips onto the floor.

He looked over. "Am I having one of those déjà vu events or are you back for something?"

"I'm back," Vail said.

"You like it when I speak French? The people are a bit uppity, but the language does kind of roll off the tongue."

Vail stepped into the room and shut the door behind her.

Rudnick sat up in his chair. "Uh oh. This is serious. Either you're going to work me over or you want some privacy."

"I want some advice," Vail said.

"Okay. I haven't practiced psychiatry in a gazillion years, but—"

"I'm serious, Wayne."

"Right. Serious. Okay, what do you need?"

Vail looked down, then up at the walls—everywhere but at Rudnick's face.

Finally, he said, "You know, your body language suggests you're uncomfortable with what you're about to ask me."

Vail nodded, then finally met his eyes. "I'm having dreams. Strange dreams." She recapped the gist of the nightmares but saved the best for last. "So the killer's straddling the woman's body, he drives the knife into her eyes, then looks up into the mirror."

Rudnick nodded thoughtfully, clearly engaged and sitting on every word. "And you saw yourself."

Vail felt herself step backward. "Yeah. How'd you know?"

"Because, my dear, you stare at mutilated bodies day in and day out. You live and breathe serial murder. It has to affect you deeply, even when you turn your brain off and go to sleep."

"But I've never had these kinds of dreams before."

"Yeah, well, don't bog me down with details."

She sighed. "I thought you'd be able to help me."

"Look, Karen, are you worried that you may be the killer?"

Vail forced a laugh. "Of course not." She chuckled again. "Yes. I mean, I don't know. I can't be, right?"

"No, you can't be. You spend all day around people who analyze behavior. Don't you think one of them would be looking at you if it were even possible?"

"A former agent on the task force thinks I'm Dead Eyes."

"*Former* agent, you say? Must be a reason why he's a former agent, Karen. Point is, you're entrenched in a very challenging case, probably the most challenging one you've ever had because you're intimately involved in it. Most of the time, you don't even get to visit fresh crime scenes, let alone investigate them personally. That guy in your unit—Mark Safarik—what's that saying he had?"

"Mark called it being 'Knee deep in the blood and guts.'"

"Yeah, that's it. You're in this one up to your *hips*. It's on your mind and you can't shut it down. You feel enormous pressure to solve it. And when you can't, you're taunting yourself in your dreams. 'Can't you see it? Study the art! Figure it out!' You're telling yourself to find the answers. Think about it a minute, objectively. I know that's hard because you're so close. But think about it."

Vail stood there, her mind flooding with thoughts when suddenly one fought to the surface; it tumbled out of her mouth as if it were a pilot ejected from a cockpit. "I can't see the killer because I'm blind, just like the victims."

"There you go," Rudnick said. "Very good." He squinted and shook his head slowly, the picture of pity. "You've been taught to empathize with the victims and think like the killers, Karen. What an impossible thing to do! No wonder you're conflicted. Your subconscious is on overload."

Vail bit her lip.

Rudnick stepped around his desk and placed a hand on her shoulder. "This is all perfectly normal, Karen. I bet if you ask some of your colleagues in your unit, you'll find that many of them have had similar dreams about this stuff."

Vail looked up, feeling a bit brighter. "Thanks, Wayne. Makes sense."

Rudnick smiled. "Of course." He bent over and retrieved his ball. He sat down behind his desk, leaned back, and took aim at the ceiling. "Now beat it so I can get back to work."

After joining Robby in the Academy parking lot, she drove him back to his car. She had planned to go to the hospital to visit Jonathan, then meet Robby for dinner. Despite what Jackson Parker had said about him being her only friend, she knew she had Robby. She felt that no matter how things turned out, he would be there for her. And her for him.

As Robby was getting into the car, his phone sounded—followed seconds later by a similar trill from Vail's BlackBerry. "Get in," he said. "I'll drive."

They arrived at the task force op center ten minutes later, ahead of Manette, Del Monaco, and Sinclair. Bledsoe was pacing, holding what appeared to be several eight-by-ten glossy photos in his hand. As soon as Bledsoe saw Vail come through the door, his face lit up.

"I feel like a kid who's just found out a really cool secret, but he's got no one to tell."

"What's the secret?" Robby asked.

"Look." He shoved the photos in Robby's face.

"Where'd you find this?"

"You're gonna love this," Bledsoe said, looking at Vail. "If we figure out what it means, it could break the case."

"Where was it?"

"In Linwood, shoved up her rear."

"In her rectum?" Robby asked.

"ME found it during the autopsy. Showed up on x-ray."

Robby handed each of the photos to Vail as he went through the stack. "What does it mean?"

Vail did not answer. She was studying the close-up photos, which depicted a heart-shaped gold locket.

"Karen? What's wrong?"

"Looks familiar. . . ." She finally looked up. "Can't place it."
Where have I seen something like this before?

"But what does it mean?"

The front door flung open and in walked Manette, Del Monaco, and Sinclair.

". . . and I'm telling you, Sears Tower has the most stories," Sinclair said.

"But in terms of actual building height," Del Monaco said, "that one in Taiwan is tallest."

"Hey, look at this," Bledsoe said.

Manette, Del Monaco, and Sinclair joined the huddle.

Vail handed them the stack of photos. "ME found this locket during Linwood's autopsy." She turned back to Bledsoe. "We already know Linwood meant something special to this guy. Somehow this is related. When an offender shoves an object up a victim's rectum, it's a very personal act. First thought is that there's a sexual component. It's symbolic. Meant to send a message."

"Another message," Sinclair groaned. "We haven't figured out the first one yet."

"I think I'm beginning to understand," Manette said. "Our UNSUB designs puzzles for *The New York Times*. He wears red underwear and likes pistachio ice cream because the nuts symbolize his mental state. What do you think, Kari, honey, *maybe? Possibly?*"

Vail ignored her. "Even though it's ritual behavior he hasn't engaged in before, it doesn't change my profile. But it does support everything we've assumed about him up to this point. If anything, it solidifies our belief that Linwood's a key. Oh—and a couple other things. The experts at BSU said the email this guy sent is likely a personal account of his childhood."

"Pretty fucked up childhood," Manette said. "Then again, isn't that the thing with these killers, Kari? They were abused by a parent, or they were pissed on by some bully, someone didn't like the color of their hair—"

"BSU also felt," Vail said, gaze firmly rooted to Manette's mischievous eyes, "that the offender definitely has artistic talent and that he's probably had some art training along the way. Could be significant. The murals show repetitive patterns, even though they're all different from one another."

"So how does all this help us?" Bledsoe asked.

"Well, for one, the more emails we get from him, the better understanding we'll have of what's making him kill. The more info we can gather on his thought process, the greater the chances we'll have of anticipating his next move, or even possibly catching him."

"Anything on the emails themselves? Are they traceable?"

"The geeks are working on it, but so far all we've got is that he's used some sort of special software that not only prevents it from being printed, but it causes the email to self-destruct after a certain period of time. In this case, approximately two minutes after you begin reading it."

"So he's a technology whiz," Bledsoe said.

"Not necessarily. It's all readily available info that anyone who's good with a computer can figure out without too much difficulty."

"Then what do we know about this software?" Sinclair asked. "Who makes it?"

"It's not software that you buy in the store. This is Internet stuff, created by people who claim that anonymous email is an extension of Free Speech, used to protect human rights, workers reporting abuses, political dissidents complaining about their government, people writing on controversial topics, that sort of thing. Most of it is web-based. There're a shitload of providers."

Manette shook her head. "So we're not gonna catch this dickhead by tracking down the source of his messages."

"Doesn't look like it. Especially since he's using a public cybercafé, logging on, sending his message, and logging off quickly. But our people are still working on it. Next time he sends us a message, we'll be better prepared to track it. If it's possible, they'll find a way."

"And the murals?" Bledsoe asked. "You said there was some significance to them."

"I've been thinking that this guy may suffer from OCD."

"Obsessive Compulsive Disorder?" Sinclair asked. "How do you get to point Q from point A?"

"The repetitive nature," Vail said. "And the amount of time he spends with the body. It's excessive, taken to the extreme. The need for perfection. To him, the victim is an art medium, the crime scene his canvas."

"And this locket?" Robby asked. "Where does that fit in?"

Bledsoe said, "I've got copies of the locket photos being circulated to area jewelers, in case any of them recognizes either the piece itself or the style of design. Maybe we'll get lucky and someone has seen something like it before."

"What about Linwood's husband?"

"We faxed him a photo. Claims he's never seen it before. I've got a uniform taking a color photo over there to be absolutely sure."

"Freaking weird if you asked me," Sinclair said.

Manette brought both hands to her hips. "Like any of this is normal?"

Sinclair shrugged, conceding the point.

Bledsoe collected the photos and handed them to Manette. "Pin these up on the wall, will you?" To Sinclair, he said, "What've we got on the blood angle?"

"We're building a database. Guy in my office is running what we've got. Some hits on infected male Caucasians in the target age range. We narrowed the list by eliminating one who was dead, another who's a double amputee from diabetes, and one who was confined to a hospice with advanced AIDS. The remaining seven we're checking out. No obvious ties to any of our vics, but we've got a lotta ground to cover. Still got a little more than half the labs and hospitals to hear back from."

"I've got a list of painters," Robby said. "And carpenters, potters, sculptors, glass blowers, graphic artists, and interior designers. Last count we were up to forty-one hundred names."

"I told you," Bledsoe said.

"May not be so bad. Next step is to cross-reference them all.

Once we start mixing in all the parameters, the numbers should drop off and leave us with something manageable."

"When can we have everything collated?" Bledsoe asked.

Robby looked up at the cottage cheese ceiling, his mind crunching numbers and estimating tasks. "I'd say three, four days. If everyone gets me their lists by tomorrow."

A groan erupted. Bledsoe raised his hands. "Hey, the longer we take to develop suspects, the longer this guy's free to roam. And the more women are at risk. I don't like body counts. As it is, I'm frustrated as hell we haven't been able to run in any mopes for questioning."

The phone rang and Bledsoe moved to answer it. He nodded at Vail, then tossed her the handset. It was the office manager at the last assisted care facility on her list that could take her mother. She had only seen photos of the place on their website, as she had not had time to tour the facility. But the woman was now assuring her that Silver Meadows was among the finest in the state, and that Vail "absolutely had to come see it for herself." Vail told her she would, then hung up.

She didn't bother telling the woman the only other facility on her list was not a viable option, that Silver Meadows was her last hope. She stood in the kitchen and thought of her mother, when it finally hit her: with her mother's mental acuity fading, her childhood house due to be sold, and her biological mother dead, the last links to her past were wilting away, drying up, and crumbling like a spent rose.

Vail made her way out of the kitchen and into the main room of the op center, where everyone had left except for Robby, who was sitting on the edge of a desk, waiting for her.

He stood and walked toward her. "Everything okay?"

She nodded, but she knew her face was betraying her. "Guess as I approach middle age, I'm having a hard time coming to grips with the issues that crop up."

"Your mother?"

"Kind of a role reversal. In some ways, she's like a child now—and I'm the parent. That visit the other day was like cold water in the face. It really shook loose some old memories, got me thinking." She rubbed at her forehead. "Going through all her stuff is going to be tough. Who knows what I'll find. Like that photo album."

Robby leaned a shoulder against the wall. "After my mom died, I had to take care of her affairs. I found some things buried in that old apartment that gave me a different perspective of who she was. Explained a lot of things, turned around everything I knew about her. It bugged me, a lot. Friend of mine suggested I go for counseling. So I did—just a few times, but it helped me out. One of the things the doc told me is that change is part of the natural order." Robby went silent a moment, then shook his mind back to attention. "Eventually, everything comes to an end."

Vail looked at the wall of crime scene photos: Marci Evers, Noreen O'Regan, Angelina Sarducci, Melanie Hoffman, Sandra Franks, Denise Cranston, Eleanor Linwood.

"Some things," she said, "end sooner than they're supposed to."

He was hungry again and fighting the urge to do something. He couldn't hold himself back much longer, which meant he needed to start planning his next target. He already knew who it had to be, but it would be a tough one. Much tougher than the others. Tougher for reasons only he knew.

But as the old man had said time and again, "You gotta be fuckin' tough." There wasn't much worth taking from the man, but that was one thing he never forgot. Because when dealing with that bastard, you had to be tough just to survive. But his definition of "tough" differed from his father's. The old man meant for others to take what he had to give, to endure the pain. Taken another way, it meant having the strength emotionally to defeat him. To eventually find a way out, an escape.

And as time passed, that way out became clear—at least, it was a method by which he could deal with it all. As he sat in his studio, the kiln cooking his class's ceramic work, he sat down at the keyboard and thought of the time when the light finally came on, when he realized who he was and how he could deal with his situation.

Like any thirteen year old, I've got my limitations in dealing with adults. They're bigger and stronger. But I'm getting bigger, too, and I'll be damned if I'm gonna let him continue to take advantage of me without some kind of consequence. So I've been putting up a fight.

But that hasn't stopped him. Now he knocks me out from behind and ties me down. I know because when I wake up I've got a bump on my head and rope burns on my wrists and ankles.

But he still hasn't found my secret room. I can get there from outside the house now, through the crawl space. Caught me a

'coon who was trying to move in on my place because it was
warm. Reminded me of Charlie, but his eyes were bigger, and I
didn't like the way he looked at me.

He's not a problem anymore. I took care of him, and that was
that. My secret room is the only reason I stay here. It's my place, I
call the shots. And I don't want anyone in here, not even animals.

Sometimes the simplest of goings-on makes you realize how
things really are, and what needs to be done. Once you see how
straightforward it all is, how the solution was right in front of you all
the time, you get mad and promise yourself you won't make the
same mistake twice. You learn from what you've done, get smarter.

As he flipped through his photos, the ones he stole from Super
Agent Vail, he realized that he'd missed out on an incredible opportunity. What a perfect way to relive the kill. He could buy a camera, take
photos of the bodies like the cops do. He could store them on his laptop and view them anytime he wanted. Even better—a camcorder—
one of those small ones—could be set up on a tripod to record
everything. Then he could watch it. Play it in slow motion. His pulse
quickened just thinking about it.

And he could walk into any store and buy one. A normal Joe buying a camcorder like any American who wants to tape his kids, grandkids, nephews, bitches.

Out to tape *his* bitches. Dead and alive.

Ultimately dead.

The tour of Silver Meadows Assisted Care was longer than Vail would have preferred. She had much on her mind, and the last thing she wanted was a sales pitch that had more shine than shoe polish. Especially since she had no other alternative. At least she could move in her mother without reservation about the quality of care she would receive. Only the monthly cost would cause her concern. But, as her mother had once told her, "It's only money."

She thanked the woman, whose smile seemed to sport more teeth than a shark, and was heading back to her car when her phone rumbled. These days, the vibration set her heart racing: odds were it meant either important news about Jonathan or the discovery of another Dead Eyes victim.

The text message belonged to Bledsoe. She was to meet him at the task force op center in fifteen minutes to discuss "a major break" in the case. Vail pulled up to the curb one minute sooner than expected, and Bledsoe met her in the street. As Robby arrived behind her, Manette, Sinclair, and Del Monaco walked out of the house and the group convened on the front lawn.

"I guess Dead Eyes is bored with sending emails. Didn't get enough of a rise out of us," Bledsoe said. "A letter was received this morning by Richard Ray Singletary at Rockridge Correctional. Ring a bell?"

"Singletary, yeah. Serial killer, North Carolina," Del Monaco said. "The Mohawk Slasher. Took out seven college freshmen before he was caught. It was one of Thomas Underwood's first profiling cases. Underwood met with Singletary a number of times. Part of BSU's program to interview serial offenders to develop an understanding of why they did what they did."

Vail said, "A lot of the stuff they learned from those interviews formed the basis for our current understanding and approach. The work was so fresh and new—and accurate—that it became legendary. So much so that some people at the BAU are afraid to embrace change and new ideas because Underwood and his colleagues' research findings are as good as written in stone."

Del Monaco frowned at her comment, and she stared him down. The others picked up on the silent interplay and kept quiet. Finally, Robby spoke. "They have the letter in custody?"

"They do now. Singletary wouldn't give it up. Said it was his ticket. His ticket to what, I'm not sure."

"Bargaining chip," Manette said. "He don't have much. Letter's a way of getting privileges."

"Privileges for what?" Bledsoe asked. "He's scheduled to be put down in five days."

"Put down, like lethal injection?"

"Like, that's all she wrote. The big sleep. End of the line."

Del Monaco shrugged. "Then something to add spice to his last few days."

Robby asked, "So what's the plan, boss? How do you want to handle it?"

Bledsoe rubbed a thick hand across his chin. "Vail and Del Monaco will go with me to meet the guy. Letter's en route by courier to the FBI lab right now. As soon as they'd found out what he had, they sealed it in an evidence bag. I don't know if we'll get anything useful out of it, because a bunch of people already handled it. But we'll talk with Singletary, see what he has to say."

Vail's eyebrows rose. "One question I have is, why him? Why did Dead Eyes send the letter to Singletary?"

"I know we're all stretched beyond our limits," Bledsoe said, "but we need someone to compile a roster of all violent offenders who've served with Singletary since his incarceration."

Manette raised a hand. "I got it."

"Good. Manny, it's yours. Get it to me as soon as possible. Okay, then. That's our plan."

"Do we have clearance to meet with Singletary?" Sinclair asked.

"Give me a few minutes," Bledsoe said. "I'll make some calls."

THE FLIGHT INTO Henderson-Oxford Airport was bumpy and turned Vail's stomach. It wasn't that she disliked the act of flying, it was the concept that bothered her. How a plane the size of a large dinosaur could slice through the air and rise, then descend slowly and land safely, was a wonderment she could never fully understand. She felt more comfortable wading through the minds of deranged killers than with the physics of aerodynamics.

As they entered the lounge area after deplaning, a CNN special report flashed across the television screen. "Convicted murderer Richard Ray Singletary claims he has received a letter from the Dead Eyes serial killer, who is reportedly responsible for Virginia State Senator Eleanor Linwood's death as well as the deaths of six other young women. . . . "

"So Singletary's leaked the story," Del Monaco said. "For what, another fifteen minutes of fame? He'll be getting that when he's executed."

"Yeah, but this is good press. Executions tend to be . . . somewhat negative," Vail said with a hint of sarcasm.

Del Monaco, Bledsoe, and Vail met an off-duty correctional officer, who transported them to the prison. They arrived at three o'clock, the way to the meeting being paved by the prisoner himself, who declined legal representation. They checked their guns and were transported to the maximum security building by bus.

Half an hour later, they were in the eight-by-ten interview room, where a small metal table sat bolted to the floor. There were two seats—one for the prisoner and one for his visitors. Vail took the chair; she wanted the center stage to ask the questions, while Del Monaco stood in the background, arms folded across his chest, content to melt into the wall and analyze Singletary's facial and body language. Bledsoe was behind a large one-way mirror in an adjacent room.

Singletary was led in by two uniformed guards. The prisoner, a slight man with close-cropped pepper hair and pleasing facial features, was shackled at the ankles and wrists. His face was a pale white, the mark of someone who had spent time in solitary confinement— or who had been restricted to his cell for bad behavior. Yet despite the dehumanizing restraints, Singletary's shoulders and hips moved with a noticeable swagger. The agents watched as the guards unshackled Singletary's hands and refastened the handcuffs to a steel bar mounted at the center of the fixed metal table.

"All yours, ma'am," the guard said to Vail. "We'll be watching. You get into trouble, just holler."

Vail thanked the men but wondered why, if she encountered trouble with the prisoner, she would need to holler if they were observing. She pushed the thought from her mind and focused on the man in front of her. "Mr. Singletary, I'm Special Agent Karen Vail, this is Agent Frank Del Monaco." Singletary had already been told who he would be meeting with, but it was a good way to break the ice.

Del Monaco nodded with disinterest, playing his presence low key, as if he did not want to be there. He and Vail had discussed their strategy in detail on the plane.

"We were told you received a letter yesterday. From someone who claims to be the Dead Eyes killer."

"That's right." Singletary's voice was smooth, his smile bright and white.

"The letter's at our lab right now, being analyzed."

"Waste of taxpayer dollars. I can tell you it's authentic."

"How's that?" Vail pulled a copy of the letter from her pocket and unfolded it. "What makes you so sure it's from Dead Eyes?"

"See the sentence 'Evil rides the ocean and the sky turns all the rivers gold'? He made that up a long time ago. It became kind of a saying for us."

"You know the Dead Eyes killer?"

"I just said that, didn't I? Man, I thought you people were smart."

Vail felt like reaching across the table and slapping the guy but kept her face neutral. "Who is he?"

Singletary burst out laughing. A smoker's cough quickly overwhelmed him, and Vail had to turn away to avoid the explosion of germs from the man's uncovered mouth. "You expect me to just give you the guy's name?"

"I thought you might, yes."

"Then you're stupider than I thought you were. But you are a fine lookin' thing," he said, then stuck his tongue out and waved it like a lizard's. "I got two demands. One is, I only talk to Thomas Underwood. Second, I want my death sentence commuted, to life in prison."

Now it was Vail's turn to laugh. She did so boisterously, purposely to annoy the man who thought he held all the cards. It was his nature to try to gain the upper hand, to seek control and power. She was not going to give it to him. "Thomas Underwood isn't with the Bureau anymore. I doubt he'd want to waste any more of his time talking to you."

"Then you'd be wrong, Agent Vail. Because Thomas has already said he'd meet with me. He said it on MSNBC, just about a half hour ago."

Vail resisted the urge to glance at the one-way mirror, behind which Bledsoe was seated. "Why Underwood?"

"The guy understands me. It's a familiar face. This is important information. I deal with him."

"You want something, you deal with me," Vail said.

"Ooh. Tough woman. That turns me on, *Special Agent* Vail. Did you know that? Because if you didn't, I can tell you Thomas Underwood does."

Vail ground her teeth. She wanted to grab the guy's jumpsuit lapels and shake him. Hard. But she counted backwards from five to calm her anger. "I'll make a call, see if I can get Underwood here. As to getting your sentence commuted, I wouldn't count on it. I can get you some T.V., a steak dinner every night—"

"Yeah, that's good. MTV. I want my MTV. Add that to the list."

"Mr. Singletary, I'll make the calls, convey your demands. I just wouldn't hold out much hope."

"I don't have much hope, sweetheart. I'm on death row. You hold out hope, you get disappointed."

She nodded, then pushed away from the table.

"Just remember," Singletary said. "You give me what I want, I'll give you the name of the Dead Eyes killer."

Vail stood there for a long moment, reading the man's eyes. Tempted to agree to the deal even though she didn't have the authority. Given all the death, the young lives taken and yet to be taken, the offer seemed too good to refuse.

But in her experience, making deals with the devil usually backfired.

Vail let the door click closed behind her. Bledsoe met her and Del Monaco in the hallway, the detective's normally olive-complected face red and strained.

"I spoke with Gifford," Vail said. "He's calling Underwood's office. We'll know soon whether or not he'll come. Bureau will pay his airfare and hotel, any expenses."

Del Monaco grunted. "We all know this deal turns on his sentence."

"And that ain't gonna happen," Bledsoe said. "Imagine the heat the DA will take if he caves and recommends leniency to the governor."

Vail shook her head. "Think about the heat he'll take if Dead Eyes murders another woman and it gets out he could've prevented it." She leaned her back against the wall, let her head touch the cold, painted cinderblock. "I think we need to make the deal. Contingent on arrest and conviction of Dead Eyes."

Del Monaco stepped forward. "The guy's set to die in five days, Karen. Delaying his execution even an hour sends a message. Once you've delayed it, it's like you've made the decision to wait till the jury comes back with a verdict. You can't suddenly decide you're going to change your mind two or three months into it. You're either in or out."

"You don't think we should do it," Bledsoe said.

"Hey, I don't get paid the big bucks to make those decisions. What I think doesn't mean diddly."

"I think Underwood's our best shot," Bledsoe said.

Del Monaco shoved his hands into his pants pockets. "There's a bigger issue. How do we know this letter is even legit? And how do we know that Singletary really knows who Dead Eyes is? He could be jerking us around. Playing us, trying to buy himself some extra time."

Vail pulled out her cell phone and began to dial. "Maybe the lab has some answers for us."

She walked down the hall, pacing, waiting for the technician to take her call. But she knew the time spent hoping they had discovered something of value was wasted when the tech told her they hadn't finished running the tests. They could tell her the type of paper it had been written on, the type of ink used to print it, and that there were no usable fingerprints other than a partial from Singletary.

"This guy dies in five days," Vail said. "Any way we'll have something soon—anything—that'll tell us if this letter is from our killer?"

"Problem is that we've got no other writing samples to compare it to, nothing where we can match syntax, or even something as basic as handwriting." The technician sighed. "But we'll do our best. If there's something to find, we'll have it for you tomorrow."

Vail walked back toward Del Monaco and Bledsoe and said, "Nothing yet."

Del Monaco was folding his phone. "Underwood is on his way. He'll be here inside of two hours. I say we get out of here, paint the town or something."

"Our knight in shining armor is on the way to save the day," Vail said with a hint of sarcasm. "Smacks of Hollywood. I can't wait."

THEY TOOK THEIR SEATS at a beat-up picnic table twenty yards from Bob's Country Store, where they'd purchased hamburgers, chilidogs, and beer. The debate over drinking while on duty died with their appetite after finding that the only greasy spoon within fifteen minutes of the prison was, in fact, a very greasy spoon.

And, as they soon learned, being in the Bible Belt meant their alcohol had to be consumed off-premises, in the chill air.

"Well," Bledsoe said, inspecting the flat head on his beer, "it seems that somewhere along the way, Underwood made an impression on Singletary."

Del Monaco tipped his plastic cup toward the light and frowned at the color of his drink. "Singletary's got a relationship with Underwood. He trusts him. Happened with John Wayne Gacy, and Dahmer, too."

Bledsoe took a pull on the beer and made a face. "I hope Underwood works his magic. I get the feeling he's more into writing books than writing profiles these days."

"Bureau pension only goes so far," Del Monaco said. "Nothing wrong with free enterprise."

"Yeah, well, looks to me like he's trying to ride the coattails of John Douglas's success."

Vail cleared her throat and leaned forward. "Frank," she said tentatively, "you ever have nightmares? Of work?"

Del Monaco swallowed a mouthful of beer as he thought about the question. "You mean like working with you is a nightmare sometimes?"

"I'm serious."

Del Monaco set down his cup and regarded his colleague. "You having Dead Eyes nightmares?"

Vail's gaze found the million-year-old pocked-wood table. "You didn't answer my question."

He shrugged. "Had a nightmare after my first murder scene way back when. But nothing since then. My brain kind of acclimated to it. Go to work, deal with this shit, come home, leave it all at the office."

She pulled her coat tight against a sudden gust of wind. "That's good you can do that," she said without further explanation.

"I've had some nightmares," Bledsoe said. "Been awhile, but I remember the last one real well. I was in a shootout and my gun jammed. Radio didn't work. And I couldn't talk. It was like my throat closed up. Woke up drenched in sweat." He shook his head. "Seemed so damn real. It's been years but I remember it like yesterday."

Vail wished she had never brought it up, because the next question was likely to be from Del Monaco, again asking if she's had dreams regarding Dead Eyes.

But he surprised her when he elbowed her and said, "Let's look at that letter again. If anyone's qualified to analyze it, it's us."

Vail pulled it from her pocket and unfolded it. She read aloud.

"I've done more than I ever thought I'd be able to do. But when you put your mind to something, you can do anything." She looked at Del Monaco, who shrugged.

"Beats the shit out of me," he said. "Nothing specific to that."

Vail continued: "I find myself overwhelmed by the power of it all. Of being able to do anything I want to. No one to tell me I can't."

Del Monaco spread his hands in acknowledgment. "Signs of power. Of control. So far, there's nothing to say it's a hoax. But, there're no details only the killer would know, either."

"It does match up with the emails he sent," Vail said. "The hunger-based need for power and control."

"But it's nonspecific," Del Monaco said. "Those are common serial offender themes."

Vail looked back at the paper: "I can't stop myself. I'm sure you know the feeling, the urges, the need for more. They may think they can stop me, but they can't. I know what they know. They'll never find me."

Vail exchanged a knowing glance with Bledsoe. All the proof she needed was right there—a reference to the stolen profile. It wasn't hard evidence, but it was enough to convince her emotionally, if not legally or logically. She cleared her throat, then said, "Well, I think those last few sentences are the most significant, because it tells us a lot about him. It confirms a lot of our profile. And it tells us he's gaining confidence, which is common with offenders as time passes. They begin to feel impervious to capture. They get sloppy and they begin to self-destruct internally. They may even get more violent."

"I thought Linwood's murder was more violent because of the personal connection," Bledsoe said.

"It was." *At least, I think it was.* "But this is something else. Many, if not most, serial killers begin to get more aggressive, more violent as the victims mount. It's almost too much, it becomes over-whelming to them. Even those who thrive on control begin to lose structure in their lives, even if they don't realize it's happening. When it gets out of hand, they surpass their ability to handle the overload. They make mistakes, lose their composure. That'll work to our advantage. Only problem is, we don't know if he'll reach critical mass at victim eight or victim twenty-eight."

Del Monaco set down his cup and wiggled a bit on the bench seat. "An offender's early murders typically demonstrate his need to engage in the thrill of the hunt. He lives for exerting control over his victim. But as he loses himself in his perception that he's invincible, the emphasis of his attacks shifts to a kind of hunger, a simple need to kill." He looked at the letter and shook his head. "There's something that bothers me, though." He picked up the paper and stared at it.

After waiting for Del Monaco to continue, Vail asked, "Frank?"

"'I know what they know,'" he said. "What does he mean by that? Who is 'they'?"

"He's talking about us," Bledsoe said.

Vail shut her eyes, bracing for the hammer to come down hard on her skull.

"He thinks he knows what we have on him," Bledsoe continued.

She opened her eyes, realizing Bledsoe was not going to reveal their secret. They brought their beer to their lips and continued ruminating over the meaning of the letter. A few moments later, Bledsoe warded off a chill, then checked his watch. "We've gotta go. Underwood should be en route and it'll take awhile to stow our handguns and get through security again."

"Show time," Vail said.

THOMAS UNDERWOOD was a fit fifty-nine years old, with a full head of ink-black hair and the boyish looks that had made him a knockout in his early Bureau days. He had the expert crime solver look Hollywood sought, and Vail was amazed he had never been offered his own television show. But his presence was electric, she had to admit, and she felt a few butterflies fluttering, though she couldn't be sure it wasn't just the cheap beer gurgling around her stomach.

Underwood smiled when he saw Del Monaco. "Frank, how you doing? Enjoying life, it looks like," he said, patting Del Monaco's round abdomen. Del Monaco huffed a false laugh.

Underwood made introductions to Bledsoe, then turned to face

Vail. "Thomas Underwood," he said, extending a hand and flashing a white smile.

"Karen Vail."

Underwood's grin widened. "Oh, you don't need an introduction."

Vail felt a flush settle across her face. She was impressed he knew who she was. Had he been following her career?

He must have read the increase in her body temperature, because he immediately clarified: "Your face was plastered across the front page of just about every major newspaper in the country."

Vail turned away to hide her disappointment and faced the one-way mirror that overlooked their subject. "You don't need an intro to Mr. Singletary either, I take it."

"No, I know Ray quite well." He clapped his hands together. "I've been thoroughly briefed on the ride over, so why don't I just get started?" He looked to Bledsoe, who nodded. "Great. Why don't you all wait here and I'll go get us some answers."

Thomas Underwood greeted Richard Ray Singletary with a firm handshake. It was awkward for both of them because of the shackles, but Underwood was clearly determined to initiate physical contact.

"Ray, how've you been?"

"As good as can be expected in a place like this, with the death penalty hanging over your head."

Vail turned to Bledsoe, who, like Del Monaco, was standing behind the one-way mirror. The gain on the microphone inside the interview room was turned up loud and picked up every utterance, every scrape of chair leg or shoe against the cement floor. The voices sounded tinny, as if they'd been run through a coffee filter.

"They're like best buddies," Bledsoe said. "How can Underwood shake the guy's hand and act like his friend?"

"Part of what made him so successful at interviewing these monsters," Vail said. "He's got the gift of gab, and he understands the criminal mind. We teach interview techniques in my unit, if you ever want me to talk to your squad."

"Thanks." Bledsoe's bruised tone told her he wasn't interested.

"You understand if I don't have a lot of sympathy for your predicament, Ray," Underwood said. "You know, it's a bed you made for yourself."

"Well, well, well. Has retirement made you a little cynical?"

"I've only retired from the Bureau, not from my life's work." Underwood flashed a smile. "So I've been told you have something to talk to me about."

Singletary leaned across the table, his eyes darting back and forth, as if he had a reasonable expectation of privacy. He lowered his voice and said, "I know who wrote the letter. I know who the Dead Eyes killer is." He raised his eyebrows and leaned back in his chair.

THE 7TH VICTIM

To Underwood's credit, he knew how to play these guys. "So who is he?"

"For a price."

"Look, Ray. You demanded they fly me out here, and I dropped everything I was in the middle of and caught the next plane. I'm here. Let's not play games."

"This isn't about games, Thomas. It's about life. I don't want to die. I've got less than five days before they kill me. That's about a hundred and fifteen hours before my life is over. They want to catch his guy, I wanna live. It's all locked up in here," he said, pointing to his head. "I give them a name, they give me my life back. That's not so much to ask, Thomas. It's really pretty simple."

"It's a lot more complicated and you know it, Ray. You're a smart guy. There's politics involved. They give in to you, it sets a bad precedent."

"They let me die with the name buttoned up inside me, and *setting bad precedent* will be the least of their problems. What politician wants the blood of more dead women on his hands?" He looked away, then back to Underwood. "Hell, once the legislature finds out I know who this guy is, they're gonna want that name so the FBI can arrest him and publicly fry his ass. It's important to show you can't kill a state senator and get away with it, right? So don't tell me about politics."

Underwood leaned back in his chair. "Let's say for a moment that they won't deal. What else can I negotiate for you?"

"There's nothing else to talk about. You want the killer's identity, that's what it'll cost you."

"The problem they have, Ray, is that there's no way of verifying his letter is really from the Dead Eyes killer. You say it is, because you recognize a phrase he used. But it could just be chance. It's not like he signed it and included a fingerprint and photo for your benefit."

"I'll give you the name and you go out and grab the guy up. Things check out, the deal goes through. It's the wrong guy, I get the needle. You can't lose."

"He's got it all figured out," Bledsoe said in the adjacent room.

"He was an organized offender," Vail explained. "High IQ.

Preyed on college girls living off-campus. He followed them to a su
permarket, then lured them away by wearing a fake cast, claimin
he'd broken his arm. He told them he needed help loading grocerie
into his van. As soon as he got them out of sight, he cracked ther
over the head with the cast and threw them into the van." Va
turned back to the mirror. "You bet he's got this all figured ou
Which is why I find it hard to trust him."

"We'll see what take Underwood has, maybe he's got a feel fc
the guy," Bledsoe said. "He knows him better than anyone."

Vail folded her arms. "For what we're paying him, he'd bette
come up with something."

"I thought the Bureau just paid his expenses," Bledsoe said.

"He's an international consultant," Vail said. "World renowned
Expenses *and* a hefty fee, I'm sure."

Del Monaco nodded. "Gifford was against it, but they worke
something out. I think Underwood saw it as an opportunity fc
another book, or at least a chapter in his next one."

". . . So give me something," Underwood was saying to Single
tary. "Something I can take to them to prove your info is good. The
won't want to cause a big media stir, then find it's the wrong gu
And even with a name, it could take a while to find him. Once the
agree to the deal, your execution is off. And if your info turns ou
bad, and they have to ramp up again and set a date for you to leav
this planet, it's damn messy. You see the problem we have here, Ray?

Singletary squirmed a bit in his seat. He had no response.

"We've got some other problems, too, Ray. Like they thin
maybe this is a hoax and it's just your way of playing with us, watch
ing us go off on a wild goose chase. Your way of getting even."

"Could be, but not likely. Even your psychobabble analysis of m
could tell them that's not what I'm about."

"They're also thinking it's your way of getting your fiftee
minutes."

"I got my fifteen minutes. I got my fifteen *years* of attentior
Thomas, some of it because of you. My name is forever engraved i
the crime journals. And in your books."

Underwood shook his head. "You're missing a huge opportunity here, Ray. Every bit of publicity you've gotten since your arrest has been negative. But 'Convicted killer gives police identity of Dead Eyes killer' makes you look good. Big headlines."

"What good is that gonna do me after they inject poison into my body?"

"I could debate that with you philosophically. Give you the Zen explanation. The concept of redemption. But I know you pretty well, so I know that's pointless." Underwood tapped his fingers on the table in front of him. "Why do you think Dead Eyes sent you this letter? My friends at the Bureau who asked me to come, they kept asking me, 'Why Singletary?'" He turned his hands palm up. "What should I tell them?"

"I tell you that, and you'll figure out who he is without me."

"You have to know they're doing that right now. Running lists of inmates who did time with you. Guys you were friends with, roomed with, played ball with, protected. Pretty soon, they're going to come across some names and start investigating. Once they do that, your negotiating power goes away."

"Then fuck them. Could be somebody I know from the outside. They think they're so smart, let them run their lists. They've got 159 hours, maybe they can figure it out themselves." The anger melted from his face, and he forced a smile. "Then again, maybe not."

"Let me at least get you something. Governor won't give you the commuted sentence. But he may give you something else."

"What else is there? What else could a guy want who's going to die in a matter of hours?"

Underwood rose from his chair. "I don't know, Ray. That's something you have to think about. But I wouldn't wait too long."

Vail pried her eyes away from Singletary and looked at Del Monaco. "Why did Dead Eyes feel the need to send that letter?"

Del Monaco stifled a yawn, then ran a couple of pudgy fingers through his eyes. "I don't know, Karen. Assuming it's someone he did time with, maybe he was coding a message in the prose. Maybe it's as simple as he knew he was about to die and wanted to say good-bye. Or maybe he knew it'd drive us nuts."

She looked down at the letter again. "Let this be a time where we conclude our daily activities, where we look inward and consider what's come before us," she read aloud. "That could be a send-off I guess."

"Or is it code? Or the ramblings of a deranged mind?"

Bledsoe snapped his cell phone shut. "Hernandez has eight thousand names on his inmate list. He's comparing it to the other lists he's been compiling to see if there are any matches. Then we'll whittle from there."

Vail said, "Problem is, Singletary's right. There isn't enough time to parse these lists. I wonder if he'd go for a 'maybe.' You know, if we can locate Dead Eyes and prove he's our UNSUB before he gets the needle, his sentence is commuted. If not . . ." She shrugged. "He gets the juice."

Del Monaco watched through the mirror as Underwood patted Singletary on the back. "No way they're going to commute his sentence," Del Monaco said. "I hope this whole exercise wasn't for nothing."

"Won't be for nothing," Bledsoe said. "Underwood gets a chapter for his next book."

Del Monaco walked out into the corridor to greet Underwood. Vail was left alone with Bledsoe, finally able to talk freely with him. "We know it's him, Bledsoe. The letter is from Dead Eyes. We know that."

He held up a hand. "Hold it, we don't know anything."

"'I know what they know.' He's telling us he knows what we know because he has the profile, he's seen the file."

Bledsoe shrugged. "It could mean a lot of things. Whoever wrote this letter ain't exactly firing on all thrusters. I don't think you can take anything at face value."

Vail sighed. "I know that. Just seems to fit, like he's trying to throw it in our faces. *He knows. We know.*"

"Which brings me back to the same question: why did he send the letter in the first place? I don't get it. Why not send you another email if he wanted us to see it? Why communicate with Singletary?" He turned from her, kicked his shoe against the wall. "Damn it. I hate this case. Usually you get a skel who commits a crime, leaves some evidence, and all you gotta do is track the leads. Half the time it's a relative or acquaintance. But this guy seems to leave nothing behind that can be traced to him. And he's hit unrelated victims. He's playing with us. Leaving us fucking riddles." He shoved his hands in his pockets and started pacing. "I don't know how you do it, dealing with these fucking serials. I did it full time, I'd have a bleeding ulcer."

The door swung open and in walked Underwood and Del Monaco. Underwood's tie was askew and his usual cheerful face looked taut and hard. "I couldn't turn him," he said. "Ray's desperate. He's got one bargaining chip, and he's not willing to give it up. It's literally life or death to him."

"Is he telling the truth?" Vail asked.

Underwood sighed, leaned both palms against the surface of the mirror, and bowed his head. "I think so. I think he really believes he knows who wrote that letter. And if Dead Eyes wrote that letter, and if his beliefs are on the money, you'd have made a big step toward solving this case."

"Too many damn 'ifs,'" Bledsoe said.

Underwood pushed away from the mirror. "That's the nature of our business, Detective. Educated guesses about what these people are thinking, about who and what they are, based on what we've seen before. There may be a lot of ifs, but a lot of the ifs have been proven right over the years. Sometimes it's all we've had to go on." Underwood grabbed the doorknob. "Agent Vail," he said without facing her. "Just wanted you to know that's a damn good profile you drew up. And I like your work on finding signature within MO. It's got a lot of promise." He turned his head and winked at her. "Keep up the good work."

With that, he pulled the door open, then walked out of the room.

. . . *fifty-nine*

The intervening five days passed with a flurry of strategy session. that included Bledsoe, Del Monaco, the district attorney Thomas Gifford, the governors of the states of Virginia and New York, Lee Thurston, and the speaker of the Virginia state legislature The posturing was intense, the political threats at times implied, a other times plainly stated.

The issues were debated, but in the end, the district attorney fel that setting aside a jury's decision to invoke the death penalty unde any circumstances devalued the very heart of the American judicia system. When the governor commuted a sentence, it was within hi power to do so according to the Constitution. Though an uncom mon occurrence, it was almost always a defensible decision. Making deals with killers due to die could be defended as well—if nothing else, to potentially prevent other women from being killed—but i was no guarantee they would find the offender even if they were given his identity. And if the whole exercise turned out to be a wild goose chase, both the district attorney and the governor would come out damaged, perhaps permanently, and lose reelection. No one would want to vote for law enforcement leaders who had been bilked by a convicted killer.

And so the argument went.

The search for an inmate who had served with Singletary was more daunting task than they had anticipated. He had not only been a resident of North Carolina's Rockridge institution, but he also spen time at Virginia's Greensville Correctional Facility. With the numbe of potential suspects with a violent background numbering in th thousands, Robby and Sinclair headed a subgroup of law enforcemen staff whose sole task was to pare the list to a reasonable number o men who could be questioned individually. But progress was akin t watching honey dissolve in iced tea. Erroneously eliminate one inmate on the list and the entire process would be for nothing. So they had to be methodical and cross-check one another's work.

With the hours dwindling, and with the Singletary decision having been made, Vail, Bledsoe, Del Monaco, the district attorney, and Thomas Underwood were invited to witness the execution. They were flown by private charter and then ushered by limousine to the prison. They were quiet, having little to say to each other. It had all been said during their earlier deliberations.

Vail had tossed and turned the past four nights, getting little sleep—and what rest she did get occurred in disturbed, nightmare-filled fits. She spent time with Jonathan each day, but there was little news to report.

It was agreed that prior to Singletary's death walk, Underwood and Vail would make one last attempt to obtain the name locked away in his brain. Upon arrival, they were led to the prison's death-watch area, where they found Richard Ray Singletary in a cell, sitting on the edge of a cot. He was dressed in a thin, short-sleeved blue cotton shirt and a fresh pair of pants, his head bowed and forearms resting on his thighs. The warden was standing outside, his face tight and drawn. There was no chaplain present.

The door to Singletary's cell was open, and three large guards stood with their hands on their belts. They were there to prevent him from harming himself, and to ensure he did not explode in one last rampage of death before he left this world.

Singletary's ankles and wrists were shackled in preparation for transport to the lethal injection chamber. Though he had been given steak dinners each night as compensation for having turned over the alleged Dead Eyes letter, his face was drawn and he looked as if he had dropped several pounds since their last visit. His head lifted upon their arrival, hope spilling from his eyes. He undoubtedly thought they might have brought news the governor had spared him.

"Thomas."

"Ray."

The two men stared at each other for a long moment, then Single-tary looked away, apparently realizing they were there not to deliver good news, but to try one last time to wrest information from him.

"We need the name, Ray. I know you're disappointed we weren't able to make the deal. No, check that. Disappointed is a bullshit word. Devastated. But I tried, you know I tried."

Vail stood to Underwood's left, arms folded, trying to will the prisoner to give up the name.

Singletary nodded.

"I'm sorry I failed." He stepped inside the open door and knelt in front of Singletary, within reach of the man's legs.

One of the guards stepped forward. "Sir, I would be more comfortable—"

Underwood held up a hand. "It's okay, it's okay. Ray won't hurt me." He looked up at Singletary and met his eyes. "Ray, I'm going to make you one last offer. I have the power to let the world know that your last act on this Earth was one of mercy. You once told me you felt sorry for the victims' families. You have a chance to make a difference, to give them a little bit of something to make them feel good. To alleviate their hate."

"Their hate is misdirected. Tell them to hate my father, who beat me every day, tell them to hate the two women who raped me when I was thirteen." A tear streamed down his cheek. "Tell them to hate the people who made me who I am."

Underwood's lips twisted into a frown. "Ray, don't do this. Don't make excuses. You are who you are, you did what you did. You're going to face your maker very soon. Wouldn't you rather face him knowing you did at least one good deed in your lifetime? Show him you made an attempt to atone for the pain you've caused."

Vail did not fault Underwood for his efforts but was sickened by the fact they had been reduced to begging for the information. Single-tary deserved to rot in hell; he deserved to be tortured the way he had tortured his victims. The way he had brought them to the brink of death, only to revive them over and over so he could torture them some more.

"This man deserves to die," Vail said matter-of-factly. "He's not ping to give us the name, Agent Underwood." She was turning the rew, driving it in, bringing Singletary to the point of no return. We've offered him what we could. The man has no desire to save mself."

Underwood sighed, then rose to his feet. "Richard Ray, you dispoint me. There's nothing to be gained by protecting this man, by king his name to your grave." He waited a moment, and for a brief cond it appeared as if Singletary's mouth wavered. "We're going to e in the chamber, in the viewing area. If you change your mind, ay, just say the name. Before you lose consciousness, say the name. ave your soul."

Underwood turned and left, Vail on his heels. They did not look ack.

The execution chamber was a clean, well-lighted circular area su
rounded by a glass viewing enclosure and a witness room spo
ing sixteen blue plastic institutional-style chairs. Already seated we
relatives of both the victims and prisoner, state-selected witness
and media representatives. Vail and Underwood took their places b
side Bledsoe and Del Monaco, who were sitting behind the gover
ment officials also in attendance.

Vail shook her head at Bledsoe, but he already knew by their d
meanor that Singletary had not cooperated. Bledsoe, desperate
clear the Dead Eyes case, had quietly lobbied the governor and d
trict attorney one last time upon arrival at the correctional facili
But they would have nothing of it.

The families of the seven women Richard Ray Singletary h
killed sat rigidly in their seats. Their faces were, for the most pa
stiff and angry, an occasional tissue being dabbed at the face. N
doubt reliving excruciating memories a parent should never expe
ence. Their daughters brutally murdered, the case file reports clea
outlining the torturous last hours of their children's lives.

The door to the execution chamber swung open and Richard R
Singletary was rolled into the room strapped to a gurney. ECG c
diac monitor leads and a stethoscope were affixed to his chest, a
two IV lines, one in each arm, had been inserted in the adjace
preparation room. The black-and-white clock mounted above t
doorway to the chamber read 11:49.

Vail uncrossed her legs and leaned forward on her thighs, han
covering her mouth, hoping for one last utterance from the mons
who lay strapped before them.

The IV lines were connected to the wall, where they thread
through an opening into a puke-green anteroom, where the hood

execution team stood amongst their drugs, a clock, and a bank of telephones—should the governor call with a last-minute stay. In this case, the governor was in attendance. Vail glanced over at the man. Judging by his rigid posture and stern face, this was not going to be Richard Ray Singletary's lucky day.

Vail knew multiple executioners were set to inject drugs into the IV tubes, but only one of them would actually supply the lethal dose. No one would know—not even the executioners—who delivered the toxic cocktail into the inmate's bloodstream and who had injected their drugs into a secondary reservoir.

At eleven fifty-five, the executioners shoved their syringes into the IV ampules, then awaited word to proceed.

The warden leaned close to the prisoner. "Richard Ray Singletary, do you have any last remarks?"

Vail closed her eyes, her heart pounding so hard she felt the pressure beating against her ear drums.

"Rot in hell, all of you," Singletary yelled.

"Thank you, sir," the warden said. "And may the same fate befall you, as I'm sure it will." He turned to the executioners and said, "Proceed."

Vail pictured them depressing their plungers, injecting a massive dose of the barbiturate sodium pentothal, the first step in Richard Ray Singletary's death. In a matter of seconds, he would be unconscious.

After flushing the line with saline, a paralyzing agent, pancuronium bromide, was then injected to deaden nerve signals to the cardiac muscle and disable the diaphragm and lungs.

Bledsoe sighed deeply, his eyes focused on the second hand as it swept around the clock face. At two minutes past midnight, with the ECG monitor registering an unending flat line, the warden pronounced Richard Ray Singletary dead.

"Shit," Bledsoe muttered under his breath.

Vail nodded. "Shit."

The flight back on the governor's private charter was quiet. No one spoke. Vail could not help thinking they were back to square one. As much as they knew, as much information they had garnered from the various crime scenes, they still had no clue as to who Dead Eyes was. No suspects. Just pages and pages of information, gruesome photos, and for all they knew, useless analyses.

Vail stretched out her legs, and a sudden spark of pain in her left knee took her breath. She pulled out a small bottle of Extra Strength Tylenol and popped two caplets. She realized she had almost finished the thirty-count bottle in less than three days. She promised herself that the next time she saw Dr. Altman she would ask him to look at the knee and give her something stronger for the pain. Even if it required treatment, she had no time. She needed to stay on top of things until they caught Dead Eyes. Along with Jonathan's condition, the case had become the focus, dare she think it, *obsession*, of her life.

She reclined her seat and thought of Robby. She missed his touch, his warmth, his scent. It was a strange feeling, losing oneself so totally in another's person. Had she not had everything else hanging over her head, she might have been able to revel in falling in love. It had been so long. She had only experienced it twice, the first time in junior high school, and then again with Deacon. Deacon happened fast, and then she quickly became pregnant with Jonathan. She didn't think Deacon was a mistake at the time, but history was not as kind in retrospect.

The Lear jet banked left and the lights of the small private landing strip came into view. She tightened her belt and turned to face Thomas Underwood, who was sitting to her right. "I enjoyed working with you."

"I wish the end result could've been better."

"Me, too."

"If there's anything more I can do, please don't hesitate."

Vail let a small smile escape the right side of her mouth. "I could use your help writing a paper on the identification of signature within MO. Would you consider coauthoring it with me?"

"Absolutely. Of course, that's assuming you're not really the Dead Eyes killer."

"Of course." She rested her head against the seatback and closed her eyes as the plane hovered above the landing strip. The wheels caught with a slight screech, and she was home.

She knew Robby would be waiting up for her.

Turning points. Turning points seem to remain with you after other memories have long since faded, like a lone flower that remains in bloom amongst a basket of dried leaves. As he sat pecking away, he tapped into the emotions that led to his establishing his independence so many years ago. For him, a turning point like this was not just a thriving blossom but an entire bouquet.

I got tired of the beatings, of the prick doing things to me I didn't want him to do. But I wasn't strong enough to fight him off. I thought if I showed him I could fight back at least once or twice, he'd get the message to stay away. But it didn't work, because he keeps coming for me. Still, I've been able to protect what's important. He'll never find the secret place. No one will ever find it.

But I realized that there were things I could do to control my own life. Like at the slaughterhouse, they use meat hooks to hang the carcasses. And I got to thinking . . . the slabs of meat are real heavy. So I asked my boss if I could work in the meat prep area. He looked me up and down and saw that I'm pretty tall for my age, but scrawny. He said he didn't think I could handle it, but I just started doing it on my own time. He saw I was determined to do it, and he finally said okay.

I've also been spending an extra half hour doing exercises with the carcasses at the end of my shift. It's as good as lifting weights, maybe even better. I've been able to lift the larger, heavier ones. So that's where I've been working the last couple of months. And I feel like I'm now ready to take on the prick. . . .

A turning point indeed. He'd gained confidence in himself, a confidence that would lead to him gaining control over his life, perhaps for the first time. He realized that if there was something that needed to be done, he merely had to find a way to do it. It wasn't a matter of *if* it could be done, but *how*. He'd always felt that way, from the time he found a way to haul the plywood from the store to his house a few miles away. But the stakes were higher then and he needed to know he could do the dirty work, confront the devil, and get the job done. Because there would be no turning back. Once he confronted the prick, it was do or die. And he wasn't planning on dying.

Now, decades later, he was facing the same demons again. Funny how life comes full circle. But he was wiser and ready for what was to come. No one would ever be able to tell him *no* again. Not anyone.

He made sure of that.

The next morning, after lying awake most of the night, Vail quickly showered and dressed, then rushed to the hospital to be near Jonathan. There were times when she needed to hold his hand, stroke his cheek, pull him into her arms. It was a longing, whenever she was away from him, that she could only liken to being without food and water. After a time of doing without them, she had to find some to keep herself going. Seeing Jonathan, even in his current state, gave her the strength to go on. As Emma used to say when Jonathan was young, seeing him "recharged her batteries." Though Vail found the analogy endearing, she now fully understood the reference.

NEARLY THREE HOURS after arriving at the hospital, Vail checked in at the op center. The lists were being crunched, but thus far there were no obvious hits. Just a few possibles, on which Robby and Manette were following up.

Vail left the op center and headed to the assisted care facility to finalize the paperwork. While en route, Vail called her Aunt Faye, who told her everything was ready for Emma's move. Though Emma's belongings were packed, there were many drawers and boxes that still needed to be sifted through, as Faye didn't know what Vail wanted to dispose of and what she wanted to keep. "Then there's your doll collection."

Vail sighed. "There's so much to take care of."

"Don't worry about the house," Faye said. "Take care of Jonathan and your mom. I'll make sure things are looked after until you're ready to put the place up for sale."

Vail thanked her and told her how much she appreciated the help.

"I'm bringing some boxes for you to look through when you

ave time," Faye added. "At least that'll be a few less for you to deal
vith when the time comes."

They confirmed their plans to meet at the assisted care facility
round three o'clock, then said good-bye.

After meeting briefly with the Silver Meadows facility manager,
/ail fought back tears as she signed the papers. The contract was fi-
ialized. Emma's room was now waiting for her.

VAIL'S PHONE RANG as she stepped into the parking lot. She wiped
ier eyes, cleared her throat, and answered the call. It was Jackson
Parker, keeping her up-to-date on the status of her case. One remark
ie made that she found particularly intriguing was whether she had
given thought to the possibility that Deacon could have murdered
Linwood. The remainder of her drive back to the op center was con-
umed with thoughts regarding this possibility: The focus of the of-
ender's attention seemed to be around her; the personal connection
vould fit. And the killings began right around the time Vail had filed
or divorce.

But how would Deacon have found out about Linwood's rela-
ionship to her? More importantly, did Deacon fit her profile? In
many respects, he did. She had to look at it objectively, removing all
emotion. It was a very difficult thing for a profiler to do. Often, any
personal involvement ruined his or her ability to keep a distance, to
evaluate and analyze without bias.

She called Del Monaco, ran the scenario by him, and he agreed it
vas worth looking into. She closed her phone and shook her head.
Once again, she had overlooked a most obvious lead, one right in
ront of her face. Regardless of whether it led somewhere, it was
omething she had not thought of. She would have to remember to
hank Parker for the heads-up.

When she arrived at the op center, she told Bledsoe of the Deacon connection and then asked about Hancock.

"We've got a guy on him and he hasn't been out of our sight. So
ar, nothing."

"And the killer's been dormant ever since you put the tail on him."

"Coincidence?"

"Guess we'll find out. Lab get anything on the stuff taken from his place?"

Bledsoe sat down heavily. "Nothing."

"I was hoping we'd find something. Lot of times the killer keeps the trophies he takes from the vics in his place, so he can play with them when the urge hits him. But sometimes they have other places just in case their houses are searched."

Bledsoe said, "Hancock knows what we'd be looking for. And as arrogant as he is, if he is Dead Eyes, he'd be smart enough not to keep his trophies in a place we'd think to look."

"Besides," Vail said, "the vics are all killed in their own homes, so the dirt and blood are all offsite. If he changes clothes and dumps them en route, they're long gone. Which leaves us nowhere."

He wished her luck on getting her mother settled into the care facility.

"Sorry for the distraction, but there's a lot of things I've got to take care of before she gets here," she said.

"Hey, it's your mother. Get her settled in, then get back on track. I need you."

FAYE AND EMMA ARRIVED a few minutes before three. They checked in Emma, unloaded her suitcases, and helped the staff orient her to her new surroundings. While Faye went to freshen up, Vail sat and tried to talk with her mother to ensure she understood what was happening and why. But Emma's lapses in and out of lucidity saddened and frustrated her.

When Faye returned half an hour later, Emma was asleep. Faye planned to stay the night on a cot in Emma's room, then drive home tomorrow. They unloaded the boxes Faye had brought from Emma's basement and bedroom closet and placed them in the backseat of Vail's car.

Vail hugged her aunt, thanked her for all her help, then drove to

Fairfax hospital to visit Jonathan. She ate dinner in his room, talked to him for a while, and told him they had moved grandma to Virginia. And like every time before this one, she told him how much she loved him.

VAIL ARRIVED AT ROBBY'S just after 8 P.M. He wasn't home, and the house was quiet. She carried in the boxes from her car and set them down in the family room. She changed into a pair of jeans and a sweatshirt, then made herself a cup of hot chocolate. She knelt on the floor in front of the boxes and sliced them open with a pair of scissors.

Inside the first box was Lily, an old doll she had played with as a child. She leaned her back against the couch and smiled. Emma was good with a sewing machine, and had spent countless hours crafting an entire wardrobe of custom clothing for her. Vail fished around the box and found that many of the outfits were still in good condition. She thought of her friend Andrea, and the hours they spent in her room, playing house with their dolls.

The electronic beep of one of Robby's wristwatches plucked her from the daydream. Holding Lily brought back many memories of her childhood and only intensified her indecision about what to do with Emma's house. She would have preferred not to sell it. With the only expenses being property taxes, insurance, and occasional maintenance, it made sense to hold onto it. But Old Westbury, while charming and serene, was five hours away, and not what she considered a vacation destination.

She put Lily aside and dove into the next box. She tried to be as selective as possible in terms of what she would keep, as her house's space was limited and she despised clutter. She put on her crime scene hat, sifting through the keepsakes and papers as if they belonged to a victim. If she did any more reminiscing, it might open the emotional floodgates—and bring on the guilt she was suppressing for removing her mother from her home and putting her in a facility . . . even though, logically, she knew it was the correct decision.

In the fourth carton, she found a locked metal cash box. She shook it, but it was heavy and she could feel the contents shifting against the interior. Her curiosity piqued, she used the scissors to pry open the box's cheap latch.

Inside, papers were piled atop each other. She dug in and found old photos of her parents when they were young—group shots, posed photos, and a few from what appeared to be a family trip. She set the pictures aside and saw a small, cloth-wrapped object jammed against the side of the box. She picked it up, spread the wrapping, and uncovered what was inside.

Her mouth dropped open. She sat there staring at it, her mind instantly numb. "Oh, my god" escaped her lips before she realized her cell phone was ringing. *Another mystery. What does it mean?*

She flashed on all the evidence they had thus far gathered from each of the crime scenes, each piece a part of the puzzle she was attempting to assemble. But there was no guide. No framework. And therefore no reference point by which to fit the pieces.

Until now.

Phone is ringing.

She pulled the handset from her pocket and answered it, her mind still tumbling over the riddle. "Vail."

"Karen, it's Thomas Underwood. I hope you don't mind me sticking my nose into your case, but I think I've got something."

Her brain was still crunching data and she was only half listening. "Not a problem. . . . "

"The message left by the offender. You were right to think it means 'It's in the blood.' The blood's the key. But it's not a blood borne disease, it's—"

"Genes," she said.

"That's right," Underwood said. "You figured it out?"

"Just now." She sat there, phone in hand, the shock of the surprise beginning to settle in. "And I know something else, too. I think I know who our UNSUB is."

. . . sixty-four

Vail turned over the metal box and dumped the contents onto a clean, plastic garbage bag. She slipped her hands into a pair of latex gloves Robby had in his desk drawer and began sifting through the items one at a time, hoping to unearth something that would help her find what she was looking for.

She discovered several other dog-eared photos of Emma and Nellie, most of which contained images of people she did not know. But on one of the pictures there was a small object hanging from both Emma's and Nellie's necklaces.

Vail picked up the gold locket she had found in the metal box and stared at it, hoping to find an inscription. There was nothing. But with the lab's color enlargement now sitting beside her, there was no doubt this locket was an identical match for the one found shoved into Linwood's rectum . . . and possibly for the objects dangling from the necklaces in the old photo, as well.

Had Vail been wearing spurs, and had she been able to kick herself, she would have done so. She had been virtually blind to something so obvious. That she hadn't seen it ate at her and ran contrary to what she prided herself on: that she knew the human psyche, could read it and evaluate it and predict certain things about it. But in this case she had been no better than a blind person who couldn't read Braille. Because like all cases, there was a key that unlocked the killer's secrets. She'd held the key—the locket—but had not realized it.

Vail put the photo aside, then continued to thumb through the spilled contents of the metal box. Something grabbed her attention: an envelope containing a scrawled note to Emma from Nellie: "Here's the photo Patrick took of us. See you soon. Love, Nell." Vail felt excitement well up in her chest. *Pay dirt! Maybe.* She thought of all the potential forensics arrayed in front of her: a first name. Finger prints, possibly saliva . . . and DNA.

She found a box of plastic bags in the kitchen and slipped the photo and envelope in their own Ziploc containers. She taped the metal box closed, then dialed Bledsoe and asked if he was seated.

"I'm in my car, I better be seated."

"Then pull over."

"Pull over? That good, huh?"

"How much do you want to break Dead Eyes?"

"More than any other case I've ever had. Why, you got something?"

"I got the killer, Bledsoe. At least, I got a first name and possibly a whole lot more."

"You're shitting me."

"Would I shit you on something like this?"

"Don't hold out on me, Karen. Who is it?"

Vail closed her eyes, took a deep breath, and told him.

"No way," Bledsoe said. "Are you sure?"

"Very sure. I connected the dots. And he fits my profile. It all makes sense, which it should, whenever you look at the suspect in retrospect, right?"

"Karen, I'm sorry."

"I never met the man, Bledsoe. It is what it is. I have no feelings either way. Let's just bag him before he kills again."

"You said you had a name."

"First name is Patrick. If he was the same age as Linwood at the time, my guess is he was born in the mid-nineteen-forties."

"That's a big assumption, but it's a start. I'll get everyone on it, see how many Patricks born in the mid-nineteen-forties show up on any of our lists. You said you've got other stuff, too?"

"I've got an envelope and a photo he may've handled. Might get some latents, possibly DNA."

"Latents would be great. I've got a feeling this guy's been in the system. If I'm right, the prints'll get us his last name, then we're off to the races. Where are you?"

"I'm at Robby's. I've gotta go by the lab to drop off the evidence. I should be back here around eleven thirty."

"Don't go home. Meet us at the op center."

"Oh, my other home."

"And Karen . . . good work."

VAIL ARRIVED AT THE OP CENTER at a quarter to twelve, having been awake for nearly eighteen hours. But she did not feel fatigued. She had been running scenarios and trying to match her profile to what she knew about her father—which was nothing. She had called

Tim Meadows and told him she had crucial evidence in the Dead
Eyes case that needed to be analyzed immediately.

"Judging by what you're bringing me, we'll need a latent person,
an image enhancer, somebody in Questioned Documents . . . I'll
have to get three people on this if you want it done yesterday."

"Tell them I said thanks."

"Oh, that'll go real far."

"Then tell them the faster we get these results the faster we'll
have a suspect in custody."

"They've heard it a million times, Karen. But I'll take care of it.
We'll do the latents first, see if we get any immediate hits. We'll take
good care of you," he told her. When she arrived at headquarters,
one of the lab techs met her at the front entrance, took the materials,
and did not say a word. He was clearly unhappy about having to
work through the night.

But her reception at the op center was vastly different. When Vail
walked in, she got high fives from everyone—including Del Monaco,
who, because of the late hour, was uncharacteristically dressed down
in sweats. Vail didn't think it possible, but by comparison his round
physique looked better in a suit.

"Guess we can pull that tail off Hancock," Bledsoe said, running
a black magic marker through Hancock's name, eliminating him
from their suspect list. "Let's connect some dots."

Vail settled into an empty chair near Del Monaco. "Okay. Here's
my theory: my biological mother, Eleanor Linwood, knew my father
was bad news. She told as much when I went to see her. If this
Patrick was my father, and he was involved with Linwood, either
through marriage or some live-in arrangement, she might have taken
me from my father without his knowledge. Another if, but if that was
the case, it makes sense he was pissed as hell at Linwood. It'd be
something he'd never forget."

"Maybe he spent his life looking for her," Del Monaco said. "To
track her down and kill her. That would explain the personal nature
of the murder, why hers was so much more brutal than the others.

Based on the old photos we have of Linwood, it's pretty obvious each of the victims resembled her. Brunet, shoulder length hair, slim build, pretty face. They were all extensions of Linwood. The way he remembered her, when she was young."

"A lot of time to hold onto all that anger," Robby said.

"Too long," Del Monaco said as he settled himself into a chair. "For someone inclined to violence, as this guy obviously was, it built to a point where he couldn't contain it anymore."

"So how do the messages tie in?" Manette asked. "Was Linwood carrier of something wicked?"

Vail shook her head. "It wasn't that at all. Blood, yes, but not a viral infection. 'It's in the blood' refers to a genetic link. Blood relative. Or maybe it refers to me working the case. And then there's the gold locket. I've got an old photo of Emma and Linwood wearing what looks like identical necklaces. Photo's at the lab now being enhanced. We found one of the lockets shoved up Linwood's rectum, and the other one was buried in Emma's keepsakes. Obviously, the killer knew about the lockets. He must've gotten hold of Linwood's and held onto it all these years."

Bledsoe lifted the telephone handset. "I'll get a uniform posted outside Emma's door at the assisted care facility until we get this guy in custody. What was the name of that place?"

Vail told him, and he began to dial.

"Where do we stand with your list?" Del Monaco asked.

Robby, who was sitting on the edge of his desk, reached behind him for his yellow pad. "Fifty-two Patricks. One of them, a Patrick Farwell, *did* show up on a roster from Velandia Correctional Facility from 1977. Did a deuce for rape, then paroled. Kind of fell off the radar sometime in the early eighties."

"This guy is how old?" Manette asked. Like Del Monaco, she was in sweats and tennis shoes, but on her slender frame, they fit well and looked cozy.

Robby flipped a few pages. "According to what we've got here, looks like we got a DOB of August 9, 1947."

Sinclair straightened. "Bingo."

Bledsoe hung up the phone and announced, "Okay, uniform i
on its way to Silver Meadows."

"Hold on a minute," Manette said. "That doesn't fit your profile
does it?" She was looking at Vail, arms spread, as if she were enjoying
that the profile was flawed.

Vail cocked her head. "The age difference is irrelevant—"

"Oh, here it comes. You give us an age range of thirty to forty
years old, and when he turns out to be sixty-one, you say it doesn'
mean nothing?"

"If you'd let me finish, I'll explain," Vail said calmly. "We know
Farwell did time for rape. If he is our guy, I'll bet he also did time
somewhere else, maybe under an alias or in a different state, for sim
ilar sexually related crimes. If that's the case, and he was in the slam
mer for a while, that would explain the age difference."

"How so?" Bledsoe asked.

"We've found that when a sexual predator is incarcerated, he
doesn't mature emotionally, even though he ages chronologically. S
even though we're looking for a forty year old, and he's really sixty, i
he's done twenty years somewhere, emotionally he's still forty when
he gets out. Since we're analyzing behavior, and behavior is a func
tion of our emotions, he actually does fit the profile."

Manette waved a hand. "Mumbo jumbo hocus pocus crap. You
got an excuse for everything, don't you? Can't you just admit you
were wrong?"

"This isn't solving anything," Bledsoe said. "For the moment,
accept Karen's explanation. Let's move on."

Sinclair's head was resting on the Michael Jordan basketball, hi
eyelids at half-mast. "Did we put out an APB?"

"And a BOLO," Del Monaco said, referring to the Bureau's "B
On The Lookout" alert.

Sinclair pulled his head up, straightened his back, and tried to
open his eyes. "Then we should be getting as much as we can on thi
guy, checking tax records, DMV files, utility companies—"

"Some of that'll have to wait till morning, when we can access their databases," Bledsoe said. "But I agree. Let's get started now on what we can. Maybe we'll have something by then. We're going to need more than a locket, a profile, and some circumstantial connections to get a search warrant."

THE SUN'S EARLY RAYS crept past the cloud cover and warmed the winter air a few degrees. Like the task force, the house's heater had worked overtime into the cold evening, struggling to blow through clogged and aged ducts.

Using the Internet, FBI, police, and tax databases, Virginia prison records, and a few favors, they were able to sift through a fair amount of information. The one promising fact was that Patrick Farwell had a history consistent with those seen amongst serial offenders. The records they sifted painted a by-the-numbers black-and-white picture, but left a great many holes that needed plugging. In the wee hours of the morning, they began reading between the lines, substituting speculation and conjecture for facts. It was a less than accurate means of proceeding, but when they stepped back and examined it, the picture they were left with did seem to support their theory.

Vail had a problem with loading theory upon thin assumptions, but everyone was tired and strained.

"Damn," Robby muttered. He was seated in front of the computer, logged onto a database that displayed Virginia real estate transactions over the past hundred years. Based on Vail's analysis and Del Monaco's theory, they had focused their attention on Virginia, hypothesizing that Dead Eyes had shown an inclination to remain within the state. They intended to look at everything but decided not to stray too far from the guidelines provided by the geoprofile as a means of narrowing their searches.

"What's wrong?" Bledsoe asked, his eyes bloodshot and his sixth or seventh cup of coffee in hand.

"I did a search of tax records, figuring if he owned a house, or condo, or some land somewhere, I'd get a hit. Came up a big goose egg."

The simultaneous rings of the telephone and fax machine shifted their attention. Being the closest to the kitchen, Vail grabbed the handset. She listened to the technician provide details on what they had found, then jotted down some notes. "And the other stuff?" She waited a beat, thanked the person, and hung up. She stepped back into the living room with a smile on her face. "That was the lab. They lifted several latents and ran them through AFIS. They got a hit." She paused for emphasis, then said, "Patrick Farwell."

"Bingo," Bledsoe said.

Manette rocked forward in her chair, then lifted the page from the fax machine. "Patrick Farwell, that's our dude." She examined the mug shot the lab had faxed, then handed it to Vail. "And he looks a lot like you, Kari."

Vail cocked her head, assessing the image, instantly noting—and regretting—the obvious likeness to herself. "Daddy," she finally said, "it's a pleasure to meet you."

The task force snacked on bagels, muffins, and a tank of coffee Sinclair had retrieved from the local café a short time after 7 A.M. It was only fifteen degrees when he left, and when he returned he babbled on about how growing up in Oak Park, Illinois, should have prepared him for days like this. Everyone was too tired to object to his bellyaching, and eventually he took his seat and hugged a large mug of hot coffee.

In fact, java flowed freely to anyone with a cup. They were now going on twenty-four hours without sleep, with no break in the foreseeable future. As they took in their fill of sugar and caffeine, they analyzed all the information that began rolling in shortly after the clock had struck eight.

They had learned that Patrick Farwell had also been arrested fifteen years ago for aggravated sexual assault of a minor. He had served time at Pocomona Correctional Facility before being transferred to the newer maximum security Greensville campus halfway through his sentence because he had been stabbed by an inmate who took his assault on the minor personally.

But his parole eighteen months ago only served to rid the system of the scourge that had been Patrick Farwell. He broke ties with his parole officer and was never seen again. As far as the Department of Corrections was concerned, Patrick Farwell disappeared. After an extensive search, it was theorized he had left the state and gone underground. But the warden had another theory, and that was that Patrick Farwell had taken on an alias and was still living somewhere in the Commonwealth of Virginia. It was only a hunch, but the warden noted that his hunches, though based only on his limited knowledge of each particular inmate, were usually accurate.

"His pent-up anger boiled over when he got out," Del Monaco said. "As soon as he disappeared, there were no controls on him anymore. No guards, no parole officers. The guy was unleashed, literally and figuratively."

Robby nodded. "And his break with parole coincides with the first Dead Eyes murder. My vic, Marci Evers."

"Any suggestion of computer skills?" Bledsoe asked.

Robby rubbed his eyes. "Like what? Classes, things like that?"

"Anything," Bledsoe said.

"Nothing I see in the record," Robby said. "But computer training is available lots of places, and most of it isn't tracked or recorded anywhere."

"And the kind of software used for the untraceable email is available online," Vail said. "Based on what I was told, advanced training isn't required."

"Well," Manette said, "I say we go for it. We've got the name, fingerprints, and background on this guy, and from what I'm hearing, he fits nicely. All we need is . . . him."

Bledsoe clapped his hands together. "Then let's get moving. Hernandez, talk with the postal inspector. Find out if there was ever a forwarding order submitted for Patrick Farwell. Sin, check with the IRS, see if any W–2's have been filed. Then check the regional jails. Possible this guy got picked up on a traffic violation or a drunk-in-public. He could already be under lock and key." Bledsoe looked at the fax. "And I'll get this circulated. Have the lab send it to every PD and SO in the state."

"Shouldn't we go national?" Sinclair asked.

"Can't hurt to get something out to NCIC," Bledsoe said, referring to the National Crime Information Center.

Vail shook her head. "Farwell's local. He's bold, aggressive, and sure of himself. He thinks he can operate without consequence, and unfortunately we've only reinforced those feelings by being unable to generate any substantial leads."

Robby held up an index finger. "Until now."

"Until now. Point is, we've given him no reason to leave his comfort zone, which is outlined in the geoprofile. For now, I say we keep it statewide. And hope we get lucky."

With the investigation now focused and well on its way toward bringing in its first suspect, Vail took a break to run over to the hospital to check in on Jonathan.

She informed the nurse she wanted to talk with the doctor, then sat and held Jonathan's hand for nearly half an hour before Altman walked in. They exchanged brief pleasantries before he said, "You remember our discussions about the importance of small steps."

"Have there been any since you last examined him?"

"Yes. Come closer." He removed his penlight from his jacket pocket and leaned over Jonathan's face. He turned on the light and brought it close to the youth's eyes.

"He blinked," Vail said. "He did that before."

"That's right. Now, watch this." Altman stepped back and grabbed a wad of Jonathan's forearm and squeezed. Jonathan moved the limb, pulling away from Altman's grip. "Purposeful movement in response to pinching."

Vail moved to Jonathan's side and instinctively rubbed his forearm where Altman had made his mark. "And that means?"

"It's a very, very strong sign that Jonathan is coming out of the comatose state."

"How long?"

"Before he's completely out of it?" Altman shrugged. "There's no timetable. Could be tomorrow, could be weeks or months. It's impossible to say."

While the agony of uncertainty would continue, at least she had substantial reason for hope. The odds that Jonathan would come out of the coma had just increased. "Thank you, Doctor."

"I noticed your limp has gotten worse. Mind if I take a look at it?"

Vail smiled. "I'd meant to ask you about it. I twisted the knee a couple weeks ago. Then I slipped on the ice, and it's been killing me ever since."

She sat down and watched as Altman moved her leg through a normal range of motion, then gently pushed and pulled in a variety of directions. Vail grabbed the arms of the chair and tried not to scream.

"Orthopedics isn't my specialty, but it looks like you've torn some ligaments. You should have an MRI and a more comprehensive exam." He pulled out a prescription pad and jotted down the names of two physicians. "Don't put it off too long, it's only going to get worse."

She took the paper and thanked him. After Altman had left the room, Vail leaned close to her son and ran the back of her index finger across his face. His left eye twitched in response. "Jonathan, sweetie, can you hear me? It's Mom. I wanted to tell you how proud I am of you. Keep fighting. You're gonna beat this."

She reached down and took his hand in hers. "I'm making progress, too, on my case. Tell you what. When you wake up, we'll ditch this place and go out for milk shakes. Just the two of us, okay?"

She gave his hand a gentle squeeze, then kissed his forehead.

"I love you, champ."

We've got Farwell's full file from Greensville," Bledsoe said, tossing it on the table in front of him. Robby and Vail had arrived at Izzy's Pizza Parlor at nearly the same time. Bledsoe had already ordered, and a large pizza pie gleaming with cheese and pepperoni sat in front of him. He moved over to allow Vail into the booth beside him. Robby's size automatically bought him the entire opposite end of the table. "Farwell was in the general population. There was a note in the file that he was particularly close with one inmate."

"Richard Ray Singletary," Robby said.

"The one and only."

Vail sighed. "Well, that makes me feel a little better. That we didn't let Singletary take the secret to hell with him. At least we found the information before anyone else died."

"What else is in the file?" Robby asked.

"According to prison records, home address is listed as a PO Box in Dale City. Manette's on her way over there to see if it's still active. If it is, she'll sit on it, see if he shows. But we also got a fifteen-year-old employment address. Timberland Custom Cabinets in Richmond."

"A carpenter," Robby said, eyeing the pizza.

"Yes," Bledsoe said, lifting a large slice from the aluminum platter. Robby followed his lead and dug in. "I take it we're on our way there after lunch."

"Already spoke with the guy. He's a real by-the-numbers prick. I put a call in to the DA to get a warrant. Should be ready by the time we're done here. Hopefully they'll have more than just a PO Box in their file."

Robby sprinkled red pepper flakes on his pizza. "Even if he doesn't, it feels a whole lot better having a scent to track. Sooner or later, we'll find him."

TIMBERLAND CUSTOM CABINETS was a sprawling industrial com plex on a potholed asphalt road that dead-ended against the back l of an adjacent lumberyard. The main structure was a tin-roofed bric building that probably had not looked a whole lot better when was new.

Vail took one last pull on the straw of her Big Gulp of Coke—hig octane to keep her mind working and her feet moving—and followe Robby and Bledsoe into the building. Bledsoe served the search wa rant and asked for the personnel records pertaining to Patrick Farwel Ten minutes later, a heavyset black woman emerged from anoth wing of the office with a dog-eared manila file folder in her hand. Sh handed it over without a word, then returned to her desk.

They thumbed through it, the three of them huddling over th paperwork, scouring it as if it contained the highly guarded secr formula for Coca-Cola.

"Same PO Box," Bledsoe commented.

"And nothing on the application to indicate he'd ever been in th slammer," Robby noted.

"You didn't really expect him to be an honest citizen when fillin out his job app, did you?" Vail asked. "Would you hire a rapist who done time?"

"So we're left with interviewing the employees," Robby said. H turned to the receptionist. "Can we talk with the personnel director?

"You're lookin' at her."

"You have any employees who've been with the company long than fifteen years?"

She looked at the ceiling, searching the exposed pipes and ventil tion ducts. "We got four. No, three. Then there's the owner."

"They in?" Bledsoe asked. "We'll need to talk to each of them."

"They're in. I'll call them."

Vail held up a hand. "Hold it. We'll take the owner first. The we'll talk with the three workers."

AL MASSIE WAS A SQUAT MAN in his early fifties. His thick, sho legs rubbed together when he walked, causing a side-to-side gait th

embled a waddle. He had a flat pencil stuck behind his right ear,
d frazzled gray hair interspersed with saw dust. His left thumb was
ssing its last joint.

"I'm Paul Bledsoe, Fairfax County Homicide. These are my asso-
tes, Special Agent Karen Vail and Detective Robby Hernandez."
asantries were exchanged. "We were wondering what you could
us about Patrick Farwell. Worked here three years, nineteen—"

"I remember Patrick. Good worker, kept to himself. Didn't know
thing about what he was doing, though. I had nothing to do with
I told the police everything, which wasn't much."

"We're not here about that case," Vail said. "We were just hoping
u could provide some background for us on Patrick. Anything you
uld tell us would be helpful."

"Don't remember much. That was a long time ago."

"How about friends he had?" Vail continued. "Was he close with
of the workers?"

"From what I remember, Patrick was a loner. There was one guy
used to work with a lot, Jim Gaston. Did a lot of finish work with
n. Jim's still here. You talk to him yet?"

"No, we figured we'd start with you."

"Jimbo's your man. If Patrick said anything to anybody, it woulda
:n to Jimbo." He looked at Bledsoe and Robby, then took a step
:kward. "I'm in the middle of a wall unit, and yes, I may own the
:ce but I still keep my hands in the sawdust. Don't like running the
siness, that was my father's job before he passed on. Anything else
u need me for?"

Bledsoe shook his head. "That's good for now. If something
nes up, we'll find you. Thanks for your help."

MES GASTON NEEDED A DENTIST. His left front tooth was miss-
;, and his lower teeth were crooked and caked with plaque. He
d a receding forehead and a strong chin, giving him almost a
:historic appearance. He, too, had a flat pencil tucked behind his
, and his apron was covered with paintbrush strokes of stain.

"I remember Patrick, sure," he said in response to Bledsoe's

question. "Strange guy. Didn't like to talk much unless he h
some beer in him. He'd sneak some during lunch, then he'd op
up. Talked about these women he'd had, but I didn't pay h
much mind. Thought he was blowing his own horn, you kno
Then when he got arrested I started thinkin' maybe he wasn't sh
tin' me."

"He ever say anything about where he lived, places he liked to
or hang out?" Vail asked.

"He lived on an old family ranch or something like that. Lo
land. Hunted fox in the winter, fished in the summer. 'Bout all I
member. We wasn't friends or nothing, just worked together on ca
inets. He was real good, though, had the gift."

"The gift?"

"Good hands. Born with it, I'd say. You can just tell. Steady han
good eye."

Bledsoe asked, "When was the last time you saw him?"

"The day they put them cuffs on him and hauled him out
here."

Robby blew on his hands to warm them, then asked, "You kno
anyone he may still be close with, someone we could talk to, may
find out where he is, or where his ranch is?"

"Don't know anyone. It's not close, I can tell you that. Big dri
to get here every day."

"Hey Jimbo," a man called from thirty yards away. "We go
move this thing outta here!"

"I gotta go," Gaston said.

Robby thanked him, then handed him his business card and ask
him to call if he remembered anything else. Fifteen minutes after
turning to the office, they had completed their interview of the
maining workers who had been at Timberland when Farwell w
employed there. None of them knew much about Farwell, but
confirmed he kept to himself and did his work with extraordina
precision.

As they got back into their car, Bledsoe said, "Gaston said Farw
had a family ranch. But when you did your search, nothing came u

"He also said the ranch was old. If we take him at his word, then s possible the ranch was purchased before the cutoff date of the cords I reviewed on microfiche. I think it was sometime around ♦00. If they bought it in 1899, I would've missed it. The other cords will have to be searched by hand."

Bledsoe turned the key and started the engine. "Then I know here we're headed."

HEY ARRIVED at the County Department of Land Records at oon. It was a typical government building built decades ago, one pry and sprawling with a sloping roof. They spoke with the clerk d half an hour later, Robby, Bledsoe, and Vail were sitting at a long poden table with volumes of bound records dating back to the late ♦00s laid out in front of them.

They each picked a volume and began searching for land owned ▼ anyone named Farwell. The task was tedious, and as the hours ssed, the combined effect of lack of sleep and stagnant blood flow gan to creep into their bodies. They had each dozed off at least ace, despite the cans of Coke they had bought from the lobby nding machine.

"I'd better go stretch my legs," Vail said. "I'm not doing much od falling asleep. I think I've read the last entry on this page five nes." But as she stood, Robby stopped her.

"Eighteen ninety-one. Franklin Farwell purchased fifty-five acres what looks like the southwest portion of Loudoun County." He tated the page and tried to get his bearings on the accompanying ap. "I'd say that would qualify as a family ranch."

Bledsoe rose from his chair with a grunt and leaned over the table get a look at Robby's find. "Got an address?" Bledsoe's button- wn oxford was ruffled, the sleeves rolled to the elbows. A large oke stain adorned the front, dating back to sometime around P.M., when he'd fallen asleep with the can in his hand. It had awak- ed him real fast.

"Got a plot number. Eighteen. Plat nine of county map four. emember, this is from the nineteenth century."

"We need a map," Vail said, "one that's up-to-date, so we c
look that up."

Bledsoe stifled a yawn as he lifted the bound volume that co
tained the Farwell ranch. "I'll bring this to the clerk in there. Let h
tell us where it is. She could probably locate it a hell of a lot fast
than we could."

After the records clerk spent five minutes triangulating the Fa
well ranch on a current map, Bledsoe notified each of the task for
members and set a meeting at the op center for one hour. His ne
call was to the Loudoun County Emergency Response Team, wh
was to prepare to mobilize in the next few hours.

The ride back to the op center was a long one, complicated
traffic caused by a motorcycle versus pedestrian accident. Ambulan
and emergency response vehicles lined the shoulder, slowing th
rubberneckers to a crawl.

Vail's heart was beating harder than normal, and even though sl
felt herself daydreaming about her bed and getting some sleep, h
energy level had risen a few notches since the discovery of the Fa
well ranch. The thought occurred to her that she must have be
there as an infant—and even though she would not, of course, have
memory of it, she realized how fortunate she had been that h
mother had snatched her from the grasp of Patrick Farwell's si
mind. It was the only decent thing Linwood had ever done for her

And for the first time, it sunk in that Patrick Farwell was *her b
logical father*. Her own genes, a rapist and sadistic serial killer. Sl
would have to spend some time chatting with Wayne Rudnick abo
this one: nature versus nurture . . . and how she turned out on tl
right side of the law, hunting down men like her father, when h
own flesh and blood had gone in the opposite direction, showing
total disregard for human life. She found the thought impossible
come to grips with.

As she wrestled with that philosophical debate, she rested h
head back on the seat and closed her eyes. The next thing she kne
they were parked at the curb in front of the op center and Robby w
waking her.

e's here now, with one of his whores. It's the one he likes, I
can tell, because she's here a lot. I started planning a few
weeks ago, started thinking that I could do what he does, and I
could do it better. I got excited thinking about it. But I'm scared.
I've never done it before. It's not like I don't know what to do or
how to do it. But something is holding me back. Yet there she is,
lying on the bed. My chest tingles. I'm short of breath.

I have to do it! I'll do what he does to me. Knock him out with
the lead pipe. I got me one at Billy's Hardware on the way home
from work. I'm ready. I'll beat him, I'll beat the whore and leave.
And I won't come back—

E SAT THERE, staring at the blank wall, thinking, remembering
at time when he was finally ready to stand up for himself. But just
he was about to act, the cops came and took the prick away. They
dn't see him, hiding in his secret room. They crunched those
ndcuffs on his wrists and slammed his face into the wall a few feet
ay from his little peephole. He thought for sure they'd find him.
t they didn't care about him. They were there for the bastard, for
at reason he never found out, because he never talked to him
ain. But the important thing was that he had the whole place to
mself. The ranch, the house, everything.

At first he wondered if he was going to come back. But as the
ys and weeks passed, he figured the place was his, and he claimed it
his own. No one knew, no one came by. It was just him. He paid
e electric bill with cash he earned from his job, and between steal-
g meat from work and making hot dogs, cheap spaghetti, and
atever else he could afford, he did just fine.

Couldn't have asked for a better place, really. Plenty of land, p[er]fect for dumping bodies, if he was into that sort of thing. But at t[hat] time he wasn't thinking like that.

He'd heard it said that with age comes wisdom. Must be true, [be]cause he'd learned a lot over the years. And he had to say he [was] pretty wise now. But one of the more important things he learn[ed] was to be able to recognize when the end had to come. He alwa[ys] promised himself he would be ready when the time came. And n[ow] here he was, about to confront it, wondering how it would feel. [It] came upon him suddenly, this need to conclude, to confront, to ta[ke] the final step.

This is where it all started. Beginnings meeting endings, endin[gs] coming full circle, the circle of life.

Life as we know it, about to end.

Life about to end, a full circle.

He wondered how it would feel.

The geoprofile was right on. Vail held it in her hand and stared at the distribution, marveling at its accuracy. Though the Farwell ranch was outside the target areas, it lay on the westernmost boundary of the report's overall geographic area.

During the past hour, Bledsoe had worked with the Loudoun County Sheriff's Office in obtaining a warrant for the ranch. The lieutenant had called out the Sheriff's Emergency Response Team, or SERT, and assigned the incident to tactical commander Lon Kilgore. Kilgore was in his late thirties, with a face that reminded Vail of something that had been chiseled from granite: severe, rugged features and a five o'clock shadow. His hands were wide and thick, but his fingers were long enough to palm a basketball.

Five years with the marines instilled in him a learned discipline evidenced by the way he walked, addressed his unit, and directed an assault on a violent suspect. Bledsoe told Vail that although he and Kilgore had disagreements in the past, none of the missions had gone sour. Bledsoe said he respected Kilgore's skills and only occasionally challenged his opinions.

Due to the size of the Farwell property, Bledsoe agreed with Kilgore's assessment that they required more accurate reconnaissance before they sent in the SERT team. They needed an aerial view of the ranch to determine what vehicles, buildings, barns, or other structures were there, and exactly where they were located. Kilgore wanted a full background on who Patrick Farwell was, and what he was capable of doing.

The task force stood around, arms crossed, tired and hungry, yet eager to help. They were at the Loudoun County Special Ops South Street office, an aging building in downtown Leesburg. A framed color photo of the sheriff, taken at the Adult Detention Center in full dress uniform, hung prominently on the wall. Vail's unpleasant visit to the ADC surged into her thoughts. She turned away and focused on Kilgore. She needed to forget about her personal problems and exert all her remaining energies on catching Dead Eyes.

"Specifically," Kilgore said, "I want to know if this guy is capable of planting mines and setting booby traps." He was standing in front of a five-foot-square enlargement of a topographic area map where the ranch was situated. "He grew up there, he knows this terrain like the back of his hand. Who knows what he's got set up there." He took a moment to study the surrounding area, then said, while still facing the map, "We're gonna need to hike it in to maintain a stealth approach. We go barreling in with a big old SERT assault truck on a dirt road, we'll kick up a dust trail that could be seen for miles."

"So we go on foot," Bledsoe said.

Kilgore turned to face Bledsoe. "*We* go on foot. You and your people stay back."

"Look, Lon, you and your men take the point, but we're going in with you. We've put too much into this case to sit back and wait here for a phone call."

"Don't you mean you've put too much in to fuck it up? Because that's what you should be thinking."

"We're detectives, Lon, not rookie beat cops. We're going in behind you." He stared the man down.

"Yes, sir," Kilgore said with a mock salute. He picked up the phone and pressed a button. "Sally, call out the whole dog and pony show. Teams Alpha and Beta. Have them meet us at the Red Fox Inn, in the Jeb Room. I want them there in one hour. Then call the manager there, she knows me. Tell her we need the room for a few hours. Oh—and ask the Air Force for a satellite image of the property." He listened a moment, then said, "No, no, that's too long. We need it within the hour." Kilgore shrugged, then said, "Fine, that'll work. Give me some large format prints ASAP."

He hung up, then turned back to his map. "We're going to use something on the Internet called Virtual Earth. It'll give us aerial and 3D views of the property. And we'll have it in a couple minutes instead of a few hours. Soon as we have it, we can start planning for deployment."

"We'll be ready," Bledsoe said.

Kilgore frowned. "I can't tell you how happy that makes me."

While they waited for Kilgore's staff to assemble the recon images, the task force members went to the lobby vending machines for coffee and snacks. They had not eaten much all day, and the prospect of downing solid food in the next several hours was dim at best.

Vail remained with Bledsoe, who contacted the local Middleburg police department to explain the nature of the operation to the watch commander. Kilgore anticipated a problem since the much larger Loudoun County Sheriff's Office had coordinated the operation without consulting the Middleburg Police. Middleburg's entire department consisted of only five men. But according to Bledsoe, the lieutenant in charge was belligerent, feeling that his territory had been trampled. He insisted his own officers be part of the action and threw a fit, claiming jurisdictional issues would be pursued with Loudoun's police chief.

Bledsoe put the guy on hold, no doubt concerned he would lose his temper and say something that would delay the entire operation for hours. He told Vail what the problem was.

She shook her head, once again amazed at how law enforcement professionals could act so petty, losing sight of the primary goal: catching the bad guy. "Men are like dogs, Bledsoe. They like to piss all over to stake out their territory. That's what this guy is doing. You've seen it a million times."

"Doesn't mean I have to like it. All it does is waste my time."

"I doubt the Loudoun chief gives a shit about turf wars. All he wants is to be able to say his people captured the Dead Eyes killer. He doesn't care whether the police or sheriff brings him in, right?"

"Right."

"Then tell your Middleburg buddy, Lieutenant *Doberman*, or whatever the hell his name is, to go ahead and call the chief."

Bledsoe issued the challenge and waited while the lieutenant was supposedly making the call. Ten minutes later, the receptionist handed Bledsoe the phone. After listening a moment, Bledsoe thanked the caller, then hung up. "'Lieutenant Doberman' said that all his investigators are busy on cases, so it'd take a while to call them in, and he didn't want to delay our op." Bledsoe grunted. "Truth is, if they pulled any of their guys in, half their district would go unpatrolled. Middleburg would use the Loudoun SERT unit anyway."

"Pissing matches and big egos," Vail said. "Next thing you'll tell me is that you guys sit around bars comparing the size of your penises."

"Give us some credit, Karen. We leave that talk in the locker room."

Kilgore took the Virtual Earth images and topographical map with him in the Full Assault Vehicle and headed toward Middleburg's Red Fox Inn. The task force followed in one of the SERT team member's cars, which was equipped with two black tactical outfits, radios, helmets, shields, infrared goggles, and masks, since the officers often reported directly to an incident site in their own vehicles.

With Bledsoe driving and Del Monaco riding with Kilgore in the assault vehicle, Vail watched as the Red Fox Inn, a four-story fieldstone Bed and Breakfast, came into view. "I've always wanted to stay here," she said.

Robby craned his neck to get a look at the building. "It's just a big old house."

"That's like saying the White House is 'just a big old house.' The Red Fox Inn has roots going back to the early 1700s. I think Washington slept here. It even played a role in the Revolutionary and Civil Wars."

"And how do you know this?" Manette asked.

"You're always challenging me, you know that?"

"Somebody's got to. You think you know everything about everything."

"I was going to book a room here about six months ago. The Belmont Suite, very romantic. You have the Blue Ridge and Bull Run mountains surrounding you, lush greenery, and the rooms are furnished like they were two hundred years ago." She gazed out the window at the passing undeveloped countryside. "Then I realized that no matter how romantic a place is, if you've got no one to share it with, it's very lonely. I threw away the brochure."

She could feel Robby's gaze burning the back of her head. He would take her there, she had a feeling, during her self-proclaimed vacation. With Dead Eyes almost in the bag, her time off was suddenly within reach. She allowed herself a brief moment to daydream.

"In case you're interested," Manette said, "your romantic getaway was around when Franklin Farwell bought his ranch."

Vail cocked her head. Manette was right. She shuddered to think how close it was, how close the young women who had gone to the inn for a special night of pampering had come to getting something they were not expecting.

A MOMENT LATER, Bledsoe followed the assault vehicle into the front lot and parked. Kilgore hopped out of the truck's cab and led the way to the inn's entrance.

As they entered the Jeb Room, the task force members took in the dark wood paneling, fireplace, and ceiling beams.

"I run all my tactical sessions out of here whenever we've got a maneuver in the area. Manager's my aunt's friend." He placed the Virtual Earth images on a long table by the far wall.

"So who was Jeb?" Manette asked.

"General Jeb Stuart, Confederate Army. In fact," Kilgore said, "General Stuart met with the Gray Ghost, Colonel John Mosby, right here in this very room, planning their strategy for the Civil War."

Manette frowned. "That don't make me feel at home."

"Yeah, no shit," Robby said.

"Political views aside," Bledsoe said, "I hope our strategy session is more successful than theirs was."

Kilgore stood the topographical map against the wall. "It will be, Bledsoe. It will be."

The seven tactical team members arrived during the course of the next hour. Kilgore reviewed the map and Virtual Earth images and formulated a plan. Coffee was brought up by management, who met one of the officers at the door. With a sensitive operation being planned, no outsiders were permitted into the room.

An hour later, Kilgore began packing away the maps while the tactical team and task force members headed down to the truck to suit up.

Bledsoe stood in front of his seat, hands on his hips.

"What's wrong?" Vail asked.

"My chair. I left it there," he said, pointing to a spot, "and now it's here." He indicated a location several feet away.

"I think you need some sleep. We all do." Vail pat him on the back, then headed out the door.

"I'm serious."

"That'd be Monte," Kilgore said. "Ghost from the 1700s. He moves things around, makes noises." Kilgore craned his neck and spoke to the ceiling: "Cut it out, Monte, you're scaring this guy." Kilgore chuckled, then headed out the door, maps in hand.

"Ghost?" Bledsoe asked. He looked around the room, suddenly realized he was alone, and warded off a chill. Then he rushed out the closing door.

A LITTLE OVER THREE HOURS from the moment they had arrived at the Loudoun Special Ops building, the tactical assault vehicle and accompanying car pulled to a stop amongst a stand of mature oaks a half mile down the road from the perimeter of the Farwell ranch. The SERT team of eight men jumped out the rear, black-vested jackets covering their torsos and sniper rifles gripped in both hands as if they were an organic extension of their arms.

The task force members were outfitted in similar garb, most of them using vests for the first time in years. Fortunately, it was a cold afternoon, and the added weight and insulation provided warmth. They did not know how long they would be outside, exposed to the elements, without supplies from the truck to tide them over.

Several of the men tossed a tan-and-brown camouflage canvas over the truck while others collected brush from the surrounding trees and gathered it around the tires. Large branches were thrown atop the team member's black car to prevent any reflection from the mirror or windows.

"Okay, listen up," Kilgore said. He positioned his headset so the mouthpiece of his two-way radio was squarely in front of his mouth. "Radio communication or hand signals only from this point forward. We fan out and establish a perimeter fifty yards off the house. When all looks secure, we'll move in and breach the place. You've all got your marks. Check in as each of you hit them. Remember, this guy is dangerous. Word is he used to hunt fox, so he's obviously a good shot. Be careful, treat the situation as if he's got an arsenal in there. We don't know what to expect. Questions?" He waited a beat, surveyed his team, then said, "Move out."

"Which team you want us with?" Vail asked.

Kilgore stiffened. "That's the problem with having you here. I've got nowhere to put you."

"We'll form our own team," Bledsoe said.

"What if I don't have extra headsets for all of you?"

"Give us what you got. We'll stay together, out of your way. But once you secure the place, we need to be in there right behind you."

Kilgore stepped to the back of the truck, lifted the canvas covering, and slipped beneath it. He emerged a moment later with six spare headsets. Handing them to Bledsoe, he said, "Don't change the frequency. And stay out of the way. Above all, don't fuck up my operation." Kilgore spun and ran off into the brush to catch up to his team.

"You gonna take that, Blood?" Manette asked.

"I did and I will. Remember the reason why we're here."

Sinclair pulled on a black ball cap to cover his shiny bald head and slipped on a headset. He motioned for Del Monaco to go first. "You gonna be able to make it?"

"What's that supposed to mean?"

"You're carrying some extra tonnage and this is gonna be a long hike."

"Extra tonnage," Manette said. "I like that. Mind if I use it, Sin?"

"Be my guest."

"The 'extra tonnage' doesn't slow me down," Del Monaco said. "I pass all the physical endurance tests the Bureau requires. But thanks so much for your concern." He motioned Sinclair ahead of him, then fell into formation behind him.

THEY TREKKED through the forested stands of pine and cedar and occasional oak, emerging at a clearing and hugging the tree-lined perimeter for cover. After nearly an hour's hike, the various SERT members were beginning to call in, stating they had reached their positions.

For the task force group, Robby led the way at the point, with Bledsoe following in the second position. Manette was third, Sinclair next, Vail, and then Del Monaco pulling up the rear. Despite his assertions about passing the endurance tests, Del Monaco had never hiked through forestland on uneven terrain after having gone thirty-five straight hours without sleep.

By the time all team members were in final position, daylight had melted to dusk. The quarter moon was hiding behind cloud cover, and the temperature had plummeted another several degrees. Their breath was vapor, a dangerous situation when involved in covert maneuvers. For the task force members, who lacked night-vision goggles, the darkness was a double-edged sword: though it provided them adequate cover, it also prevented them from seeing unknown objects in unfamiliar territory.

From what they could see in the failing light, the house appeared to be a medium-sized clapboard two-story home that looked very much its one hundred and fifteen years. The paint, or at least what was left of it, was peeling and faded. The porch decking was cracked and dry. It was for this reason that Kilgore had wanted the Virtual Earth photos: he saw what appeared to be decking and knew, from his years of experience, that wood and nails and the ravages of weather produced noises one had better not encounter when attempting to launch a surprise attack. Due to Kilgore's diligent intel, the team members were prepared and followed a preplanned route around the deck.

Vail bent her mouthpiece away from her face and asked, "Now what?"

Bledsoe stood beside her, both of them hunched behind a large-trunked redwood. "Now I kick myself for not asking them for night-vision goggles."

"Most important thing is that they have them."

"How's your knee?" Bledsoe asked.

Robby had seen her pop a couple Extra Strength Tylenol just prior to beginning the hike, but she had shrugged it off. "I'm not going to let a little pain stop me."

"A *little* pain?" he had asked.

"Okay, a lot of pain."

Now, after the long hike, she framed it with level-headed realism. "As long as I don't run out of pain pills, I'll be fine."

"When this is over," Bledsoe said, "we'll get a chopper in, fly you out of here."

"Not exactly how I'd pictured my own private limo." She inched to her right and watched as the first tactical officer moved to the left of the front door frame. Though the other four team members had gone around to the back door and were engaged in similar maneuvers, they were outside Vail's line of sight. She pressed the earpiece against her head. She didn't want to miss this.

"Unit one in position and ready to move," the anxious voice said over the headset.

"Unit two, three, and four ready." Vail immediately recognized Kilgore's voice.

Vail's heart was slamming against her chest.

"Unit five, six, seven, and eight ready."

"Hold all positions," Kilgore whispered. He moved his fist in

ont of the door and banged it hard several times: the knock-and-
otice. "Patrick Farwell, this is the sheriff," he shouted. "We know
ou're in there. We've got the place surrounded. Come out with
our hands up."

The house remained dark, the air still.

"Flash bang, sir?" asked one of the officers.

"No." Kilgore's voice was stern. "Stick to tactical."

Another voice over the radio, probably from the back. "Unit
ight reports no sign of movement."

"Roger that," Kilgore said. "On my mark." After waiting a beat,
e said, "Go!"

The first position moved aside and the second officer stepped up
ith a Stinger battering ram. "Second in position. On my mark.
io!" He swung back the thirty-five-pound steel cylinder, then arced
forward and breached the door, sending shards of splintered wood
ying in all directions. The position three team member, Lon Kil-
ore, rushed the house.

Vail put her head down and concentrated on the voices coming
hrough her headset:

"Entryway, clear."

"Kitchen, clear."

"Living room—hold it—body, I got a body. Male, looks to be in
is late fifties maybe." Pause. Then: "Dead. Rest of living room,
lear."

Vail turned to Bledsoe. "What the hell?" She bent the mike back
 front of her mouth. "How long has he been dead? What's the ap-
arent COD?"

Kilgore's voice crackled through her headset: "Get off the damn
adio!"

"Shit," she said, rising and moving out from behind the tree.

Bledsoe grabbed her left arm. "Wait here, Karen. Let them clear
he house, then we can go in."

She pulled herself free with a windmill of her shoulder. She
anked the Glock from her side holster and stepped toward the
ouse. "I'm going in now."

Robby, ten feet back behind another tree, emerged and followe her forward. "We're coming in," Vail announced.

"Upstairs bedroom, clear. Holy shit—"

Vail stopped, instinctively raised her weapon with both hand "What?"

"This is one sick fuck," the tactical officer said. "All sorts of sh hanging around up here. And I mean hanging. Five severed hand strung up from the ceiling. Holy, Jesus."

Vail exchanged a knowing glance with Robby, then proceeded u the steps toward the fractured front door. She moved slowly into th living room, where she came upon the body.

"Upstairs bedroom two, clear," another voice said somewhere i her ear. But she was not listening. She was staring at the face of Patric Farwell.

Her father.

The Dead Eyes killer.

Frank Del Monaco knelt beside Vail and matched her gaze.

"I don't get it," she finally said.

"He unraveled," Del Monaco said. "Just like the others."

"What others?" Robby asked. He was standing behind them, his hat and headset dangling from his left hand.

"All the serial killers. They reach a point where the killing gets to be too much even for them to handle. Even though they have no moral sense, deep down they know what they're doing is wrong. It's not enough to stop them, but the pressure builds to the point where they can't deal with it. It's an end game."

"But suicide?" Robby asked.

"They get sloppy," Vail said. "Their fantasies get more violent, their order disintegrates into disorder. Organization into disorganization. That's how we caught Bundy. If we hadn't caught him, he might've eventually done himself."

"Linwood's crime scene certainly was an indicator," Del Monaco said, "though we didn't see it that way. I think we still called it right. The personal connection, the overkill."

"But the violence wasn't just because of that," Vail said. "He was coming undone at the same time. Maybe killing Linwood, the woman who took his daughter from him, was too much for him to handle."

Del Monaco shook his head. "More like he had done what he needed to do, what he'd fantasized about doing, for the fifteen big ones he'd done in the slammer. He got out and bang, he saw women who reminded him of Linwood when she was younger, the way he remembered her the last time he'd seen her. Even though he may not have consciously been aware of it, he killed them because he was killing *her*, over and over again."

"Then he somehow found her. Found Linwood. And he went after her."

"What's the COD?" Sinclair asked, walking into the room.

Del Monaco answered: "Gunshot wound to the forehead. Lots of stippling on the face. Close range, an old thirty-eight. Gun's still in his hand. Looks like a suicide."

"How long ago?"

"Just a guess, but I'd say a day, maybe a little less."

"Let's get a powder residue, just to be sure," Sinclair said.

"Karen," Bledsoe called, "you should see this."

She rose and followed his voice up the stairs to the bedroom. Five left hands hung from the ceiling with thin fishing line. In the lighting, they appeared to be floating in mid-air. "Five . . . tell the lab we need to know which one's missing."

Bledsoe nodded. "Then there's this." He led her down the hall into the bathroom. Scrawled on the mirror in lipstick were the words "It's in the blood."

Vail sighed deeply. She looked around the old bathroom, the toilet the kind that had a wall-mounted water tank and a pull-chain flush mechanism.

"Looks like we got our man," Bledsoe said.

Vail nodded. "Yeah."

"You okay?"

She pouted her lips. "I thought I might feel something, like I've been here before. Because I have, I must have been. I was an infant here, till Linwood had the sense to get the hell out." Her eyes bounced around the bathroom and into the hallway. "But I don't feel anything."

"You were a baby. What do you expect?"

"I don't know, Bledsoe. I just thought I'd feel something. Then again, there aren't that many things that move me these days."

Just then, she noticed Robby standing in the doorway. "I'll move you," he said, taking her hand.

She followed him out of the bathroom and whispered up toward his ear, "You already have, Robby. You already have."

... *seventy-three*

Gifford stood at the head of the conference room, addressing the profiling unit, Vail at his side. "I think we all owe Agent Vail sincere thanks for a damn fine job in helping break the Dead Eyes case. And for standing by her convictions. I know we all doubted her at various times in the past eighteen-plus months. I'm as guilty as anyone else, and for that I apologize." He looked over at Vail, who felt that Gifford was genuine in his apology.

"Thank you, sir. I appreciate it."

Applause broke out for a brief moment but stopped at Gifford's raised hand. "Let's all get back to work." He leaned over and whispered into her ear. "Meet me in my office in ten minutes."

THE MANNER IN WHICH GIFFORD had approached this morning's recognition of her efforts, in front of the entire unit, was completely unexpected—and was thus something Vail had been unprepared for. Though it meant a great deal to her, she could not fully appreciate it because both her body and mind were in fairly rotten shape. She felt as if she had been run over by a truck and wanted nothing more than to crawl back into bed and sleep for several days.

Following the episode at the Farwell ranch, Vail had been airlifted off the property by a county chopper and taken to a waiting cruiser at the Fairfax County Police Department's Mason District Station. She then had been driven back to Robby's house, where she took another two Tylenols and fell asleep in bed, without even changing out of her dirty clothing. She had awakened to a call at 9 A.M. from Gifford's secretary, asking her to report to work in one hour.

Now, as she sat in Gifford's office, the haze of the past forty-eight hours still hovered over her like a thick fog. What did he want to talk to her about? Reinstatement? Not possible with the charges still pending against her. Then what, a commendation? Not likely, for the same reasons. Commending an agent whose ass was still on the line for assault was . . . poor timing.

Gifford strode in and sat down behind his desk. He leaned back and sighed. "I know you and I have not always seen eye-to-eye, but I'm ready to move past all that. You came through big time. I know there were others on the task force, but you were a big part of the winning team. Good work, you made us proud."

"Thank you, sir."

"There is something I wanted to talk to you about. It's a step toward regaining your job, assuming, of course, you're cleared by judge and jury." He scanned his desk, moved a file, and found the document he was looking for. "Here's a list of three Bureau psychologists. Pick one and make an appointment."

She took the paper. "A shrink?"

"A shrink. It's for your own good. Anger management, for one. OPR will want to see that in order to clear you of their own investigation. Also, given all the crap you've just been through, and are still dealing with . . . it's for your own good, really."

Vail pursed her lips. *She couldn't argue with that.* "Okay, sir. I'll make an appointment."

Gifford nodded, then his phone buzzed. "Go home and get some sleep. Get that knee of yours examined. I want you back full strength when the time comes."

She smiled, arose gingerly from the chair, and then left.

Vail walked, or rather hobbled, back to her car feeling no pain. And it was not just from the Tylenol she kept popping. It was because for the first time she could remember, she had been afforded the respect she thought she had always deserved but had never received. She climbed into her car, pulling in the left knee slowly, then headed out of the commerce center's parking lot.

She intended to heed Gifford's advice about getting some sleep, but first she needed to make a stop. She arrived at the hospital, made her way up the elevator to Jonathan's floor, and heard "Code Blue! Code Blue. All available personnel. . . ."

Her brain still in a stupor, her mind suddenly focused on a grouping of white lab coats at the entrance to Jonathan's room. "Oh, my God!" she gasped, then took off down the hall, fearing the worst. Thoughts pored through her mind as she whizzed by the rooms along the long corridor: *he was doing so well! Small steps, pieces to the puzzle. My son, my son. . . .*

A group of hospital personnel in scrubs ran past her down the hallway. In the back of her mind, Vail realized the emergency was for another patient on the floor, not Jonathan. But she was not completely tuned into her thoughts yet, and she fought through the mass of white coats congregated in the doorway, grabbing and pushing bodies aside. The interns were huddled around Altman, who stood beside Jonathan. Her son's eyes were open and he was smiling.

"Mom!"

"Jonathan?" She stepped forward, arms outstretched, and an instant later felt his hands on her back, patting her gently. Finally, she released him and leaned back to look at him.

"We thought you'd come sooner," Altman said. He was standing off to Vail's right, smiling.

"Sooner?"

"I had the nurse call you last night. When you didn't answer, they left a message on your machine."

"I was inaccessible," was all Vail said. She turned back to Jonathan, who appeared thin, pale, and drawn. "You look tired."

"I am. I've been sleeping but I feel exhausted."

"I *haven't* been sleeping, and I'm also exhausted." She hugged him again. "It's so good to have you back, sweetheart."

"Let's let him rest," Altman said. He looked out amongst the medical students who were still gathered around the doorway. "Anyone have any questions?" No one spoke. "Okay, let's find out where that code was, and see how it's going." The crowd began to disperse, and Altman turned to Vail. "We've got a few days of testing and monitoring to do, and then he should be ready to go home." He placed a hand on her back, indicating it was time for her to leave.

"One thing—" she looked at Jonathan. "Do you remember what happened, how you ended up in the hospital?"

He bit his lip, eyes moving up, then left, then down again before landing on Vail. "Last thing I remember is going home after school. That's it. Wait, dad was angry about something. About you, I think." His eyes drifted back off to the right, then he shook his head. "Why can't I remember?"

Altman patted Jonathan's shoulder. "Don't worry about it. That's quite normal. If you're lucky, your short-term memory will come back. Today, tomorrow, the day after, it's hard to say. There's also a chance it won't come back at all."

Altman told Jonathan he would return later, reminded Vail she need to let him rest, then left.

Vail placed a hand on her son's. She did not say it, but she was torn. She hoped with her strongest convictions that Jonathan's memory did return as it would validate her claim of Deacon's abusive nature and put him behind bars for a long time. But she did not want her son to be scarred with the memory of his father pushing him down the stairs.

"Get some rest," she said, then planted a kiss on Jonathan's forehead. "I'll be by a little later."

Before leaving the hospital, Vail flagged down Dr. Altman and told him she wanted to take him up on his referral for a surgical evaluation of her knee. Within the hour, Vail was sitting in the orthopedist's office. Thirty minutes later, the surgeon had examined her, walked her over to radiology, and informed the technician she was to squeeze in Vail between patients for an MRI.

Two hours later, the radiologist told her he had reviewed the images and found tears in the medial meniscus and medial collateral ligament. He informed the orthopedist of the findings and Vail was scheduled for surgery the day after next. She marveled at how quickly the medical machinery moved when one had a few inside connections.

AFTER LEAVING THE HOSPITAL, Vail returned to Robby's place and threw her laundry and clothing in her suitcase and moved back into her house. With the Dead Eyes case solved, the thought of being back in her own home was inviting. She enjoyed the days spent at Robby's and was confident she would be spending much of her future time there. But retaking her house, after having been driven from it, was a moral victory—even if she did not intend to sleep there until Jonathan came home.

Following dinner later that night, Vail and Robby visited Jonathan at the hospital. On the way, Robby detoured to an electronics retailer. The store was closing, but Robby told the owner he needed to buy a gift for his friend's son who had just come out of a coma, and they made an exception. Robby knew exactly what to get.

When Vail walked into Jonathan's hospital room, she found him asleep. But it was a different scene than when he had been lying in bed, helpless, hooked up to tubes and machines. His face was peaceful now, and he lay curled up on his side, just like when she would come home at night, plant a kiss on his little forehead, and tuck him in.

With Robby waiting down the hall giving her some one-on-one mother-son time, she gently sat down beside Jonathan's bed. But the rustle of the shopping bag caught his attention. He stirred, then fluttered his eyes. He tried to focus on his mother but kept blinking, as if he was unsure she was really there.

"Hi, champ."

"Mom. What time is it?"

"Eight-thirty."

"I'm so tired." He stretched and yawned. "I've been sleeping the whole day."

"Have you eaten?"

"I think they woke me for lunch, but I'm not sure."

"I'll buzz the nurse, have them bring you some dinner."

Robby walked in, carrying a small bag. "You must be Jonathan," he said.

"This is Robby Hernandez," Vail said. "He's a good friend of mine. A detective in Vienna."

"Glad you're doing better, man. You had your mom very concerned."

"Oh," Vail said. "We got you something." She reached down for the bag.

"What is it?"

"Sorry we didn't have time to wrap it. I didn't think you'd mind." She pulled the box out of the bag.

"Xbox 360! Cool!"

"Have to admit, it wasn't my idea. I had some help."

He turned the white box round and round, looking at the circular lime-green graphics. "I've wanted one since before it came out."

Vail smiled. "Well, now you've got one. But I don't want you playing around with this thing and neglecting your homework."

"Mom." He drew the word out and glanced at her sideways, as if trying to hide his embarrassment.

"You'll need this to play it," Robby said, handing him the bag.

Jonathan flung the bag aside, revealing a green *Rainbow Six Vegas 2* game case. "Cool!" He flipped it over and looked at the back. "This is hella tight, Robby, thanks."

"You're welcome, kiddo." He nodded to Vail. "I'll pick you up tomorrow, around one-ish, okay?"

"I'll be right back," she said to Jonathan.

Her son was intently studying the back of the game case.

"I don't think he'll miss me," Vail said.

As they strolled out into the hall, Robby took her hand. "You should probably tell Jonathan we're more than just good friends."

"I'll talk to him about it later. I'm sure he won't mind. You scored big with that *Rambo* game."

"Rainbow. *Rainbow Six.*"

"Whatever."

"Hey, you heard. It's hella tight."

They reached the elevator and Robby hit the button. "Tomorrow night is ours, okay?"

She leaned forward and gave him a kiss. "You don't have to ask twice."

It was two in the morning when Jonathan started shouting and thrashing his arms. Vail was off her adjacent cot immediately, taking hold of his hands and calming him. "Shh, it's okay. It's okay, sweetheart. It's just a dream." She thought of her own nightmares and realized how unfeeling her comment was . . . how real they feel when you're the one going through them.

Jonathan sat up in bed and hugged her so firmly she thought he was going to squeeze the air from her lungs. Finally, his grip loosened and she pushed back to look at his face. "Are you awake?"

He nodded. "I remember what happened."

While waiting for him to continue, she took a tissue and dabbed at his moist forehead. The door opened, letting in a slice of light from the hallway.

"Everything okay in here?" the nurse asked.

"Nightmare," Vail said. "We're fine."

The door slipped closed. Jonathan wiped his eyes with the back of a hand, sniffled, then spoke. "Dad was angry, said you'd kicked him and broke his ribs. He said you were going to make the court take me away from him. I told him that's what I wanted."

She touched his forearm. She was proud her son had stood up to Deacon. He had intimidated Jonathan, abused him for too long.

"He didn't say anything. But a few minutes later he told me to get a can of beans from the pantry in the basement. As I started to go down the steps I felt him push me. That's the last thing I remember."

Vail sat down on his bed and gathered him close. While holding him, she reached for the phone to call Bledsoe. He answered it on the fourth ring.

"Sorry to wake you, but I'm at the hospital with Jonathan. He remembers what happened. You're going to want to hear this."

Bledsoe arrived twenty minutes later, wearing sweats and a leather jacket. He reintroduced himself to Jonathan and listened intently to the youth's version of events. "Are you sure this isn't something you dreamt? I mean, not to say I don't believe you, but you woke up screaming. Sounds like a nightmare to me."

"I remember hitting my elbow on the metal railing." He pushed the gown back and turned his arm to look at it. There was a large scabbed wound overlying the joint. He held it up for Bledsoe to see.

"Okay." He pulled a cell phone from his jacket pocket and dialed a number. "Hey, this is Bledsoe. I need you to find out what magistrate is on duty." He waited a long moment, placed a reassuring hand on Vail's shoulder, then pulled his face back to the phone. "Yeah, I'm here. Tell Benezra I need an arrest warrant drawn up."

AN HOUR LATER, Bledsoe called Vail from his station house. "Just wanted you to know I dispatched two officers to pick up your ex. He should be in the system real soon."

Vail was standing outside Jonathan's hospital room. Though he had fallen back asleep, Vail remained awake—which had become a bad habit these past few days. "Bledsoe, I owe you."

"Shit, Karen, you don't owe me anything. It'll be a pleasure seeing this monkey greased."

"At least he won't be hurting Jonathan anymore. It should solve the custody issue once and for all. And maybe even the case he's got pending against me."

"One thing's for sure. A jury's going to be a lot more inclined to believe you and piss on Deacon's version of what happened."

Vail thanked him, left Jonathan a note, and hobbled out to her car using the crutches the orthopedist had given her. She felt uncoordinated and looked even worse, she was sure. At least she would be rid of them soon.

She headed home to try to get some sleep so she did not fall asleep in Robby's arms later in the evening. She wanted the date to be perfect—knee pain aside—and had gone food shopping yesterday to stock up on the items she needed to prepare a special meal she found in one of her gourmet cookbooks. She even bought a large bottle of Korbel champagne to celebrate Jonathan's recovery and their cracking the Dead Eyes case. Now, with Deacon's impending arrest, they had one more reason to make it a special occasion.

As she slipped beneath the covers, the morning light started slicing through her blinds. But a minute later it didn't matter, because she was already fast asleep.

"We haven't been able to find your ex." Bledsoe stood at Vail's front door, leaning against the porch railing. "I don't know he's just out of town, or if he somehow knew this was coming own and fled. We've got a guy on his place. We started pulling one LUDs, home and cell, to see who he might've talked with re-ntly. It'll tell us when the last calls were logged, give us an idea if 's been home lately." He looked out at the street for a moment. ny idea where he might have gone? Relatives? Friends?"

"Brother in Vegas. Hasn't spoken to him in years. No friends I ow of." Vail was wearing a faded FBI sweatshirt and ragged jeans e had thrown on when the doorbell rang. Though she had napped r several hours, she felt worse now than when she had been pump-g her sleep-deprived body full of caffeine. She rubbed at her burn-g eyes and said, "Neighbors?"

Bledsoe shook his head. "No one's seen anything. Him, his car, hers around the house, nothing. For days."

"I wish I could tell you where to look."

"We'll find him," Bledsoe said. "When we pick him up, I'll let u know." He smiled. "Must be my breath or something. First ancock disappears, then your ex. Still can't find Hancock, either."

"Turn over some rocks. They'll both probably be crawling in the uck like slugs. What do you want with Hancock?"

"With Farwell in the bag—literally—he's obviously off the Dead ves suspect list, but I wanted to make sure he was clear for Lin-ood. Del Monaco thinks I'm wasting my time. He said everything s and I shouldn't beat a dead horse. Actually, I think he said a dead rpse."

"The locket sealed the linkage."

"Maybe I just want to get in the prick's face again. Stir him up.

Gotta get my kicks somehow. You were right from the get-go. Guy's a first class asshole."

Vail winced. "I've gotta get off my feet. Knee's killing me. Surgeon gave me Tylenol with codeine, but I hate the thought of taking narcotics. Goes back to my beat days."

"Hey, the Tylenol's legal. If the doc gave 'em to you, use 'em. No reason to be in pain. You've suffered enough these past few weeks."

Vail turned and hobbled down the hall to grab a seat. "Ain't that the truth."

An hour after Bledsoe left, Robby showed up at Vail's house with a bouquet of white roses, along with a bottle of V. Sattui's Madeira, not realizing Vail had already procured the champagne.

"We'll start with the champagne," he said, "then work our way to the madeira. A friend of mine brought it from Napa a couple months ago. He said it's real good after dinner. Wine fortified with brandy. Not too sweet, but very smooth."

"I gotta warn you, Detective Hernandez, I don't handle my booze very well."

"Oh, yeah? And what happens?"

"I get drunk and disorderly."

Robby's eyebrows raised. "I think I can deal with that, Agent Vail. I've got my cuffs with me."

"And I get really horny."

Robby smiled. "Then we've got everything we need."

She laughed. "Come on in, you can help me finish cooking dinner."

THE FAMILY ROOM FIREPLACE was crackling, lit candles were flickering, and the smell of a merlot-based tomato basil reduction sauce filled the entire house. Vail removed the garlic bread from the oven while Robby drained the linguini noodles.

And they were already on their second glass of champagne.

Vail swiveled her head. "You know, I had some paperwork from the hospital somewhere, but I can't find it. I've looked high and low and everywhere in between. Everywhere and in between," she said, drawing out the last word.

Robby smiled. "Maybe it said not to mix alcohol and pain pills before surgery."

She could feel a slight bead of perspiration on her forehead, her movements free and a bit easier than usual. The alcohol had hit her bloodstream.

"No shit, Sherlock. I know that, but Bledsoe told me to take my pain meds, codeine, can you believe that? I'd be, like, totally flying now if I'd done that. Codeine and alcohol. You know what that would've done to me? Can you believe how that would feel? I'd be, like, shit-faced right now."

Robby placed his fingers on her lips and smiled. "Shh . . . I don't know if I should tell you this, but you're already shit-faced."

"Not me. Not after only two glasses of champagne."

"You're a lightweight, Vail. I'm in total control of you."

She pulled him close. "And what are you going to do with this control, you detective agent Rob-me Horny-andez?"

He pulled her from her chair and carried her out of the dining room into the adjacent living room, where he laid her on the couch. "I'm going to take advantage of you."

"Oh, should I call a cop?"

"What's a cop going to do about it, help us cop-ulate?" He chuckled.

She giggled.

"Maybe he'll use these," he said, pulling the handcuffs from his back pocket. But they dropped harmlessly to the floor as he leaned into her and planted a long kiss on her lips. She wormed her arms around his neck and held him close, continuing the kiss, the alcohol melting away the stresses of recent weeks. No, it wasn't the alcohol, she suddenly realized as he unbuttoned her blouse. It was passion. Love. The release of letting oneself go so completely without fear of total consumption.

They made love over the next hour, the candles flickering above them, hearts fluttering within them. Warm bodies and hot breaths forging a union she had been yearning for all her life, but never had found. Until now.

They lay on the floor in each other's arms, the fire dying out and

he cool air chilling their naked bodies. She drew a throw blanket
around her while Robby crawled to the coffee table, where he then
peeled away the smooth, red wax sealing the bottle of madeira. He
poured a glass for her, then for himself, and they both drank simultaneously. "Ooh, this is good," Vail said. "Really good." She instantly
felt the rush as the brandy-infused wine slid down her throat.

"I'll have to thank my friend—"

He was interrupted by the warble of his cell. Vail's went off a second later. They shared a confused glance, then Robby rose to retrieve his phone. He helped Vail to her feet, but she let out a loud
cry and crumpled in his arms. "My knee. Shit. I shouldn't have been
sitting on the floor like that. It's locked. Shit."

"I'll get you some ice." He carried her into the kitchen and set
her down on a stool.

"There's a gel pack in the freezer."

He wrapped the pack in a paper towel, then handed it to her.

"Thanks." She nodded toward the coffee table, where his cell sat.
"Who's it from?"

Robby made his way back to the family room. She watched his
butt move as he walked, a pleasing sight that seemed to ease the pain
a bit. But maybe it was just the freeze from the ice.

He lifted the phone and checked the display. He looked at Vail,
his face turning pale, his eyes conveying confusion.

"What's wrong?"

"Text from Bledsoe. Dead Eyes code."

She sat there on the stool, fighting through her alcohol haze to
process the meaning of this. Finally, she managed, "Can't be." Vail
reached for the phone and dialed Bledsoe. He answered on the second ring. "Bledsoe, what's—"

"All I know is first cop on the scene said it looks like a Dead Eyes
job. I asked him, is the left hand severed, he said no. I asked if there
was any writing in blood on the walls, he said no."

"You're thinking copycat?"

"That's what I'm thinking. I'm in my car. Meet me there ASAP."

She hung up and relayed the info to Robby, who had already gotten dressed. He was strapping on his shoulder holster, when she threw the ice aside and announced she was going to go with him.

"Don't be ridiculous. You've got surgery in the morning. Besides, you can't even put weight on the leg. Stay here, ice the knee. I'll call you as soon as I get there, walk you through the scene. I'll take some photos and video and you can review it all as soon as I get back."

"You okay to drive?"

"Hey, you're the lightweight. I'm fine."

"I hate being like this. I need to go and do, not sit around. I can't just stay here."

He shrugged on his wool overcoat and gave her a long kiss, then pulled away. "I'll call you as soon as I look over the scene." She grabbed his hand as he turned to leave. He looked at her over his shoulder. "I love you, Hernandez. Be careful."

ledsoe was the first of the task force members to arrive. He relieved the patrol officer, who had responded to the call and roped
off the surrounding area with yellow crime scene tape.

"Lights were off inside," the cop said. "I used my flashlight,
didn't touch anything. I even put the bedroom door back the way it
was when I walked in."

"Good," Bledsoe said.

"My partner's canvassing. He radioed in a few minutes ago.
Nothing to report."

"Who discovered the body?"

"Neighbor. But 911 didn't get a name. They're analyzing the
tape now. It was a short call, sounded garbled like it came from a cell
phone. They gave the address, said they were a neighbor, and then
the signal dropped and we lost the call."

"Male? Female?"

"Operator thought it was male, but wouldn't swear to it."

"What do we know about the vic?"

"Place is registered to a Laura Mackey. DOB 5-9-69. Dark brown
hair, best I could tell with my flashlight. Looked like someone did a
chop job on her hair, though."

A chill bolted up Bledsoe's spine. He nodded, then turned toward the front door.

"It's bad, sir. Real bad. Be perfectly honest, I had to come outside
and get a breath of air before I called you. Felt like throwing up."

"I know the feeling." Bledsoe patted his pocket, felt the air sick-
ness bag, and said, "Okay, take your position. No one through except the task force. Forensics should be here soon." As Bledsoe
turned away from the cop, Robby and Manette pulled up to the
curb. He waited for them at the front door.

"Sinclair and Del Monaco are on their way," Bledsoe told them. He produced a bunch of latex gloves from his pocket and handed them out.

"Karen's not coming," Robby said, wiggling his left hand into the glove and snapping the rubber to position the fingers properly. "Knee's real bad. She can't even stand."

Bledsoe looked up from his gloves. "Shit. I was really hoping she could give us some insight as to what the hell is going on here."

"Her *insight* will just be a lot of might this and maybe that," Manette said. "Won't do us no good. See where it got us?"

"We don't know anything till we look everything over," Robby said. "Let's not jump to any conclusions. We can't have any biases."

Manette leaned back. "You been spending too much time with Kari, I think. You beginning to sound just like her."

Bledsoe frowned, then opened the front door. They filed in slowly, eyes roaming every square inch of the entry area and hallway. Looking for signs of a struggle—scrapes on the walls, broken glass on the ground, and blood . . . just about anywhere.

But there was nothing.

They continued through the house, clearing room by room until they reached the one at the end of the hall. The door was partially closed and obscured the view of the bed. Bledsoe glanced at Robby, then turned back to the door, squared his shoulders, and nudged it with his shoe.

It swung open with a creak.

And before them lay a young woman, brutalized in a way that had become all too familiar to them. They took a few steps into the room and stood there staring at the body. Bledsoe bent over and barfed into his bag. Blood was everywhere . . . pooling on the bed, dripping to the floor. Smeared on the walls. But not painted.

"There's no message," Robby said.

"Maybe he's already made his point. We know what it means, so there's nothing left to say."

Just then, a noise down the hallway pricked their ears. Bledsoe instinctively drew his SIG Sauer nine millimeter. Then he heard the deep voice of Sinclair and the heavy footfalls of Del Monaco, and his heart slowed toward a more normal rate.

Sinclair's eyes found the body. "Holy Jesus."

"Fuck," Del Monaco said.

Bledsoe found himself agreeing with Del Monaco. A simple four-letter word, but the emotions it conveyed in this particular instance just about summed it up.

"Okay, Frank. Tell me what you see. Tell me what you think. Karen's not coming, so you're it."

Del Monaco swallowed hard, took a few seconds to compose himself. "It appears to be the same offender, but there are some key elements missing. Hand isn't severed, there's no message, and the blood isn't painted on the wall. It's kind of smeared."

"Yeah, we can see all that. When I told you to tell me what you see, I didn't mean literally. I meant, you know, what do you see that we don't?"

"I know, I know what you meant." He dragged a hand across the sweat on his brow, then took a step closer to Laura Mackey. "Key is focusing on the ritualistic behaviors we didn't make public. We didn't release anything about the hand, right?"

"Right."

"And the hand isn't severed. So maybe that indicates copycat."

"Here we go with the maybes again."

"Give me a break, Manette. You think this is easy? I'm flying by the seat of my pants here. You got anything better to offer than smart alec remarks?"

"Let's take it down a notch." Bledsoe said. "Go on, Frank."

Del Monaco swallowed and turned back to the body. After a few seconds of observation, he said, "Knives driven through the eyes. That would also go in the copycat column. Same with the smeared blood. But the knives . . . I'd want to know if there are similar knives in the kitchen. Dead Eyes always used the vic's own knives. That wasn't released to the press."

Bledsoe nodded to Sinclair, who left the room in search of the answer.

Del Monaco continued. "Body left in the vic's bed. No significant signs of struggle. Copycat or not, this guy knew what he was doing. There's confidence in this scene. He's organized, methodical. He's killed before. This isn't the work of a beginner."

The forensics team arrived and immediately began setting up their halogen lights in the bedroom to take their photos and collect their evidence.

Sinclair returned holding a steak knife. He held it beside the victim's body and compared the handles. "Looks the same."

The task force members were lost in thought as the technicians set up their equipment. Finally, Robby stepped beside Del Monaco and said, "I thought smeared blood, blood all over the crime scene could indicate disorganization."

"Yes, it can," Del Monaco said. "But this guy got this woman into her bedroom without much of a struggle. I don't even see head trauma. Won't know for sure till they shave her head, but if I'm right he probably used verbal means to con his way in. That indicates intelligence and planning. There may be some disorganization in the postmortem behavior, but this guy is high IQ."

"None of this makes any sense. Dead Eyes is dead," Bledsoe said.

"There is another explanation," Del Monaco said. "Someone on the inside."

"On the inside?" Manette asked. "What drug you on?"

"It's happened before. Could be a forensic tech, too. Someone who's been at the crime scenes, who knows what we'd expect to find. Or a lab tech who's worked on processing one of the vics."

Sinclair shook his head. "Let's not go off half-cocked here—"

"Half-cocked. Hancock."

Everyone turned to Bledsoe. He had said it softly, but the word caught their attention.

"Hancock," Del Monaco said. "Yeah, it's possible. Let's bring him in for another chat."

"Wish we could, but we pulled the tail off him a couple days ago once we had Farwell. I tried reaching him about Linwood, just to ride him a bit, but couldn't find him."

"And now this."

Robby squinted at something that caught his attention. "What the hell is that?" Something white, illuminated by one of the halogen lights. He moved toward the body and peered between the legs of Laura Mackey. "Tweezers?"

"Chuck, pair of tweezers," Bledsoe called to the head technician.

Chuck walked into the bedroom and handed them to Robby, who deftly held them near the victim's vagina and extracted a tightly rolled piece of paper.

"How the hell did you see that?" Manette asked.

"Caught the light." Robby unrolled it, then unfolded it into a full size sheet of paper. "Holy shit." He turned to Bledsoe. "What the hell does this mean?"

Bledsoe came up alongside him and looked at the document. He turned to Robby, his jaw clenched. "Oh, man. This is bad."

Robby pulled his cell phone from his pocket and punched in a number. "Come on, Karen, answer the damn phone."

"What's the deal?" Sinclair asked. He crossed the room with Manette and Del Monaco to look at the paper.

"She's not answering," Robby said, his voice rough and tentative.

"Let's go," Bledsoe said, then started to run out. "Call all available units," he shouted over his shoulder. "Have them report immediately to Karen's house. Hurry!"

Vail watched the minutes tick by. Angry at her body for betraying her when she needed it, frustrated that she had to remain behind. Concerned they may have made a grave mistake.

As her cold pasta sat in the pot in front of her, she stared at the clock in a daze, running all the Dead Eyes facts through her mind. It all fit. It all made sense. So why was she filled with this sense of unease?

It was a copycat killing, it had to be. All they had was a beat cop's first-on-the-scene impressions. He wasn't a homicide detective and he wasn't a profiler. The finer points of behavior strewn out across the victim's bedroom would be lost on him, just as they would be on the new agents she taught each month.

But the unease ate away at her. And Robby had not called. She was tempted to phone him, but her better sense told her not to. She needed to let them evaluate the scene without interference. He said he would call . . . he'll call, she just had to be patient.

But being patient was not part of Karen Vail's makeup. Acknowledging she needed to divert her attention, she limped over to the stove and began placing the food into containers. She sniffed the sauce and caught a whiff of the fresh pasta and garlic. It would have made a special meal. But with Robby gone, she had lost her appetite.

She slipped the food into the fridge, then pulled the stool in front of the sink. She turned on the hot water and began washing the dirty dishes and pots. It was more difficult to do from a sitting position, but at least it kept her mind off the crime scene, Robby, and her knee pain.

As she placed a dish into the drainboard, she heard a noise somewhere behind her. She stopped the water and listened. Her eyes bounced around the room, noticed the fireplace had completely

urned out and was now a smoldering layer of embers. Perhaps a
piece of wood had fallen from the rack.

She turned around and returned to the dishes, moving on to the
pots. As she maneuvered one into the sink, she heard a *clunk!* and
quickly brought a hand up to the faucet, shutting the water again.
She swiveled on the stool and squinted into the family room.

Nothing.

She thought of where she had left her Glock. In its holster, in her
bedroom. She slid off the stool and lowered herself to the floor, then
wobbled down the hallway, moving slowly, eyes wide and her body
ready to react. Question was, *react to what? To whom?*

"THIS IS PAUL BLEDSOE," he shouted into the handset in his car.
Robby's hands were locked on the dashboard as Bledsoe maneu-
ered through the traffic. "Get out an APB on Chase Hancock.
Info's in the computer. There's an active case open under my name."
He handed Robby the mike and put his other hand on the wheel just
in time to swerve away from a pedestrian. "Shit. What the hell's going on here?"

Robby chewed on his lower lip, holding his thoughts.

Bledsoe accelerated. "Who could've gotten hold of the profile?"

"We know who got hold of it," Robby said. "Dead Eyes."

"We got Dead Eyes. He's deader than a doornail." He glanced at
Robby. "No. *Someone* broke into Karen's house and stole it. *Someone*
left a message on her wall. We just assumed it was Dead Eyes."

"Who the hell else would it have been?"

"I don't know, Hernandez, I don't know. Her ex? Screwing with
her head? Hancock? Same reason?"

Robby sighed. "Whoever broke in is whoever stole the profile.
Same person rolled it up and shoved it into Laura Mackey."

"So who are our suspects?"

"Hancock. Deacon Tucker. And an UNSUB."

Bledsoe swerved onto the shoulder of the roadway and passed
several cars waiting to make a left turn. He was on surface streets,
headed to the Interstate, trying to make the best time possible.

"Try Karen again."

Robby pressed redial. "No answer." He shook his head. "The line must be cut."

"Maybe she's just not home."

"She's home. Her knee's real bad. She's got surgery tomorrow morning, she wasn't going anywhere. Plus, she's got a machine."

Bledsoe gripped the wheel tighter.

Robby tried the line again, cursed under his breath, then slammed the phone shut. "Can't this car go any faster?"

VAIL MOVED INTO HER BEDROOM and saw the holstered Glock sitting atop her dresser. She strapped the shoulder harness across her body then flipped on the overhead light. Everything was as it should have been. She left the light on and moved into Jonathan's bedroom and glanced around. Nothing unusual.

Next she checked her study, where the message was still scrawled on the wall. She would have to get some paint and get rid of that, and soon. It gave her the creeps. It reminded her Dead Eyes had been here, had violated her space.

She moved back down the hallway, using the walls for support. As she stepped into the great room that contained the kitchen at one end and the family room at the other, she wondered if she was just being paranoid. Noises in the house. She hadn't spent the night here in several days, ever since the profile had been stolen. She was unnerved, is all. A killer had been in her home, touched her things. Now she was back here at night and got spooked.

She hobbled through the living and dining rooms, turning on lights. Everything was in its place. There were no messages scrawled across the walls. She chuckled silently, amused at letting herself get so worked up over nothing. *Shame on you, Vail. You should know better.*

She sat back down at the kitchen sink and continued washing the pots.

"WHAT'S OUR ETA?" Bledsoe asked.

Robby looked around at the dark landscape flashing by outside the car. "Man, I don't know. I never go this way. If I had to guess, five minutes, maybe ten."

"When are they going to invent flying cars, huh? Make our jobs so much easier."

"Were there any available units in her area?"

"Different jurisdiction. Dispatch was putting out the word. Did you try her mobile?"

"I texted and called her three times. I was kicked right into voice mail."

"Try the landline again."

Robby hit redial and waited. A moment later, he closed the phone. He didn't need to say anything. Bledsoe already knew there was no answer.

THE SMELL OF BURNT WAX and smoldering wicks irritated Vail's nose. *A draft must have blown out some of the candles.* She hated that odor—she always tried to put a cup over the candle before it had a chance to burn out. Vail shut the water and reached for the dish towel to dry her hands.

But it was not where she always kept it.

A noise behind her, in the family room—and she grabbed for her Glock. Her wet hands fumbled with the leather strap, but she finally yanked the pistol from its holster. Three point stance, hands thrown out in front of her in a triangle. She slid down off the stool and immediately felt the pain of her body's weight bearing down on her left knee. She swung around, keeping her hands fixed in front of her, moving in an arc. But she saw nothing.

"Who's out there?" she yelled.

A flash of light to her extreme right caught her eye, and she spun and fired her gun in one movement—but suddenly the house went dark. There was no longer a doubt of *if* there was an intruder.

Someone had cut the lights. The only questions were who—and where—he was.

Then something else occurred to her. Vail knew she had pulled the trigger. But her pistol did not fire. In fact, it felt light. She pressed the release button with her thumb and the magazine dropped into her opposite hand. She stuck her index finger into the opening, feeling for the rounds. But there were none. Whoever was in her house had emptied her weapon.

Shit.

She shoved the magazine into the pistol and backed toward the sink to grab one of her large knives, but her foot caught the stool's leg and she fell, the Glock flying from her hand. Her initial reaction was to feel for it in the dark, but she realized there was nothing to be gained. She pulled herself up, the pain in her knee now toothache-intense, and moved toward the counter where she kept her knife block.

She realized too late that if the intruder had been smart enough to empty her Glock, and stealthy enough to move her kitchen rag, he probably had also removed other weapons of opportunity. Her knives.

"Hancock, show yourself!" She shouted it into the dark air, hoping to elicit a response. Hoping for a chuckle if she were wrong, a voice if she were right. Something to give her a sense of direction.

But before she could plan her next move, she heard a shuffle of feet. She threw her hands up and bent away from the noise bracing for impact—and got what she expected. *Whack!* Across the hands. Then a swift kick to her left knee. Pain ignited, burst through her leg, like fireworks exploding in her brain. She let out a groan, in that instant knowing there were going to be more fierce, angry blows.

She crumpled in pain and was driven backwards to the floor, as a lineman would tackle a quarterback. And then she felt the weight of a body atop her.

Vail swung her arms hard and hit something, something metal, and heard the object clunk against the floor. She immediately threw her hands up and grabbed clothing—then pushed the man back, away from her. Her eyes were now accommodating to the darkness and could make out what looked like nylon pantyhose stretched across his face.

"Son of a bitch!" she shouted as he grabbed her neck with strong, ice-like hands.

She tried to maneuver her legs to kick him, but he was sitting on her abdomen. Pinning her pelvis to the floor. He had done this before, she was sure. Highly intelligent, excellent planner . . . thirty to forty years old . . . her profile flittered through her mind while she tried to pry his hands loose.

As the air left her lungs.

Bledsoe swerved, his tires crying in protest. He broadsided a parked Honda but continued on, the rear of his car dovetailing as he accelerated.

"We're close," Robby said. "Maybe half a mile."

"I just hope dispatch got through to the sheriff's office—"

Just then, a police cruiser came speeding up behind them, strobe lights whipping in dizzying rhythm.

"He's either after us for hit-and-run or he got dispatch's message."

"Let's hope he got the message," Bledsoe said, "'cause I ain't stopping for nothing."

Bledsoe killed the lights a half a block away; the tailing cruiser followed suit. Bledsoe pulled up at the curb with a heavy foot on the brake while trying to avoid squealing the tires. Robby was out his door before Bledsoe and covered the postage-stamp lawn in four strides. Bledsoe motioned the cop in the patrol car toward the rear of the house.

They drew their guns and stood on opposite sides of the front door. Bledsoe nodded to Robby, who stepped up and unleashed a wicked front-on kick.

The door splintered inward. Bledsoe charged in, followed by Robby. They crouched low and moved quickly through the family room, their roving LED flashlights throwing an eerie flicker through the darkened house. Bledsoe tried the light switch. Nothing. He motioned to Robby to move on, toward the back of the house where the bedrooms were located.

Robby started down the hallway—and saw something on the kitchen floor. Vail's Glock. He knelt beside it, reached into his pocket and pulled out a latex glove, and snapped it on. He lifted the

weapon, held it up to his nose. It had not been fired. He removed
the magazine. *Empty.* "What?"

Bledsoe came up behind him.

Robby motioned to the gun. "Magazine's empty. No shells.
Hasn't been fired."

Bledsoe squinted confusion. He turned and continued on through
the house, his flashlight's narrow beam bouncing around the walls.
Robby remained where he was, trying to piece together what had
happened. *Why would she empty her weapon? That doesn't make sense.
Unless someone emptied it for her.* Concern welled up inside his chest;
his blood was pounding in his neck, in his head, in his ears.

He moved toward the garage, using his small but powerful flashlight to peer under boxes and around corners. Vail's car was still there;
the hood was cool to the touch. *Come on, Karen, where are you?*

He moved back into the house and met Bledsoe. "Anything?"

"House is clear."

"Car's in the garage," Robby said. He rested his hands on his
hips. "So where is she?"

Bledsoe held up Vail's BlackBerry. "Turned off. That's why you
didn't get through." He scrolled through the numbers stored in
memory. "Three missed calls. All yours."

"I think we can assume she didn't leave of her own choosing."

As they stood there, the looming silence between them was
deafening.

Finally, Bledsoe turned and headed toward the garage. "Let's get
these lights back on and take a good look around."

To Robby, that course of action seemed severely inadequate. But
at the moment, he had nothing better to offer.

. . . eighty-two

Vail's head was bowed. Her shoulders ached and her neck was on fire. As consciousness returned, second by passing second, she realized why she was in pain. Her wrists were encircled by handcuffs secured to a beam, her body suspended above the floor, a few inches off the ground. Her ankles were shackled together, the loose chain dragging impotently beneath her.

And she was naked.

A single bare bulb stared her in the face, a few feet from her head. Close enough to feel the heat radiating from it. The remainder of her body was cold, the air chilled and drafty. A strong mildew scent tickled her nose.

She blinked, trying to clear her blurry vision. She did not know what had happened to her after she fought for her last breaths. She remembered an intense electrical shock ripping through her chest. The only likely scenario was a stun gun.

But there was so much that remained unexplained . . . chief of which was how Dead Eyes could have been resurrected. She had seen Patrick Farwell's body on the ground. And the most telling evidence of all, the left hands.

But what if the man lying there had not been Farwell? Their only photos of him were mug shots from twenty years ago. What if Farwell had found someone who resembled himself, took him back to his house, and executed him, disguising it as a suicide and expecting the police to draw the obvious conclusions, that the body was that of the Dead Eyes killer?

If it was not, in fact, Farwell's body, then the crime scene had been staged: making it look like something it was not. Staging was a telltale sign of an organized offender. That Vail did not see this sooner bothered her. Another missed sign. She had never wanted to accept that she was fallible. Yet as the pain in her shoulders and wrists increased, it served as a constant reminder of just how flawed she was. Kidnapped by the Dead Eyes killer, however, her fate was far worse than imperfection.

Such a fate was not something she was willing to accept. Not yet.

She closed her eyes for a moment, attempting to reinvigorate her night vision. The bright bulb, seemingly the only light source, had blinded her, and she wanted to be able to look into the darker recesses around her. Hopefully to gain some clues as to where she was.

Closing her eyes provided a secondary benefit: it focused her senses. She swore she smelled something, a light perfume, more a suggestion than a statement. It was a scent she had smelled before. But where?

When Vail opened her eyes, she looked to her extreme left, where a narrow shelf sat mounted to a bare plywood wall. The space was about eight feet across, the ceiling perhaps eight feet high. It almost had the look of a closet, though slightly larger. She moved her head and looked over her right shoulder. The underside of steps. This was some sort of basement, or dead space beneath a staircase. Dead space for Dead Eyes. The irony was not lost on her.

Also not lost on her were the crime scene photos stolen from her house. Hanging to her right were pictures of the Dead Eyes victims: marked with what appeared to be red lipstick: their names, their identification, their personality—who they were as people—reduced to mere numbers on darkly grained plywood. They were all there, Marci Evers, Noreen O'Regan, Angelina Sarducci, Melanie Hoffman, Sandra Franks, Denise Cranston; and a newspaper photo of Eleanor Linwood, two knives protruding from the wall. Stabbed through the eyes.

Vail now knew where she was: in the killer's lair. She closed her eyes and tried to think. Tried to block the pain coming from her shoulder joints, which felt as if they were going to snap like the dead twigs she used to crunch beneath her heels in her parent's yard in Old Westbury. What a far better place to be now.

But her situation was not going to be solved by visualizing better times or reliving the past. She was a spider caught on a web, hung out until the predator could come along and eat her alive.

Her legs, though cuffed at the ankles, were still free to move about. But the tractioning weight on her left knee was substantial. Which hurt worse . . . her shoulders and wrists or her knee . . . it was difficult to say. At the moment, none of that mattered. She had to shut off all pain, all thoughts of defeat.

Visual examination of her surroundings told her there was nothing she could use to her advantage, no walls or stools, boxes or handles for her feet to gain purchase. She would have to use her legs to kick and, hopefully, win her freedom.

Questions flooded her thoughts: Where was she? Down the street from her house or in another state? In the middle of nowhere? She thought of the bank, of the Alvin look-alike, of how there was no tactical team outside backing her up. Yet standing there with her Glock trained on the man's head, she'd had control, she'd had power. What she would give to be back there.

Because as precarious as it had been, staring down the barrel of a crackhead's .38 Special, it was nothing compared to this.

BLEDSOE WALKED BACK into the kitchen and joined Robby, who was kneeling beside a forensic technician.

"Anything?" Robby asked.

Bledsoe shook his head. "Nothing of use. There was a struggle in the kitchen. That's about it. No obvious signs of forced entry."

"Anything on your end?"

The technician looked up from his toolkit. "About the best news I can give you right now is that there's no blood. We found a few footprints in the soil outside that don't match any of your shoes. Sneakers, size nine, Reeboks, if I had to guess." He stood from his crouch. "Latents galore, but it'll be a while before we can sort them all out. Sorry. I wish I had more to give you. We may have more later."

"Later . . ." Bledsoe griped. He walked off with Robby.

"So where does this leave us?"

Bledsoe rubbed tired eyes. "We thought Patrick Farwell was Dead Eyes. Everything pointed to that, even the shit at his place. But he's dead—"

"Is he?" Robby asked.

"Look, Hernandez, I know it's late and we've been pushed up against the wall, but you're not making sense. You saw the bullet wound. His body's lying at the ME's office on a slab."

Robby was waving his hands. "No, no. You're missing the point. *Someone* was shot dead in that house. What if it wasn't Farwell?"

Bledsoe sat down on the family room couch, eyes searching the floor. "It sure looked like him. We had his mug shots—"

"Yeah, from twenty years ago. Humor me. Call the ME, find out where they are in processing the body. See if they've run the fingerprints yet."

Bledsoe dug out his cell phone, then punched in the number.

Robby stood there, trying to work it through. Feeling he was missing something, but not sure what. Then he realized what was bothering him. The email from the offender. He played it back in his mind: *The hiding place smelled musty . . . it was small and dark. He watched everything through little holes in the walls.* It had to be. If he was wrong, they would lose valuable time. But at the moment, there were no other leads to pursue.

Bledsoe's shoulders fell. "Can you run them ASAP?" he said into the phone. "The body may not be Farwell's. Soon as you get something, call me." He shook his head, then closed his phone.

Robby grabbed Bledsoe's arm. "I know where she is."

"You *know*? Or you think you know?"

Robby hesitated. He had asked himself the same question. But he was relying on intuition . . . intuition and analytic logic. "How soon can you get a chopper here?"

"If there's one in the air, ten minutes. If not, longer."

"Make it ten. Karen's life is at stake."

THE PAIN WAS STARTING to reach her limits of tolerance. Vail tried pulling herself up to alleviate some of the strain on her shoulders. If

her arms had been separated by just a few more inches, her position
would be the same as the leg pull-up exercises she did to strengthen
her abdominal muscles at the Academy gym. But because her hands
were locked so close to one another, the increased strain on her arms
only worsened the wrist pain.

"Shit," she said. It was her first utterance . . . but not her last
Figuring that the intelligent offender would have gagged her had he
thought her screams could be heard, she knew that calling out for
help would be a useless exercise.

She did it anyway.

But after her first plea, she was stopped short by the feeling that
someone was behind her. She spun her head around and saw, in the
dim recesses of the small room, a figure dressed in dark clothing
Vail's body swung from her sudden movement, allowing a sliver of
light from the bulb to catch the shiny nylon of the pantyhose
stretched across the offender's face.

"Won't do you any good," the voice said. It was rough and
strained, but confident.

"Who are you?" Vail shouted.

"I gave you more credit than you deserved." He moved slightly
to his right, making it more difficult for Vail to see him. It was a
move of power, Vail was sure of it. He talked; she had to listen but
could not look at him.

"Are you the Dead Eyes killer?"

"You still don't get it, do you? Crack profiler, supervisory *special*
agent and you ask a dumb question like that. What good is the title
'special' if you're as stupid as the rest of them? Of course I'm the
Dead Eyes killer!"

There it was again. The scent. She tried to force it from her mind
but it popped back in. The backyard. Sandra Franks's yard, when she
felt as if the killer was watching her, when she had run through the
brush and sprained her knee.

"It *is* you," Vail said.

"The light comes on. How very promising. Now for the million
dollar question: Do you know where you are?"

"I'd say the million dollar question is *who you are,* not where I am."

A snapping sound flicked in Vail's ears before the searing sting of a whip slapped against her bare skin. "I ask the questions here, Agent Vail. *Karen.* Sweet little Karen."

The bite from the whip was still throbbing and overrode all other pain; she bit her lip to contain the whimper that threatened to escape her mouth. She was not going to give him that.

"I'll tell you where you are. You're in the same place we grew up, the place where we watched father through that peephole in front of you. The place we hid, too scared to come out."

"We?" Vail clenched her jaw, trying to will away the pain, trying to put it all together. *Come on, Vail, think!* An accomplice. There had been many serial killers who had a friend or spouse as their partner in crime. Then: "Where is he? Is he afraid, too scared to come out?"

The whip snapped again, this time striking the flesh over Vail's low back and buttocks. Tears squeezed from her clenched eyes.

"I'd hoped to make you work for it, but I see you're too stupid to get it. And I'm not interested in playing twenty questions."

The offender moved in front of Vail, the light beating down on the pantyhose-covered head. Vail squinted at the figure before her, bracing for what might come next. Pain was a state of mind now, coming from nowhere . . . and everywhere. Her abdominal muscles, which seemed to be stretched beyond their limits by the weight of her lower extremities, were cramping. She needed to lift her legs somehow, to lessen the strain on her stomach.

But suspended as she was, there was little she could do to defend herself. Instead of harming her, however, the offender merely reached up and pulled off his nylon veil.

And in that instant, the profiler in her vanished. All thoughts, all emotions, all words left her mind. Seconds passed before the shock wore thin enough to speak. And even then, she was only able to whisper one sentence: "Oh, my god."

*H*ow could this be?

The lighting was poor, her vision blurred by pain. But from what she was able to see, the offender's hair was short, the face hard, the brow prominent, and the mouth drawn down into a scowl.

Vail finally summoned the strength to speak. "Who are you?" But the name was unimportant, Vail realized. The physical appearance, the hair color, the face, the eyes. . . . There was no need to ask who it was. The answer was obvious. Vail hesitated a moment, then said: "I . . . I'm a twin? I have a twin sister?"

"I'm not who you think I am," the Dead Eyes killer said.

"You have to be," Vail insisted. It was all coming together. The nightmares . . . could it be possible they weren't merely dreams, but some kind of "psychic connection," the kind documented between twins? She'd always doubted such phenomena, but now she wasn't so sure.

Of course. "Nellie took me and left you with our father."

Another snap of the whip, this time across the legs. "Does it hurt? Do you feel the pain? It's just like the pain you caused. *You.* You're the one responsible. You and that dead queen bitch. The lying Eleanor Linwood. Or should I call her Nellie Irwin?"

The bare bulb cast a harsh light on Dead Eyes's head, causing deep shadows to fall across the remainder of her face.

"I can help you," Vail said.

A laugh. A deep, guttural laugh. But no response. The killer moved out of the penumbra holding a Tupperware container. "Do you know what this is?"

Vail strained her eyes downward.

The killer removed the top and held the container up to Vail's face. Inside was a left hand. A man's hand.

Vail immediately recognized the thick scar across the knuckles. "Deacon—"

"An ugly SOB, if you don't mind me saying. And mean—man, I tell you, it was a totally different experience. All those bitches were soft-talking sitting ducks. But your Deacon, he was a bit more challenging. I thought it would be fun to go to his house, make him think I was you. At first, it worked. He thought you'd come to fight, and he got nasty with me. Reminded me of father. So I gave him what he deserved." Dead Eyes looked down at the hand and shrugged. "I took a little souvenir. *A trophy*, I think you called it in your profile." She looked down at the container, tilted it in the dim light. "It turned out to be more satisfying than I thought it would be."

Vail stared at the hand, embarrassed by her momentary relief over the discovery of Deacon's death. She pushed the thought aside, realizing she needed to find a way out of this, for she had no desire to join him. "The eyes," Vail said. "Did you stab the eyes because of how you think mother looked at you? Because she left you and took me?"

The killer forced a tight smile. "'It's in the blood,' Karen. Do you get it now?"

"I got it. I thought the genetic reference meant father. The letter to Singletary threw us off."

"Wasn't that absolutely brilliant? I found some letters from Richard Ray in the house. He and the bastard were obviously good friends. But friendships only go so far. I knew if I sent Richard Ray a letter, he'd try to use it to save his sorry ass. Between that and the locket, I knew you'd end up here."

"You killed father for revenge." It was more a statement than a question.

"The bastard deserved it, for what he did. I wanted to do something special to him, but I knew his 'suicide' would be worth more. It gave me an opportunity. I had to control my desires so I could take advantage of the situation, use it for the greater good. It's always about control, isn't it?"

Always about control. In many cases, it was.

At the moment, Vail had to control the pain. Fight through it. Focus. "What was the greater good?"

"Going after you, of course. Once I killed the queen bitch, you became the ultimate prize."

Vail leaned forward and locked eyes. "It didn't work out, though, did it? I'm still here."

A growl, then Dead Eyes swiveled away from the light, toward the shelf, and returned with a small, black, rectangular object.

Vail instantly knew what it was. A stun gun. And she now knew another thing: her earlier suspicions had been correct: Dead Eyes had used the device to get her here.

But it was not going to be the way she would die.

Dead Eyes studied the stun gun as if teasing her, then looked up at Vail. "My guess is that you already know what this is. But don't worry, I won't kill you all at once. You're different than the other bitches. I'm going to have some fun first, play with you for a little while."

If Vail was ever going to do something, this was the time. She had to override the pain and summon the strength to move.

"The longer I hold the probes against your skin, the more scrambled your brain gets. So I'm going to start with a few quick jolts to make sure your mind is clear. I want you to know what's happening to you. I want you to *feel* it." She smiled. "In a few minutes you're going to beg me to kill you. And I'll be glad to accommodate your wishes."

Vail's eyes were riveted to the stun gun. "You don't have to do this."

"Really! You read those emails, you know what the bastard did." The killer jabbed her breast with the stun gun. Vail screamed.

"Don't you understand?" Dead Eyes yelled. "It should've been you!"

Vail bit her lip, trying to contain her fear. She had to turn her thoughts inward, separate mind from body. She closed her eyes. *There is no pain. I'm feeling no pain.*

"Don't shut your eyes on me! I want you to watch!"

Another jab, this one to the stomach. Her leg muscles twitched fiercely. She was starting to lose consciousness. *No, fight. Think of Jonathan. Of Robby.*

Another jolt. She opened her eyes.

On the shelf was a steak knife, the silver blade catching the orange incandescence of the bulb. Her eyes shifted to the stun gun as it again moved toward her—

And she drew her legs up, thrusting them outward and catching Dead Eyes in the chest. The killer reeled backward, her head slamming against the wall.

A growl. Blazing eyes. "Bitch!"

She righted herself and came at Vail. This was it—perhaps her only window of opportunity. Her mind screamed *Now!* as she lifted and spread her legs as far as the chain allowed. She forced her thighs over the killer's head and slammed them onto her shoulders.

Dead Eyes writhed and pulled, grabbing at Vail's legs, trying to loosen her hold. The weight of her body transferred from her wrists to the killer's torso, relaxing the pull on Vail's arms. Vail grabbed the overhead pipe with her right hand, giving her more control over the movement of her body. But Dead Eyes was putting up a valiant fight: Vail felt like a cowboy riding a bucking bronco, summoning every last ounce of strength to hold on.

Remembering that the leg muscles were the strongest in the body, Vail tightened her stomach and brought her thighs together. But as she squeezed, she felt the killer's hands pulling on her ankles, trying to pry the legs apart.

It was a smart move, because gripping the legs down low gave her leverage, leverage that Vail found hard to overcome. Sharp knee pain shot up her thigh. Her muscles started to shake. And her legs slowly parted. "Damn it!" she screamed, desperate to keep her hold. "Ahhh!"

It was all she had left. In the seconds that followed, all she could think about was how much she wanted to live. Jonathan and Robby. She filled her mind with those thoughts as her legs spread apart. Dead Eyes twisted free and fell to her knees. Coughed spasmodically. Then grabbed the stun gun from the floor, stood up, and swung hard, smashing the light bulb.

Vail hung there, her leg strength spent, her stomach muscles cramping. Overriding pain just about everywhere.

In total darkness.

Awaiting the searing jolt of electricity.

With the chopper's high-intensity spotlights swirling over the Farwell ranch below, Robby spied an older model Audi parked perpendicular to the front porch.

"This is it!" he yelled into Bledsoe's ear. He thrust a finger into the helicopter's window, indicating the vehicle below.

Bledsoe craned his neck to have a look, then leaned over the pilot's shoulder, pointing at the ground. "Set her down! Set her down!"

The helicopter descended rapidly and touched down in the clearing, thirty feet away.

"Air Unit Four," Bledsoe shouted into the mike, "positive ID at Farwell ranch. Requesting backup."

"We're not waiting till they get here," Robby said.

"Hell no. Let's go!"

They climbed out of the chopper, weapons drawn, and ran without cover toward the front door. Had someone been crouched anywhere nearby with a rifle—or even with a pistol and a steady hand and a good eye—Bledsoe and Robby would have been tin cartoon characters in an old fashioned arcade game.

But they reached the door without drawing fire. They threw their backs up against the clapboard siding of the house and watched the helicopter lift up and away to search the immediate area in case the offender had attempted to flee.

Robby motioned to Bledsoe that he would take the point. After receiving a confirmatory nod, he crouched low and stepped through the splintered doorway.

Into pitch darkness.

Bledsoe followed and tried a light switch. On-off, on-off. Shook his head. Nothing.

They pulled their flashlights and swept the narrow beams across the path ahead of them. "You go up," Robby whispered into Bledsoe's ear. "Once you clear it, meet me back down here."

Pistol in hand, Bledsoe proceeded up the creaky stairs as Robby moved through the rooms slowly, relying on his ears as much as the tightly focused cylinder of light. After their initial analysis, the forensics crew had crated everything and moved it out for additional evidence collection at the lab, so clearing the house was efficient and quick. Less than a minute later, Bledsoe descended the stairs. Robby met him at the landing.

They pivoted 360 degrees.

"Any ideas?" Bledsoe whispered.

Robby leaned down to Bledsoe's ear and said, "I'll take the closets. You look for crawl spaces."

Bledsoe trained his light on the worn wood flooring to search for an access point. A broken trail of caked mud littered the ground. He turned and tapped Robby's arm. Nodded at the soil tracks. They both checked their shoes: no dirt.

Robby followed the mud with his flashlight as it trailed from the house's rear door through the downstairs hallway. It ended at the entryway coat closet, built into the back of the staircase. With everything having been removed, Robby knew it would be empty. He motioned to Bledsoe and they positioned themselves on either side of the door. Bledsoe yanked it open.

Robby swept the area with his pistol and flashlight, then shook his head: nothing. Bledsoe started to close the door, but Robby stuck out his arm. His eyes caught a straight-cut line in the wood floorboard. He followed it to his right, where it met the wall . . . and another seam. He craned his neck up and around. They were beneath the staircase. He looked down again and followed the seams in the flooring. Then it hit him.

A hidden room. His thoughts flashed back to the contents of the vanishing email Vail had received. The UNSUB mentioned "a hiding place . . . musty . . . small . . . dark." Robby moved into the closet and knelt in front of the side wall. Putting the narrow flashlight into his mouth, he traced the seam up and around: it was approximately

ur feet high and nearly two and a half feet wide, the bottom of the
ctangle being formed by the floorboards. He reached into his back
ocket and removed a long, black handcuff key. He stuck it into the
am and pried outward. The section of wall moved.

Robby traced the edges with his fingertips and noted a roughened
ea along the left side: whoever had built the hideaway had pried
ainst the same spot numerous times while using it as an entry point.
n close examination, based on its texture, Robby figured a section
the wall had been replaced with a rectangle of painted plywood.

He looked up at Bledsoe and motioned him into the closet bend him. Robby extinguished his light and continued prying at the
all. When it was sufficiently loose and ready to be removed, he
pped Bledsoe twice on the leg. Bledsoe, nearly a foot shorter than
obby, would be the logical choice to enter first.

Bledsoe crouched and waited as Robby tapped his leg once, then
ice, then three times. Robby yanked back on the wall and the rec-
ngle popped into his hands. A musty odor wafted toward them.
ledsoe, weapon out in front of him, remained by the opening and
aited. Listened. Then he climbed in.

LTHOUGH ROBBY THOUGHT he had prepared himself for just
out anything, he knew that whenever you crawled into a dark
ace in a house that belonged to a sexual offender, you could not
ssibly anticipate what you were going to encounter.

But the pained scream that emerged from Bledsoe's mouth
ught Robby off-guard. He flicked on his flashlight and held it
ainst the side of his handgun. Bledsoe was facedown, sprawled
ross what appeared to be two small steps leading down into the
awl space beneath the house. Bledsoe was moaning, his body con-
lsing. Robby shined his light up and around, his Glock moving
th the beam. He saw something, something that made his racing
art skip a beat.

A woman's body, apparently hanging. But he could only see the
ngling ankles and feet, as she was suspended below the staircase,
d his view was blocked. *Karen?*

Bledsoe's convulsing had slowed to intermittent twitching. What the hell had happened to him? *A stun gun.* It was the only thing that could incapacitate someone so rapidly and leave telltale signs of transient nervous system disruption.

Robby again ran his light around the small space. Was it safe to go in? Clearly not. To take out Bledsoe with a stun gun, the offender needed to touch him: he had to be nearby.

But he couldn't retreat and wait for backup, either. If that was Karen a few feet away from him, and if she was still alive, he had to get to her. *Now.*

He reached forward and grabbed Bledsoe by his belt and yanked him back into the closet. He was heavy and he banged up Bledsoe's face on the rough edge of the cutout, but Robby's concern was getting to Vail.

Glock firmly in hand, he squeezed through the opening feet first. If he was going to get zapped, this would be the time. But he made it in and quickly swung his light and pistol around the space. Nothing. Swiveled it toward the woman's body.

My God.

He stood face to face with Vail. Shined his light: eyes at half-mast. He moved behind her to keep as much of the area in his view as possible, stuck the small flashlight in his mouth, then fumbled for his key. He unlocked the handcuffs and gently lowered her to the packed dirt ground in a sitting position against the side wall of the stairwell. A spasmodic tic rattled her body.

A voice in the darkness: "So good of you to drop in."

Robby spun, swinging his Glock in the direction of the voice—but an electric shock jolted him, like a lightning bolt attacking his muscles. He convulsed.

Pain shot through him. His arms spasmed, his body went numb, and his mind exploded into a mess of disorientation as he dropped to his knees.

"Thanks for coming," Dead Eyes said. "How nice it is to kill you."

What happened? Where am I? Who's talking?

A voice, in the distance . . . and a feeling that something as terribly wrong.

"I'm saving you from the evil this bitch would've brought upon you, Detective. It's an evil that's generational, an evil that must be urged. An evil that spreads, invades, and infects. You're infected . . . you must be killed like a germ."

Robby's muscular twitching and fatigue were still pervasive. The tense vertigo and numbness, however, were clearing and his senses ere coming back to him: he smelled a rank odor . . . felt raw nerve in flaring in his shoulder . . . saw a dark figure looming, leaning own toward him—

And heard a woman's scream: "No!"

Robby instinctively threw up his arms to protect himself. But his ovements were still slow and ineffective. The assailant brought his m down—

—and then crumpled to the ground, beside Robby, atop Vail's lap. Standing there was Bledsoe, a thick two-by-four in his hands. ou okay?"

Robby's eyes shifted to Vail, who just sat there, apparently lacking e strength to move. His twitching ceased, the pain subsided, and nor-al vision returned. "Karen. . . ." He rolled onto his side and clumsily alled the handcuffs from his belt. He got them around the wrists of ead Eyes and ratcheted them down. Bledsoe grabbed the offender's rso and dragged the unconscious body toward the opening.

Robby removed his windbreaker, draped it around Vail's shoul-rs, then drew her close. "I was afraid I was going to lose you."

She squeezed him softly, with all her remaining strength. "That's ver gonna happen."

Karen Vail stood behind a large one-way mirror in the Special Needs cell block of the Fairfax County Adult Detention Center. Chase Hancock had been found in New Jersey, laying low and looking for work. As for Vail, her wrists were wrapped in cock-up splints and she was wearing a figure-eight support on her shoulders and hinged metal brace on her left knee. High-dose Motrin floated in her bloodstream. The ER physician prescribed Vicodin, but she wanted to be lucid, in complete control of her surroundings.

It's always about control, isn't it?

Beside Vail stood Paul Bledsoe, along with Thomas Gifford and the rest of the task force squad. Vail was transfixed on the scene unfolding behind the glass, where Behavioral Science Unit criminologist Wayne Rudnick had begun questioning a shackled Dead Eyes killer. Normally, one or two task force members would be in the interview room with their quarry. That was just the way it was done: those who tracked and caught the killer were given the opportunity to interrogate. It was like the reward, the dessert for eating your vegetables. But due to the complexity of the offender's psychological condition, Bledsoe had reluctantly deferred to the BSU specialist.

The Dead Eyes killer abruptly stood and shouted. "Get her in here! Fucking bitch. Where is she? I'll kill her!"

"Sam," Rudnick said, maintaining his calm, "Please relax. I need you to sit, Sam, so we can continue to talk."

"I don't want to talk. All I want to do is kill her! Where is that bitch?" The chair went flying and the metal table overturned, knocking Rudnick to the floor. Four guards rushed the room, moving to restrain the killer—who was still fairly well contained by the shackles. But it was a raucous and adrenaline-spilling situation nonetheless.

"You okay?" a guard asked.

"I'm fine," Rudnick said, his voice tinny through the speaker. Even through the one-way mirror, Vail could see Rudnick's face was ~~red~~ from embarrassment. She watched him brush back his wild, ~~ti~~ghtly coiled hair and shrug his shoulders to reseat his worn, corduroy sport coat.

Upon Vail's arrival, Bledsoe had told her they had just completed ~~a~~ nightlong search of the ceramics studio and loft, and found a bogus FBI shield fashioned from brass. An old copy of *U.S. News*, with a close-up photo of a genuine Bureau badge, served as the model.

Vail's gaze returned to the Dead Eyes killer, Samantha Farwell. Her twin sister.

The short red hair was parted to the side, the voice was deep and ~~r~~ough, and the actions were aggressive and consistent with male offenders she had faced in the past. In fact, everything in the killer's behavior was consistent with that of a male. Above all, a true female serial ~~k~~iller was nearly unheard of. But it was now clear there was a great deal ~~m~~ore going on.

Rudnick was back at the table facing Sam, who had calmed. The ~~g~~uards had left the room on Rudnick's insistence. "Sam, I would like ~~t~~o talk with Samantha."

"And what's she going to tell you that I can't?"

Rudnick shrugged matter-of-factly. "How she felt, what it was ~~li~~ke growing up."

"I can tell you everything you need to know."

"I'm not here to hurt her, Sam, you know that. I realize you can ~~a~~nswer my questions, but I'd really like her perspective. Please."

Sam's chin dipped a bit and his head tilted to the side. The brow ~~s~~oftened, the face lost its hard edge—became more feminine—and ~~t~~he shoulders slumped inward.

"Samantha?" Rudnick asked. "Is that you?"

Her head remained still, but her eyes darted around the room be~~f~~ore coming to rest on Rudnick's face. "Who are you?" The voice ~~w~~as smooth and melodic, as different from Sam's as the scent of a ~~r~~ose is from a clove of garlic.

"Whoa," Sinclair said, watching through the mirror. "No offense but your sister's loony tunes."

Manette whistled. "Man, she is definitely off her rocker."

Loony. Off her rocker. Convenient colloquial terms, but inaccurate. "Samantha has classic DID," Vail said. "Dissociative Identity Disorder. To understand what it is, you have to understand who she is, where she came from. Her father, Patrick Farwell, was a sadistic man; Samantha had to find a way of dealing with him. My guess is she was young and weak and ill equipped to handle his abuse. Eventually, her mind created a stronger personality, what psychiatrists call a *protector persona*. Sam, a male, was better equipped to withstand the abuse and probably found a way to fight back. He became dominant and Samantha remained tucked away, safe and sound."

"Sounds like more psycho bullshit to me," Manette said.

Vail spun to face her. "It's a well-documented condition. It usually begins during childhood as a defense mechanism to severe abuse. And it mostly hits women. Don't take my word for it, look it up in the journals. Hell, check the DSM-IV manual, it's in there, too." She turned back to the glass. "And I've seen it before."

"So have I," Del Monaco said. He had been standing in the background, engrossed in the interview. "Once. Absolutely blew my mind."

"So Samantha was *asleep* for twenty-five years?" Bledsoe asked.

"Not asleep," Vail corrected. "Dormant, probably for a little while. Patrick Farwell was arrested when Samantha was about thirteen. My guess is that when Sam felt it was safe, Samantha reemerged. When Farwell got out of prison eighteen months ago, he must've found Samantha. Sam reemerged, older and wiser, able to carry out the fantasies he'd created as an adolescent." Vail continued to watch her sister through the glass. "Unleashed and unchecked, Sam acted on those fantasies. He set out to kill the woman he considered responsible for Samantha's fate—her mother. He started killing. The first victim came easy. It was intensely satisfying, and he killed again. And again."

Del Monaco nodded. "Each victim was similar in appearance to the way Eleanor Linwood looked as a young woman. To Sam, each victim *was* Samantha's evil mother."

"What keeps every killer from claiming they've got this 'identity disorder'?" Manette asked.

"Nothing," Del Monaco said. "Gacy tried to claim DID as a defense, but not once, in all the interviews I conducted with him, did I ever see evidence of an alternate personality. Gacy was bullshit. From what I'm seeing here, Samantha Farwell is the real deal."

Vail couldn't help but think how fortunate she was. If Linwood had not been able to wrest her from Farwell's grasp, she, too, could have ended up like Samantha. And what of her sister? What would happen to her? Shipped off to a state mental institution's maximum security ward, possibly for the rest of her life. Slim chance of rehabilitation or recovery.

Recovery. Vail knew the treatment for dissociative disorders involved merging the different personas into one. Even if technically possible, how could Samantha integrate a serial killer into her personality? How could she recover from the knowledge that she'd brutally murdered eight innocent women? Vail rested her head against the one-way mirror and sighed deeply.

"You okay?" Bledsoe asked.

"Let's see, I find out I have a twin sister who's a serial killer, my mother's really my aunt, my biological mother is brutally murdered, and my worst fears about my biological father are confirmed. I'd say it's been a kick-ass week."

Manette nodded. "Sometimes, Kari, life just sucks the big one."

Vail was lying in recovery, her left knee bandaged and slightly elevated. She had regained consciousness a few minutes ago, her senses coming back to her in stages. She was hungry and felt dehydrated.

"Knock, knock." Vail smiled. Robby's voice.

"Come in."

Robby stuck his head in from behind the curtain and grinned. "How you doing?"

"Better, now that you're here."

His head ducked back for a second before reappearing. "I have present for you."

Her eyebrows rose and her head tilted. "What is it?"

Robby pulled back the curtain and Jonathan stepped forward. He was thin, but he looked well. His face was bright. He hesitated at the foot of her bed, his eyes taking in the bandaged knee and the brace on her wrists before finding her face.

She lifted her arms, taking care not to snag the IV line, and motioned to her son. Jonathan moved to the side of the gurney, then melted into her embrace.

"It's over," she whispered. "We get to start again, a new life for us."

"Are you okay?" he asked.

"A little banged up, but nothing I won't get over." She looked down and noticed something in Jonathan's hand. "What's that?"

He pushed away and showed her the small package. "Robby got me *Too Human*." He must have noticed Vail's quizzical look, because he elaborated. "It's an Xbox game, mom."

"Oh. Hecka tight, right?" she asked.

"Mom," he said, rolling his eyes.

Robby cleared his throat. "You're embarrassing him."

"Give me a break. I can speak the groovy lingo with the best of them."

A nurse appeared at the foot of the gurney with a large bouquet of flowers. "A messenger dropped this off for you at the front desk," the woman said, then handed them to Robby, who thanked her.

Vail pulled the small card from the porcelain vase. As she read it, a smile teased her lips.

"Who's it from?" Robby asked.

Vail eyed him curiously. "Do I detect a note of jealousy?"

"More like a couple of notes."

"Hmm. Haven't heard that tune in a while." She winked at him. "It's from Jackson Parker, my attorney. He told me to get well soon so he could face me in court again. And, he wanted to let me know that everything's going to be fine."

"What's going to be fine?" Jonathan asked.

Vail gently touched her son's face, then reached out to take Robby's hand. "Everything, sweetheart," she said. "Everything's going to be fine."

acknowledgments

I'm indebted to the following individuals for their time and assistance. Any errors (or literary license I may have taken with some minor facts/locations) are solely my responsibility.

FBI Profiler Mark Safarik, recently retired Supervisory Special Agent with the Bureau's Behavioral Analysis Unit. My work with Mark goes back twelve years, and during this time he's helped me gain a deep insight, not just into the life and work of a profiler, but into the serial offender's mind as well—perceptions and observations that can't be gleaned from textbooks. In ensuring the accuracy of the material, characters, and concepts used in *The 7th Victim*, Mark's unending assistance and attention to detail were invaluable.

FBI profiler Mary Ellen O'Toole, Supervisory Special Agent with the Bureau's Behavioral Analysis Unit, for being candid with me about her experiences as a profiler both on and off the job; for her insight into the mind of a killer; and for offering me a woman's perspective on the unique issues she faces not only in her unit but as woman packing a large weapon . . . with the attitude and skill to use it.

Lieutenant William Kitzerow, City of Fairfax, Virginia Police Department, for his extensive tour of his police department and hospitality in making sure I had everything I needed—including being "my eyes" in extensive follow-ups; there's nothing better than having a veteran police lieutenant interview people on your behalf for information.

Major R. Stephen Kovacs, Commander, Court Services Division, and **Lt. Stacey Kleiner,** Fairfax County Sheriff's Office, for giving me a private tour of the cell blocks and booking and processing areas of the Fairfax County Adult Detention Center. They were courteous, open, honest, and invaluable resources.

Fairfax County **Police Officer First Class Micheal Weinhaus,** Mason District Station, who not only answered my unending questions but who took me on a behind-the-scenes tour of his facility and then welcomed me into his cruiser for a hoppin' midnight shift ride-along. I'm confident one day he'll be able to get my finger impressions out of his dashboard.

Fairfax County **Police Officer Jeff Andrea**, Mount Vernon District Station, for his assistance and explanation of prisoner booking procedure and transport; **Sergeant Jamie Smith** of the Vienna, Virginia, Police Department for his tour, candor, and contacts; **Major H. D. Smith** and **Detective Twyla DeMoranville**, for taking me behind the scenes at the Spotsylvania Sheriff's Office and Criminal Investigations Division.

Kim Rossmo, PhD, Research Professor in the Department of Criminal Justice at Texas State University, and the Director for the Center for Geospatial Intelligence and Investigation. That's a mouthful—but bottom line is that Dr. Rossmo is the father of geographic profiling. I thank him for his time in discussing with me the concepts of geoprofiling, for lending his name to the manuscript and for reviewing the relevant portions of *The 7th Victim* for accuracy.

Rodger Freeman, Community Outreach Assistant for Women Escaping A Violent Environment, who provided me with insight and perspective on domestic violence issues. **Marion Weis**, for relating her real-world experience in dealing with people who have been stricken with Alzheimer's Disease. **Matthew Jacobson**, my Xbox and Internet guru, for ensuring I got my references and terminology correct. **Shel Holtz**, principal of Holtz Communication + Technology, for his information on anonymous email. **Michael Berkley**, ceramicist, for providing me the framework for Dead Eyes's occupation.

Michelle Sallee, PhD, psychologist for San Quentin's death row inmates, for her input on, and experience with, Dissociative Identity Disorder (DID). **Jerry Gelbart, MD**, psychiatrist, for information pertaining to the diagnosis, treatment, and incidence of DID. **David Seminer, MD**, for orienting me as to the diagnosis, prognosis, and treatment of coma.

Bill Caldwell, retired police officer, armorer, and firearms instructor, for assisting me with the nitty gritty details on firearms.

Army Lieutenant Cole Cordray, Hostage Negotiation Team, for being my jack-of-all-ordnance and research guru. **Pamela Midthun**, manager of the Red Fox Inn, for her tales of Monte the ghost and other facts regarding her Bed & Breakfast. **Bob Campbell**, Work First coordinator with North Carolina's Henderson-Vance Chamber of Commerce, for being my "eyes and ears" in Warren County and the fictitious Rockridge Correctional Institution.

Frank Curtis, Esq., for his sound legal counsel and astute editorial input.

C. J. Snow. He's not only a man of integrity, but a fabulous bookseller and a skilled editor. His early critique of the manuscript helped me craft a finer product.

To those who've helped me get my novels into the hands of my readers—I'm sincerely grateful: Tom Hedtke, Poppy Gilman, Lonnie Blankenchip, Dave Gabbard, Ben Coombe, Lyn Caglio, Lia Boyd, Stephanie Burke, Anthony Horsley, Erika Cowan, Karen Brady, Carol Stonis, Sheila Gordon, Mary Jo Corcoran, Joan Wunsch, Joan Hansen, Barbara Peters, Terry Abbott, Kathy Coad, Ed and Pat Thomas, Fall Ferguson, Betty Ubiles, Lita Weissman, Ben Coombe, Amanda Brooks, Nelson Aspen, Connie Martinson, Marianne McClary and Nick Toma, Bill Buckmaster, Dawn Deason, Glenn Mason, Dan Elliott, Jennifer Smith, John St. Augustine, AnnMarie Iasso, Kristin O'Connor, Norm Jarvis, Tony Trupiano, Vicky Lorini, Linda Keough, Jean Kelley, Stacey Kumagai, Brent Deal (Doodle Films), Brandy Jones (NAYABIS Productions), and Robert Grossman (Focus Creative Group).

Kevin Smith, editor extraordinaire, who tweaked and refined but didn't destroy. Any author who's read and reread his or her own work a gazillion times—yet still misses a repeated word—knows how invaluable an editor is with Kevin's exceptional skills.

Anais Scott, my copyeditor, for her keen eye and attention to detail. A good copyeditor is vital to giving a novel that last buffing before it hits the presses.

Roger Cooper. Roger is not merely a veteran of the publishing industry. He's a visionary who understands the transformation that has occurred across entertainment the past couple decades, and who's acted on it. I owe Roger a lot—and you, my readers, owe Roger a lot, too—because without his foresight, *The 7th Victim* might not have lived to see the light of your bookshelf.

The staff at Vanguard Press/Perseus Books—including **Georgina Levitt, Amanda Ferber, Janet Saines, Joshua Berman**, and the entire sales, marketing, and design departments—for successfully seeing this project through the various phases of production with skill and professionalism. You've been fantastic and have made it look easy—and I *know* it never is.

Peter Rubie. It was many years ago that I first stumbled upon Peter's nonfiction book, *The Elements of Storytelling*. Its influence remains ingrained in my writing DNA.

My brother, **Jeffrey Jacobson, Esq.**, for all his tangible and intangible support over the years. Always willing and able, there's no one I'd rather have in my corner than my brother.

My kids, who have seen me daily (before leaving for college) and who've been with me through all my career highs, lows, and highs. You're a gift. I've tried my best to give you what you need in life to succeed—but you've given me as much, and more.

Ultimate thanks goes to **Jill**, my wife and life partner, without whom I'd be incomplete. Jill's stood beside me every step of the precarious path that accompanies the journey of getting three major novels published. It's a road filled with landmines, but each time we've found our way through, together. Third time's a charm. In more ways than one.

If I've left out anyone, the omission was unintentional; please forgive me. Stated facts, if they differ from the truth, were changed for reasons of National Security, under the threat of prosecution. Actually, no facts were knowingly altered (aside from a tiny bit of harmless literary license). If something's wrong, it just means I blew it. I worked hard to ensure accuracy, so I sure hope you don't find any errors.

PREVIEW CHAPTERS OF THE FORTHCOMING

CRUSH

A NEW KAREN VAIL NOVEL BY

ALAN JACOBSON

ONE

ST. HELENA, CALIFORNIA
The Napa Valley

*T*he crush of a grape is not unlike life itself: You press and squeeze until the juice flows from its essence, and it dies a sudden, pathetic death. Devoid of its lifeblood, its body shrivels and is then discarded. Scattered about. Used as fertilizer, returned to the earth. Dust in the wind.

But despite the region in which John Mayfield worked—the Napa Valley—the crush of death wasn't reserved just for grapes.

John Mayfield liked his name. It reminded him of harvest and sunny vineyards.

He had, however, made one minor modification: His mother hadn't given him a middle name, so he chose one himself—Wayne. Given his avocation, "John Wayne" implied a tough guy image with star power. It also was a play on John Wayne Gacy, a notorious serial killer. And serial killers almost always were known in the public consciousness by three names. His persona—soon to be realized worldwide—needed to be polished and prepared.

Mayfield surveyed the room. He looked down at the woman, no longer breathing, in short order to resemble the shriveled husk of a crushed grape. He switched on his camera and made sure the lens captured the blood draining from her arm, the thirsty soil beneath her drinking it up as if it had been waiting for centuries to be nourished. Her fluid pooled a bit, then was slowly sucked beneath the surface.

A noise nearby broke his trance. He didn't have much time. He could have chosen his kill zone differently, to remove all risk. But it wasn't about avoiding detection. There was so much more to it.

The woman didn't appreciate his greatness, his power. She didn't see him for the unique person that he was. Her loss.

Mayfield wiped the knife of fingerprints and, using the clean handkerchief, slipped the sharp utensil beneath the dead woman's lower back. He stood up, kicked the loose dirt aside beneath his feet, scattering his footprints, then backed away.

TWO

As Karen Vail walked the grounds of the Mountain Crest Bed & Breakfast, holding the hand of Roberto Enrique Umberto Hernandez, she stopped at the edge of a neighboring vineyard. She looked out over the vines, the sun setting a hot orange in the March chill.

"You've been quiet since we got off the plane. Still thinking about your application to the Academy?"

"Am I that transparent?" Robby asked.

"Only to a sharp FBI profiler."

Robby cradled a tangle of vines in his large hand. "Yeah, that's what I'm thinking about."

"You'll get into the Academy, Robby. Maybe not right away, with the budget cutbacks, but I promise. You'll make the cut."

"Bledsoe said he could get me something with Fairfax County."

"Really? You didn't tell me that."

"I didn't want to say anything about it. I don't really want it. If I talk about it, it might come true."

"You don't really believe that."

He shrugged a shoulder.

"Fairfax would be a step up over Vienna. It's a huge department. Lots more action."

"I know. It's just that there's an eleven-year wait to become a profiler once I get into the Academy. The longer it takes to get into the Bureau, the longer I have to wait."

"Why don't you call Gifford," Vail asked. "I thought he owes you. Because of your mother. Because of their relationship."

"That was Gifford's perception, not mine. He promised her he'd look after me." Robby looked off a moment, then said, "He doesn't owe me anything. And I don't want any favors."

"How about I look into it, quietly, under the radar, when we get home?"

Robby thought about it. "Maybe."

"I can call first thing in the morning, put out a feeler."

"No. We're here on vacation, to get away from all that stuff. It'll wait."

They turned and walked toward their room, The Hot Date, which was in a separate building off the main house. According to the information on the website, it was the largest in the facility, featuring spacious main sleeping quarters, a sitting area with a private porch and view of the vines, and a jetted tub in the bathroom. A wooden sign, red with painted flames, hung dead center on the door.

Vail felt around in her pocket for the key they'd been given when they checked in fifteen minutes ago. "You sure?"

"Absolutely sure. I'm wiping it from my mind right now. Nothing but fun from here on out. Okay?"

Vail fit the key into the lock and turned it. "Works for me." She swung the door open and looked around at the frilly décor of the room. She kicked off her shoes, ran forward, and jumped onto the bed, bouncing up and down like a five-year-old kid. "This could be fun," she said with a wink.

Robby stood a few feet away, hands on his hips, grinning widely. "I've never seen you like this."

"Nothing but fun from here on out, right? Not a worry in the world? No serial killers dancing around in our heads, no ASACs or lieutenants ordering us around. No job decisions. And no excess testosterone floating on the air."

"The name of this room is The Hot Date, right? That should be our theme for the week."

"Count me in."

"That's good," Robby said. "Because a hot date for one isn't much fun."

Vail hopped to the side of the bed, stood up precariously on the edge, and grabbed Robby's collar with both hands. She fell forward into him, but at six foot seven, he easily swept her off the bed and onto the floor, then kissed her hard.

He leaned back and she looked up at his face. "You know," Vail said, "I flew cross-country to Napa for the fine wine and truffles, but that was pretty freaking good, Hernandez."

"Oh, yeah? That's just a tasting. If you want the whole bottle, it'll cost you."

As he leaned in for another kiss, her gaze caught sight of the wall clock. "Oh—" The word rode on his lips and made him pull away. "Our tour."

"Our what?"

"I told you. Don't you ever listen to me?"

"Uh, yeah, I, uh—"

"The wine cave thing, that tour we booked through your friend—"

"The tasting, the dinner in the cave." He smiled and raised his brow. "See, I do listen to you."

"We've gotta leave now. It's about twenty minutes away."

"You sure?" He nodded behind her. "Bed, Cabernet, chocolate, sex . . ."

She pushed him away in mock anger. "That's not fair, Robby. You know that? We've got this appointment, it's expensive, like two hundred bucks each, and you just want to blow it off?"

"I can think of something else to blow off."

Vail twisted her lips into a mock frown. "I guess five minutes won't hurt."

"We'll speed to make up the time. We're cops, right? If we're pulled over, we'll badge the officer—"

Vail placed a finger over his lips. "You're wasting time."

They arrived five minutes late. The California Highway Patrol was not on duty—at least along the strip of Route 29 they traversed quite a few miles per hour over the limit—and they pulled into the parking lot smelling of chocolate and, well, the perfume of intimacy.

They sat in the Silver Ridge Estates private tasting room around a table with a dozen others, listening to a sommelier expound the virtues of the wines they were about to taste. They learned about the different climates where the grapes were grown, why the region's wind patterns and mix of daytime heat and chilly evenings provided optimum conditions for growing premium grapes. Vail played footsie with Robby beneath the table, but Robby kept a stoic face, refusing to give in to her childish playfulness.

That is, until she realized she was reaching too far and had been stroking the leg of the graying fifty-something man beside Robby, whose nametag read "Bill (Oklahoma)." When Bill from Oklahoma turned to face her with a surprised look on his face, Vail realized her error and shaded the same red as the Pinot Noir on the table in front of them.

"Okay," the sommelier said. "We're going to go across the way into our wine cave, where we'll talk about the best temperatures for storing our wine. Then we'll do a tasting in a special room of the cave and discuss pairings, what we're about to eat, with which wine—and why—before dinner is served."

As they rose from the table, Robby leaned forward to ask the sommelier a question about the delicate color of the Pinot. Oklahoma Bill slid beside Vail, but before he could speak, she said, "My mistake, buddy. Not gonna happen."

Bill seemed to be mulling his options, planning a counterattack. But Vail put an end to any further pursuit by cutting him off with a slow, firm, "Don't even think about it."

Bill obviously sensed the tightness in her voice and backed away as if she had threatened him physically. Judging by the visible tension in Vail's forearm muscles, that probably wasn't far from the truth.

They shuffled through the breezeway of the winery, their tour guide explaining the various sculptures that were set back in alcoves in the walls, and how they had been gathered over the course of five decades, one from each continent. When they passed through the mouth of the wine cave, the drop in temperature was immediately discernable.

"The cave is a near-constant fifty-five degrees, which is perfect for storing our reds," the guide said. The group crowded into the side room that extended off the main corridor. "One thing about the way we grow our grapes," the woman said. "We plant more vines per square foot than your typical winery because we believe in stressing our vines, making them compete for water and nutrients. It forces their roots deeper into the ground and results in smaller fruit, which gives more skin surface area compared to the juice. And since the skin is what gives a red varietal most of its flavor, you can see why our wines are more complex and flavorful."

She stopped beside a color-true model of two grapevines that appeared poised to illustrate her point, but before she could continue her explanation, a male guide came from a deeper portion of the cave, ushering another group along toward the exit. He leaned into the female guide's ear and said something. Her eyes widened, then she moved forward, arms splayed wide like an eagle. "Okay, everyone, we have to go back into the tasting area for a while." She swallowed hard and cleared her throat, as if there was something caught, then said, "I'm terribly sorry for this interruption, but we'll make it worth your while, I promise."

Vail caught a glimpse of a husky Hispanic worker who was bringing up the rear. She elbowed Robby and nodded toward the guy. "Something's wrong, look at his face." She moved against the stream of exiting guests and grabbed the man's arm.

"What's going on?" Vail asked.

"Nothing, signora, all's good. Just a . . . the power is out, it's very dark. Please, go back to the tasting room—"

"It's okay," Robby said. "We're cops."

"Policia?"

"Something like that." Vail held up her FBI credentials and badge. "What's wrong?"

"Who say there is something wrong?"

"It's my job to read people. Your face tells a story, señor. Now—" she motioned with her fingers. "What's the deal?"

He looked toward the mouth of cave, where most of the guests had already exited. "I did not tell you, right?"

"Of course not. Now . . . tell us, what?"

"A body. A *dead* body. Back there," he said, motioning behind him with a thumb.

"How do you know the person's dead?"

"Because she cut up bad, señora. Her . . . uh, *los pechos* . . . her . . . tits—are cut off."

Robby looked over the guy's shoulder, off into the darkness. "Are you sure?"

"I found the body, yes, I am sure."

"What's your name?"

"Miguel Ortiz."

"You have a flashlight, Miguel?" Vail asked.

The large man rooted out a set of keys from his pocket, pulled off a small LED light and handed it to her.

"Wait here. Don't let anyone else past you. You have security at the winery?"

"Yes, ma'am."

"Then call them on your cell," Vail said, as she and Robby backed away, deeper into the tunnel. "Tell them to shut this place down tight. No one in or out. No one."

━━━━━━

As A FEDERAL AGENT, Karen Vail was required to carry her sidearm wherever she traveled. But Robby, being a state officer, transported his weapon in a locked box, and it had to remain there; he was not permitted to carry it on his person. This fact was not lost on Vail as she removed her sidearm from her Velcro fanny pack. She reached down to her ankle holster and pulled a smaller Glock 27 and handed it to Robby.

They moved slowly through the dim cave. The walls were roughened gunite, dirt brown and cold to the touch. The sprayed cement blend gave the sense of being in a real cave, save for its surface uniformity.

"You okay in here?" Robby asked.

"Don't ask. I'm trying not to think about it." But she had no choice. Vail had developed claustrophobia after the recent incident in the Dead Eyes Killer's lair. Though she never had experienced such intense anxiety, it was suddenly a prominent part of her life. Going into certain parking garages, through commuter tunnels, and even into crammed elevators became a fretful experience. But it wasn't consistent. Sometimes it was worse than others.

Overall, it was inconvenient—and no fun admitting you had such an irrational weakness. But she was now afflicted with the malady and she did her best to control it. *Control?* Not exactly. *It* controlled *her. Manage* it was more accurate. Take her mind off it, talk herself through it until she could move into roomier quarters.

Sometimes, though, she thought she might actually claw through walls to get out. Getting squeezed into an elevator was the worst. For some reason, people didn't mind cramming against you if the alternative meant waiting another minute or two for the next car.

Vail slung her purse over her shoulder so it rested on her back, then moved the weak light around, taking care not to tread on anything that might constitute evidence.

"Maybe we should call it in," Robby said. "Let the locals handle it."

"The locals? This isn't exactly Los Angeles, Robby. I seriously doubt they have a whole lot of murders out here. If the vic's been cut like Miguel says, the local cops'll be out of their league. They're going to look at the crime scene but won't know what they're seeing."

"Beyond the obvious, you mean."

"The obvious to me and the obvious to a homicide detective are not the same things, Robby. You know that. When you encounter something unusual—no matter what profession you're talking about—would you rather hire someone who's seen that unusual thing a thousand times, or someone who's only seen it once or twice?"

"If we do find something, we won't have a choice. We've got no jurisdiction here."

"Yeah, well, we'll cross that bridge when we come to it."

They turned left down another tunnel, which opened into a large storage room of approximately a thousand square feet. Hundreds of French oak barrels sat on their sides, stacked one atop the other, three rows high and what must've been fifty rows long. A few candelabras with low-output lightbulbs hung from above, providing dim illumination. The walls and ceiling were constructed of roughened multicolored brick, with multiple arched ceilings that rose and plunged and joined one another to form columns every fifteen feet, giving the feel of a room filled with majestic gazebos.

A forklift sat dormant on the left, pointing at an opening along the right wall, where, amidst a break in the barrels, was another room. They moved toward it, Vail shining the flashlight in a systematic manner from left to right as they walked. They stepped carefully, foot by foot, to avoid errant hoses and other objects like . . . a mutilated woman's body.

They entered the anteroom and saw a lump in the darkness on the ground.

Robby said, "That bridge you just mentioned? I think we just came to it."

"Shit," Vail said.

"You didn't think Miguel was pulling our leg, did you? He looked pretty freaked out."

"No, I figured he saw something. I was just hoping it was a sack of potatoes, and in some kind of wine-induced stupor, he thought it was a dead woman."

"With her breasts cut off?"

"Hey, I'm an optimist, okay?"

Robby looked at her. "You're an optimist?"

As they stood there, Vail couldn't take her eyes off the body. She'd come to Napa to relax, to get away from work. Yet lying on the cold ground a little over twenty feet away was an all-too-obvious reminder of what she'd come here to escape.

Then she mentally slapped herself. She was pissed at having her vacation ruined. The woman in front of her had her life ruined.

Vail took a deep breath. "You have cell service? We need to call this in."

Robby flipped open his phone. "No bars."

"No bars in Napa? Some other time and place, that would be funny." She shook her head. "I can't believe I just said that."

"Humor is the best defense mechanism. Honestly, this sucks, Karen. You needed the time away. It was my idea to come here. I'm sorry."

"As our colleague Mandisa Manette is fond of saying, 'Sometimes life just sucks the big one.'" Vail's thoughts momentarily shifted to Manette, how she was doing in recovery. It didn't last long, as the snap of Robby's phone closing brought her back to the here and now.

"Okay," Vail said, "one of us goes, just to see if she's alive. We don't want to totally destroy the crime scene."

"Might as well be you," Robby said. "Get a close look, see if you see anything worthwhile."

Vail stood there, but didn't move. "I already see stuff that's worthwhile." She sighed in resignation, then stepped forward. "Like you said earlier, nothing but fun from here on out."